Judex ergo cum sedebit, quidquid latet
apparebit, nil inultum remanebit …

*(When the judge takes his place, what is hidden
will be revealed, nothing will remain …)*

D0907938

BURDEN
OF TRUTH

A Birdie Keane Novel

BURDEN
OF TRUTH

TERRI NOLAN

MIDNIGHT INK
WOODBURY, MINNESOTA

FIRST EDITION
First Printing, 2013

Book design and format by Donna Burch
Cover art: Open field: iStockphoto.com/Jamie Evans
        Los Angeles, CA skyline: iStockphoto.com/John Crall
        Palm and date trees: iStockphoto.com/DNY59
        Police badge: iStockphoto.com/Mel Stoutsenberger
Cover design by Kevin R. Brown
Editing by Connie Hill

Midnight Ink, an imprint of Llewellyn Worldwide Ltd.

Library of Congress Cataloging-in-Publication Data

Nolan, Terri.
  Burden of truth : a Birdie Keane novel / by Terri Nolan. — 1st ed.
     p.   cm.
  ISBN 978-0-7387-3582-5
  1. Women journalists—Fiction. 2. Cold cases (Criminal investigation)—Fiction. I. Title.
  PS3614.O474B87   2013
  813'.6—dc23   2012028475

Midnight Ink
Llewellyn Worldwide Ltd.
2143 Wooddale Drive
Woodbury, MN 55125-2989
www.midnightinkbooks.com

Printed in the United States of America

For Scott

FAMILY TREE

The Keane clan:

Gerard (Birdie's father)

Maggie (Birdie's mother)

Birdie Elizabeth (aka Bird, Tweety)

Louis (Gerard's twin)

Nora (wife to Louis)

Thomas (1st-born child. Aka Thom.)

Aiden (Thom's twin)

Arthur

Madigan Birdie (aka Madi)

The Whelan clan:

Frank Senior (patriarch)

Mary (matriarch)

Frank Junior (aka Father Frank, Junior)

Michael

Eric

Colin

Emmett

Matt

Patrick

Mary Junior—deceased

ONE OF THE CONCEITS of the journalism profession is that every story is a nut. Crack it open and discover what's inside. The kernel can be ripe or rotten, true or false; sometimes a little of both. Police Officer Matthew Whelan always said, "The process to find the truth is methodical, precise, and, in the end, provable." But often the absolute truth is not always knowable.

—ELIZABETH KEANE
Preface of *Darkness Bound*

ONE

Lake Henshaw, CA
Saturday, January 7

Matt Whelan sat on the edge of the bed shivering from the frigid mountain air that found tiny passageways into the bedroom. He had attempted to turn on the heat. The man with him said no. The cold would preserve his body.

Matt took a hard toke off a nearly done joint, inhaled toxic smoke deep into his lungs and held his breath. An uncomfortable suffocating feeling settled in and he blew it out. THC dulled his mind, calmed the muscle spasms. Too bad it didn't kill the guilt of what he'd done.

The man snatched it. "That's enough. The scent will linger."

"I'll be dead soon. Why should I care?"

"Don't you care what she thinks?"

"She already knows I'm a stoner."

"What about the other stuff?"

Oh, that. He did care. A lot. But really, what did it matter now? He'd already put his plan into motion. The one the man didn't know about.

He picked up a favorite photograph taken the day he met *her*. Birdie Elizabeth Keane. His entire existence had twisted sideways the day he met the then fifteen-year-old. It was the worst day of his life. And the best. In the subsequent years Matt never discovered how a teenage girl incarcerated his heart, locking it away from all others. She gave him the best of herself without expectation. He tried to reciprocate, but always came up short in his estimation. Even now, all he wanted was her happiness—more than life itself, and so he purposely betrayed her with a promise he wouldn't keep.

She was first introduced to him as Bird. Her cousin, Arthur, was Matt's new partner. They were LAPD patrol cops working Rampart Division. Matt was twenty-seven then and married. By the time Bird reached legal age Matt was divorced and they could pursue a romantic relationship. But by then he was the steward of a devastating knowledge so powerful it could destroy a family and shake the department with another scandal. Because Bird was fiercely protective of her family, he caged his love to spare her the anguish of dividing her loyalties.

Matt felt woozy. He no longer sensed the fingers of cold caressing his bare skin. He looked up wistfully at the man who would execute his penalty.

"You have a few minutes," the man said.

3

Matt watched Birdie standing against the service door, allowing her eyes to adjust to the dark. She had an unerring nose. She'd smell the marijuana seasoning the moist air of a recent rain. He didn't usually dope and drive, but this was an unusual circumstance. Something needed to be done and his spine was a broken spring.

He moved into the light.

She approached with an impatient, long-legged trot. "It's about time you showed up. What's up with the surreptitious beckon? Where the hell have you been this past week? You missed a PT session." She grabbed his arm. "Come on. The midnight jig is in twenty minutes."

He captured her in a fleecy hug. "Can't a guy have a quiet moment with the birthday girl without the whole of Molly's watching?"

"It's a private party. Family and friends. The usual suspects."

"I have a special present that requires privacy."

"Oh?"

"But first a Q-and-A." He backed her against the pickup truck and took a step away. The outer rim of the lamplight lit her face but not his; better to veil his anguish.

She exhaled into her palms. "It's cold out here. Get on with it."

He took her hands in his and rubbed them. "Shush. Why are you always in a hurry?"

"Is that question one?"

"Okay, here goes. Are you in love with George?"

"No."

"Would you be willing to break up with George?"

"For what reason?"

"I ask. You answer."

"Sorry. I forgot the rules."

"Bullshit. It's not in Bird's nature to go with the flow. Now answer the question."

"I'd break up with him for the right reason."

"What is the right reason to compel you to break up with George?"

When they played this game, Birdie always framed her responses to gain more information before answering the original question. Matt counted on this.

"You already know," she said.

"That's not a proper answer." He tapped her chest. "Rules."

Her eyes sought his hidden in the shadow. She nibbled her lower lip in consideration. "If the man I love loved me back, I'd break up with George."

"Who is the man you love?"

"You."

Matt thought his heart might break under the pressure. *Courage, Whelan.* He caressed her jaw. "And I love you." He leaned his body into hers and kissed her forehead. "Past." He kissed her nose. "Present." His lips swiped hers. "Future."

"Don't tease me."

He delicately ran the tip of his tongue over her lips—a seductive caress before a nibble. She opened her mouth and accepted him. A breathless sensuality broke loose. They kissed like long separated lovers. Deep. Penetrating. Turbo-charged. The kiss combusted into caressing and quickly ignited into full-on making out. Matt lifted her and she wrapped her legs around him, gyrating her pelvis against his manhood. His fierce passion broke free of the leash. He wanted to ravage her. Now. Without severing the seal of their mouths he reached for the handle on the cab door. He managed to jerk it open and attempted to maneuver Birdie into the front seat.

"NO." The stinging echo of the word stopped them both cold.

Matt heard a dull crack—the sound of his heart splitting. He despised himself and was on the verge of wailing. He did what he could to conceal his self-loathing—he bent down and slowly rose with his hands on his chest. "Wow, Bird. You're gonna give me a heart attack."

She snuggled his neck and whispered, "Our first time together is not going to be in a pickup truck like fumbling teenagers."

"We almost got away from ourselves." And he nearly forgot a vital detail of the despicable plan. He reached into the pocket of his fleece jacket and pulled out a tiny envelope. He slid his hand into the back pocket of her jeans, squeezed her ass, and deposited a message.

"It's been a long time since we've kissed like that," she said.

"Eleven years. You were nineteen."

"Was that my present?"

Could she see Matt's upper lip vibrating with self-hate? He moved into shadow and rubbed his eyes before the welling tears had a chance to fall. He cleared his throat. "This is the prologue. I have business this weekend. Take it to break up with George. Be gentle. Then come to me Sunday night. We'll be together. Forever after. 'Till death do us part."

"Forever after."

Later, as Birdie jigged her way back to the birthday party, Matt noted he had never seen her so ebullient. If he had his handgun in the truck he might've just put himself out of his misery.

Lake Henshaw, CA
Saturday, January 7

Matt held up another photo. Birdie posed in the middle of a lemon grove. The trees were ripe with white blossoms. The first fruits were still tiny green buttons. Matt closed his eyes and remembered the tart fragrance that mingled with dirt kicked up by Birdie's hiking boots. He heard the buzz of bees and insects and the occasional rustle of leaves.

"It's time," said the man, taking the photo and replacing it with a glass of stinky opaque liquid. "Drink it."

Fetid vapors of rot stung Matt's nose and eyes. He hacked, nauseous before taking a single swallow. He pinched his nose and gagged down the crap. He sputtered and coughed. His insides were going to explode. He clutched his stomach and groaned, falling back in immeasurable pain—a minor penance for unleashing hell's devastation.

The man knelt over Matt where a catheter port had already been attached to his chest—the needle mark hidden under a jagged, reddish scar. The man uncapped a syringe, slid the needle into the port and slowly thumbed the plunger.

"Just so we're clear," said Matt, already feeling the sedation of the drug injected so close to his heart, "it's not murder or suicide."

"Accidental drug overdose."

As Matt drifted into oblivion he smelt the lemons and began to weep.

"It's too late for that," said the man. "Much too late."

TWO

BIRDIE KEANE AWOKE FEELING happy. She cracked open her eyes and saw the familiar glow-in-the-dark stars on the ceiling. The plastic galaxy above her bed a favorite thing.

The blue numbers of the digital clock glowed 9:10 a.m.—still early by weekend standards. She thought about getting up to raise the blackout shades, but decided against it. She stretched and relived the memory of last night.

Yesterday was her birthday. Her family threw a party at Molly Malone's. The Mulligans performed Irish standards for the older generation, folk and rock covers for the younger crowd. Matt Whelan had arrived late and asked the bartender to pass on a message: meet him outside.

She'd been in love with him for fifteen years. He loved her too, she was certain of it, but he never said it in a way that suggested

9

more than intense friendship. Last night the words rolled off his tongue. Their lips came together in a fusion of two people radioactive with years of suppressed desire and longing.

She ran her hand down her belly and twiddled between her legs, summoned a quick erotic response and remembered the melting knees, the lurch in her heart, the silken strokes of his hands on her breasts. Her groin grew moister and she removed her hand. She'd save it for Sunday night. She covered her face with a pillow and laughed with joy.

Birdie tumbled out of bed, warm feet on cool mahogany, and then across the hallway to the guest bedroom. She propped against the doorframe and watched George straighten his necktie.

"Morning," she said. "Working on Saturday?"

George checked the 9-mil and shoved it into the rig under his left arm, clipped the police badge to his belt. He pulled on his suit jacket and turned dark eyes on her.

"I'm disappointed," he said. "I saw you and Matt making out last night."

"Geeze … I'm sorry. I was going—"

"I've been betrayed by two people I trust."

"George—"

"Stop." He threw up his palm. "Do you love me?"

He had never asked the question because he already knew the answer.

"No."

"What have we been doing these months?"

"Dating."

"You go clubbing with Matt. You cruise flea markets with Matt. You go to movie premiers with Matt. That's dating. We eat out and have sex in the guest room. I'm not even allowed to sleep in your bed. It's upside down."

George sat on the chaise, ran slender fingers through his short dark hair. "I can't be with you anymore. I thought I could be the man to bust through the invisible barrier that you and Matt built—the one that prevents either of you from forming emotional attachments. What an ego I have." He winced at his own words.

A quick siren wail came from the street below. "That's Thom. We've got a guy in the box."

Thom was one of Birdie's cousins. George and Thom were partners. Detectives. They worked Robbery/Homicide Division.

"Ironic, isn't it? The man who introduced us is the one standing between us." He pressed his tall sinewy build next to Birdie and took her face into his hands. He presented his lips and she accepted the consolation prize.

A few minutes later another failed relationship walked out her front door.

George Silva saw the Technicolor version of the same reel another ex-boyfriend, Denis Cleary, took two years to see: No man had ever been able to measure up to Matt Whelan. She wished George hadn't seen the physical manifestation. Besides being an excellent lover, George was a good friend. He deserved better.

Birdie punched buttons on the kitchen phone and got Matt's answering machine. "Hi, it's me. George broke up with me this

11

morning. Call me." She dialed his cell and got voicemail. "It's me. I just left a message on your house phone. George and I are officially broken up. Call me." Anxious, she dialed the number to his weekend house in Lake Henshaw. No answer.

Finally, she dialed another number and stuck the phone between ear and shoulder. There were two rings before a woman's pleasant voice answered, "Rectory."

"Good morning, it's Birdie Keane. Is Father Frank available?"

"Please hold while I check."

Birdie dumped four heaping scoops of dark roast into the coffee filter then filled the carafe with water, concentrating on steadying the shaking of her hand as she gently poured it into the reserve. She opened the leaded glass window. It had been raining for the past three days and her large thirsty lawn rejoiced with bright green growth. She inhaled the fresh rain-scrubbed air perfumed with the romantic scent of camellias.

A soothing voice came on the line. "Hello, Bird."

Father Frank Whelan was her friend and priest. The eldest of seven Whelan brothers and one of a handful of non-family allowed to use the nickname of incessant adolescent teasing.

"Frank," she said, "last night Matt came to Molly's. We finally said 'I love you.'"

The silence that followed was far longer than Birdie felt comfortable with. Finally he said, "I'm pleased for you both."

"I'm walking on air."

"What about George?" said her moral barometer.

"He broke up with me this morning." She wondered if she should tell Frank the rest. It was silly, really, because she told

Frank everything—whether in the confessional, in person, or on the phone, he heard it all eventually.

Impatient for morning brew she poured the first coffee drips into a porcelain cup, and took a burning sip in preparation for part two of the after-party recap.

"We're going to be together Sunday night. I think he's going to ask me to marry him."

"It'll be a matrimonial Mass and you'll get pregnant on the wedding night."

Birdie laughed at the absurdity.

"You're one tough customer," he said.

"I love you for trying to save my soul. I'll be happy with purgatory."

"Come to confession."

"For the sin I'm going to commit Sunday night?"

Frank blew out an exasperated snort. "I see your point. *Dominus vobiscum.*"

"*Et cum spiritu tuo.*"

Birdie entered her home office and ripped the top sheet from a pad of paper mounted on the wall. 239 in bold black appeared. Just over eight months of sobriety. She wadded the paper into a ball and slam-dunked it through the miniature basketball hoop. She sat at the desk and powered up the computer. Checked her schedule. Nothing pending. No important e-mails awaited. She hit the remote and turned on the television, flipped channels until she had clicked through them all and turned it off. Nothing interesting. She picked up a new pack of gum and zipped it open, popped two pieces in her mouth and dropped the foil wrappers next to the dish filled with silver balls of used gum.

The anticipation of making love with Matt or an engagement ring on her finger wasn't enough of a distraction to keep her thoughts from what she knew she had to do. Work. She looked up at the number on the wall. 239 days since she wrote her last word.

No articles. No features. No essays. No OP/ED pieces. No work done on the outstanding cases she followed for the crime books in progress. Boxes of court documents sat unopened. Editors stopped calling. Contacts neglected. Some days she sat for hours and meditated on the emptiness in her head.

Ambition and success surrounded Birdie. Three true crime books published, *Mississippi Serial*, *Real Evil*, and *As Crime Comes*. A fourth to be launched later this year. Three more in the pipe. One in the deep freeze. Two movie adaptations: one produced with her screenplay, the other garnered an Academy Award for a lead actor. Her biggest achievement, the one that gave her a puff of pride: the Pulitzer. Awarded for excellence in journalism. The gold medallion framed on her wall represented the pinnacle of sacrifice and hard work.

Done drunk.

All of it.

The computer's screen saver scrolled across the monitor: What's new with Paige Street?…What's happening?…Any leads?…Get to work! Fuchsia lettering on a pale blue background…What's new with Paige Street?…What's happening?…Any leads?…Get to work!

14

Birdie jiggled the mouse. She looked up at the tin mobile that hung off the corner of a bookcase. It represented the pieces and parts of the Paige Street Murder. The one in the deep freeze. Sixteen years cold. The one resolution she desired the most. The one she should have. After all, she knew some of the players. It had been her obsession since she was fourteen.

Where is that drive? What happened to your brain when you quit drinking?

"Beats the hell out of me," she said aloud. "Maybe Frank is right. I should get pregnant and become a mom. Try something new. Maybe that's how I'll reinvent my sober life."

She spit out her gum and carefully wrapped and rolled it into a ball and added it to the pyramid in the dish.

Birdie checked the Caller ID on the ringing phone. Henshaw House. Matt calling from his house in Lake Henshaw.

"Hey, you got my message."

"Birdie. It's Jacob Hoy."

"Jacob! Long time. Still putting that medical degree from Yale to work at the coroner's—"

A feeling of wrong pushed its way into her heart.

"There's no easy way to say this," he said.

Birdie's insides turned liquid. She huffed out a high-altitude pant. Matt's mysterious disappearance ... the secretive reemergence. Her throat spat out a cry of abandonment.

"Jacob—please ... no."

The declaration of love ...

"I found him a few hours ago on his bed."

The kisses …

"What happened?"

The promise of forever love …

"Drug overdose."

'Till death do us part …

"Oh, God, please … it's not true."

The grand goodbye …

"I'm sorry, Birdie. So sorry."

A rumbling sensation worked its way up her chest. Birdie convulsed out a howl so powerful it could cause an avalanche. She dropped the phone, ran to the toilet, and vomited.

THREE

Hollywood Freeway South. East Interstate 10. South Interstate 15. East State Highway 76. A primitive navigation system in Birdie's head controlled the excessive speed and assertive lane changes. She clutched the steering wheel without thinking about the route or being able to see it through the mascara mixed with sticky tears.

Five miles of single lane, unimproved fire road, and a quarter mile of ballast driveway was the final part of the journey. The usually locked gate to the fire road was wide open. Responding to steady pressure on the accelerator, the Ford Taurus banged its rpms up the rough road, leaving behind a wake of mud clods. Up and over the hill and around slick paperclip curves, Birdie pushed the sedan's suspension to its luxurious-highway-travel limits. The car bounced on ruts and grooves and slowed in murky puddles. What normally would take thirty minutes took twenty impatient ones.

The approach to the ballast drive was too fast. She jerked the steering wheel left. Momentum forced the back end of the car to fishtail. A wave of crushed rock splashed the pine tree marking the entrance. She manhandled the steering wheel hard right. The car straightened and careened as gravel bounced off the undercarriage.

When the house came into view, she knew she was too late. A San Diego Sheriff vehicle was all that remained.

No fire truck.

No ambulance.

Matt's body was already gone.

Birdie's mouth stretched wide with a scream that vibrated with an agonizing crescendo to the adrenalin-activated thrill ride. The fury and pain bounced around in the car with an awful echo.

The tantrum got the attention of a deputy. A cigarette dangled from his mouth as he leaned over the hood of the squad tapping a laptop. He stopped to watch her.

What kind of twisted sense of the morbid did Birdie possess that forced her into a law-breaking, no-win-if-she-were-caught scenario, in the hope of seeing the man she loved dead? She wondered how in the hell he could tell her he loved her, promise a life together, and then pull the rug from under her. She took Matt's death as a personal affront. How could she not? His visit had served one purpose: to say goodbye.

Birdie punched the dash, then took several deep inhalations of calm. Tilting the rearview mirror, she checked her face. Puffy and red. She licked a finger to rub the black from under her eyes. It spread.

The furious gum chewing made her jaw ache. Still, she spit the stale piece into the foil wrapper and popped a fresh one. Stretching her head side-to-side, she forced herself into a disciplined frame of mind. She plucked press credentials from the passenger visor and looped the lanyard around her neck.

The car door opened to pine-scented air, thick with heavy moisture that glossed the landscape with mist and laid down spun water webs. Under different circumstances it'd be a fanciful setting, full of wonderment.

The smoking deputy flicked his cigarette, stepped on it, and then picked it up and stuck it into his trouser pocket. He closed the computer and tossed it into the squad.

Birdie sized him: six-three with muscles gently pressing the sleeves of his tan uniform shirt, no bulletproof vest, gun worn on the left, taser on the right thigh, nose almost too big for his face with a horizontal crease connecting his eyes at the bridge, buzz-cut hair, military fashion, forehead high and smooth, face clean-shaven, fine lines at the corner of deep-set hazel eyes. The name-tag read R. Hughes.

"What does the R stand for?"

"Ron." He handed her a business card: San Diego County Sheriff's Department. Deputy Detective R. Hughes.

"Detectives wear uniforms out here?"

"Not usually. I was called in from a PR gig."

She stuck the card into the back pocket of her jeans and held up credentials. "Elizabeth Keane."

"I was expecting a woman named Birdie."

"Birdie is my given name. Elizabeth is the name I use professionally."

"This is an official visit?"

"Actually, no." Her cheeks bloomed. "Old habit. I suppose Jacob told you I'd come?"

"Yes, ma'am, he was certain of it. He asked me to extend every courtesy. You made good time. What was your top speed?"

"I hit one-ten on the 15."

"That's ballsy considering you have a suspended license for DUI."

"You put that laptop to good use."

"There's no service out here. Jacob Hoy told me."

"Why would he do that?"

"I asked." Hughes flicked his thumb toward the house. "You're practically immortalized in there."

"What else did Jacob tell you?"

"He said you're a fair-skinned, blue-eyed brunette with long Veronica Lake waves, a lusty laugh, and you were an alcoholic. He also said you have more curiosity than a cat."

"We know what happened to the cat, don't we? Anything else?"

"He said you're a brilliant investigative reporter who received a Pulitzer for a series on domestic slavery and now your fulltime occupation is writing true crime."

"I'm surprised he didn't give you my bra size."

Deputy Hughes smiled wide. Birdie sensed a bit of nervousness that was endearing. "Well, ma'am," he said, "I'm sure he would have if he knew it." His voice was like Puerto Rican rum— smooth, authoritative, unthreatening—and it irritated the hell out of her that she found him attractive.

"I'd like to take a look around."

"Have you been here before?"

"Many times. But not under these terms. Talk me through it?"

Birdie walked the perimeter of the ranch house and inspected a single set of boot prints in the rain-soft dirt. Detective Hughes said the treads were his. "Windows, doors, locked. No forced entry. No unknown tire tracks. Hoy arrived just before noon. They had made plans to hang out. He knocked, got no answer, used the spare under the potted geraniums to open the back door."

Matt's F-250 was parked in its usual location; backed up next to the shed. Hughes produced a key from his shirt pocket and dropped it in her palm. "I spoke with Mr. Whelan's father. He said you could take anything you wanted."

"That was especially kind of him."

"May I ask why?"

"He's a hard man. Let's leave it at that."

Birdie unlocked the cab door and stepped up into the driver's seat—the one Matt had attempted to wiggle her into. Now she was sorry they didn't do it. She had no idea that would be her last chance. She checked the glove compartment: owner's manual, warranty information, vehicle registration, proof of insurance. In the center console: Swiss Army knife, aviator sunglasses, satellite radio guide, flashlight, and a zippered change purse.

"Matt kept a Beretta in here. Did you find it?"

"There are no firearms on the premises."

She counted the money in the purse—eighty-nine dollars and thirty cents. She took a battered *Thomas Guide*. "Maps and short-cuts. One of his favorite things."

Hughes made a discreet notation into a portfolio.

"Keeping an inventory of what I take?"

"Yes, ma'am."

The shed door was ajar. She went in and flipped on the light. Matt called the property Henshaw House. His escape from reality. It was located behind a ridge on several acres of heavily wooded property that butted the Mesa Grande Indian Reservation and Cleveland National Forest. Modern devices were few and out of sight. The only phone, sans answering machine, was located here. Jacob called her from it. She picked up the phone to verify a dial tone. Birdie used to tease Matt about all the crap he stored in the shed. Like the two-way radio that hadn't worked in years. Now all the stuff seemed like discovered treasure, even the old trash barrel that smelled of rotting leaves and pine needles.

There were new photos tacked onto the front edge of a shelf, ones she hadn't seen: Matt and Jacob fishing, Matt and Birdie on a hike in a desert wash, a group shot of family, Matt with three guys in the snow, and Matt and Birdie celebrating her eighteenth birthday. She unpinned each. Hughes cast a panicked gaze as he watched. She braced her cheeks and turned away from him, her back shaking as she stifled the cry. After many minutes she finally slid the photos into her back pocket and faced the deputy. He flashed a smile of reassurance and made another notation in the portfolio.

"Matt loved his photos," she said, her voice trembling. "Shall we go inside?"

Hughes hesitated at the back door. "I have some face masks in the squad. A squirt of aftershave on the inside helps with the smell."

Birdie stepped back. She had focused her energies to get here and didn't properly consider what would occur next. Sure, she'd smelled death, seen the mess up close, experienced the suffocating horror of it, but not of a loved one. She shoved her shaking hands into her jacket and reminded herself why she had come: to find an answer.

"I'm okay," she said bravely.

Wide plank oak floors, antiques, cozy leather upholstery, handmade wool rugs, and creamy silk draperies gave the house a distinctive design. By no means was the décor feminine, yet its owner would never be guessed a bachelor. They walked through the kitchen and dining area. Birdie gasped. A foul smell hung in the air, clung to the rugs, polluted the silk. She squeezed her eyes shut. Just then rain started to fall. The reassuring sound of water on the roof took the edge off the oppressive greeting.

Detective Hughes waited patiently for her to adjust.

"What happened after Jacob entered?" she said, trying not to breathe through her nose.

Hughes switched on lights. "He knew immediately something was wrong."

"Because of the smell?"

"He followed it to the bedroom. Saw obvious signs of death and called the resident sheriff in Warner Springs."

"From the phone in the shed?"

"Yes, ma'am. The sheriff dispatched a deputy from the Ranchita sub-station. Then me. The three of us independently verified death. Hoy reported his preliminary finding of drug overdose to the coroner. SOP states that he doesn't come out for natural deaths.

But considering Whelan was a peace officer he asked for a thorough inspection and report for his review."

"No criminalist?" said Birdie.

"The department doesn't have the funds to send one for a drug overdose."

Birdie's instinct told her that Matt's goodbye indicated suicide. She clearly stated the question and held her breath in anticipation of the answer.

"There are no indicators."

"So you're leaning toward—?"

"Accidental drug overdose. He was probably in pain."

Indeed. Matt had been in constant pain. Six months ago he was shot during a domestic violence call. The first bullet hit Matt from behind, just right of the spine. It ripped the trapezius, blew apart the scapula and a couple of ribs. The force spun him around, and the second bullet hit him on the left side of the chest, pierced the lung, and barely missed his heart. He was in intensive care for weeks and almost didn't make it.

It wasn't the first time Matt had been shot when responding to a call for service. During the Paige Street incident, sixteen years ago, a 40-caliber round—fired by a suspect who got away—hit Matt in the head, ricocheted off the skull, and scraped three inches off his scalp.

Yeah, Matt was in pain. Still, Birdie couldn't get brainwaves around an overdose. It ground against everything Matt believed.

"Who determined the cause of death?"

"Hoy. He is a medical examiner."

"He was also Matt's friend. It's a conflict of interest."

"Like thrusting your credentials in my face?"

"Point taken."

Hughes waved his hand toward Matt's bedroom. She reluctantly followed.

FOUR

AT THE END OF the hallway hung an intricately carved square panel of dark wood. Buddha sat cross-legged in the center with one hand raised in greeting. Birdie reflexively waved back as she always did.

"There was no trauma to the body," said Hughes, turning into the bedroom. "No sign of struggle. His position indicated that he was sitting, legs off the edge of the bed, and fell backward." Remnants of excreta and bits of vomit remained. Smelly liquid soaked the sheets.

Birdie turned her head and swallowed the bile that crept into her mouth.

"What drugs did you find?"

"Methadone and marijuana."

"He used them for pain management. He had prescriptions for both."

"Methadone has a long tail. It's easy to overdose. Perhaps if he were high—"

"He was extremely careful with his drug use."

She opened his bureau drawer, looked through his boxer briefs, socks, caressed the cotton T-shirts. Opened the closet door. "Where is his wallet? Cell phone?"

"Not here. Three keys were loose on the bathroom sink. The truck key, the one to this house, and another that Jacob said belonged to his L.A. residence. I understand you are likely to have a duplicate. May I verify?"

Birdie took the keys from her jacket pocket; showed Hughes which one was Matt's and watched as he compared the two. "Yes. It's the same."

Birdie couldn't stand it any longer. She spun around and ran into the great room.

On the console table near the front window sat an eight-by-ten photo in a silver frame. Matt and Birdie were cheek-to-cheek, smiling broadly. She had never seen that photo either, but remembered it was taken Christmas Eve at a gathering hosted by his parents before midnight Mass. Thirteen days ago. Surrounding the photo were recent cuttings from a pine bough and an arrangement of cones. At the edge of the console several sticks of incense of various lengths were stuck into a burner.

"It looks like a shrine," said Hughes. "Perhaps you can see the reason behind my inquiries."

"People don't construct shrines for the living." She studied the odd decoration. Not his style. He preferred clean lines in which to highlight art or objects. She picked up the picture. Clutched it to her chest. Outside, the rumble of far-off thunder mimicked her heart.

"What was your relationship to Mr. Whelan?"

Should she tell him that she had loved him for fifteen years or that she pined for him, placed him on a pedestal, admired him, worshiped him? She decided to go with the less painful option.

"We were best friends."

"When was the last time you saw him?"

"Last night in Los Angeles. Right before midnight."

A puff of displeasure escaped Hughes nose. The downy hairs on the back of her neck stiffened. She regarded him. He returned the intensity of her gaze and offered her a look of compassion. One that said, it's tough, I know. Losing someone close.

"Was he melancholy?" said Hughes.

"I didn't detect sadness, but he was more intense than usual."

"Hoy informed me that Mr. Whelan didn't like taking drugs, which could account for the absence of OTCs in the house. If he were unaccustomed to taking medications—"

"He wasn't an idiot."

"I'm not suggesting—"

"Toxicology will be administered?"

"Yes."

"Where will the body be taken for autopsy?"

"There won't be one."

"Isn't the blood for a tox taken from the heart at the time of autopsy?"

Hughes wasn't surprised she knew this. "Correct. Hoy collected it here using a heart syringe."

"If Jacob discovered the body, how is it he happened to have a heart syringe?"

"You should direct your body inquiries to Hoy. That's his purview. Mine is the scene and manner of death." Hughes handed her Jacob's business card. On the back was a hand-written phone number. "He asked that you call when you're done here."

Despite Hughes' assessment that Matt's death was accidental, his behavior last night was not. It was out of character. In retrospect, contrived. Suggesting his death was planned. But why would Matt do that? Perhaps her dependable instinct failed her on this occasion. She needed further inspection of her feelings, time to mourn, time to look back with a clear-headedness not muddled with the emotional turmoil inside her.

She determined that she wouldn't find the answer just now, just here. But she would. Her emotional stability depended on it.

"Mark it in your pad, Detective. I'm taking this picture." Then she offered her hand. "Thank you for waiting. I appreciate your indulgence and patience. This isn't easy."

"It never is, Miss Keane. I'm sorry for your loss." He took her elbow and gently escorted her out.

When Birdie figured she was in an area that had cell service, she pulled off the highway and dialed Jacob's number.

"I was hoping you'd call soon," he said. "I'm ready to get drunk and have a good cry."

"I saw Matt last night. Just before midnight. The situation was unusual ... he, um ... well, long story short, he was saying good-bye. I think he committed suicide."

The silence was so long Birdie thought the call had dropped. "Jacob?"

"Sorry. I'm kinda blown away at the moment. Midnight you say? That fine-tunes the TOD. He likely died between two and three a.m."

"There you go. Proof."

"Proof of what? Self-termination? He didn't have to drive to Lake Henshaw to do that. He could've done it in Koreatown. And you know as well as I that despite Matt's interest in Buddhism he was devoted to the Catholic Church. We were altar boys together. Took catechism together. I know he'd never test church doctrine in that way."

"He wasn't devoted to the church as much as he was devoted to his brother. Father Frank is a popular pastor. I mean, his Tridentine Mass is so well attended by Whelans and Keanes that we have our own pews. His other Masses are standing room only. Matt's attendance was based more on tradition than spiritual enlightenment. He sought that elsewhere."

Jacob blew out a frustrated sigh. "That may be so, but still, self-termination can only be called such if there's evidence to suggest it. Can you be sure you're not letting your feelings for him cloud your judgment?"

"Can you?"

"Alright then. Let's say he exercised his God-given gift of free will. It doesn't change the fact that I found my friend dead. Dead is dead."

"Geeze, Jacob!"

"I'm sorry, Birdie, I've had a hell of a day and you're not helping."

"I'm sorry, too. Really. My brain is numb. I'm pretty sure I'm in shock. At least tell me what happened from your perspective."

Jacob reported the details in a surgically precise monologue that resembled the one delivered by Detective Hughes. "Expelled vomit blocked the airway and he suffocated. He was unconscious when this occurred. Matt didn't suffer."

"Do the bowels always empty?"

"Not always."

"How do you determine time of death?"

"It's a calculation based on eyes, lividity, fixed rigor, and core temperature. I estimated he had been dead nine to thirteen hours. Considering you saw him at midnight and if he made no further stops and factoring drive time, that puts his death between 0200 and 0300. Like I said."

"The evidence?"

"Delivered to the lab."

"Hughes told me you collected blood from the heart. How is it—?"

"I have a crash kit in the trunk of my car. It's a toolbox of sorts that contains the instruments of my trade."

"Where's Matt's body now?"

"Frank Senior dispatched Junior with a private ambulance. They took him to Holy Cross. Follow my example, Birdie. I'm putting away the medical examiner. Put aside the journalist. Go home and have a long cry."

Exactly.

FIVE

Sunday, January 8

BIRDIE AWOKE DISORIENTED. IT took a moment to remember why. Yesterday, after returning from Henshaw House she turned off the phone ringer, put a do-not-disturb note on her front door, and dialed down the doorbell to zero for those who—despite reading the note—would insist on condoling. She buried herself in a blanket cave and lost herself, fighting the unconsciousness of sleep until exhaustion forced it upon her. As she reluctantly drifted off she became vaguely aware that scales took root on her skin and an icy sheath enclosed her heart.

She looked at the clock. 8:30 a.m. Mass in half an hour. She'd never make it in time. Not like she wanted to go anyway. She wasn't in the mood to sit through a morose service with a grief-stricken congregation. She'd rather lock down and suffer in private.

Biology forced her up to pee. Once up, she required coffee. And, what the hell, after getting adequately caffeinated, and not so brain dead, she might as well check her messages and get it over with. She went into the office and immediately ripped off a page on the wall. 240 days sober. Just get through this day.

Amazing how fast the news of death spread. The voicemails and e-mails were plentiful and kind. The whole of her universe knew what Matt meant to her. Most of the messages began with, "I know how you felt about Matt …" or "I know how important Matt was to you …" It seemed the whole of their mutual acquaintance were in tune with the way the couple felt. Everyone voiced some variation of the same theme: they knew they loved each other, wondered why they weren't together, always thought they'd be together.

There were two unexpected callers. The first was an ex-boyfriend, Denis Cleary. The last time she saw him they were in a judge's chamber where he swore to hate her forever. The second was Matt's ex-wife, Linda, who blamed the teenage Birdie for the destruction of her marriage. Despite the past ill will, Birdie took comfort by their willingness to reach out.

The last message was from Frank Senior, Matt's father, and it froze her bones.

"Come to the house after Mass. Business. Brunch."

A beckon she dare not ignore.

She practically sprinted up the stairs to her bedroom above the office. Frantic, she picked up jeans from the floor and shook them out to test their wear-worthiness. At the exact moment she decided to wear a dress to Frank's obligatory meeting, small items flew from the pocket. A tiny paper envelope caught her immediate attention.

Matt used to write sayings on a piece of paper, fold it into an envelope and leave the surprise for Birdie to find later. She pounced on the last note Matt would ever write. She reveled in the weight of it. Felt the slick texture of the colorful Asian wrapping. Held it to her heart. He must've snuck this one into her pocket Friday night when they were making out behind Molly's.

She carefully unfolded the creased paper. Inside was a brass key. Larger than the average house key, the head was square and etched with the words DO NOT DUPLICATE. In his precise script Matt wrote a Latin phrase on the white side of the paper: *Judex ergo cum sedebit, quidquid latet apparebit, nil inultum remanebit.* The words filled her with dread. They were part of a Requiem Mass and translated: The Lord of judgment on his throne shall every secret thing make known, no sin escapes that once was sown.

The Latin simply meant that upon death there would be an accounting of earthly behavior. Coupled with the key it had a more sinister connotation. Birdie slumped to her knees in moral agony. Matt had done something wrong and he wanted Birdie to know about it.

The note and key wasn't the only wicked surprise. The shake-out also dumped Detective Hughes' business card and the photos from the shed. As she picked up the photos a grave foreboding enveloped her like a heavy shawl.

In the snow picture four men stood side-by-side. Matt wore the red parka she had given to him several Christmases ago. Jacob Hoy was also there and another man she didn't know. The shock came when she identified the fourth. The one standing next to Matt. An attractive man with an engaging smile.

Deputy Detective R. Hughes.

Was it possible that Hughes' nondisclosure and his castaway look had a hidden meaning? Birdie would consider all possibilities. But not now. She'd quell the questions until after she met with Frank Senior.

Her hands shook. A clear sign of alcohol craving. She envisioned the numbers. 240. 240. 240. She tucked her hands under her knees and forced herself to breathe.

The Whelan family home was a grand formal residence in Beverly Hills. Matt's mother, Mary, came from old Irish money, and the Whelan clan owned successful textile mills. Frank Senior and Mary never took their moneyed heritage for granted. They had working class values and drilled a strong work ethic into their seven sons.

By L.A. standards, the drive wasn't long from her house to theirs, yet by the time she arrived she had a massive headache brought on by deception, a brain that wouldn't shut up, and pesky sobriety.

Several people with clipboards loitered on the broad walkway waiting for instruction. A fashionably dressed woman blasted out of the house and skipped across the porch and down the steps. She barked into a wireless headset, "Fast track the permits. Tents and deliveries are Wednesday. Event on Thursday. I'll hit the neighbors." She started clapping as if to gain control of an unruly classroom. "Get Sal off his fat ass and tell him to round up his

A/V guys." She pointed a manicured finger at one of the idle persons and said, "Set up a rain contingency."

Only in L.A. would an event planner be hired to put together a post-burial wake.

Birdie pushed open the heavy oak door. The vast entry was empty. The murmur of saddened voices from the kitchen and family room filled the massive space with a leaded moodiness. Not wanting to participate with the family's sorrow she tiptoed down the central hall toward the powder bath in search of an aspirin.

She opened the door. On the sink was her cousin, Madigan, dress over her hips, legs wrapped around Matt's youngest brother, Patrick, whose pants were around his ankles.

Birdie gasped and slammed the door shut. Their hushed conversation of surprise could be heard through the door. Both thought the other had flipped the lock.

Patrick was the youngest of the brothers, a patrol officer working Hollywood Division—the same division where Birdie's father worked. A few minutes later the toilet flushed and a red-faced Patrick exited the room. He quickly moved down the hall.

"Patrick," Birdie said to his back. "I'm sorry for your loss."

He stopped, not turning. "I know. And you, too."

Then she remembered the picture. "Patrick."

He reluctantly turned. His puffy undereyes matched hers. She held out the photo. "Can you please tell me who these men are?"

He pointed. "Matt, Jacob Hoy, Parker Sands. I don't know the other."

"Who is Parker to Matt?"

"A friend from St. B. He's a mortician at Holy Cross. Junior took Matt's body there."

Another conflict of interest.

"Please don't tell Father," he said. She didn't need to ask of whom he referred.

Madi pulled her inside the powder bath. Though Birdie had their paternal grandmother's name, she and her cousin had an equal share of her resemblance. Born one month apart—Madi the elder—they were more sisters than cousins and were often misidentified as twins.

"Babe," said Madi, "I'm so sorry." She hugged Birdie tightly and stroked her hair. "I can't believe Matt's dead. It's so sudden."

This was exactly the kind of condoling Birdie wanted to avoid, but understanding Madi's fondness for Matt she returned the hug and uttered sympathies in her ear, which had the dual effect of comforting herself.

When Madi pulled away to blow her nose, Birdie took advantage of the opening. "You and Patrick?"

"Don't tell anyone. We've been together since Thanksgiving."

"I'm happy for you both. It's perfect."

Madi's lifestyle was romance killjoy. She was a brand. An in-demand stylist as hip and famous as her celebrity clients. With the Hollywood award season nearing high gear she was home for now. Come April, she'd be getting her passport stamped in exotic locales. The work always took precedence over relationships.

"Why hide?" said Birdie.

"Patrick wants to go public, but I'm new at this, a little more cautious. Besides, I don't need the family pressure of marriage and babies."

"That's the problem with dating Catholic men. They're traditional and want the complete package. George certainly did. So did Denis. I'm determined that my next boyfriend is going to be an atheist."

Madi put a multi-ringed hand over Birdie's mouth. "Don't say that."

Birdie pushed her hand away. "Oh, come on. You have to admit how much easier sex would be without two-way guilt."

"Yeah, right, like you've ever felt guilty about sex."

Birdie responded with a mischievous grin. "His brother just died. It seems an odd time to bang it out on the bathroom sink."

"Stress relief."

"Yeah, I always like a good screw when I'm stressed."

"Don't tease. What do you mean by next boyfriend? What's up with George?"

"He broke up with me. Couldn't compete with Matt."

"No man could."

"You in love?"

"I think so. I get this fluttery feeling in my belly every time he's near."

"Love or lust. In either case you can't go wrong with Patrick. He's a good man like his brother. You're lucky."

Birdie felt genuine happiness, but envy wouldn't be denied. Matt and Birdie wouldn't be the couple who'd legally bind the two families.

She shook two aspirin from the bottle, swallowed them with a palm of water and chased them with a piece of yellow Fruit Stripe gum.

"I've got to go. Frank Senior called me to a meeting."

Dread washed across Madi's face. "What for?"

"He didn't say." She kissed Madi goodbye. "Wish me luck."

Frank Senior was a heavy-handed, black-and-white kind of man; an alpha-dog patriarch who demanded obedience. His opinion was the only one that mattered. Frank didn't approve of Birdie's liberal education—which gave her a progressive, open-minded view of the world that didn't fit Frank's chauvinist standards— and by default, Birdie herself. She operated in shades of gray in regard to the personal. Her professional side was strictly B&W, but that wasn't the half that mattered to Frank.

Birdie followed the cigar smoke into Frank's study. A man's room: wood-paneled walls, leather couches, plaid chairs, rifles in racks, handguns in a case, photos in tarnished silver frames, a haze of smoke yellowing the crown molding, ancient books moldering on dusty bookshelves. As she entered the room, two sets of eyes studied her and she felt like she'd just been sent to the headmaster's office.

"Come in," said Frank Senior with his usual formality. He closed the door with a soft click, then took her hands into his. She flinched. This was the first time they'd had physical contact. He offered silent commiseration and she relaxed in the palms of his old-soul strength. His eyes were dry, but bloodshot and swollen with a recent bout of crying. With a final squeeze he let go and waved for her to sit.

"I've always known that Matt loved you." He patted his chest with his fist. "I always thought he'd marry you. I gave my blessing despite my concerns." He nodded at her in a way that suggested she knew to what he referred.

"Yet why did he always back away when we got too close?" she said.

"I wish I could give you the answer. Matt kept his own counsel. Well, that's not entirely true. This gentleman is Mr. Martin Reidy of Deeney, McMahon, and Desmond."

A lawyer.

Reidy gave her a firm handshake. "I apologize for the suddenness of my business at this terrible time. Matt left explicit instruction. He made you heir to his estate."

Her breath stopped. The only sound in the room was the tick tick tick of the clock on the fireplace mantle. Equilibrium snapped and the room began to spin. She was in a state of confusion. There was already too much to bear.

"You've been given a tremendous responsibility," said Reidy. "If you're unable to take on the task, we have the authority to manage the estate until you're ready."

"I'm flabbergasted," she managed to say.

"Even in death my son continues to take care of you," said Frank. "That's proof of the depth of his feelings."

Frank's words spoke part of the truth. They were as close as two people could get without physical intimacy. He had always been an important presence in her life. Her trusted friend. The one she called when she needed bail money. But his heir?

"What do I have to do?" she said to Reidy.

"I'd like to come to your home tomorrow morning with some boxed possessions he left in my safekeeping. We'll need to go over the terms of his trust. There are papers to sign. I expect we'll need a couple of hours."

"Tomorrow is as good as any day I suppose," she said. Then to Frank, "Did you know?"

"Yes. Matt began the process while still in the hospital after the domestic."

Reidy added, "It's not uncommon for people to think about their loved ones after a medical crisis."

"How do you feel about it?" she said to Frank.

His cheeks moved upward in a rare smile that spread out like an alluvial fan from the corners of his eyes. A beautiful sight. "I didn't approve at first. But he had a persuasive argument and I conceded to his decision. Know this, Birdie, the Keanes and Whelans are like family, and families stick together. Regardless."

Birdie waited. The balance went unsaid.

"We'll give you some privacy," he said. "Come eat when you're done in here."

Reidy handed her an envelope and a business card. "Monday's are tough traffic-wise. Is a thirty-minute warning sufficient notice?"

"I'll make myself available."

When they had gone, Birdie inspected the envelope. Matt's monogram was engraved in the upper left corner: a gold M interlaced with a black W, the W had an arrow pointing upward like on a stock graph. It looked like a corporate logo. She opened it with shaky hands.

The letter was written in Matt's neat cursive:

Dearest Bird,

The day I met you was a beautiful and dire day. The temptation of you pulled me to pieces. From then forward my life has been divided in two: before Bird and after Bird. We certainly can't control with whom we fall in love and I fully understood its forbidden nature.

I watched you stumble in your efforts to become a part of the adult world. I've seen you blossom into a successful, determined woman who has a huge capacity for love. I've experienced firsthand the stubbornness, tenacity, and fierceness with which you protect the people you love.

Now it's my turn. I'm obviously gone and can no longer be a physical presence in your life, but I will be with you today and forever in spirit.

Every conversation and every moment we spent together has been precious to me. Even if you received a fraction of the happiness you've given me over the years then you, too, have been blessed. You were not the first love of my life, but you are the greatest and the last. Please continue to dance and follow your heart—it won't betray you.

I love you now and forever, M

She crumpled the letter and looked up at the family portrait above the fireplace. It was brown, faded with age, and covered with ashy grime. Frank Senior and Mary flanked their seven sons. In birth order: Frank Junior (the priest), Michael, Eric, Colin, Emmett, Matt, and Patrick. All, excluding Junior, were cops, and they had inherited equal shares of the glamorous movie star appearance of their Irish parents. As she stared at the faded portrait, she became angry at what could have been and the trick Matt had played.

"Damn you Matthew Francis Whelan!" She double-fingered the portrait. "It's too late. Hear me, asshole?" She sobbed. "Why'd you lie to me? Do you think this is adequate compensation for my broken heart? Huh? Answer me!"

The bitterness of profound grief stuck to the roof of her mouth. If Matt loved her so much as demonstrated with words and kisses, a love letter, and an inheritance, then why would he betray that promise of forever love by taking his own life? Was the answer behind the wrong thing Matt needed to atone for? Was it so bad he *had* to take his life?

As questions swirled in her head, a terrible realization crashed down on her. Matt Whelan's life wasn't as slick and shiny as she'd thought. It was darker. Baser. She hated the flat sensation that nothing was as it seemed. Worst of all, he robbed her. A futile, loveless, emptiness lay in her future.

SIX

I<small>F ONE WERE TO</small> look at a map and draw a straight line from Birdie's historic neighborhood of Hancock Park to downtown L.A., the line might cross over Matt's house in Koreatown. He spoke fluent Korean, Spanish, and Mandarin and loved the languages of his ethnic neighborhood. A step through the front gate transported one back in time. The Kyoto-like courtyard was hedged by bamboo, Japanese boxwood, ferns, and ficus. Dormant pink jasmine and honeysuckle wound around redwood lattice. Come spring, they'd fill the air with sweet fragrance. A large variety of exotic acacias provided winter blooms of cream and yellow. The courtyard offered a private sanctuary and transition from the street. On the right side of the porch, a copper rain chain hung from the edge of the roof. Rain water gently twinkled down the teacup-sized bowls and into a large, round basin. The overflow spilled over the sides and disappeared onto black, shiny rocks.

Birdie let herself in. The interior was tidy as usual. Clean-lined Asian furnishings in muted colors were punctuated with ornate accessories, statues of Buddha, and a large Wheel of Dharma. Matt practiced Catholicism, but was especially taken with Buddhism after finding the wheel at a flea market. In the days before statues of Buddha were made, the wheel was the object of worship. Eight spokes represented the right view, right thought, right behavior, right speech, right effort, right livelihood, right mindfulness, and right meditation. The wheel became Matt's compass.

Birdie had been here last week. She had brought Chinese. They danced in bare feet on the bamboo floor of the great room. During breathers they drank Orange Crush from glass bottles. Matt inadvertently sprayed soda from his nose. This gave them the simples and they laughed until their sides were sore. He seemed relaxed and happy.

She yearned to go back in time and grab that opportunity to express how she ached for him and admired him and trusted him. How she felt his presence flow through her body, as if life-giving. Maybe if they had expressed their love then things would be different now.

Birdie perused Matt's home. Looked for locks and touched his things as if pieces of his soul could be transferred to her. In the library, she caressed his beloved writing desk that once belonged to his maternal grandmother. It was pear green with a Dutch-style still life painted on the front of the flip down. Randomly plucking a book off the shelf, she opened the pages and stuck her nose in the gutter. The dusty smell of wood pulp and printer's ink filled her nostrils with one of her favorite scents.

Framed photos eased past the periphery of her vision as she walked down the hall to Matt's bedroom. She slid open the screened closet door, sniffed the leather polish used to clean the Sam Browne, fingered his pressed uniforms and smiled at the immaculate spit shine of his boots. She bent down and unhooked the handcuff key attached to the boot laces. Part talisman, part just-in-case, he'd worn it since his academy days. She attached it to the chain around her neck. It clinked next to the medallion of Saint Francis de Sales.

She pulled back the coverlet of his bed, shook off her mules and slid between the cool sheets. She rubbed her bare feet together to warm them. The bed smelled like Matt after he did some light work at her house—a heady earthy kind of smell. A delightful scent. She buried her head in his white, silk-covered pillow, took a full breath of him and fantasized that they had spent the night together. Matt lay next to her, rested from love-making. In profile, his eyes were closed and his breath as soft as a butterfly's wake. She ran a finger down his forehead, traced his nose and his full lips. He bit her finger in a playful gesture, turned on his side, and placed his warm hand on her bare hip and pulled her close. He combed fingers through her hair, gazed at her with lovely green eyes.

Her eyes welled as she remembered the day they met.

Birdie was a jaded fifteen-year-old who thought she had the world figured out. She disregarded her parent's strict rules and her surliness often earned restrictions. Mostly, she was bored.

Madi had gone to Ireland to visit relatives and every one of Birdie's friends seemed to be on European vacations.

There she was, in her favorite red-and-white bikini, floating on a silver raft in the middle of the pool, hiding behind dark sunglasses and ignoring a Fourth of July party. One hand lazily dipped into the cool blue water that contrasted with the smoggy gray sky. The palm trees that bisected Magnolia Street, and towered over the house, looked dirty. She gazed at the white, square beast of the house called Magnolia Manor (so named for the street and often shortened to the Manor). It was the home of her dad's brother, Louis—also a cop—and his wife, Nora, a nurse/homemaker.

The Keane family and their friends didn't need a reason to party, but the holiday was a good excuse for swimming, barbeque, drinking, loud music, and Irish dancing. It wasn't yet noon and already the party was noisy and raucous. It'd be only a matter of time before the neighbors called the police. It happened every time. The dispatchers would tire of the neighbor's complaints. They'd tell the callers that the cops were already on scene. It was as true then as it was today. The Keanes were a cop family that hung with other cop families.

Birdie loved parties. But not that day. She felt an electric restlessness as if on the verge of a big bang. She wasn't interested in a bunch of drunken buffoons with loaded guns. That is until her cousin, Arthur, showed up with his new partner.

The first time she laid eyes on Matt Whelan he stood near the French doors greeting other cops. He was the handsomest man she ever saw: tall with slender muscles, clean-shaven, with dark hair that hung in wisps on his forehead. His lips had a broody, sexy pout. His poise suggested a peacefulness that was disarming. His gait smooth and even. She watched from her silver island and pretended to be nonchalant and unaffected by the newcomer.

Arthur pulled a couple of chairs next to the pool and motioned Matt to sit.

"Bird," he said, "get your ass outta the water and meet my partner."

She pushed the glasses on top of her head and exited the pool with a push-up from the side. She stood as close to Matt as space would allow while water slid down her body.

Never one to buy into her precocious bullshit, Arthur said, "Give it a rest. He's too old for you. Besides, he's married."

Maybe. But Matt took a long hard look at her. If nothing else, he noticed. Ding ding ding. Matt stood and extended his hand. "It's a pleasure to meet you."

"And you," said Birdie, returning the firm grip.

He held her hand briefly and studied her face with his bright shamrock-green eyes. That's the moment she fell in love. Arthur would later say that he felt the current pass between them.

As the afternoon wore on, partygoers were getting drunk in typical Manor fashion. Birdie was no exception. A handsome cop and a hazy veil of alcohol had resuscitated her day. When her dad called for more lime daiquiris, she begrudgingly stumbled into the kitchen for bartending duties. Deep in thought, she didn't notice that someone had entered behind her. Nor was she expecting an arm to suddenly wrap around her neck. Matt. Misunderstanding his advance, she allowed her body to relax, thinking he was going to kiss her.

"Never go limp," said Matt. "An attacker will dominate you."

"Huh?"

"Hasn't your cousin taught you the simplest of self-defense moves?"

"What do I need self-defense for?"

Matt spun her around. "You're a very pretty girl who drinks and flirts. Liquor compromises good judgment. Boys will take advantage. Pay attention. We're family now. You're my little sister."

"I don't want to be your sister."

Matt blinked with helpless fascination. "Do you at least know how to scream?"

As a response, she screamed as loud and shrill as she could. Before she was finished, a dozen men with firearms stormed the kitchen.

Matt threw up his hands.

"Yeah," she said, "I know how to scream."

Matt didn't wear a wedding ring and Birdie conveniently forgot he was married, and it was at that moment his wife arrived at the party. The gunslingers parted for an exquisite woman. No introduction necessary.

Linda was a female version of him—long and lean with grace and serenity. Her long blonde hair shone against her luminescent pale skin.

Linda's eyes perforated the kitchen. Her red-faced husband, hands in the air, stood next to a bikini-clad teenager who wore a broad smile of satisfaction. Even an impetuous girl could see the hurt, and Birdie quickly wiped the smile off her face. After a brief conversation with her husband, Linda left the party the way she came—alone.

∞

Every Fourth of July since was a private anniversary. Matt stated in his letter that his life was divided in two. So was hers: before Matt and after Matt. Getting up from his bed to continue her search, she reflected on how people divided their lives. Was it possible that Matt was the man she always knew him to be except in this bizarre situation? Maybe he purposely hurt her to pique her interest. After all, the key and note were obviously intended to be found after his death. But the pesky whys bothered her.

Birdie walked to the other side of the house through the small dining area to the kitchen. A sudden chill of cool air caressed her arms. She spun around and saw a shadow move across the window. She pressed against it, gazed into the backyard. No one was there. She shook it off.

On the kitchen counter, next to the rice cooker, five items were in a neat row: his wallet, cell phone, keys, Beretta handgun, and a change purse. The items missing from Henshaw House laid out so deliberately.

The wallet contained no cash. All the credit cards seemed to be in their proper slots. She picked up the Beretta, did a press check, put the unloaded gun on the counter. She turned on the cell and scrolled through the incoming and outgoing calls. Nothing unusual. She opened the change purse and counted out eighty-nine dollars and thirty cents.

Four twenties, one five, four singles, a quarter, and a nickel.

The same amount and the same denominations as the money found in the truck.

Finding that amount of money in one location wouldn't be memorable. Two? Neon sign.

She retrieved Deputy Hughes' business card and punched the number.

"Elizabeth Keane," she said in greeting.

"Official for real this time?"

"Absolutely. This is no longer personal. Tell me about your relationship with Matt and don't leave out any details."

"We didn't have a relationship. I met him in Mammoth. It was a ski trip organized by the Southern California Gun Association so there were lots of enthusiasts on the mountain. Matt was there. I was there. We met. I didn't see him again until yesterday."

"Why didn't you tell me?"

"I didn't intentionally conceal it—the topic never came up."

"What about Jacob?"

"Our paths cross every now and then over a dead body. I've known him for years. I hope you're not worried about integrity. Jacob—"

"—knew Matt. You knew Matt. Both of you were there at his death."

"Correction. We were there after his death. As was another deputy."

"Why didn't you search Matt's Koreatown house or send someone up to do it?"

"Matt died in Lake Henshaw, not in Los Angeles."

"He was a cop."

"Cops aren't allowed to die?"

"Guess what I found at his house?"

"His cell phone, wallet, and that gun you mentioned?"

"And another case of money in the exact amount, in the same denominations, as the cash found in the console of his truck."

"That's random."

"Matt didn't do random. Or accidental. Or coincidental. He micromanaged his life. The items were laid out in a row so the money would be noticed. It means something."

"It means he was organized. He laid out his stuff to check it before putting it into his pockets. Only he forgot. His father is a retired cop. Don't you think he'd go himself or send an investigator if he were suspicious of his son's death?"

This fact stopped her cold.

"It's validation of an accidental overdose," he continued. "How else do you explain ingesting too much pain reliever? He was distracted or absent minded."

"You sound like you're trying to make it fit."

"The coroner will determine the manner of death."

"Based on your report."

"And the evidence collected by Jacob. By the way, I'm coming to L.A. on Wednesday. I'll be attending the funeral Thursday."

"Why?"

"Because I'll prove my conclusion and disprove all other explanations. I'm crossing my Ts and dotting my Is. May I come by your place on Wednesday?"

"Why?"

"Same reason."

"Okay, fine."

"Anything else?"

"I don't care what you say. A dead man left behind a clear message to decipher. So, by all means, come to town, make sure you have it straight because I'm going to be on your back, Detective Hughes."

"I must warn you. I have a Saker watching my back."

"What does that mean?"

"Maybe one day you'll find out."

"Your attitude is condescending. And I find your dismissal to be offensive."

"I apologize. Look, your friend's death has no sinister connotations. Don't create something out of nothing."

"If you're a good detective, you'd check out all the angles."

He snorted with impatience. "I know my job. You sound more like a spurned lover than a concerned friend."

That was closer to the truth than he knew.

SEVEN

Birdie traced a finger across the etched name in the granite monument. WHELAN. Only one marker graced the family plot. Mary Junior. Frank and Mary kept having sons until they were blessed with a daughter. Unfortunately, the child was stillborn and Mary would conceive no more. People don't think of death until it happens. So Frank bought the biggest plot available in a Catholic facility in which to inter his family. There was room for thirty-six Whelans and Mary Junior would soon have company.

Holy Cross Mortuary was located on Slauson Avenue next to the cemetery in Culver City. A depressing place full of soft sobs and morose voices. Fake roses scented with perfumed oil couldn't mask the stale air. Soft piano music filtered through hidden speakers. Birdie glanced through an open doorway into a visitation room. A mourning family, clutching paper programs, sat awkwardly in padded folding chairs lined up in front of a flower-laden casket.

A woman with a sad smile approached and offered a program.

"I'm here on another matter," Birdie whispered. She held up her press credentials. Oftentimes it opened doors because reporters are hunter gatherers, truth seekers, unlike cops who can legally lie. "Is Parker Sands available?"

She glanced down at the ID and squinted. "Your name?"

"Elizabeth Keane."

The lady dropped the programs onto a round table and exited through a wood-paneled door. A few minutes later she opened another door and motioned Birdie over. "Please have a seat. Mr. Sands will be right with you."

On the walnut desk sat a brochure: *The Catholic Family Funeral Guide*. Birdie imagined a friendly man sitting across the desk. He'd talk about the importance of musical compositions. He'd provide binders with full-color photographs of caskets and flower arrangements. He'd start with the plainest selection and flip through the book until the family settled on the best and upgraded to the $40,000 fancy model with the real silk lining.

Birdie cupped the snow photo in her hand and studied the face of the man who walked into the room. It was him. He offered his hand. "Hello, Ms. Keane. I'm Parker Sands. You're inquiring about Matt Whelan? Were you a friend?"

"Yes. I understand you are as well." She slid the photo across the desk.

Sands picked it up as he sat. "Where did you get this?"

"At his house in Lake Henshaw. Have you ever been there?"

"No."

Birdie took out a reporter's notebook and a pen. "When was the last time you saw him?"

"I'm sorry," he said. "Who are you exactly?"

"Elizabeth Keane. Matt's best friend."

"I thought Jacob Hoy was his best friend."

"So you know Jacob."

"Yes. We all went to St. Bonaventura together." His eyes dropped to the ID hanging around her neck. "Why are you here?"

"I'd like to see his body."

"There is no viewing scheduled."

"That's wrong," she said, losing her composure. "They're usually on the day before burial."

Sands clasped his hands. "Viewing the departed gives closure to those who grieve, but his brother, Junior, gave us explicit instructions based on Matt's wishes."

"I understand. In lieu of a formal viewing will you let me look at him?"

Sands had a practiced smile. "As a licensed mortician I cannot permit that."

"You embalm bodies and prepare them and dress them for burial. Just a peek?"

"I'm sorry, but your request is not sanctioned by the laws, restrictions, and common practices of my profession. I wouldn't even allow it for his family."

"Junior is his brother."

"He's a priest who performs a religious service."

The conversation wasn't going the way she intended. Time to regroup. "It must have been strange to receive a body of someone you know."

Sands' shoulders relaxed. "It was a shock when Matt's father called. Junior seemed especially grieved when he arrived with the body. Matt survived near fatal gun shots and ended up dying from an accidental drug overdose. What are the odds?"

Birdie stiffened. There hasn't been an official proclamation of death. "Who told you that Matt died from an accidental drug overdose?"

Sands' right eye twitched. "I believe Junior did. He must've heard it from Jacob."

"And he used that exact wording? Not overdose? Not unde-termined?"

"I believe so."

"Please don't be offended," said Birdie, "but I've never heard Matt mention you."

"Matt and I were casual friends. Our paths have rarely crossed since school."

"So, you're a gun nut like Matt?"

"No."

"Then how is it you ended up on Mammoth Mountain on the exact day with a bunch of members of a gun association?"

"I was Jacob's guest. We keep in closer contact."

"Have you spoken with Jacob in the last day?"

"He called sometime after Junior arrived. He said to take extra care of Matt. I would anyway, but I think it gave Jacob some com-fort to express it." Sands abruptly stood up. "I really must go now. I have a family to attend to."

Birdie licked the powder from a stick of orange Fruit Stripe be-fore folding it in thirds and sucking it. She set the timer on her phone to see how long it took to start chewing—a little game to distract her from the demon on the office wall called a dry erase board. The massive white board was where she made notations for her work; a place to riddle out the puzzles of a crime or keep track of timelines or beats to a story. It represented the vast wilderness of nothingness her life had become when she lost her voice—her work—since becoming sober. It lay hidden underneath a roll-up shade of gray metallic fabric—but even covered, the empty board taunted her.

She convinced herself to roll up the screen just to see what would happen. When the walls didn't come tumbling down she picked up a black Expo marker and wrote.

The process to find truth is methodical, precise, and provable.
Intuition is not evidence!

A good start she determined. So she continued.

Matt = suicide → pain relief? self-punishment? why promise Birdie?
accident = accident
Key = unlocks secret thing/sin → why be sneaky?
Layout of gun, wallet, cell, keys = notice same amount of money @ two locations.
$89.30 = ?

She circled $89.30 and rewrote it.

89 30 = coordinates? reference?
8930 = code? pin? suffix? password? address?

As soon as she wrote "address" she dropped the marker and jumped back in surprise. Her eyes shot to the Paige Street mobile hanging from the bookcase. In the sun position was a piece of tin stamped with **8930 Paige Street**. The house where the incident took place.

There must be new information regarding the cold case. Something Matt wanted her to know.

EIGHT

Monday, January 9

DAY 241. JUST ONE more. The rising sun shone pink through a crack in the storm clouds. Birdie opened the front door to the sharp scent of wet grass and clean, smog-free air. She took a deep breath of it, pulled it down into her lungs. She took another, sat on the damp brick of her front porch, and picked up the *Los Angeles Times*. She flipped to the obituaries just as a Crown Victoria pulled in the driveway.

Her dad, Gerard Keane, stepped out from the passenger side of the vehicle. His adjutant, a Sergeant II—three pointy stripes and a curved one at the bottom, called a rocker, on his sleeve—rolled down the window and waved. She waved back.

Gerard was captain of Hollywood Station and had been a suit for the bulk of his police career so she was surprised to see him in uniform. He always presented a rugged youthfulness when he wore it. The sun hit his full head of silvery-white hair, creating a halo of light. Premature gray hair and clear blue eyes were a familial trait all the men shared. It was a shockingly good-looking combination.

A smile of pride split Birdie's face and she wolf whistled. "My, my, my. Look at my handsome father. I do believe, sir, that you're walking with a bit of swagger. Is that because you're wearing the blue today?"

He laughed and sat next to her. Gave her a hug and kiss. She leaned into him. He had a quiet strength that emanated from deep within. It gave her a feeling of safety.

"What brings you out here?" she said.

Gerard handed her a white paper bag. "Running on fumes?"

When was the last time she ate? Saturday morning?

"There's an egg sandwich in there." He noticed the open paper and frowned. "Don't be reading his obit. You know who Matt was."

"It's not in here anyway." She folded the paper closed. "Maybe tomorrow."

Gerard put a condoling arm around her shoulder and kissed her head.

"You really came out here to bring me food?"

"Just wanted to see how my girl was doing."

"You wanted to see if Matt's death sent me back to the bottle."

"Can't fool the reporter. Mom and I missed you at Mass. You okay?"

"Define okay. I got notified of Matt's death and immediately drove to Henshaw House. I looked at the scene, met the detective in charge. Yesterday, Frank Senior beckoned me to the house and introduced me to Matt's lawyer."

Gerard nudged her. "You've been too busy to hit the bottle. Whatever helps, sweetheart."

"Frank actually touched me. Took my hands."

"Really? Did his son's death thaw the ice king?"

"Something melted."

"Why the lawyer?"

"Matt left me his estate. I'm his heir."

Gerard whistled. "What a class act."

"The lawyer is from a Beverly Hills law firm. He'll be coming by today to bring me some boxes of stuff that belonged to Matt. Papers need signing. Lawyerly business."

"Your mom will be happy to help."

"I'll call if I need it. Was Father Frank the celebrant yesterday?"

"No. Father Gabriel said he's on bereavement. He'll be back Wednesday."

"Being a priest doesn't spare him the heartache of losing a beloved brother. Why the uniform today?"

"Wearing it all week in honor of Matt." He touched the black band around the badge on his breast.

She decided to run the money amount past her dad. Verify and double check. "Does eighty-nine dollars and thirty cents mean anything to you? Maybe a monetary value for something specific or a police code?"

Gerard thought a moment. "Hmm. N.I.R." It was a running family joke. N.I.R. is LAPD shorthand for "no independent recollection." It was also Keane shorthand for "I don't know."

"8930 is the Paige Street address."

"Is that so? Why is it relevant?"

"Matt left that amount of money in his truck and the exact amount in his kitchen."

"Probably a coincidence." Gerard flinched. Matt's anal nature was legendary. "Mom's hosting her card group tomorrow night. I've been ordered out of the house. How about dinner with your old man at the Westend like we used to?"

"Sounds good. Six o'clock?"

"Perfect." He kissed his daughter on the nose. "Okay. It's off to work for me. I love you, sweetheart."

"I love you too, Dad."

Birdie flipped through a worn copy of *The Los Angeles Police Department Manual* that she'd filched from her Uncle Louis' basement—a place she was forbidden to be in the first place. The theft cost her a month's allowance and worth every cent. The manual became an invaluable resource during her crime reporting days.

Under VOLUME 3 – MANAGEMENT RULES AND PROCEDURES, numbered headings listed 890 and 895. No 893, nor 8930. Skipping ahead to VOLUME 4 – LINE PROCEDURES the highest numerical heading was 871.

Well, the numbers didn't refer to a police procedure. She closed the book and called her cousin, Arthur.

"Is the pin still in place?" she said.

"Don't worry, the grenade hasn't gone off."

Arthur used to have anger issues and a fast temper. His behavior improved when he took up mixed martial arts: a dangerous combination of boxing, street fighting, kung fu, and wrestling. And now he was a cruiserweight champion of submission moves.

Arthur and Matt's pairing at Rampart Station occurred because of the Paige Street Murder—so named for the street where the incident happened. Matt and Hugh Jackson were partners working Hollenbeck. They responded to a 211 hot shot and radioed in two armed suspects. Jackson was killed during the encounter. Matt returned fire and killed the shooter. The other suspect got away. The guy Matt killed turned out to be an off-duty cop, Antonio Sanchez, who worked narco in Van Nuys. His partner was Arthur Keane. They had the unfortunate nickname of Double A because both had quick-to-fire electric personalities like the standard battery. This fact alone made Arthur the number one suspect. The one that got away.

After Paige Street, the commander of Central Bureau, a big dog named Ralph Soto, orchestrated Matt's transfer into Rampart Division. Ditto Arthur's. He coupled the pair, making them partners. It was a strange setup from the get-go that still had gossipy cops talking. But Arthur and Matt defied all the scrutiny and rumors. They not only worked well together, their friendship and socializing bonded two families. They also had the unique distinction of having the longest-running partnership in the department.

Matt's death didn't just hit Birdie hard. Arthur was surely feeling intense sorrow.

"Are you staying off the mat?" said Birdie.

"Kidding me? That's my salvation, baby. The bag, the mat, it's where I work it all off. You staying off the bottle?"

"Yeah, but I've been chewing down my teeth."

"Have stock in Wrigley's?"

"I wish. They're owned by Mars, which is a private company."

"Hmmm," he said, distracted.

Birdie heard the distinct sound of ice clinking in glass as Arthur took a drink.

"I always expected him to come back after the domestic," he said. "I never thought it'd end this way."

"When was the last time you saw him?"

"Couple weeks."

"Did he seem depressed?"

"Naw. But he wasn't the same after the shooting. He disappeared into himself. Almost paranoid."

"Really? I never saw that."

"You wouldn't. Matt always put on a happy face when you were around. He wouldn't burden you with his junk. You'd already been through hell with a cold-turkey withdrawal before he was shot."

Right. Birdie had just begun to feel whole. She even resumed jogging. When Matt got shot she took all the energy she had been spending on herself and focused it on his recovery.

"Listen, Bird," continued Arthur. "I know this has been a hard-ass year for you. Matt's death doesn't have to make it worse. Don't dwell on the loss. He wouldn't want that."

Wrong. Matt wanted her to dwell on something.

"I'll pass that advice back to you. It's too early in the day to be drinking."

"Busted."

"As always. Hey, I have to get ready for a meeting with Matt's lawyer. He's delivering some of Matt's property this morning. Before

I hang up, does the amount eighty-nine dollars and thirty cents mean anything to you?"

"Not as money. Take away the decimal."

Birdie's heart beat fast. Verification on the way. "I looked in the manual. Nothing matches."

"Eight. Nine. Three. Zero," said Arthur with slow and deliberate enunciation.

"I must be dense," she lied.

"Man, you are out of work mode. It refers to a big scandal. The one you want to solve."

"It's the Paige Street address."

"Bingo."

She told Arthur about the money left behind by Matt in his truck and at his house.

"This pisses me off. Definitely not nice of him to leave you a hint like that, what with your natural predilection of getting tangled with crap. He's a bastard—God rest his soul."

"It doesn't matter anyway," said Birdie. "I've already investigated Paige Street along with every crime reporter in this city. The damn blue wall is intact and the one inside the investigation isn't talking."

"We've been through this a million times. I can't tell you anything about it because I wasn't there. For two-and-a-half years the taskforce and the FBI made my life miserable and came up with zip. End of story."

"Maybe Matt found something relevant and wants me to re-examine the issue."

"There's nothing more." Arthur took a gulp of his drink, followed by a hard swallow. "Why now? What transpired that he couldn't tell you in person? Or in a phone call? Or an e-mail? He knew better than anybody how obsessed you were with Paige Street."

The answer lay with Matt's personality. He always weighed the pros and cons of every decision. Nothing was left to chance. Yet, Birdie might have to reconcile the real possibility that Matt wasn't the man she knew. There was a sinister aspect here that made her sick.

"Dad thinks it's a coincidence."

"When did you speak to him?"

"He came by a little while ago. Brought me food. We're gonna meet up for dinner tomorrow night."

"Since we're still close to the topic of Paige Street I'm going to tell you something and I need your promise that you won't freak out."

"What?"

"It was just a rumor that went around for a while. But now that Matt's dead, it's resurfaced. About a year into the Paige Street investigation money checked into evidence was stolen. There was a very quiet internal probe because of the large amount."

"How much?"

"Two mil. Never found. No suspects. It eventually faded away. Since Saturday, the rumors are floating around again. Word is, Matt took it way back when and was close to getting caught so he offed himself."

"No way," she hissed.

"He's being called a bad package."

Birdie felt like Arthur delivered one of his famously sneaky undercuts to the ribs. Her hands shook, making it difficult to hold the telephone receiver. A package is a cop's employment file. Bad package was slang for dirty cop.

"Look, Bird," said Arthur, "I can hear you seething. Don't get mental and start drinking. That moniker makes me guilty by association and I'm not freaking out. I'll be doing my best to talk it down."

"Why tell me? Should I pull out my file drawer of research and give Paige Street another look?" Which she had already done. "Or should I investigate missing evidence money?" Which she was going to do.

"Neither," said Arthur, his voice stern, "you're likely to hear it yourself so I wanted to warn you. In the end it means shit."

Like hell. It means something to me.

NINE

Birdie met Mr. Martin Reidy of Deeney, McMahon, and Desmond in the driveway. "A three-story house with a turret," he said. "May I have a tour?"

Tours of her house were standard requests from first-time visitors. Though she felt wrung out after Arthur's call she'd do her best to be gracious.

"You mentioned possessions. Is there something I can help carry?"

Reidy opened the side door of a panel van. Inside were seven banker's boxes. Six sealed with red packing tape. "They're quite heavy," he said despairingly.

"Don't worry. The house has a lift. We'll load in the garage." She punched a code into the electronic keypad. A filigreed wrought iron gate fanned inward. Birdie walked down the drive while Reidy followed in the van to the garage located at the back of the house.

They each grabbed a box. "What's in these?"

"I've no idea," said Reidy. "Matt was seriously concerned that you get them immediately in the event of his death. They were delivered to me as you see here, except for this last box; it holds the material we'll be going over today."

"How long have you had them?"

"Two weeks."

"And the letter you gave me yesterday?"

"The same."

"Don't you find the timing odd Mr. Reidy?"

"It is a strange coincidence."

She didn't need further evidence that Matt's death was deliberate. She needed the reason. Birdie suspected the boxes contained his journals and thus the answer.

It didn't take long to unload the boxes and deliver them to the third floor. From there they were moved to an unused bedroom. Then like a well-practiced docent, Birdie started the requested tour. She had the spiel memorized.

"The house was built in 1904 by the Catholic Church. All of the stained glass, mahogany, travertine, marble, and brick are original. There are five bedrooms on this floor." She led him down the hall and descended the turret to the second floor. On the way down, Reidy closely eyed the collection of religious objects: crucifixes, the antique tabernacle housed in a niche, another with old chalices. The morning light wasn't bright enough to illuminate the beauty of the stained glass, but he oohed and aahed anyway.

Birdie wished the showcase would've afforded her an opportunity to let go of the grief for a while, but it didn't. Matt's death hung heavy over her world. On the landing they passed a three-foot-tall marble statue of St. Joseph—the patron saint of the home—and entered the living room. Birdie's office was directly to the right, straight ahead the library, at the end the entrance to the kitchen. A breakfast nook and formal dining room were on the backside of the house.

Birdie directed Reidy to put the unsealed document box on the dining room table. "I'll show you the view." She led him into the library. The corner windows offered a stormy sky view of the city, including a corner of downtown.

"Beautiful," said Reidy.

"Follow me downstairs and I'll show you the pot farm."

"The what?"

That always shocked people.

She led him down the marble service stairs to the first floor. "The previous owner was a movie producer who had turned the old chapel into a screening room. He went broke and converted it into a greenhouse." She opened a pair of glass doors and flipped a switch. Row upon row of suspended growing lights buzzed and flickered to life to illuminate an empty massive space. "I understand marijuana is harder to grow and harvest than people think."

"The first floor is nothing?"

"Correct. All the living spaces are up. But there is a nice lanai and a gym down here. Now you've seen the house. Shall we get started?"

"I must say," said Reidy, as they made their way back to the dining room, "you live very nice. You must make a lot of money."

"Not really. Movie money helps."

"Didn't Matt help you buy this house?"

"I'm the only person in my family to attend college. After I graduated my maternal grandmother gave me a large monetary gift. I wanted real estate. Matt did the research and found this place. I bought it from the bank."

"It's big for one person."

"Too big. I rattle around. I bought it as an investment and didn't think the size would be an issue. Despite having an alarm system I convinced myself that someone could break in and I wouldn't even know it. I heard strange sounds all the time, started carrying a loaded gun. The house speaks. It took a couple of years to figure out what it was saying."

"Which is?"

"I'm old and creaky."

Reidy laughed. "How big is the lot?"

"Over an acre. I'm sorry now that I bought it. It's too much expense with maintenance and property tax and such. I live in a mansion on an upper-middle-class income."

Reidy took a seat and laid out several pens. "You won't have to worry about that anymore. Mr. Whelan's estate is significant. Four million."

Birdie nearly choked. "You're joking, right?" Stolen evidence money no longer seemed unbelievable.

Reidy hummed. "After you settle the estate and pay the taxes, you'll be lucky to net three. You're also the beneficiary on a life insurance policy worth a mil. I checked with the company this morning. Accidental death is covered. You'll have to wait for the death certificate before filing a claim."

"Out of curiosity, what if he had committed suicide?"

"Wouldn't be covered."

Sonofabitch. He really did do it. She felt pinched. Miserable. Knowing a truth didn't make it easier to swallow. Birdie reached for the bowl holding packages of Doublemint.

"Does his family know his worth?" she said, unzipping a new pack.

"Not likely. He was extremely private when it came to fiscal matters."

She wondered if Frank Senior would've been as encouraging if he knew what his son was worth. Then she berated herself for the disingenuous thought.

"It's pretty straightforward—" Reidy went over the will, terms and statement of trust and just about every power imaginable. He gave her a ring of keys, deeds, investment portfolios, an address book of advisors, pink slips, numerous contracts, riders, life insurance policy, statement of receivables and payables. Reidy tapped a pen on a copy of his and Linda's divorce decree. "They were legally divorced. She has no rights."

There was a vast inventory of possessions with notations of assignment. Matt left items to nieces, nephews, his parents, brothers, sisters-in-law, friends. Tithe to be split between two churches: St. Joseph and St. Bonaventura. He left items specifically for Birdie, the rest was to be disposed as she saw fit. Even Birdie's now ex-boyfriend, George Silva, was left with first rights of purchase for Matt's Koreatown residence. It was an exacting list with one exception.

"Mr. Reidy, Matt left one dollar to his brother Emmett. That's out of synch with the rest and seems petty. Can you explain?"

"He wanted to exclude his brother entirely. I suggested he leave Emmett a dollar so there'd be no appearance of an oversight that could give Emmett an opening to sue the estate for a larger share."

"Why? As far as I know they got along."

"As far as I know they didn't. Matt didn't specify the reason behind his decision, but he expressed his adamance." He patted her hand. "Don't worry."

It wasn't Emmett she worried about.

TEN

Birdie stared at the boxes in the empty bedroom. She held Matt in high esteem. On a pedestal. Okay, she'd already determined that he wasn't the man she thought he was. But what if he turned out to be two-faced? Monster on one side, affable human on the other. She'd had enough crushing emotions. She didn't need more. And yet, she was compelled to enter a place that could lead to greater hurt. After a long stretch of indecision, she decided to start small and seek the explanation for an incident that occurred when she was nineteen.

She cut the tape.

Each box was numbered. One being the oldest. It contained boyhood drawings, schoolwork with big red As across the top, reports, BB gun targets, photographs, a cigar box with scout badges and patches. A pinewood derby car. When box one was filled, he moved to box two and so on. Each item was marked with a number for the corresponding box. Even as a child, Matt's propensity for order was well established.

Based on his meticulous numbering and dating system she knew where to look. She fingered through the journals. No Moleskines here. These were custom made. Boards were covered in smooth leathers. Gold leaf on the top edge of the archival paper. Paisley and decorative frieze papers created with special pigments and oils covered the pastedowns in which Matt's black and gold monogram was stamped into the middle. Birdie stuck her nose in the gutter of a slim volume, pencil lead with a hint of green tea and incense.

Saturday,

Today I pushed away the person I love above all. At the time I thought I was doing the right thing. Will Bird forgive me? Probably. But will I ever forgive myself?

One moment she was helping me fold laundry and the next we were entangled in an embrace and a passionate kiss.

We tumbled onto the bed. Bird moved her hips to the soundless rhythm of our hearts. There were no words. Only desire. Her breathing labored as I did my dance upon her body. We began the hip hustle to wiggle out of our clothing. We were all over each other. One breath. One heartbeat. One mind.

The word took me by surprise. I didn't feel it coming. "Stop. We can't do this." We wrestled as our lips locked again. "NO." Then the wail came, "Stooooop!" And then the shove and slap. She lay on the hard floor holding her face. Too stunned to move. Shock in her eyes. Tears welled. The flush of my handprint grew on her cheek.

It was my voice and my actions that put her on the floor.

She curled her body, covering her breasts and began to cry. She whimpered, "I'm sorry." It is I who should be sorry. I told her I wasn't mad; it wasn't her fault. She gathered her clothing. I saw my rejection in her eyes.

I pleaded with her to stay. She left.

I wanted to tell her that I love her. Hold her in my arms. Stroke her hair and caress her lovely face bruised by my own hand. I needed to explain that I'm afraid of the power she wields, that I'm afraid it will consume me. I wanted to tell her that she is the most important person in my life. How deep my feelings go. That I worry about her. How I want her close at all times.

I did not say these words. I couldn't bring myself to say them aloud. Speaking them would curse her as I am cursed.

I drove to Bird's apartment. Her roommates hadn't seen her. I left messages. She hasn't returned my call. I'm heartbroken and worried. What have I done?

This evening as I sit here and write, I know I will never marry again. I realize that Linda was a prize to win. Bird is not a prize. She is a gift. And I'm not worthy.

Birdie held the journal to her chest in awe of the enormity of Matt's feelings. She knew him to be a Renaissance man. He had proficiency for languages, business, the law, all matters spiritual. He read literature, collected art, studied religions. He was also a man of action, a cop. He rarely spoke of feelings. His emotions were hidden. But here, written in his hand, was a deep well of love. She gasped for breath, overcome that he was much more complicated than he ever revealed. She truly didn't know the deepest parts of him. The parts that mattered most.

Matt's account mirrored Birdie's memory. To see the emotion behind the words, to relive the excruciating pain, cut her deeply. She fell to the floor and wept for everything that was lost.

∽

Sunday,

Bird missed Mass. I searched her haunts. She is nowhere to be found. I questioned her roommates. They were in agreement: she had not returned.

Bird lives on her own. Her family wouldn't know she was missing. I was tempted to call Gerard, but didn't. I couldn't face my culpability. How could I tell him that I injured his daughter in punishment for my weakness in wanting to be intimate with her?

All I want is her safety. Where is she? Please God, don't forsake us.

∽

Monday,

Today I did something I've never done. I called in sick. It's true. Bird is still gone.

∽

Tuesday,

Arthur came by to check on his sick partner. It's been nearly 72 hours since I pushed Bird away. I couldn't stand the uncertainty. I confessed all. According to him, his whole family knows how I feel about Bird. He said our love is transparent. He practically gave me permission to pursue a relationship with his cousin. Is it that simple? In the end, regardless of intent, I'd be asking her to make a choice. I could never harm her in that way. Yet, in my attempt to protect her, I may have inflicted greater hurt.

Wednesday,

I surveilled Bird's apartment and watched as one by one her roommates left for the day. Several hours later Bird came home. Ninety-six hours since I saw her last. She wore the same clothes and looked haggard. Her posture bent.

Pent up frustration, fear, concern, and terror escaped. I cried for an hour before mustering the courage to go to her door. She wore a bathrobe, fresh from a shower. She smelled of powder and sweet perfume. The right side of her face was purple, her manner cold.

I tried to explain what happened. She had no desire to hear me. She said, "It's over. I forgive you." Her blue eyes had grown gray. She said, "We will never discuss this again." I reached out to touch her. She stiffened and pulled away. I left her apartment brokenhearted.

At eight p.m. I called her. I hung up after the first ring. I didn't know what to say.

Evidenced by smudges, Matt had cried as he wrote, just as Birdie cried now.

When she'd found herself on his floor, rejected in such a violent way, she was embarrassed and hurt. At nineteen she wasn't a stranger to sexual activity, but she'd never been tossed out of bed.

What Matt didn't know, and would never learn, was that when she left his place, she went to the Keane family doctor. Matt had hit her so hard that the velocity rolled her over. She landed on her hip. That bent posture he noticed was actually a limp.

After she left Dr. Ryan's, Birdie drove to a liquor store friendly to minors. She drank all the way to Palm Springs, checked herself into a motel, and had her first bender. She drank for three days—trying to understand why Matt had pushed her away.

Even now she didn't have a clear answer and was confused about a "choice." But she took comfort in the knowledge that he suffered too.

The echoes of boyfriends, men past, came to visit Birdie like shadows of perceptions. That incident impacted her future relationships. She'd share her body. Not her bed. Nor her heart. That vulnerability had been the core reason she shut down the soft parts of her soul.

Birdie explored the journals that represented Matt's life. Full of wonder and reaching and learning. He shared his spiritual quest with archival paper. He composed poetry from snip-its gleaned from the streets. He wrote about citizens he had positively influenced or vice versa. Time became lost. Hours passed. Then a day. She had sought something personal and found it. But the journalist eased into the light. There was another matter of import.

She dug through the journals and papers. She sought key words: Paige Street, Montecito Heights, Hollenbeck, investigation, money, murder, lawsuit, drugs. She looked for relevant players: Hugh Jackson, Arthur Keane, Antonio Sanchez, Martine and Monica Alvarado, Dr. Ryan, Ralph Soto, Narciso Alejo. Her efforts became frantic and she searched for acronyms: LAPD, FBI, FID, PSB, SID.

She found nothing. Not even a hint.

She understood the occupational hazard of taking work home. Matt had spoken of it often. But nothing?

Birdie went to Matt's last journal entry, dated three weeks before his death.

Friday,

It's done. The project is complete and I am renewed. The agility and flexibility I once had is slowly returning. Labor at Bird's house has helped my strength. Her gym is a work of art. The lumber for the gazebo is being delivered tomorrow and the blueprints are straightforward. I'll keep trying to convince her to build a pool. –M

Birdie read it again out loud. Compared to the other writings, the last entry read more like an instruction. True, Matt used his disability time to labor at Birdie's house. He practically built her home gym singlehanded. She gathered that he apparently felt physically better. It also indicated that he'd be around to build the gazebo—a contradiction of suicide—because the fiscally responsible Matt wouldn't have had Birdie purchase the lumber otherwise.

But that last line floored Birdie. They'd never discussed building a pool. Not once.

She didn't have the heart to explore deeper.

Put it away for now.

She repacked each box and closed the lids.

ELEVEN

Tuesday, January 10

Day 242. The Westend was a family-owned restaurant and bar on the west side of downtown's shadow. Other than a new generation allowing the older to retire, it hadn't changed much since it opened in the forties. The bar was long, the pour generous. It was an in-the-know kind of place. The kind with no signage, hidden behind a dingy exterior and a scrubby street. Inside was another world: burgundy leather banquettes, wood-paneled walls, white linen tablecloths, and stained-glass windows that shielded the interior from the street.

Birdie entered the bar. Jimmy, the bartender, let loose a loud whistle. She acknowledged him with an air kiss and pushed her way toward her cousin, Thom. He leaned on the bar in his usual spot, drink in hand. A glass with a coaster on top saved the spot next to him.

Thom was barely the eldest of four children. Behind him by one minute was his twin, Aiden. Then Arthur. Then Madigan. Thom was the bossy one—took the role of firstborn seriously. And since Birdie was an only child he bossed her too. The familial gray wasn't an asset to Thom. It made him look old. His penetrating blue eyes split the difference so that he became distinctive, but not handsome.

They kissed. "We're drinking twelve-year-old Redbreast in Matt's honor."

Birdie leaned toward the glass and inhaled deeply. "Pot stilled. Blended. Linseed, sherry, resin. Hint of oil and fruit. Rich."

"How do you do that?"

"It's a gift. Who is we?" she asked, nodding toward the unattended glass.

"Arthur. He's in the head. You know, George regrets breaking up with you."

"Not my problem."

"That's cold. He saw you and Matt making out. You can't do that to a man. Now he's pining and it's driving me insane. At least talk to him for my sake."

"I'll call him tomorrow just to make you happy."

Two sinewy arms of sharp-edged strength wrapped around her waist from behind. "My little Bird," said a voice washed rough around the edges. The man snuggled his nose in her hair. Arthur. They had always shared a mutual affection. Birdie turned and kissed him. He held her in a conciliatory hug of grief from which both received comfort.

When Arthur released her she stepped sideways so he could reclaim his seat next to his brother. Arthur's hair was cut so short the gray appeared blond. She rubbed his scalp like a good luck charm. His grown-up, Dennis the Menace appearance that worked well on televised MMA matches, relaxed. Birdie was glad to have run into him. Arthur hugs were a good thing.

"The pin's still in," he said.

"I see that," she said. "Take it easy on the Irish whiskey."

"Will do, boss."

She said goodbye to her cousins and shouldered her way toward Jimmy. He reached across the bar with damp, sticky hands, pulled her face toward him and planted a sloppy kiss on her lips. "Sobriety looks good on you, but don't turn into one of them bony girls. You gotta eat."

"Hey, that's what I'm here for."

He winked. "Glad to hear it. How 'bout the usual?"

It used to be a vodka martini on the rocks with green olives. Nowadays, her usual was sparkling water with a splash of Rose's limejuice. Pushing the drink toward her he whispered, "There's a lot of talk going around about Matt. You know how it is—cops and gossip."

"What's the word?"

"That he was dirty. Got caught. Killed himself. I don't believe it meself."

Arthur had already warned her. Still, she didn't like Matt's reputation being disparaged.

"Let me know if you hear anything else."

"Aye." He patted her cheek. "Gotta get back to work. Very busy."

"Seen my dad?"

"In the restaurant with a retired dog named Ralph Soto. Know him?"

"Who doesn't? Thanks for the mud, Jimmy."

"Don't be a stranger, Birdie."

Gerard and Soto sat at a two top. Gerard with his back toward the restaurant; a supplicant position in deference to the senior man. As Birdie approached, Gerard's head nodded in response to something Soto said.

Ralph Soto was a tough guy. Not a knuckle breaking, choke-hold kind of tough. His toughness came from being a hardliner. Some went so far as to say that he avoided the top job of Chief because he didn't want to get his hands dirty.

As Commander of Central Bureau, Soto ran an operation that encompassed sixty-five square miles in the most culturally diverse area in Los Angeles. Almost a million people lived and worked under the jurisdiction of Central.

He liked un-jaded recruits—took them fresh out of the academy. The men and women who endured Soto's training became disciples of righteousness and straightforward ethical behavior. They became hardliners like Soto. Matt was one of his boys. So it made no sense that bad package gossip was being batted around.

Soto wore black slacks and a tan sweater. Rheumy-eyed, a pair of glasses dangled from a chain around his neck. His posture erect and regal. "Ah, Elizabeth. It's so nice to see you. Since you're no longer dogging my office for Paige Street information, may I call you Birdie?"

"It's nice to see you, too." She extended her hand. "Yes, please call me Birdie." She pulled over an empty chair and motioned for him to stay. Kissed her dad.

"Since you mentioned it … I'm doing some follow-up on Paige Street. Despite retirement, I'm sure you have enough pull to set me up with the taskforce lead, Narciso Alejo. In fact, I'd like to see the murder books."

Gerard guffawed. "My girl sure has a set."

The great Ralph Soto sat frozen with his mouth nearly open. "What do you expect to find that hasn't already been reported?"

"I have new information that I'd like to check out."

"Share."

"I can't just yet."

Soto wetted his lip. Considered the matter. "Okay. I'll talk to Alejo. See what happens." He vacated the seat and grasped Gerard's hand. "I won't delay your dinner any longer. Gerard, always a pleasure. Let me know about the party." Soto nodded at Birdie as he departed.

Birdie returned the chair, eased onto the warm cushion, and said, "What party, Dad? Thinking about retiring again?"

"Hell, Bird, I've earned my pension. But I love the job."

Before telling her dad about meeting with Reidy, she swore him to secrecy. Gerard and his brother, Louis, gabbed all the time. Once something juicy reached either of them it went directly to Thom, then to Arthur, and then the whole family. And it worked in reverse. The Keane men were worse than a knitting circle. Aiden moved to Brooklyn several years back, but even he wasn't out of the loop via the miracle of modern communication.

The upside was that they were a reference library; they knew everything, remembered everything, and if they didn't, they knew how to get what Birdie needed—just like Monday when Arthur pulled the Paige Street address off the top of his head. Gerard knew how to keep a confidence; he just had to be told as such.

Birdie didn't leave details behind when she told him about the boxes and Matt's estate. "… After Reidy left, I lined up all the keys. The one Matt gave me doesn't match any of them. Dad, I thought he had two houses: Koreatown and Henshaw House. He also has property in Indio. Indio!"

Gerard's attention had wandered. "I'm sorry Bird. I'm stuck on four million."

"I looked at a report compiled by his financial advisor. It goes back twenty years. He was a value investor and got in on IPOs. He made a fortune. I mean, on the surface, it looks legit. But there's rumors circulating about stolen evidence money and Matt's culpability."

Gerard waved his hand in dismissal. "Cops are a brotherhood. Like real brothers there's sibling rivalry. Don't let rumor distract you from what you know to be true."

It felt good to hear Gerard defend Matt's honor.

"Well, anyway," she said. "I've been looking through his stuff since yesterday. Henshaw and Koreatown are to be disposed of. I haven't found the documents for the Indio property yet—who knows what he wants done with that. He itemized possessions and assigned stuff to people. Everything was inventoried. When did he have the time?"

It was a rhetorical question. Matt could operate on a few hours of sleep. While the city slumbered, he was getting shit done.

After dinner Birdie wasn't surprised to see Thom and Arthur still sitting in the bar hunched together in conversation. She spotted Soto, too. Sitting on the opposite side, eyes glued to the television over the bar.

"Let me say goodbye to Soto," said Gerard. "I'll be right back."

Birdie waited outside on the sidewalk. The forecast called for another storm. She lifted her nose and inhaled the heavy air. Yep. It was coming.

"Hey, sweetheart," said Gerard, when he finally emerged. "There's a new action flick I'd like to see. Want to join me?"

"I think I'll pass, Dad. I'd better get home. A hard rain is coming."

"Remember the Tuesday father/daughter date nights? We always saw a movie after dinner. You know your mom prefers that Indie crap. I need my high body count and explosion buddy. Please."

Birdie liked hanging out with her dad. Sharing a bag of popcorn. Listening to his glee-filled chuckles during especially big fire-filled explosions. Despite not wanting to go out and see a movie, she agreed. What's the best thing that could happen? She'd enjoy herself? There was no downside.

TWELVE

THE WEATHER REPORT WAS right for a change. A fast-moving rainstorm swept into the basin by the time Birdie started the drive home. Hard rains were a favorite thing. As a child she'd lay in front of the glass slider and watch the water dance on the patio. She especially liked lightning and thunder. The tempest outside reminded her of rainy day games: creepy crawlers, dominos, solitaire, cardboard box caves.

Arriving home at nearly eleven, Birdie went straight to her office. Two voicemails waited. The first from Father Frank: "Hello, Bird, I know how much you are suffering. I'm praying for you and have every confidence that you'll persevere during this difficult time. I'll come by tomorrow. *Dominus vobiscum.*" The second from Hughes: "Detective Ron Hughes confirming a visit to your residence tomorrow. Time unknown." *Okay, then.*

She raised the screen covering the no-longer-blank dry erase board. She changed it slightly.

The process to find truth is methodical, precise, and provable.

Intuition is not evidence!

Matt = suicide → pain relief? self-punishment? why promise Birdie?

Key = unlocks secret thing/sin → why be sneaky?

8930 = Paige Street → why now? something new?

Last entry = ???

She'd dwell on the last entry later when she wasn't tired. She attached the guys in the snow photo with a magnetic clip. Funny how all three men pictured with Matt had some part in handling his dead body. She tried not to be suspicious even when circumstances were extraordinary, but curiosity came with being a journalist.

A flash of lightning preceded a blast of thunder. The adjacent living room lit up. Stepping out of her office, she sat on the landing and looked up at the stained glass dome over the turret. Every flicker of light illuminated gold, red, green, and blue. The brief flashes created reflective, strobe-like snapshots of an Old Russian icon. Birdie enjoyed Mother Nature flexing her muscles. During pauses in the tempest she listened to the overgrown sycamore scraping the brick façade. The wind chime at the corner of the house. Wind whistling through a poorly fitted window. Footfalls. Huh?

Don't be paranoid. It's one of the mysterious groans of a house over a hundred years old. She got up, away from the turret's echoes and stepped back into the office. Without realizing it, she pulled the screen down over the board and listened with a well-trained ear to the sounds.

Footfalls. Above her on the third floor. No mistake.

Birdie eyed the alarm panel on the wall. It hadn't been triggered. No one's in the house, she told herself. Then she heard it again. A steady creak. She knew the squeaky portions of the floor. These were carefully moving toward the turret. She opened the top right drawer of the desk and pulled out a Sig-Sauer P239, preloaded with a magazine of seven 40-caliber Smith & Wesson rounds. She thumbed off the safety.

A shot of adrenaline, released into her blood stream, forced her heart to work harder, breath came fast and even. Without thought—as if she did this every day—and with a self-confident excitement, she hugged the wall and ran in the opposite direction toward the marble service stairs. She stopped just long enough to remove the cowboy boots and soundlessly sprinted up the stairs in her stocking feet. She crabbed to the landing and peeked around the corner to view the hallway.

At the far end was a dark figure with its back to the wall. Damnit, hissed Birdie. She'd hoped her imagination had gotten away from her. She waited for a flash of lightning. It shone on a curly haired man leaning sideways toward the stairwell. The way he pressed against the wall indicated he didn't want to be discovered. A robber? Prudence said err on the side of safety.

She backed down the stairs and ran back to the office. He was positioned almost directly above her. Wasting no additional time, she slammed her palm against the panic button. Alarm horns wailed. The security company would notify the police. She dialed nine-one-one anyway. "Help. A man is in my house. He's got shoulder-length curly red hair. I'm on the second floor, in an office." She put the phone down—the line active. Wilshire Station serviced her neighborhood. Their response time would be mere minutes. The second phone line began ringing. The security company. She let it ring.

The alarm prevented her from knowing the location of the intruder and the office didn't have a door to close and lock. A heavy curtain held open with tasseled tie-backs separated the office from the living room. But she had a gun. And she knew how to use it.

She backed against the file cabinets, facing the curtained archway. Birdie gripped the gun in her right hand and wrapped the left over it. With the Sig securely in place, she spread her feet for balance, swiveled her hips, stood in a classic isosceles position, and hoped she wouldn't puke.

Wailing sirens cut through the din of the alarm. The reflection of light bars and hazards pulsed red, blue, and amber on the wet living room windows. The police banged on the front door. It was three inches thick. An Army platoon with a battering ram wouldn't get through.

Her legs shook. She widened her stance.

With nothing to do but wait she concentrated on the sounds. Her ears weren't as refined as her nose and she couldn't discern the location of the thumps and shouts until they got closer. Then she heard heavy, deliberate footsteps coming down the hall. One masculine voice called out "police." She put her hands in the air. She caught a quick glimpse of his head as he checked the room. He stood behind the wall and yelled, "Put the gun down. Step out toward me." Another cop joined him on the other side of the doorway, gun drawn.

She put the gun down and stepped over it toward the cop. "This is my house," she said.

They didn't care. When she passed the curtain, one of them grabbed her neck and pushed her down. She was quickly hand-cuffed, brought to standing and frisked. He pushed her back in the office and said, "How do I shut it off?"

She nodded toward the keypad. "Punch seven-nine-zero-six and enter."

He did and the alarm silenced. Then he brought her back through the doorway, positioned her facing the wall and pushed her down on her knees. He stepped on her foot. A tactic designed to prevent a suspect from standing up.

Other voices called out, "Police" and "Clear" as they worked through the house. Birdie didn't have any ill will toward the cop. He was doing his job. As soon as the house was cleared, he'd con-firm her identity and uncuff her.

Echoes of harsh-sounding foreign words bounced up the tur-ret. The inflection was instantly recognizable even though she hadn't heard it since her grandpa died. The intruder was an Irish-man, cussing in Irish Gaelic.

She got it. The intruder had run down the turret and hid in the entry coat closet. He didn't know it, but it was the best place to hide. The cops didn't come through the front door. The entry would be one of the last places checked.

She thought she heard pops and thumps and glass breaking, but the thunder messed with her ears. She wasn't sure. Voices from indistinct areas shouted. "Out Back." "Police." "Put the gun down." "Stop now."

There came a long silence. No commands. No thunder. As if Mother Nature turned off the stereo.

She wanted to know what was happening. Her knees hurt. Her foot hurt.

The cop's radio crackled to life.

Suspect down.

THIRTEEN

BIRDIE SAT IN A living room chair under the watchful eye of a
uniform. Her identity had been verified. She'd been uncuffed.
Two suited men approached. One knelt in front of her and said,
"Are you okay, Miss Keane?"

She looked at the badge around his neck then glanced up at
the face. Crinkled eyes, brown skin, mustache. Kind. "What is
your name?"

"Detective Nunez. I need to ask you some questions."

She looked up at the other man. No police badge was visible.
"And you are?"

The man didn't answer. He looked down at her with an air of
superiority that she took an instant dislike to—especially since
he was in her house. His face was familiar though: bent nose,
straight eyebrows, scarred complexion, dark eyes. She'd seen him
before, but couldn't remember where. He gave her the creeps.

Nunez said, "Tell us what happened here this evening."

She pointed a shaky finger at the suited man. "Who is he? If he doesn't identify himself, I won't talk in his presence. My father is Captain Gerard Keane from Hollywood Station." Her voice went up an octave. "I know you have a job to do, but I have rights, and I don't have to talk to anyone who presents the color of authority, but won't identify himself." The adrenaline had worn off long ago and her hands shook violently.

The man smirked, whispered in Nunez's ear, and walked away.

"Do you need something before we continue?" Nunez said.

"I'm an alcoholic. I need my chewing gum," she said, hiccupping back a sob.

Nunez reached into his front pocket and pulled out a small pack of peppermint. He handed her a piece. She thrust it into her mouth and began chomping like her life depended on it.

"Take your time," said Nunez, sitting down. "Start at the beginning."

Birdie made a good witness. She told him everything without embellishment.

"How long have you lived here?"

"Eight years."

"You live alone?"

She nodded.

"How many times has your house been broken into?"

"Just tonight."

"Why would you feel the need to have a loaded gun in your desk?"

"I have several guns in the house." *Oh, you shouldn't have said that.* "They're all registered." Her voice picked up speed. "I've been threatened in the past ... because of my work ... I have a

CCW." *Stop talking. Don't* ever *offer unasked information to the police.*

Another uniform approached and spoke to Nunez. "There's a mess in a room upstairs; storage boxes overturned, papers everywhere."

Matt's boxes. Everything seemed wrong. What could the intruder have wanted with those? They didn't contain anything worth breaking in for. The unidentified man appeared within Birdie's sightline and he seemed interested in the report.

"What's upstairs?" said Nunez.

"Bedrooms. Bathrooms."

"I'd like you to accompany me upstairs to get an indication of what he was after."

They toured Birdie's bedroom. It was as she'd left it. Ditto the guest room across the hall. The one that held Matt's boxes was a disaster. The contents of every box were dumped. Journals, yellow pads, files, papers, awards and memorabilia littered the room. The intruder was definitely looking for something. Birdie felt an overwhelming protection toward the materials that represented Matt's life. She made an instant decision to lie to Nunez. She was a skilled and clever liar. Most functional alcoholics were. There could be serious consequences of lying, but she didn't care. All that mattered was Matt's privacy.

"What's all this?" said Nunez.

Okay, Birdie, you can do this. Don't twitch, don't wink or avert your eyes. Don't rub your hands together. Don't change your posture; don't change the pitch of your voice; don't take an obvious breath. Just let the lie flow easily.

She shrugged. "Nothing of importance."

Nunez raised an eyebrow and said, "Obviously he was looking for something." He made the correct assumption that the intruder made the mess. Looking at the apparent neatness of the rest of the house, it was a good call. But Birdie wasn't about to confirm it. If she did then the contents of the boxes would become evidence, and she wouldn't allow that.

"I should clarify," she said. "Nothing of importance to anyone other than myself. I'm a reporter. Those boxes contain notes, research material, copies of stories, stuff like that." *You're taking a big gamble. What if he decides to look closely?* "As I said before, I'm an alcoholic." *Go ahead, lay it on thick.* "Today was a bad day. I got frustrated. Made a big mess."

"What about jewelry, cash, or other valuables?"

"In the gun locker in the garage."

"We'll look at that, too. Let's continue."

"Are you going to tell me what happened downstairs?" she said.

"Your intruder got cornered and killed himself in the backyard."

"Why would he do that?"

"That's what I intend to find out."

They finished inspecting the house. Birdie determined that nothing was missing, but she wasn't 100 percent sure that the intruder didn't take something from Matt's boxes.

The yard had become a hive of activity—uniforms, suits, guys with tackle boxes, lights on tripods, cameras—the dead body business.

A familiar voice came from the kitchen. "Where is she? Bird?" Thom appeared. "Are you all right?" He swooped her into a hug. "I came code 3."

"I'm glad to have some friendly company." She gave Nunez her best evil eye, even though he was just doing his job.

"Gerard's on the way," said Thom.

"Oh, let's not get crazy," she said.

Nunez piped in. "Yes, let's not get crazy. You are?"

Thom flashed the badge and gave Nunez a business card. He wasn't impressed. He said, "Well, Detective Keane, RHD, Wilshire has it under control, but it was nice of you to come."

"Come on, Bird, we're going to the library." He ticked his head at Nunez. "You know where to find us."

Birdie found herself leaning on Thom. She turned and looked for the man with no name but couldn't see him. She worried that he had moved upstairs to check out Matt's stuff.

"Have any hooch?" said Thom.

"In the cabinet."

She didn't specify which and he didn't seem to care. He opened several doors to find the stash. Birdie stood at the door watching the stairway to see if anyone moved up or down from the third floor. So far nobody had.

"Pay dirt. You shouldn't have this shit here."

He found a bottle of her ex-favorite liqueur, B&B. It was an 80-proof blend of Benedictine and brandy made with over seventy ingredients that included herbs, citrus peel, and honey. Yum. A recovering alcoholic shouldn't have liquor in the house, but she'd convinced herself that she kept it for Father Frank—really, it was her in-case-of-emergency stash.

"You want hooch, I give you hooch, and then you scold me for having it in my house. Don't drink it then."

"Heck no. This is good stuff."

He poured the deep amber-orange liquid into a Waterford snifter. Swirled it in the glass. The pungent aroma wafted up Birdie's nose into her sinuses, moved to the back of her eyes, and up into her brain. An instant euphoria washed over her and she didn't even taste it with her lips. She remembered the slow, warming movement down the back of her throat, the warmth of the liquid lingering in the middle of her chest, the peppery after-taste. She reached for the glass.

The unnamed man appeared in her peripheral vision. She flinched and turned to look at him. He looked past Birdie's shoulder and caught Thom's eye. Birdie swiftly turned toward her cousin. His eyes diverted to the glass. Ahhh, now she remembered . . .

Birdie often stayed with her cousins at Magnolia Manor on holiday weekends. One Saturday night after she and Madi said goodnight to the adults, the teens slipped out the front door to attend a house party. The girls drank too much, smoked pot, and got totally wasted.

By the time they returned, the Manor household was tucked in for the evening. They'd been stupid enough to leave without a house key. They managed to jimmy the window above the kitchen sink and crawl in just as the phone rang. Moments later there were shouting voices. Birdie and Madi barely had time to slip into the pantry before Louis and Nora came crashing through the swinging kitchen door. The girls watched the action through the louvered doors.

Nora unlocked a cabinet and pulled out a tarp, quickly shook it out and laid it on top of the oak breakfast table. Louis filled a kettle with water and put it on the stove. Nora systematically laid papers towels on the countertop and began to line up what looked like surgeon's tools. Just as the boiling water in the kettle began to whistle, two men burst through the kitchen door. Both wore the familiar blue uniform of the LAPD.

A man held up Thom's bloodied body. Louis helped the man lay his son onto the table. Louis poured the water into a large bowl and placed a stack of small white towels at Thom's head. Nora scissored away his bloody shirt. She placed a wooden spoon into his mouth. As Nora wiped away the blood from Thom's torso, she calmly gave instructions.

"You, hold his legs. Don't let his hips move."

"Louis, hold his arms above his head. Keep him still. Don't let him squirm."

Birdie and Madi huddled together, too petrified to move, but compelled to watch Nora perform an illicit surgery on her eldest son, on her very own kitchen table. It didn't take long. Thom's muffled cries rang in their ears as they watched Nora work. The girls saw the terror in Thom's eyes as he writhed in pain. Finally, there were whoops from the men when Nora pulled a bullet from his side.

After Thom was stitched and bandaged, he was stripped of remaining clothing and Nora gave him a shot in the butt. He was cleaned and carried away.

Long after the kitchen went dark, the girls were still too scared to move. They held on to each other long enough to fall asleep.

Some time later, the kitchen light woke them. The louvered door opened. Thom stood there, attempting to stay standing. He said, "I cover for you two. You cover for me. We never speak of it. It never happened." Then directing his eyes at Madi, he said, "Little sister, you have ten seconds to get upstairs to your bed." Madi bolted, leaving Birdie alone with Thom.

She attempted to leave, but he placed his hand on her chest.

"Cousin," he said, "do you understand?"

"Yes, sir," she managed to squeak.

"You don't tell anybody. Not even your parents."

"Yes, sir."

"You have six seconds."

It was her turn to bolt.

Birdie's memory of the kitchen surgery wasn't that specific. Her young self filled the holes. Accuracy could be debated. She and Madi never had the courage to discuss it and compare experiences. And they'd never asked Thom. That was a scary thing. Time passed. Birdie had other, more pressing matters to pursue. The finer details faded.

After all these years, she relived the important parts. The man who brought Thom into his parents' kitchen was younger then. And he didn't have the same position he had today. But it was the same man. The one in her home. West Bureau Deputy Chief Theodore Rankin.

A two-star boss.

Birdie also remembered the one thing that always bothered her about that night: clean cops don't get bullets removed on kitchen tables. She turned to look at Thom. His eyes were on the window with the view, seemingly avoiding hers. One question invaded her thoughts: was this long-ago incident with Thom and Rankin connected to the intruder?

FOURTEEN

Detective Nunez needed the front door unlocked and an explanation of how the alarm system worked. Birdie punched a few buttons and the electronic lock buzzed, unlatching the front door. Then she examined the master control panel. It hadn't been touched since she left to meet her dad. There had been no storm-related power loss; even if there had been, a battery backup would engage.

"It's an electronic and manual system," said Birdie. "A code can be entered into a touch pad to unlock a door—each door has its own pad. The key, which works on a pin and tumbler system, can also be used, but the key isn't ordinary. It has a transponder embedded in the body that emits an electronic signal to prevent duplication.

"The windows stay armed unless a specific zone of the house is turned off," she continued. "If the house were broken into a silent alarm would be triggered and the security company would attempt to reach me via phone. Then they'd dispatch the cops."

"Have you ever been billed for false alarms?"

"Never."

"To get into the house without tripping the alarm someone would have to have a code or a key. Any idea how the guy got in?"

"I assume that a master thief might know a way to bypass the alarm. I'd have to talk to the company about that."

"Why don't you have a better system?" said Nunez.

Birdie shrugged, slightly confused. "It came with the house. I thought it was good."

"A good system could time stamp enter and exits. A good system would have video. Basic security protocols recommend motion-detection flood lights. Considering that you're a single woman living alone in one of the largest houses in the neighborhood, you have a crap system."

Birdie gulped. Other than family heirlooms she didn't have anything worth stealing so she had never scrutinized the security system.

"Um … I feel really weird asking this—after all, a guy died, but … do I need to call a clean-up crew or something?"

"I'm not certain. I'll give you a referral list."

A forensic man approached. "Ma'am, I need to check your hands and clothing."

"She didn't fire her weapon," said Nunez. "But what about the DB on her grass? After the coroner transports the body, is there something she should do with whatever is left?"

"In this case, no," he said. "There'll be blood and tissue and some tiny bone fragments left behind in the grass. I mean, we can't scoop it all up. But nature will take care of it. First there'll be flies. Then maggots will consume the biologicals. The bits of bone will be swept clean of contaminants by other insects that will eventually feed the soil. Come spring that patch of grass will be greener and healthier than the rest."

"That's gross," said Birdie.

"Beauty in simplicity," said the man. "It'll happen fast, but there might be an odor. I'll tape off a large area. Stay off it and let the bugs do their jobs."

"What's going on here?" asked Thom—drink in one hand, unlit cigarette in the other.

"No need to get protective," said Nunez. "We were getting a forensic lesson."

A voice from the other room called out for Nunez. He departed and took the forensic guy with him.

"Come on," said Thom. "It's only drizzling. Let's go outside so I can smoke this sucker."

They leaned on the rail and looked down at the coroner's investigator inspecting the body.

"I never thought my home would be the scene of an active investigation. Why all the fuss? Matt's su—death didn't get this kind of attention."

"It's a force investigation. A man killed himself in front of a bunch of cops while being chased. The department will check the gun of every cop on scene. Including backups. They will determine, absolutely no doubt, that he actually killed himself."

"You think a cop shot him?"

"No. But the department will do its due diligence."

"Seems like a waste of money."

"It is. But if they don't and this guy's family screams foul and sues the department it will cost more in the long run. Lots of families get rich off the city in settlements alone."

Nunez stuck his head out. "My captain has a few questions for you. Follow me, please."

Birdie ended up back in the same living room chair. The captain stood over her and asked the same questions. She gave the same answers. When he seemed satisfied, he said, "We'll need you to come into the station to make an official statement."

"No, she won't."

The man spun, irritated, then he quickly smiled and extended his hand. "Captain Keane. How are you? I didn't realize there was a family connection."

"This is my daughter."

"I see. Well, it's straightforward enough."

Gerard nodded his head. "We'll be in the library if you need anything."

Thom poured some B&B into a crystal snifter for Gerard.

Gerard took a sip and said, "You look tired, sweetheart."

"Tired? I look tired? What the hell, Dad? Some dude broke into my house. His dead body is on my lawn!"

Gerard swept her into a hug. "Shush, sweetheart. I'm sorry. I'm sorry, Bird. It's the cop in me speaking." He held her until she calmed down and then led her to the couch to sit.

"What was he after?" said Gerard.

"Those boxes I told you about at dinner," said Birdie. "The ones that belonged to Matt."

"What did they contain?" said Thom.

"Stuff. Six boxes of it. You know, Eagle award, school reports, journals, photo albums, like that."

"Man, I must not have a life. I have only one box of shit."

"You possess enough common sense to throw crap away."

"Nunez will want to look at them. He'll have an obligation to inspect those boxes. After all, they were the reason for the break-in."

"I'm not going to let that happen," said Birdie.

"My guess is that Bird's protecting Matt's privacy," inserted Gerard.

"He has no privacy," insisted Thom. "He's dead."

"I'll get the tab if there's hell to pay," said Gerard.

"How big is that tab?" said Thom with a slight sneer.

"Doesn't matter anyway," said Birdie. "I lied to Nunez. I told him it was my crap."

Thom shook a finger at Birdie, "You're a troublemaker. You can get arrested for that."

He sat down and promptly stood up again. "Shit. Anne will be worried. I've got to get home."

Birdie lay down on the sofa.

Gerard said, "I'll talk to Thom. We won't say anything about the boxes. Now tell me everything."

For the third time she retold the tale. Gerard listened intently. Finally he said, "Matt was on disability. What could this guy be looking for? Then he offs himself instead of answering questions? He was scared. Definitely not your typical burglar."

"Maybe he was hired by someone and he was afraid of *that* person."

Gerard nodded. "Let me think on it."

Gerard shook Birdie awake. Dull morning light shone through the window.

"You fell asleep," he said. "It's morning."

"I hit a wall." She got up, rubbed her face. "Cops still here?"

"Left at dawn. Your neighbors will be talking about this one during the next HOA meeting." He handed her a cup of black coffee.

"I feel filthy. Will you stay while I take a shower?"

"Of course, sweetheart. Take your time. I'll fix some breakfast when you're done."

Birdie's job as journalist was dichotomous: her best day was someone else's worst. This time the two halves belonged entirely to her.

She slid back the carved wood screen separating the shower enclosure from the rest of the bath and turned on the cold water. She stepped in, clothes and all, and sat down. The frenetic activity of last night came crashing down along with the icy water. She shivered. She used to do this when she felt strung out and needed a quick pick-me-up. When the despair dissipated she turned the knob until the water was piping hot. The heat gave her a sense of forced bravery. And she'd need all she could get in the days to come.

FIFTEEN

Wednesday, January 11

DAY 243. ONE DAY and one day only.

Birdie's long wavy hair took forty minutes to blow dry and straighten. She didn't mind spending time on a mindless chore. Her brain needed the reboot.

The Mason Pearson paddle brush with the nylon and boar bristles that she pulled through her hair was a seventeenth birthday present from Matt. Her mother, Maggie, considered a hairbrush to be an intimate gift. She thought an older, newly divorced man giving such an item to her underage daughter was inappropriate and told Matt as much. He came to the house, apologized, and delivered a substitute gift—a generic mall gift card. Maggie asked Birdie to return the hairbrush. She refused, and a shouting match with a lot of tears ensued. Birdie almost laughed now as she pulled the brush through her hair. That seemed a lifetime ago.

Since then, Maggie regarded Matt with high esteem. Loved him. She wanted him as a son-in-law, to father her grandchildren.

"Camelot has died, Mom." Birdie said aloud. "There will be no babies now."

It didn't surprise Birdie that past events had new meaning. Death could do that. One is compelled to look back as a form of condoling. Remember the sweetness. The tiny moments that brought smiles. Hear the soundtrack of a relationship. In her case, dance music. Matt and she liked to dance together. Of course, it was Matt's guilty pleasure. If his cop brothers found out he'd be razzed big time.

After dressing in a favorite pair of woodland camouflage pants and baby-blue T-shirt, she returned to the kitchen. The smell of fried eggs and toast made her hungry.

"I know it's not much," said Gerard, pouring orange juice.

"It's perfect," she said, taking a seat at the bar.

He slid an official damage report across the countertop. "It's an inventory of what got damaged last night. The laundry room door and jamb will have to be replaced. Also a stained-glass door was broken. I swept up the pieces and put them in a box in case it can be repaired. You can use this for the insurance company."

"Thanks, Dad. I hadn't given any thought to this."

"Why should you? You've had other important matters to deal with." Gerard eyed the artsy graphic on the tee. *Boys like Catholic girls.* "Is that a photo-shoot hand-me-down from Madi?"

"It was a gag gift from Matt." She stuck a corner of toast into the egg yoke and stuffed it in her mouth while her dad washed the skillet.

"I liked Matt much better than any man you've dated," he observed.

"We were friends, Dad. George and I dated."

"Like hell. Why George put up with it is beyond me, but then he is a longhaired faggot."

Birdie suppressed a smile. Poor George. When he worked vice he did undercover work as a drug-addicted male prostitute who wore his hair long. Off duty he was a dapper dresser; a good-looking man who took care of his image. Designer suits and fitted shirts in bright colors, florals, patterns—Miami style. The cops couldn't square his undercover work with his personal life and ragged him relentlessly. Birdie knew him to be straight, but hey, it's not like she discussed their sex life publicly.

"Geeze, Dad, I never knew you didn't like him. And you know he doesn't have long hair anymore."

"Well I didn't like it, I don't like him, and I didn't like him with my daughter. That snake Denis was worse. And that black prosecutor is a cop hater that listens to that pack of pinkos on the Police Commission." Gerard kicked a cabinet door. It shuddered under his boot. "Goddamn waste of a good man!"

Gerard checked his emotions. His verbal missive unnerved Birdie. He flicked his wrist and said, "I have to get home and change before going to the station." He kissed her on the nose. "I'll call you later. Oh, a guy named Ron Hughes called. Said he'd be here at twelve. Who is he?"

"The detective investigating Matt's death."

"Glad to hear a cop will be here. I'll worry less. Love you, sweetheart."

Birdie had just finished what was left of her breakfast when Thom called. "Your burglar is a ghost. He had no wallet, no ID, no money, no keys. Not even a scrap of paper with your name or address."

"The intruder was after the contents of Matt's boxes and would've needed transport if he had found what he was looking for."

"Unless he was looking for something small that could fit in a pocket."

"Good point. Just in case, call Nunez and have him check for abandoned cars. There might be a parked car nearby with keyless entry. Speaking of … I've gone over and over it. He either bypassed the alarm or had my house key."

"He had no keys."

"Maybe he had a wheelman that got scared off when the patrol units arrived. Maybe that guy had the key."

"How would he have gotten it?"

"Beats me."

"Dig this; the curly red hair on his head was a wig. And he had no fingerprints. He might've been a professional thief."

"This means he'd have the skill to bypass the system—I'll notify the alarm company. They have this upgraded program that could tell me what time any door or window is opened. Maybe I'll get that and video surveillance." Birdie paused to think. "You know what? About a year-and-a-half ago I was out of town and Denis stayed here while his house was being painted. I gave him a spare. I'm not sure I ever got it back. Damn. That means I have to call him."

"I'm sure he's forgiven you by now."

"He left a sympathy message."

"That's progress. Why are you so sure that the burglar was after Matt's boxes?"

"When I heard him he was upstairs. Matt's boxes were the only thing touched. It wasn't a random break-in. He must've seen Reidy make the delivery. I didn't leave the house until last evening. He waited until I'd gone."

"Doesn't make sense. If he had prior knowledge, he could've intercepted them at the source or carjacked the delivery."

"There's less risk the way it went down."

"Still doesn't add up. We'll have to wait for his ID to find out if he had a prior relationship with Matt. The gun the guy had? A Sig P229, the heavier version of yours."

"40-caliber?" said Birdie.

"Yep."

"Speaking of which, the cops took mine. See if you can get it back sooner rather than later?"

"You have other guns."

"It's my favorite. Hey, I appreciate you doing all this legwork. It saves me from cajoling Nunez."

"No prob. I'll call with anything new. Don't forget your promise to call George."

Birdie grimaced. She didn't want to.

Birdie stood over the tornado that represented Matt's life. He had entrusted his history to her and her alone. She was now the curator of his legacy. There was no way Nunez could find out she lied about the ownership of the mess spread out on the floor—unless he or Rankin or one of the other cops examined the contents. If they had, and if a relationship between the intruder and Matt was established, then he'd have probable cause to compel the surrender of the boxes. She couldn't allow anyone to rifle through the private life of Matt and those he knew. A possessive responsibility to his memory made the decision for her. She repacked the boxes. She put aside a pile of photos to add to the others from Matt's shed. She plucked the last journal to have a look at the final passage. Rereading it didn't provide a light bulb moment, so she carefully ripped the page out and tucked it safely into the cargo pocket on her pant leg. She followed Matt's numbering system, but it wasn't nearly as pretty. Stuff bulged and the lids teetered.

By the time she had loaded each box into the lift, she knew exactly what to do.

In the garage she unlocked the wheels of a Sears workbench and pushed it aside. Behind it a hidden panel led into a narrow crawlspace. It'd been found shortly after she moved in and de-moed a cheap storage cabinet made of fiber board that had warped under too much weight. When it came off the wall she discovered the passageway hidden behind it. It led to a cavern about the size of a bathroom under the stairwell, abutting the entry coat closet. It was the perfect hiding place.

The remnants of Matt's life would be safe under the stairs.

SIXTEEN

Birdie had just finished concealing the panel with the workbench and was slapping off the dust when the phone rang. She picked up the extension in the garage.

"It's Detective Hughes. I'm here. You must not have heard the doorbell."

"I'm in the garage. On the left side of the wrought-iron gate is a postern entrance. I'm unlocking it now." Birdie punched a code into the panel next to the gun locker. "Follow the drive to the back of the house. I'll meet you there." Birdie closed the garage door and waited.

When Hughes strode around the corner of the house Birdie was surprised to see him in civilian clothes. He wore casual black shoes and Levis. A black T-shirt fit snug against his muscles and highlighted his tan. The day-old scruff on his face was a rugged accessory. A partial of a colorful tattoo on his right bicep peeked from under the sleeve. His firearm was holstered on his left hip and the deputy badge clipped to his belt. He wore a watch and a silver cuff on his right wrist and carried a portfolio. He waved at himself. "I dress casual for travel," he pointed at the hardware, "but I'm on call."

"Guns don't bother me."

"What shall I call you today?"

"Birdie."

His smile was quick and wide. "Call me Ron. This is a big house. Live here alone?"

"Mostly. Would you like coffee?"

"Yes, ma'am, I mean, Birdie."

As they neared the plot of grass staked off with yellow crime scene tape she smelled damp grass with a twinge of iron and cordite and something sickly sweet. Ron broke away to take a closer look, disturbing shiny green flies. They buzzed, manic and irritated. "What the hell happened?"

Birdie decided she had no obligation to tell the full story. She shoved her hands into the front pockets of her pants and shrugged. "A man broke into my house. I surprised him and triggered the alarm. He tried to elude police and killed himself instead of allowing capture."

"Melodrama. You okay?"

"Not really. Why would someone do that? It makes no sense. Of course, my imagination is going wild." She leaned back on her heels. "Mind if we not talk about it?"

"I can respect that."

She jerked her head. "Kitchen's upstairs."

When they entered the house Ron's gaze fell immediately to the black wainscoting in the breakfast nook. "It's hideous." His eyes grew round with disbelief. "I can't believe I said that out loud. I'm so sorry."

Birdie puffed out a grunt of surprise at the tactless remark that morphed into a chuckle. She forced it to the back of her throat, but it spat back out in a surprising laugh. Ron's face went blank with confusion. The laugh grew in strength and she snorted, which caused her to laugh harder. She knew it was an inappropriate response to an unfiltered remark, but she couldn't help herself. With each second of laughter Birdie felt a vapor evaporating from her skin—the tonnage of grief lightening its load.

She sat in one of her grandmother's antique chairs to compose herself. Ron had a look of *what the hell did I do?*

"Nothing like a little levity to break the ice," she said.

Ron gave a tepid nod.

"Oh, yes, coffee." Birdie hopped up and waved Ron to sit. "If it makes you feel any better, I don't like the black either."

Ron sat and stretched out long legs and crossed his ankles. While she made coffee she checked out the reflection in the sink window. Birdie watched Ron's eyes clock her. Then he inspected the cabinetry, the appliances, the antique mirror. His eyes settled on a cardboard crate of fruits and vegetables on the counter. He got up and examined the contents.

"You're a whole foods eater?" he said in a hopeful tone.

"No."

"Then why would you have this box of goodies?"

"My version of goodies is cupcakes and cookies."

He chuckled. "As it is to most people. Why have it then? It's a lot of food."

"My cousin, Madi, is under the mistaken impression that I've developed an eating disorder since I stopped drinking." She opened a cabinet and pulled out two cups. "I've been dropping pounds and the busybody in my family is worried. She's a vegan and that box is her way to get me to cross over to the dark side. She has a box delivered every Friday from an organic co-op. Sad thing is, it goes to waste, but she refuses to suspend the delivery. And don't ask me why losing weight has anything to do with fruits and vegetables, because I don't understand her way of thinking."

"You're what? Five-eight? One-twenty?"

"Exactly right. Madi's thinner than me so where she gets off thinking I'm skinny is beyond my logic. I think she's just used to seeing me as a puffed-up alcoholic."

"You look very healthy," said Hughes, leaning against the stove.

"Thank you. How do you like your coffee?"

"Black, please."

She poured and handed him the cup. "What is a whole foods eater?"

"I try to eat only what nature provides, not what man makes."

"Sounds boring. What about meat and bread?"

"Grilled steak, a fat piece of fish, chicken—good stuff. Certain breads are okay."

Birdie poured herself a cup and sat down at the bar. She pointed at the portfolio. "Where do we begin?"

His face couldn't conceal the disappointment of getting to the business. He slid the portfolio off the bar onto the countertop. "I have an update on the tox screens. The alcohol came up negative. Marijuana positive. Do you know what 6-acetylmorphine is?"

"Sounds serious."

"It's the base compound of most natural and synthetic opiates, such as codeine, heroin, methadone, or morphine. The lab did an immunoassay, which is a preliminary opiate test. Matt tested positive, which confirms the conclusion that he took an overdose of the methadone."

"Could it have been one of the other opiates you mentioned?"

"Sure, but only remnants of methadone were found in the house. I'd like to get more background, but do we have to discuss it now? I was enjoying talking with you."

"Fine. Hang out here long enough and you'll get to meet Matt's brother. He's a priest."

"I met Frank when he came for the body."

"I'd forgotten."

"Are you hungry?" said Ron. "Would you like to grab a bite?"

"That's a nice offer, but Frank doesn't carry a cell phone and I don't know when he'll be here."

"I'm pretty good with chow. I'd be happy to make a hearty soup with that box of goodies. I'll make enough for Frank, too."

Birdie felt slightly destabilized. What an odd circumstance on an entirely different scale. The deputy investigating her best friend's death offers to make her food. Then again, nothing about this death has been ordinary. Not like she knew what an ordinary one felt like. In her experience they were all important and extraordinary.

She wanted to be taken away. To forget for a while. Ron wasn't scary or intimidating. His presence gave her a sense of security and peace of mind. And he wasn't bad to look at either. Ah, what the hell.

"Soup is a good thing. Do you need me to show you where stuff is?"

"I'm good with kitchens. I'll figure it out. Company would be nice."

"Actually, I need to make a few phone calls."

"Do what you need. I'm in town for a while. We have time."

Birdie had dated Denis Cleary before George. Their breakup ended with judicial involvement and they haven't spoken since.

Denis was a civilian contractor with the city. A pilot. He owned three helicopters. He contracted one to the LAPD, the other to a local television station, and when he wasn't working in the city, he flew for an oil company.

He had a handler named Mica. She had brown skin, exotic dark eyes, and a curvy figure. Her duties included scheduling, dispatching, and logistics, to which she added fornicating. Birdie caught them having sex, and a raging, violent fight took place.

By then, Birdie was nearing rock bottom in her alcoholism. She had begun blacking out. Late that night, after the big fight, Birdie tried to run over Denis with her car. Broke his leg. She had no memory of the incident and a part of her really wanted to believe that he staged the whole thing. But she was forced to face her problem and pay the consequences. Through a series of frantic negotiations she got off easy. That is, she served no jail time. But it was expensive. And there's nothing easy about getting dry.

Even if Denis never returned her house key, she didn't think he had anything to do with her home invasion, but checking facts was an ingrained character trait. She left a voicemail on his home phone. Ditto his cell phone. Impatient as always, she dialed the one person who would know his whereabouts.

The familiar accent answered. "Cleary Flight Services. Mica speaking." Her mesmerizing voice had Birdie forget for a moment why she called.

"Um … hello, Mica. This is Birdie Keane. I'm trying to reach Denis."

Mica relaxed the formality in her voice, and, as if there'd been no history between them, said, "Birdie, what a surprise. It's been forever." There was no hesitation in her voice and her greeting was genuine. English was her second language, and though it was rough, she told Birdie that Denis was out of town. He was on a tour ferrying engineers between offshore oil platforms in the Gulf of Mexico. She gave Birdie a number where he could be reached.

"That's terrific, Mica. More than expected. Thank you."

She dialed the number and was put on hold.

Birdie shook her foot. Stuck two pieces of gum in her mouth. As the clock ticked she became more nervous. Their last communication—prior to the sympathy message—was nasty and contentious. After several minutes of silence her call was transferred and Denis came on the line.

"Cleary speaking."

"Hey, you."

"Birdie. Is everything okay?" Pleasant tone. So far so good.

"Why do you ask?"

"You wouldn't call me otherwise. And you would've called Mica to get this number."

"Well, I wanted to thank you for your voicemail. It meant a lot."

"When's the funeral?"

"Tomorrow."

"I'll miss it. What else is going on?" On-point as always.

"Remember when I was working on *As Crime Comes*, you stayed at my house while yours was being—"

"Painted. What of it?"

"I'm missing the copy of my house key."

"I gave it back."

"I don't remember. But I was going downhill pretty fast back then. Anyway, I can't account for it."

"Sorry. On that topic, you never did return mine."

"If I recall, I threw it at you. We were fighting about Mica. Well, anyway, I took a shot. Thanks for taking my call," she said.

"You want to have lunch when I get back to town?"

"Sure. That'd be nice. Call me."

She knew he never would.

Birdie then called George's cell. "I want to say again how sorry I am."

"I can't get the image of you guys practically doing it out of my head," said George. "I trusted him. I trusted you."

"If it makes you feel better, it took me by surprise, too."

"Matt was my friend. As sorry as I am that he's gone, we now have a real chance of making our relationship work."

"It makes no difference. I'm not ever going to love you."

"Why? Didn't I treat you right? Wasn't I forbearing in allowing you the freedom to go out with Matt, knowing how close you two were?"

"You were a great boyfriend. And I thought that I could love you. When I saw Matt Friday night, I realized that I want the giddy, walking on air kind of love. Not the kind that grows from familiarity and comfort. I need to feel it deep in my soul."

"I appreciate the honesty, not the sentiment."

"Thanks for being understanding."

"I don't have a choice. So, I heard Matt made you his heir."

"The gossip circle's working. He wanted you to have first crack at his Koreatown place."

"I've always loved that house." George choked up. "That's cool of him. I'm definitely interested."

"It's a special house and someone special should have it."

"Thanks."

Birdie spit her gum into the foil and balled it up, added it to the pile that had grown to resemble some kind of sick sculpture. She contemplated working on her board; she had new stuff to add. The intruder. His interest in Matt's boxes. His death. Rankin, an unknown variable. She could sort through the photos. See if the burglar's in any. She should. But she didn't.

The man in her home was distracting. He was in the kitchen, she in her office, yet she felt his presence, sneaking up on her. She began to feel itchy, like a sense of something new might be imminent. She wanted to be near him, watch him make soup, and maybe earn an emotional respite. So she returned to offer company. The kitchen smelled like a brisk, windy day at Grandma's house in Ireland, redolent of herbs and celery and cabbage. Of vacation and simple times.

Too bad the country-comfort wouldn't last.

SEVENTEEN

Madi's arrival was unexpected, but not unwelcome. She had heard about the break-in from Arthur who heard it from Thom. After greetings and introductions and "what the hell happened?" And after Birdie insisted she didn't want to discuss it, Madi turned her attention to Ron and began the interrogation while he attended the soup.

"The blue Audi must be yours," said Madi. "Nice car. Married?"

"No, ma'am," said Ron.

Madi winked at Birdie.

"Ever been?" said Madi.

"No, ma'am."

"Girlfriend?"

"No, ma'am."

"How old are you?"

"Forty-four."

"You're obviously domesticated. And damn good-looking. Oh shit, you're gay."

"No, ma'am."

"What's wrong with you then?"

"Nothing."

Birdie was tempted to rescue Ron from Madi's galloping pace, but she enjoyed that Ron was willing to charm his way through Madi's questions.

"You an atheist?" she said, giving Birdie a knowing look.

"No, ma'am."

"What then?"

"Marines are force-fed God-Country-Corps, but I don't know. I'm more an agnostic."

"Close enough," said Madi with another glance in Birdie's direction.

Ron said to Birdie. "Did I pass the litmus test?"

She held up her hands and shrugged.

Then Madi said, "Do you dance?"

"No, ma'am."

Madi frowned. "You were doing so well, too. So, let's see this tat." She reached for Ron's right arm. He flinched away. "You modest?" she said.

Ron scratched the stubble on his face and said to Birdie, "Is this the way it always is?"

Again, Birdie held up her hands.

Madi said, "Look mister, you're in my cousin's house—"

"With her permission," said Ron.

"Doesn't matter," said Madi. "You're here sharing our misfortunes. We're good people and it's my right to make sure you're okay. As long as you're in Bird's home, you have no privacy. Got it?"

"Why not just strip search me?" said Ron.

"Tempting. But I'll leave that to Bird."

"That's enough," Birdie finally said. "Give the guy a break."

Then Patrick Whelan arrived. Welcome and serendipitous. Birdie would have an opportunity to question him about Emmett and Matt's relationship. Maybe find out why Matt only left him a dollar. Since he worked Hollywood—under the umbrella of West Bureau—she'd also ask him about Rankin.

Patrick entered with a bottle of Jack Daniel's Old No. 7. Birdie used to keep a bottle of the whiskey in the freezer and she'd have a splash with her morning coffee. Distilled in Lynchburg, Tennessee, and aged in charred white oak barrels, the amber liquid was mellow and went down easy. He gave Birdie an 80-proof kiss and handed her a bottle of port that he pulled from his waistband. "It's for Junior. He's on his way."

Birdie introduced Ron and they shook hands. Patrick slid his arm around Birdie's waist turning her away from Ron and pulling her into a hug. "Is that the guy from the photo? In your kitchen? *Cooking?*"

"He's a detective," she whispered. "Called out to Matt's scene."

"Freaky," said Patrick.

"*Excuse me,*" said Madi.

"We'll talk later," said Birdie.

"Don't be jealous, my love," said Patrick. He gave her an open-mouth kiss.

"Out of the bathroom?" said Birdie.

"Actually, yes," said Patrick. "I told Father."

"And?" said Birdie.

"Didn't give me shit. I think Matt's death gave him a bit of mellow."

"If there were ever an excuse for patricide," said Madi to Ron, "he'd be it."

"Madigan," Birdie scolded.

"You know it's true. His own sons hate him."

"That doesn't make it right."

Patrick unscrewed the cap, took a swig of Jack. "It's time to start drinking."

"As if you hadn't already begun," said Birdie. "You best join us for food."

Patrick scowled, took another swig, and passed the bottle to Madi. She also took a swig and offered it to Ron. He declined with a wave.

Birdie handed the port back to Patrick. "Take this to the library?"

"I've a better idea," said Patrick with a twinkle in his eye. He took Madi's hand and led her to the service stairs. They went up.

"They're gonna bang one out," said Birdie.

"Ooo-rah."

"How long were you in the Marine Corps?"

"Twenty years. Retired. Now I'm a gay domesticate posing as a detective."

"Sorry 'bout that."

"Hey, you make an excellent straight man."

The doorbell rang. "That'd be Frank." She buzzed him in and pressed the intercom and said, "Frank, we're in the kitchen."

An unfamiliar voice replied. "Miss Keane? It's Detectives Seymour and Morgan. We'd like to talk to you."

Birdie was taken aback. "That's strange. The detective here last night was a guy named Nunez."

Ron slapped the hand towel he'd been wearing over his shoulder onto the counter. "I'll check their IDs."

Birdie followed close behind. Ron held out his hand in a protective gesture as they descended the curving mahogany stairs to the entry. He confirmed their identities and introduced himself. Birdie escorted them to the living room and asked Ron for privacy. Told him she could handle two suits. He reluctantly returned to the kitchen.

They were Robbery/Homicide detectives. This troubled Birdie. Upgrading the intruder's self-inflicted gunshot to an elite division indicated seriousness and gravity. The man of medium height with the receding hairline and wearing an olive green suit was James Seymour. The other man was just Morgan. Short, muscular build, shaved head, dressed in black.

Birdie sat on a couch. Seymour sat opposite her on another couch. Morgan stood off to the side with crossed arms. Birdie fiddled with Morgan's card: M. Morgan. "What does the *M* stand for?"

"Just Morgan, ma'am."

"Your name is Morgan Morgan?"

"Miss Keane—" Seymour began.

"Hold on," said Birdie. "Morgan is obligated to tell me his first name because I asked."

After a brief silence Morgan finally said, "Mortimer."

"That wasn't so hard. I see why you use Morgan. It's a better fit."

Morgan suppressed a smile.

"Miss Keane—" Seymour began again.

"Hold on," said Birdie. "You need to know that my cousin, Thom Keane, works in RHD too."

"We're aware of the family connection," said Seymour. "Now to why we're here. A representative from the Beverly Hills law firm of Deeney, McMahon, and Desmond came to visit you on Monday. Is that correct?"

"Yes. Martin Reidy."

"What business did he have with you?"

"Tell me why you want to know," said Birdie.

"He's dead," said Seymour without ceremony.

"What the hell?" Birdie felt a dangerous foreboding.

"He was discovered in Little Tokyo. He'd been shot. We're investigating his homicide."

Birdie felt the levity slip away, replaced with a dose of harsh reality. "Excuse me." She put a hand over her mouth and ran into the kitchen. Birdie shook out her hands. "Oh, God. Oh, God."

"What happened?"

"Matt's lawyer was shot," she stammered. "He's dead. Murdered." She zipped opened a fresh pack of gum and stuffed three pieces in her mouth. Spittle drooled down her chin. Ron wiped her mouth with the dish towel in the same manner a parent would clean up a child.

"Was he a friend?"

"No. I'd just met him."

"His relationship with Matt makes it appropriate for me to join in. I'll let you know if you shouldn't answer something."

Birdie was thankful to have the buffer. She returned to the couch and Ron chose the dominant seat, the one with eyes on the whole room.

"Did Reidy indicate where he was going after he left here?" said Seymour.

"No, sir."

"Did you observe his vehicle?"

"Yes. He drove a white panel van. Was he found in the van?"

"He was. What business did he have with you?" repeated Seymour.

"Mr. Reidy was the lawyer of my friend, Matt Whelan. He died Saturday. I'm his heir." She glanced at Ron for his reaction. Nothing. "Reidy delivered some boxes and we went over the terms of Matt's will and trust. It was legal business and that's all I'm going to say about it."

"Tell me your whereabouts and activities starting from Sunday the eighth through yesterday," said Seymour.

"Hum ... I went to the Whelan family home where Frank Senior introduced me to Reidy. I went to Matt's house in Koreatown, to the mortuary. Then home. I didn't leave again until yesterday evening at five-fifteen."

"Tell us what happened when you arrived back home."

"You can get her statement from the other detective," said Ron.

"We've talked to Nunez," said Seymour. "We want to hear it direct."

Ron nodded his okay.

As Birdie re-told the story of the break-in once more, she kept glancing at Ron for his reaction but couldn't get a read.

Seymour pulled a photo from his jacket pocket. "Is this the man who broke into your home and shot himself?"

A non-smiling bald man glared at the camera in what appeared to be a mug shot. She imagined him with a curly red wig. Even so, she couldn't be certain.

"I don't know. It was dark. Who is he?" she said, dropping the photo on the coffee table.

"His name is John O'Brien. He's a jobber from Belfast."

"Jobber?"

"Someone you hire when you want someone killed or robbed or beat up."

"Is he the guy who killed himself on my lawn?"

"Confirmed," said Morgan.

She sat on her hands. It was wrong. A hardcore professional with the skill to break into a house undetected wouldn't hide from the single woman who lived alone. Nor would he take a quick and efficient exit from life.

"Tell me about the boxes Reidy delivered to you," said Seymour.

"What specifically do you want to know?"

"What was in them?"

She'd already lied to Nunez about the ownership of the boxes. She also knew that detectives asked questions they already knew the answer to. She didn't dare lie again. "Personal property belonging to Matt Whelan."

"With your permission we'd like to take a look."

"The boxes contained memorabilia, awards, journals, stuff. You know about stuff, don't you, Detective Seymour?"

"Why did you lie to Nunez? You told him the boxes contained your work."

Ron's stoic expression gave no hint of his thoughts.

"An unidentified man who was with Nunez frightened me." She'd keep Rankin's presence off the record for now until she figured out what brought him to her home and why he and Thom didn't acknowledge each other though they had past history. "I had looked at the contents, but didn't inspect every item thoroughly." That was true. "There are some rumors going around that Matt was a bad package. I wanted to protect my friend from anything that might disparage his reputation." Also true. "As it turned out, the contents were benign and of no concern." Maybe true. Truth was, Birdie really didn't know. Especially in regards to the last entry.

Seymour scribbled in a portfolio. "Something important enough was in those boxes to bring out a hired jobber. We'd really like a look."

"The boxes are no longer in my possession." Birdie was going to have to start keeping track of her lies.

"What did you do with them?"

"I can't tell you that."

Morgan sneered. "You've interfered with a murder investigation. You've lied to an investigator. We can get a warrant for those boxes."

"Don't try to intimidate her," said Ron. "She's done nothing wrong and has no obligation to talk. She extended a courtesy, return the favor."

Seymour and Morgan's sharp glares left no doubt they didn't like his interference.

"I appreciate Detective Hughes' chivalry," said Birdie. "But I didn't know that Reidy had been murdered. I didn't know there was going to be an investigation. I am the legal heir to Matt Whelan's estate, so it's within my authority to do whatever I wish with his property."

"Miss Keane..." said Seymour, sighing.

"I'm sorry, but there's nothing I can do." She crossed her fingers hoping they were bluffing about coming back with paper and she blessed heaven that she had already hidden them. "Can we go back to something? Is there a possibility that Reidy's death is connected to O'Brien and possibly Matt?"

"How do you mean?" said Seymour.

"Everyone who has had contact with those boxes is dead, including the man who had them the longest."

Ron interjected. "We've ruled out homicide in Mr. Whelan's death."

"Undetermined, according to my information," said Seymour.

"Officially, until the coroner signs off," said Ron.

"Do you know who killed Reidy?" said Birdie.

"We don't have conclusive proof of the shooter's identity. But we have the weapon that killed him. O'Brien used it on himself."

"A ballistic comparison? Already?" said Birdie, indignant, not believing the fairy tale thrown at her. "How could you have even known to look? O'Brien's gun was with Wilshire."

"And you're able to jump the line and have a tech willing to do a speedy comparison?" said Ron. "Do you have a personal crime lab?"

"I don't know how things work in San Diego," said Morgan, "but we have resources."

"O'Brien might be connected to Reidy with the gun," said Birdie. "Reidy was connected to Matt as his lawyer. What connects O'Brien to Matt?"

Seymour stood. "Triangular thinking is premature. We don't know if there's a connection."

"And even if there were," added Ron, "it may not be relevant to what might have occurred between O'Brien and Reidy."

"That's right," said Seymour. He plucked the mug shot off the coffee table and slipped it into his portfolio. "Thank you for your time, Miss Keane. We'll be in touch."

Morgan snorted in agreement.

Ron escorted them out.

Birdie's hands shook with a tight jittering. RHD doesn't launch an investigation unless the crime is significant. A dead lawyer? A nonviolent break-in? What makes these two events important? How did they connect the gun so soon? It was too convenient. Birdie felt there was a splinter of explanation working its way out. Tiny. Piercing. It was an irritant she couldn't reach.

Warm hands were on hers. "You're shaking," said Ron.

Birdie's breath snagged the moment she felt his hands holding hers. They were big. Thick-fingered. Hard-working. Strong. Yet gentle as they stilled hers. She liked them and she liked them touching her.

Madi and Patrick's post-coital chuckles swirled from above. They came bounding down the stairs in drunken ignorance and bliss. Ron quickly dropped Birdie's hands, a look of interest passing between them.

"Babe," said Madi to Birdie. "We must consider the possibility that you'll be photographed tomorrow. What are you wearing to the funeral?"

"The Phillip Lim trench dress."

"The sheer, pale gray one with the black weaving? Perfect. Wear a flesh-colored sheath underneath and you'll stand out from the usual funeral black. Wear the silver mantilla for the church and take that webby black hat and Jackie O's for the graveside."

"Madi's been styling me since we were kids," said Birdie to Ron in response to his expression of perplexity.

The doorbell rang. Madi yelped, "That's Frank. I'll get it."

Birdie whispered to Ron, "No need to tell everyone about Seymour and Morgan's visit."

"Roger that."

EIGHTEEN

It HURT TO LOOK at Father Frank; he wore Matt's absence on his face. Four sleepless days gave his usually sharp green eyes a weepy appearance with inky reminders like crushed paper underneath the lower lashes. Frank's ash hair, salted with gray, was in need of a trim. His mouth taut in a downward pull. He raised his palms over the dining table. "Let us pray." Birdie placed her hands on her lap. Patrick took Madi's hand. Ron lowered his head.

"Lord, our beloved Matthew Francis has left us. We experience his loss as a traumatic injury. Please grant us the strength to heal, to take care of our bodies, and our spiritual health. Please forgive us when we strike out against you in our anguish. See us through the good days and the bad. By your grace, please do not let us sink into depression and overindulge in grief. Let us not feel the guilt when we experience the light moments. Please grant us the courage to laugh.

"Lord, when the well-wishers have departed, the food has been eaten, the trash barrels are filled with empty bottles, after the stories have been retold, the photos passed around, please grant us the strength when the loneliness creeps back. Grant us the wisdom to push aside the regrets and second guesses.

"Bless us, oh Lord: Patrick Thomas, Madigan Birdie, Birdie Elizabeth, our new friend, Ronald, and your humble servant Francis Owen Junior, and these thy gifts which we are about to receive from thy bountiful hands, so lovingly created by Ronald, through Christ our Lord. *In Nomine Patris, et Filii, et Spiritus Sancti. Amen.*"

"Amen."

Frank raised his glass. "To friends and fellowship and this wonderful soup."

Everyone's interest focused on Ron. Being the newcomer to the table, he answered questions about his career in the Marine Corps with a gracious shorthand that suggested he was uncomfortable being the center of attention. His voice was soft spoken but had a tenor that suggested one used to barking commands or throwing his voice to the back of the room. Birdie became aware of his every gesture. The way the corners of his mouth turned upward when he smiled. The way he swiped his mouth with his napkin. The way he flicked quick glances in Birdie's direction. The way his hazel eyes seemed to hide behind his lashes. The way he held his spoon ambidextrously in his right hand.

There was an exciting buzz in the dining room, an oblivious distractedness from suffering and grief. Like an exchange of pain for stories about being the youngest child, the only boy, in a household of women with an absentee father.

"Well, we know where you learned domestic skills," said Madi, "but it's peculiar that you entered into such macho professions. First the Marines and then the cop business."

"No, it's not," said Patrick. "He had to swing to the far side to avoid being a swish."

That made Ron blush and Birdie thought it was cute as hell.

Birdie dried a bowl and stacked it atop another in the cabinet. Patrick maneuvered a hand towel around a fist full of spoons. Stopping the drink and eating the thick, stew-like soup was sobering for Patrick.

"Why do I always get stuck with washing? I'm the one that needs pretty hands," said Madi.

"Don't be such a diva," said Patrick.

"There's lotion under the sink," said Birdie. "The good stuff you sent from Italy."

"Where'd Frank and Ron disappear to?" said Madi.

"The library," said Birdie. "Ron's getting background for his report. I need to steal your boyfriend for a few minutes." She slid her arm around Patrick's.

"Great," said Madi. "Leave me slaving away."

Birdie led Patrick to her office. "I hope you know what you've gotten into."

"Don't worry 'bout me," said Patrick. "I know she can be a handful."

"You won't be able to tame her."

"I wouldn't want to."

"I'm happy to hear that. Madi's strong personality is uniquely hers."

"So, what's up with Ron? Did he know my brother?"

"He says they met just the one time," said Birdie. "The photo was taken during a ski trip. Does it bother you that all three men in the photo were either at the scene of Matt's death or handled his body?"

"Luck of the Irish. If I were to die, I'd like my friends handling me instead of complete strangers. Why does it bother you?"

"I don't like coincidence."

"Matt didn't either, but not everything in life and death can be managed."

"Speaking of management ... I need some information and I need you to keep our conversation private. What can you tell me about Theodore Rankin?"

"Chief Rankin?" Patrick raised an eyebrow. "He's more politician than cop. Why are you asking?"

"He was here last night. After the break-in. He was here when the dude killed himself, too. He seemed extremely interested in what had happened."

Patrick shrugged. "Wilshire is one of his divisions. You're the daughter of one of his captains. We look out for our own."

"He wasn't wearing a badge and he wouldn't identify himself."

"Don't take that personal, he's an arrogant ass. What say Gerard?"

"Rankin had gone by the time Dad got here." Until she figured out what was what between Thom and Rankin, she'd rather keep the incident quiet. "Forget I asked. Please."

"Consider it forgotten."

"About Emmett … why weren't he and Matt getting along?"

"That's a can of worms."

"Tell me everything."

"E was a wee bastard. Too much like the old man. He'd bully Matt. Call him sissy, homo, weakling. He'd trip Matt, break his toys, spread rumors at school. Once, Matt got a beautiful new baseball mitt for his birthday and E shredded it with a razor blade. Dad allowed his boys to scrape and shove our way through childhood. But after the mitt episode, Mom had had enough of E's meanness and persuaded Dad to intervene. His response was to beat the shit out of E for picking on Matt and to beat Matt for not fighting back. After that, Matt became extremely competitive when it came to E. He had to get better grades, date the cuter girls, shoot better, run faster, study harder."

Matt's early box was full of childhood memories. Birdie wondered if his rough relationship with Emmett was the catalyst for his unwavering order. Had he been forced to box up the precious, the good, and lock it away to keep it hidden and safe? She imagined him sneaking into a dark corner of the attic to spend time with the things that gave him a sense of pride or comfort. These thoughts made her sad.

"They settled into a truce after E married Eileen," continued Patrick. "Then Matt married Linda and all the old shit surfaced. E once had a thing for Linda but couldn't close the deal. Matt did. And what really burned E's hide was that—from his perspective—Matt practically threw his marriage away after he met you. E called Matt a pedophile and cradle robber. It was apparent to anyone with a pulse to see how you felt about Matt. Matt tried to hide his feelings about falling for a teenager. E's constant belittling and name calling just made it worse. The truth is Matt worked harder at making his marriage work. He went to counseling. Took Linda to a marriage encounter. In the end, it was Linda who walked away."

"I had no idea," said Birdie.

"Matt's emotional downfall was his problem not yours. He protected you with a fierce desire to keep you from blame."

But she wasn't blameless. Birdie was an impetuous teenager. Cocksure and aggressive. When she was sixteen she surprised Matt with an open-mouth kiss. His return kiss was unrepentant. For a few seconds anyway. Afterward, she scolded him for wrecking her. How could she date boys her own age when she felt the power of a real man? "I know you're married and it'd be wrong," she had said, "but I want to be your girlfriend." She saw the flash of consideration cross his face, but he told her no. It was a few months before she saw him again. For her part, she was encouraged. Matt wanted her, and yet, he couldn't have her, which made him want her more. His absence was proof of his desire—he had to stay away because of the temptation.

"What's the prevailing gossip about why we never got together?"

"I got a sense that Matt was embarrassed from carrying around the shame for so long, but he told me it was a complicated issue and he refused to elaborate."

She wondered if years of guilt made it complicated. Or was it the secret thing? But they had gotten off track. "Did Matt have problems with the other brothers?"

"Just E. Eventually, they settled into a neutral existence."

"Do you have problems with Emmett?"

"We get along fine."

Childhood was difficult enough in a strict and traditional household without the added burden of a brother's hatred. Birdie became dispirited to hear Matt had such a hard time and wondered why she didn't read much about their relationship in his journals. Then again, she'd sought specifics about herself. She read tidbits out of sequence and context. At least now she knew why she had a sixth sense that Emmett didn't like her.

"I think I know why you've asked," said Patrick. "Matt left E out of his will and you're wondering why."

"Exactly."

"Matt got the last word. Good for him. Whatever you do, don't give Emmett anything."

"Is he going to ask?"

"Probably."

Birdie entered the library. "Madi and Patrick have gone. Ron, they say thanks for the excellent soup. Frank, they'll see you tomorrow."

"Come in," said Frank.

The curtains were open and the city lights stretched farther than usual, twinkled brighter in the rain-washed clean air. Frank sat in his favorite wingback chair; the one that allowed him to gaze at the city view and see the rest of the room. The advantage spot. He may be a priest, but he learned a thing or two from his cop father. "I think we've picked apart my brother's brain thoroughly enough to fill three files of background."

Ron nodded his head in agreement.

Frank yawned. "I must get back. Tomorrow will be a busy day. Bird, I invited Ron to the funeral. He said he was already scheduled to attend. You both may ride to the cemetery from the church in one of the family limos if you like."

"I find limos uncomfortable," said Birdie. "I'll drive myself."

"You have a suspended license," said Ron. "I'll be happy to escort you."

"What clothes will he be buried in?" said Birdie.

"His Class A," said Frank. "The department will have a large presence."

"Who's the celebrant?"

"Me."

"What?"

"Why are you surprised? He's my earthly brother, and I can care for his soul better than Father Gabriel or Ignacio."

"Competition even in priesthood."

Frank snorted in dismissal. "Ron, I must have a private moment with Bird. Do you mind?"

Ron excused himself and closed the library door. Birdie sat in the vacated warm seat.

"I want you to invite Ron to stay the night." There was earnestness in his voice. "I inquired and he said he hadn't yet made arrangements so I know he'd be amenable. I know, Bird, you're going to say he's a stranger and you hardly know him, but he won't let harm come to you. Let a grieving priest rest his eyes in peace knowing you'll be safe."

"I don't need a man to protect me. John O'Brien, that was the intruder's name, didn't break into my house to hurt me, and he had ample opportunity. It's over. Please don't worry."

Frank was too tired to even attempt to disguise his concern. She could see it in his face. It was clear in the way his eye twitched and the pleading expression. A shiver pricked her arms. "Frank? What are you afraid of? What do I need to know?"

He lowered his head and shook it vigorously. "For once, will you please just acquiesce without argument!" he said sharply.

"Okay. I'll invite him. But don't be mad if he declines the offer."

"He won't. I'm not blind to the way you two look at each other."

"Are you setting me up?" Birdie teased, trying to lighten the mood.

"Certainly not." He stood. "I really must go now. Thank you for a fine afternoon. *Dominus vobiscum.*"

"*Et cum spiritu tuo.*"

NINETEEN

RON WAS AN ENGAGED speaker with an audience of one. Conversational lulls were rare and there was no awkwardness. His speech was kind and thoughtful in a chivalrous way.

They sat at opposite ends of the couch. Ron scooted closer and pointed at the silver chain that disappeared under her shirt. "What's that you wear around your neck?"

"Sentimental juju." She untucked it and held it out for him. He fingered it. "It's a medallion Frank gave me for memorizing Latin prayers. This is Saint Francis de Sales, the patron saint of journalists and writers. I wear it near my heart."

"It's nice," he said. "And a handcuff key?"

"Matt's lucky charm."

The probing look in his eyes suggested that he wanted to ask questions. About her faith? Or Matt? She'd freely tell him anything. But she had to be asked. The moment drew out too long so she moved on.

"I know you didn't want to show Madi, but I'm curious what kind of tattoo a deputy detective wears. The part that's visible looks like snake skin."

Ron rolled up his sleeve. "It a coiled serpent." Tiny scales were outlined in thin black lines and colored gold and red. The head of the serpent had one green eye open, one closed. Two carefully curved scripts followed the contour of the creature: *Semper Fidelis* and *Semper Paratus*.

"Always faithful and always prepared," she said.

"Always faithful or always ready; depends on the translation."

"Is it okay to say beautiful in regards to a tattoo on a man?"

"It's fine. Remember the Saker I mentioned? Would you like to see it?"

"The one watching your back? Okay."

Ron turned his back toward her and lifted his shirt. The broad expanse of his upper back and shoulders was covered with a large, bird-of-prey in flight, coming right at her. Birdie pushed back in reflex. "Whoa."

She'd never seen anything like it. The bird had brown upperparts with contrasting grey flight feathers. The head was a paler brown with streaks and spots running down its chest. The thighs were thick and ended at sharp talons. The tattoo was so detailed and fine with the various shades of brown, gray, and tan that she swore Ron pasted a photograph on his skin.

"The first time I saw a Saker falcon was in Central Asia," he said, as he pulled his shirt down. "Then I saw one in the Middle East. Sakers are aggressively fierce hunters. Popular with falconers."

"How long did it take to do?" she said.

"'bout forty hours."

"Ouch. The same artist did both?"

"The serpent was done in Southeast Asia and the Saker done at home in Oceanside."

The phone rang. Birdie silently cursed the intrusion.

"Hey, Birdie, it's Jimmy from the Westend. You wanted me to call, remember?"

"What do you have?"

"Nothing about Matt. Something else. When you were here with Gerard, that retired cop, Soto, stayed the whole time and watched you from the bar. And Thom and Arthur watched him. I figured Soto for a dirty ol' man. After Gerard said goodbye to Soto, Thom got in his face. He and Soto had a heated discussion. I couldn't hear what was said."

"Then how do you know it was heated?"

"Body language. Arthur watched it and stood as if he were about to get involved when it suddenly broke off and Soto left. Anyway, I got busy 'cause my bar back had to leave early and I forgot about it 'til this evening."

"Thanks Jimmy. I'd appreciate your discretion."

She could ask Thom about the fuss, but he'd know that Jimmy had called. Bartenders were like priests. There was a code. Hear everything, repeat nothing. She wouldn't want to make things uncomfortable for Jimmy. Besides, the encounter probably meant nothing. Still …

"Problem?" said Ron.

Birdie shook her head. "Don't think so."

"Then why are your hands shaking?"

She hadn't realized they were. "Alcohol withdrawals. But really, anything can make them quiver: nervousness, agitation, a craving, stress."

"A suicidal jobber breaking into your home?"

"That will do it." Birdie clenched her fists.

Ron pointed to the gun and badge that he still wore on his belt. He unclipped the badge and placed it on the library desk. The gun holster was not only clipped to the waistband of his jeans, but it was also threaded by the belt. He unbuckled the belt and pulled it through the loops, freeing the holster. The way he shed the hardware of his profession seemed deliberate. Like undressing. Everything that followed would be personal.

"I'm goofy footed with damsels in distress," he said, spreading his lips into a nervous smile. "But I'm a great hug." He opened his arms.

She didn't answer. She pressed her body into his. They stood together, arms wrapped around the other. Comfort. Birdie's head pressed tight against Ron's chest listening to his heart, a ballad chasing away the uncertainty and confusion. She felt connected to him. Here was a man she was just beginning to know, yet she felt secure in his arms. She perceived a sensation of compassion and trust. It was scary. And thrilling.

Birdie allowed her hands to gently move up his back, feeling the taut skin underneath the soft cotton of his shirt. Down his spine and around the small of his back. He didn't protest, so she allowed her hands to move under his shirt, her fingertips lightly touching his smooth skin and iron-man strong muscles. He inhaled. One of his large hands cradled her head; his fingers grasped some hair as he applied a very slight pull.

Birdie's pulse quickened with the rush of warmth that precedes sexual awakening. Ron presented a physical manifestation of the same arousal.

Her fingers spread out as she moved them up his side, thumbs pressed harder as her hands traveled upward toward his underarms. He sucked in his breath at the increased pressure.

Suddenly Ron pulled her head back, twirled her body and gently pinned her against the wall. Hazel eyes locked on Birdie's blue ones. His mouth centimeters away. His body didn't touch hers yet it was close enough that she could feel his heat.

"What do you want?"

What could she say? That she was attracted to him, but felt like she was betraying Matt? Or that she wanted him to screw her so that she could feel grounded and stop thinking about the brain bits that were on her lawn. Or that she desired to ravage him to take her mind off Reidy's murder or the mysterious key Matt left behind or the unsolved Paige Street murder. Or should she tell him that Frank's fear had scared her and she simply wanted his strong body next to hers.

She opened her mouth in invitation for a kiss. Her lips grazed his and she felt them twitch. *Kiss me*, she pleaded silently.

"Tell me," he said.

To hell with it. She pressed her lips to his.

Big hands moved to her face and pushed her head back.

"I want to have sex with you," she said. "Is that clear enough?"

"Why?"

She interpreted his question as a rejection. "Forget it." She pushed him off. What kind of slut would ask a man to have sex with her just days after the man she loved died? Yeah, she had boyfriends. Sexual partners. But that was before she and Matt had said the words. Everything was different now that the words were floating in the ether.

"Don't take it back," said Ron. He grabbed her arm and held her so close that she thought he would steal her breath. He whispered in her ear, "I'm already off the reservation. Still, I'm a little old-fashioned. Please understand that I need to know it's me you want. If your only interest is a ready dick then I'll make a call and get you a number for a safe stud service. Otherwise ..."

Birdie couldn't quiet the noise of silence. She did want Ron. No conflict here. Humans are hard-wired for sex and she was attracted to Ron in a natural, earthy way, like bees to lavender. But there was something else that lingered: an overwhelming emotion that bubbled its way to the top of all of the others. She'd felt it only once before. It was that part that made her feel unclean. But before she could retreat and apply some logic, the words spurted out. "I want *you*," she said.

Ron took her face into his hands, smoothed back her hair and kissed the hollow of her throat. There was no ambiguity in his lips or desire as he twirled her around and explored her shoulders, neck, and the back of her ears. His tongue tasted the base of her scalp even as his hands moved across her belly, up to her breasts.

Birdie's flesh was hungry and her knees quaked. She felt certain she was going to faint.

"I ... I'm going to fall."

"Let me catch you."

At two a.m. Birdie awoke to an unfamiliar sound. A muffled purring. In the twilight of a hard sleep she thought it was George's cat performing some nocturnal kneading until she remembered she was home. Slowly the reality set in. It was the vibrating buzz of a cell phone, loud in the slumbered night. Her eyes swept across the nightstand. Ron's cell phone rested silently next to the house phone. He must have another.

She became aware of Ron's body comfortably wrapped around hers. Oblivious to the sound. Marines must learn how to sleep with any amount of noise. When the buzzing stopped, she expected to hear the beep of a new voicemail, but the phone started again. The caller obviously didn't want to leave a message.

She nudged Ron. "Your phone."

He reached across her to pick up his cell.

"The other one," she said.

Birdie heard a puff. The sound of displeasure pushed out his nose. He carefully extricated himself from Birdie and quietly tumbled across the bed. He got up and dug through his duffle resting on the chaise. In the glow of the phone, Birdie watched him check the number and then turn it off. It wasn't uncommon for cops to carry two cell phones. Thom did. One personal. One business.

Despite the hour, it must not have been urgent.

"Who calls at two in the morning?" Birdie mumbled.

"Only an asshole," whispered Ron, resuming his spoon position. He put his hand on her hip then slowly massaged it down around her butt, across her thigh, back up and forward, down her belly and reached between her legs.

Birdie felt him harden against her backside. She scooted forward and rolled over.

TWENTY

Thursday, January 12

Day 244. This day was gonna be a tough-ass day.

Birdie was agitated. Forty minutes of hard running on the treadmill didn't help. She was disturbed and angry for giving in to her physical desires at a time of emotional upset. *I love Matt. Not Ron. I love Matt. Not Ron.* The words were the rhythm of her cadence. One-two-three, one-two, one-two-three, one-two. Like a dance step that missed the forth beat.

Two floors above her head a man was asleep in her bed. The place she had saved for Matt. She had never shared it with men for sleep or sex; that's what the guestrooms were for. Last night she'd led Ron upstairs to the room across from hers. He sat on the bed and bounced. Then he walked across the hall and sat on her bed, repeating the bounce. He declared that he preferred her rack and that's where they were going to be for the night. There was no discussion. Other men had asked for the same privilege of sex in her bed and every one had been denied. She wasn't sure why she relented so easily to Ron and this upset her.

He was also the first man she ever slept with. The previous routine was sex in a guest room and afterward she'd get up and sleep in her own bed. Sure, it caused hard feelings, but her terms weren't negotiable. She felt that sleep was the most intimate and vulnerable act two people could share. It took a complete trust to lay unconscious, baring the body and soul to the unknown of sleep. The rule was a way to stay emotionally detached from her lovers. Like she really needed it—she loved Matt and that alone kept her from loving any other.

The two a.m. wake-up call aside, she experienced a deep sleep with a virtual stranger. What frightened her more than the entire sum of events in the last five days was a fledgling emotion that Ron brought out in her. Though it was a strange sensation she recognized it immediately. She was falling for him.

As a lover, Ron was brutal, kind, hard, giving, all at the same time. Birdie ravaged him with an intensity she never knew possible. It was so raw that she cried with repressed emotional energy that preceded rapture. And the tenderness he showed after a mad session of sex was a smooth nightcap.

She finished the run just as Ron arrived. She pulled open the multi-paned glass wall that separated the gym from the lanai.

He held her chin and gave her a lingering kiss. She could taste herself on his tongue.

"Good morning. Thank you for last night."

"Are you always this nice the morning after?"

"Yes, ma'am."

"Let's sit outside."

The sharp morning air was a refreshing bite on her hot skin. The skies remained clear overnight yet the patio furniture was still damp. She sat on a brick step and wrapped her arms around her bare legs. Ron sat next to her.

"Nice gym," he said.

"Matt built it." She pointed to a mound hidden under a blue tarp beyond the patch of grass marked with the yellow tape. "That's a pile of lumber. It was to be his next undertaking. It's supposed to be a gazebo. The plans are in my garage."

"I'm confused about your relationship."

"We were each other's life project."

Ron screwed his face in noncomprehension.

"Our relationship can't be compressed into a simple answer."

"Tell me a story then."

"About eight months ago a two-year relationship ended. Right after, I did something stupid that could've landed me in prison. I got lucky when a judge ordered me to rehab. I took the deal, but escaped after one day. Matt vouched for me with the court and brought me home. He made a drunk tank in the empty room next to mine. Put a mattress on the floor. A lock on the door. He maintained a vigil over me for an entire week while I suffered delirium tremens." Birdie fought back the tears. "It was awful. I sweated, and shit, and pissed, and threw up in that room. I yelled obscenities and assaulted Matt. I screamed in pain and wanted to die. Yet he fed me, cleaned me, gave encouragement, prayed with me. He never complained or argued. And here I am, my body purged of poison and still suffering withdrawals."

"That takes a true friend," said Ron, "but I have a few who'd do it for me."

"In turn, I cared for him. You already know about the domestic. When Matt was released from the hospital, I brought him home, helped him with his physical therapy. Including the civilian time, he had twenty-seven years invested with the LAPD. He loved the job. Tried to go back. The physical pain was overwhelming and interfered with his duties. They moved him inside, but he felt claustrophobic. He loved the streets and couldn't hack it on the inside. Then one day he had a seizure and had to go back out on disability. The gym, the future gazebo, they were a way to keep his mind and body occupied until he figured out what he was going to do."

Ron interlaced his fingers with hers. "You said a lot and still didn't answer the question."

"Not to your satisfaction."

"Hum. I guess what I want to know is … well, there were photos of you all over his house. Hoy told me how much he loved you. How much you loved him. You mention boyfriends. Wasn't he your boyfriend?"

"We never had sex if that's what you want to know."

"I was curious about that. What kept you apart?"

She reclaimed her hand. "Ron, I'd like the answer to that, too. Since his death, I've discovered a side of him that I never knew existed. I have to figure that out."

Ron cracked an imaginary egg over her knee. The simple tactile sensation tickled and she laughed. Yeah, he'd snuck up on her, but the relationship was doomed. Like the rest. She respected him enough to end it sooner rather than later. He was an excellent respite amid the turmoil of the last five days. But she had work to do and he had become a distraction she couldn't afford.

How you gonna pull this one off, Bird? Screw up some courage and get moving.

She rubbed the goose bumps on her legs. "About last night—"

He heard the dismissal in her voice. "It looks different in the daylight?"

"I'm emotionally unbalanced. I don't need nor want a relationship right now."

"That's a quick slice to the essence of things. Look, I don't want to complicate your life and I sure as hell can't compete with a dead man."

"If Matt were alive, last night wouldn't have happened."

Ron got up and scratched his scruffy face. "Yes. But if Matt were alive we never would have met." He began to pace.

"What? Don't tell me I hurt your feelings."

"Even though we skipped the audition and went straight to the play, I do want a relationship."

"It won't work."

"Why not?"

"Well, for one thing, you live, what? Ninety miles away? And I'm grieving the loss of the only man I've ever loved. Let's add my commitment issues and that I feel guilty for enjoying myself with you. I really like you. I do. But I don't want to give you any false hope."

"You're an independent woman. I'm an independent man. You like your space, I like mine. We're a perfect fit."

"Wouldn't work."

"Give me a good reason."

"I just gave you several, but okay, here's another, even if I don't feel an emotional connection with the man I'm with, I have to have a monogamous understanding. That's what I require. The geography alone prevents that. For argument's sake, let's say we give it a try. We'd be spending so little time together that when we did hook up we'd spend all our time in the sack. As much as I like you as a sex partner, I need more than that."

"What makes you think I don't require the same?"

"I know guys like you. You're good looking, fit, smart, literate. You navigated my body like a master. You respected me and the boundaries I set. You have a charming aw-shucks demeanor that's very attractive. I suspect you have no problem getting laid."

"I get it. You think I'm a player. Look, I've spent twenty years in a military uniform working shows all over the world. I considered myself lucky if I caught the eye of some diplomat's wife."

"That's not my problem."

"Didn't our lovemaking mean anything?"

"We didn't make love. We had sex. There's a difference."

"You're wrong." He pointed his finger in an accusing way. "I saw it in your face. Felt it in the way you moved. You let go and were with *me* one hundred percent all the way. Slow, fast, everything in between. And now you're shutting it down before we have a chance to see where it'll take us."

He was right. Birdie felt the heat of the truth in her core. But this was her modus operandi. She fulfilled the passion and moved on. There had been too many similar morning-after conversations. But this one hurt. The guilt of such an intense sexual interaction with a man so soon after the death of her love couldn't be erased with Matt's deception and the horrible events since his death. Too bad she wasn't a Libra. Maybe then she might have the skills to balance her life. But she was an all-in woman—used to taking risks with every aspect of her life except her heart. She reserved it for a man who kept her close but not close enough. And now he was dead. She didn't know how to behave.

"Life is lived but once," said Ron low and deliberate. "I can't change what's happened in recent days and I understand what you're saying and why you're saying it." Ron squatted in front of her. "You'll pull the emergency brake no matter how compelling my argument. But I'm asking for a yield. Attach your fate to mine for the duration of this day and this night. Tomorrow morning I'll drive away. Give you the space to do what you need."

The tattooed former Marine had an expression of boyish hopefulness so endearing that Birdie caved. Despite her best efforts he managed to earn a reprieve. There was a small place in Birdie that wanted to see where this would go. Her beating heart pumped happy colors of pink and red to that very space.

But … it would end in ruin.

Of that she was certain.

And she dreaded the repeat of this conversation tomorrow.

TWENTY-ONE

BIRDIE AND RON ARRIVED late. The procession had already lined up in the portico of St. Joseph. She pulled at Ron's arm. "We're going to use the vestibule off the nave. It's a hidden way in. I used it to sneak out of Mass after communion when Father Frank wasn't looking."

"Such a rebel," said Ron.

Birdie's breath caught when they entered. She had never seen the sanctuary so full. St. Joseph wasn't a large church, and it bulged at the seams. The stained glass depicting the Stations of the Cross bathed the congregation in colors. Dust shimmered in the light. It was breathtakingly beautiful and magical.

She covered her head with the lace mantilla, and they moved down the side aisle looking for a seat. Her family's pews were full. So were the Whelan's. Emmett, his wife Eileen, and their four children sat two rows behind the rest of his family. Eileen waved the pair over. Birdie knelt and crossed herself before entering the pew, forcing everyone in the pew to scoot and sit thigh-to-thigh.

Ron rotated his wide shoulders sideways to fit his frame into the row.

Birdie leaned around Emmett to kiss Eileen. At the end of the row sat Linda. Matt's ex-wife. She was more stunning now than when Birdie first met her. Birdie flicked her gaze back to Eileen and kept it there, ignoring the ex.

"Thanks for squeezing us in."

"Nice dress," said Eileen. "Who's the handsome guy?"

"Ron Hughes. San Diego Sheriff Deputy."

"Matt's detective?" said Emmett.

Birdie nodded and pressed her back against the pew in order to make an introduction. Ron had to press his elbow into Birdie's ribs to shake Emmett's hand. He expressed his condolences, then gave Birdie's knee a squeeze in apology.

Knowing that Emmett suffered with insomnia, she said, "You sleeping?"

He shook his head and a few tears fell loose onto the hat of his Class A uniform that lay on his lap. Birdie never got a sense of innate sincerity from Emmett. After hearing Patrick's tale of Emmett's abuse toward Matt, she felt inclined to dislike him. But watching him cry for his brother, she had a little more compassion.

The music changed, signaling the congregation to rise for the procession's entrance. A young acolyte—one of Matt's nephews—held the processional cross followed by another gently swinging a gold vessel with burning frankincense.

The long line of solemn men and boys in ceremonial robes slowly shuffled up the middle aisle.

"Fascinating," whispered Ron. "Do they always wear black?"

"This is a Requiem Mass. They wear black for the dead."

At the foot of the altar, Father Frank blessed himself. *"In Nomine Patris, et Filii, et Spiritus Sancti. Amen.* I will go in to the altar of God. To God who gives joy to my youth. Our help is in the name of the Lord, who has made heaven and earth …"

An LAPD color guard directed traffic into Holy Cross Cemetery—a green sanctuary surrounded by buildings of commerce and rows of houses. White-gloved uniforms directed the funeral procession around the cemetery in an orderly manner.

The limos transporting immediate family had already arrived and were parked on the street nearest the gravesite. As Ron slowly drove past, Birdie saw Frank Senior and Mary exit the first car. As Ron's Audi snaked around the roadway, she was struck by the enormous number of people in attendance. There was even a KCLA news van and a small video crew standing discreetly off to the side. The last uniform waved them to the next parking space. Organized like Disneyland.

Ron reached into the back seat for his navy suit jacket and camera.

"Why the camera?" said Birdie.

"I'm a wannabe photojournalist. If it bothers you I'll leave it behind."

Cameras at funerals weren't that unusual. She had taken photos at her Grandpa's funeral that she later shared with distant family who couldn't attend.

They picked through the soft grass toward the folding chairs set up in front of the casket.

"There's Jacob," he said. "If you don't mind, I'll escort you to your seat and meet you after."

Fine. She was surrounded by family and friends. After Mass she had spoken with the majority of them and introduced Ron. But she hadn't seen Arthur and couldn't find him now amid the multitudes of reverent police officers in dress blues with hats slung low over their eyes. Together they formed a sea of blue that overwhelmed the funeral black. She also scanned the crowd for Linda. Birdie became irritated that she'd allowed that woman to invade her attention.

Birdie sat at the end of a row next to her mom, Maggie. There were too many people. Birdie's lungs clenched. They shouldn't be at a cemetery. Matt shouldn't be lying in the casket with a reproduction of his badge on the lid. Her breath rasped out quick gasps. This was a mistake. A misunderstanding. She leaned forward to stave off a panic attack. Maggie grabbed her daughter's hand, a strong anchor that allowed Birdie to catch her breath.

Arthur and Matt's partnership brought sociality to the two families and soon the two clans were linked by the brotherhood of copdom and shared heritage. Both patriarchs were Irish-born. There were five Keanes and now five Whelans currently working for the LAPD. In police circles, they were collectively known as the Irish Mob. They spanned all sworn personnel levels from patrol uniforms to two star politicos, with one civilian—Birdie's mom.

Privately, Birdie took pride in the Irish Mob moniker. Being a cop was a tough job. Each member of her family, immediate and otherwise, relied on one another for emotional support and camaraderie. So it was today at the gravesite of one of their own. But in the cop bars and the suburban backyard barbeques of captains and commanders, it was a real force that was discussed. The Irish Mob had become a machine to be reckoned with.

The service ended when Frank chanted the words: "Eternal rest grant unto him, O Lord. And let perpetual light shine upon him. May he rest in peace. Amen. May his soul and the souls of all the faithful departed through the mercy of God rest in peace. Amen."

All police radio frequencies were put on hold for an end-of-watch announcement. Birdie held onto Maggie. Gerard wasn't close at hand to provide a hug to his girls. He stood with the rest of the mob and saluted. Afterward the Los Angeles Drum and Pipe Band played taps. The moaning, emotive quality of the bagpipes stabbed at Birdie's heart. A pain caught in her throat. She felt the brace in her cheeks and couldn't contain the loss. Her shoulders shook as she cried.

The Irish Mob was down one man. Birdie was down the best man she ever knew.

TWENTY-TWO

BIRDIE EXPECTED MATT'S WAKE to be a classy affair to match the Whelan family sensibility. What their money bought was a giant block party with a fair-like atmosphere. Sweet smoke from ribs, hamburgers, hot dogs, and sausages floated in the air. Row upon row of tables were laden with food. There were plenty of tables and chairs for eating. The bar tents located at either end of the street already had long lines.

The Mulligans played on a stage at the north side of the street accompanied by a troupe of girls in traditional Irish dress that performed various jigs in front of a large dance floor. A balloon archway marked the entrance to a tent laid out with couches in front of a huge movie screen on which Matt's life played out in home movies and photos. It was right next to the jump house. Potted hedges were brought in to hide the long row of porta potties.

Ron whistled at the spectacle. "Is this a wake or what?"

"Or what," moaned Birdie, in no mood for a crushing party that wouldn't end 'till dawn. "I can't be here. I feel claustrophobic."

"Frank Senior wanted to meet with me first thing. If you can hold on for a little while I'll take you home right after."

Birdie thought she could so they wove their way toward the house located mid-block. A flash of blond hair caught her eye.

"Ron, look. Over there."

"Who is that?"

"That's Linda." Birdie paused for emphasis. "Matt's ex-wife."

Linda held the hand of a mini, five-year-old version of herself. She turned and caught Birdie and Ron starring. She boldly walked over and gave Birdie an awkward embrace. They exchanged shallow hellos and nice to see yous, then Birdie introduced Ron.

"This is my daughter," said Linda, caressing the girl's head. "April, say hello to Birdie."

The eyes that looked up at her were shamrock green. Just like Matt's. Birdie stared with astonishment into the little girl's eyes then up to Linda's blue ones, smug with satisfaction. Birdie was familiar with enough Whelan grandchildren to know she was looking at one. Birdie felt threatened and off balance. Angry even. Her left hand began to shake and Ron slid his into it and held tight. Now she knew why Reidy had made a point to say that Linda had no rights. Linda held Matt's heart in her hands long before Birdie, and Matt loved Linda in a way he never loved Birdie. Now Linda had a part of him that would outlive them all.

"You have a funny name," said April.

"Yes. I do."

"You're pretty."

"Not as pretty as you." Birdie poked the girl in the belly and she squealed with delight.

"We've got to go. It was nice to see you, Linda." She'd be damned if she'd allow Linda to see her discomfort.

"Birdie—" Linda halted as if contemplating, "would you like to have lunch sometime? To talk?"

"I don't think so."

"What the hell was that?" said Ron as Birdie led him away.

"Matt was married to her when he met me."

"You said you hadn't slept with Matt."

"I didn't. But wives know when their men fall for someone else. She wouldn't forgive him the emotional indiscretion."

"Can you blame her?"

"Of course not. But I won't sit through lunch and listen to her self-righteous gloating."

"What do you mean?"

"Forget it." She suspected April to be Matt's daughter and she just couldn't go there.

They found Frank Senior on the front porch leaning down and speaking to his eldest son, Frank Junior, who sat on a porch bench.

"Frank," she said, as they approached. "This is Ron Hughes."

"Ah, yes," said Frank Senior. He shook Ron's hand. "I'm glad you found me straight away. Let's get this nasty business over with. Join me in the study for a brandy and cigar."

"Thank you, sir." As Ron disappeared into the house he turned and mouthed at Birdie, *You okay?*

Birdie gave him a thumbs-up and sat down next to Father Frank. "How are you feeling?"

"I'm fine," said Frank. He put his arm around her shoulder. She leaned into her confidant, her compass, her priest, and together—the sinner and the pious—watched the festivities from the porch. Frank sighed. "Matt is in a good place, but I miss him terribly."

"Me, too, but that didn't stop me from having sex with Ron last night."

"I have to say, Bird, that of all my parishioners you sure are the fastest confessor." He kissed her head. "But I already knew. I'm not blind. I see the afterglow."

"I'm glowing?"

"No. Ron is. That man is too dang happy."

"I feel bad about my lusty desires at this terrible time."

"Oh, child, do you honestly believe Matt would begrudge you a small measure of happiness? He wouldn't want you to stop the forward momentum of your life to wallow in the misery of his loss. Me, I'm less happy with you. I'm obliged to give you a lecture about pre-marital sex. You remember how it goes. Don't forget to say your penance."

She couldn't help smile. That's what she loved about Frank. He understood her, yet accepted and loved her anyway.

"And remember that shame and guilt are powerful toxins," he added.

Emmett approached, followed closely by Arthur and Thom. "Hey, Bird. Hey, Frank, nice service," said Thom. He leaned down to kiss Birdie and dropped the Sig he had claimed from Wilshire Station into her lap.

Arthur gave her a kiss as well and then squeezed Emmett's shoulder. "Have a minute?" he said.

"Sure," said Emmett, wincing under Arthur's strong grip. "Let's go inside."

Frank and Birdie were alone once again.

"Have you met April?" said Birdie. "Linda's daughter?"

"I haven't. She quit coming to church after the annulment. Why do you ask?"

"She's here. She was at Mass, too."

Frank frowned. "Let us hope that Mother doesn't cross her path. I'm afraid her Christian charity doesn't extend to her ex-daughter-in-law."

Ron exited the house in a shroud of richly perfumed smoke. Frank gave Birdie a quick hug and excused himself, denying Birdie an opportunity to press him about Mary and Linda. Ron eyed the handgun.

"It's mine from the other night. My purse isn't big enough. Do you mind?" Ron did a quick press check, then slid it between his belt and waistband. He smoothed the jacket over the bulge.

He handed her a cigar. She examined the band. In the center was Matt's image. His birth and death date were on the left side. On the right, a police shield, and the words *rest in peace*.

"That is a premium cigar from the Dominican Republic. Probably made from tobacco stock imported after the U.S. embargo of Cuba. Very nice. This one—" he discretely lifted it from his breast pocket—"is a genuine Cuban. Not a counterfeit."

"What a clever idea," she said, handing it back. "Did you like his brandy?"

"Oh, yeah. So this is how the really rich live."

"He's satisfied with the specifics of Matt's death?"

"As much as a man who lost a son can be. You ready to go now?"

"More than anything."

TWENTY-THREE

Friday, January 13

THE DAY WOKE TO the promise of renewal and hopefulness. The rain had washed away the smog and cleaned the streets of grime. The trees were a bright, shiny green, the grass thick with new growth. Birdie's visitors had departed and the phone wasn't ringing. It should've been a good day. There were no distractions to prevent her from digesting the disastrous week and working on Matt's secret.

Except thoughts of Ron.

They said goodbye in the pale glow of dawn. She didn't have to repeat the previous day's *I'm not ready for a relationship* talk. Instead, he held her a long time, kissed her tenderly, and asked her to call him when she was ready. Then he was gone; headed back to a life in a city far away. It made her miserable.

Taking her morning coffee into the office she ripped a page off the wall. 245. She flicked on the television, the volume muted, and powered up the computer. An e-mail pinged for her attention. Narciso Alejo, head of the Paige Street taskforce, agreed to meet her tomorrow. She sent a confirming response and then sent a thank you to Ralph Soto for arranging the meet.

Images of Ron kept inserting themselves into her thoughts like a stubborn virus: his nervous smile, the strength of his touch—the way his hands stilled hers, his attentive nature. She didn't want to remember the soft, fleecy prick of his hair on her fingertips, the glistening tattoos, or the way he moaned when he came, or the jaw stubble scratching the delicate soft spots between her legs. And she certainly couldn't avoid the leftover smell of latex mingled with his musky smell on her skin. She didn't want to remember the feel of his muscles under her fingertips. She didn't want to remember that he was a fine specimen of a man.

She didn't want to like him.

Mostly, she didn't want him pushing memories of Matt out of her mind.

Ron's words replayed in her head, "I can't compete with a dead man."

Matt's mere existence had been a protective emotional bubble that stood between her and every man she'd ever been with. Matt was dead. And still in the way.

A familiar image on the television caught her attention. She punched the mute button on the remote.

"… was laid to rest yesterday at Holy Cross Cemetery in Culver City. Hundreds attended the graveside memorial of the decorated police officer who was on leave due to near-fatal gunshot injuries incurred as the result of a domestic violence call. Authorities say his death is not related. The exact cause of death is not known at

this time; however, a family spokesperson says that foul play has been ruled out.

"Officer Whelan and his partner were the first patrol officers who responded to a call in the still unsolved scandal that became known as The Paige Street Murder. Police officer Hugh Jackson lost his life in the shootout and off-duty police officer, Antonio Sanchez, was also killed in the commission of the crime. A second suspect who allegedly shot Officer Whelan escaped and is still at large.

"Officer Matthew Whelan is survived by his parents, six siblings, and numerous nieces and nephews. His father, Frank, is a retired police commander and five of his brothers serve in the LAPD. In other news ..."

Birdie switched off the television. Paige Street was located in Montecito Heights, east of downtown. The hilltop neighborhood was an island surrounded by criminal street gangs: "El Sereno" and "East Side 18 Street" were on the east. "The Avenues" were on the north. "Lincoln Heights" and "Clover" on the west.

Young families moved up the hill to buy houses with views, not knowing that they were surrounded by the highest concentration of gang violence anywhere in the city and had to drive through gang territory to get to their homes.

Montecito Heights bordered Ernest E. Debs Regional Park and a smaller local park, Rose Hill. Footpaths criss-crossed and connected the parks. The Rose Hill housing project was located on the eastern edge.

Birdie opened up Matt's battered *Thomas Guide* and studied Montecito Heights. She had driven that neighborhood too many times to count. The streets were narrow and curvy. There were many dead ends in the area; including Paige Street, which dissolved into parkland at the northern end. Matt had marked a pencil X where the crime occurred.

Matt would often say, "To solve a crime is to be a mathematician. The process to find the truth is methodical, precise, and in the end, provable."

She raised the screen covering the massive dry erase board and reviewed the convoluted math formula.

Matt = suicide → pain relief? self-punishment? why promise Birdie?

Key = unlocks secret thing/sin → why be sneaky?

8930 = Paige Street address → why now? something new?

Last entry = ???

To this she added:

Bad Package = stolen evidence $
Matt → Reidy → O'Brien → Matt?
O'Brien = key or alarm? → suicide → WHY?
O'Brien = Matt's boxes → why?
O'Brien is a key link! What is his connection to Matt?

Off to the side she wrote:

April = ?

She stared at the guys in the snow photo. Despite Patrick's reassurance it bothered her. Matt tacked it to a shelf beside friend and family photos. Why would he pin one up with a man he'd only met once, and a man he hadn't seen much since high school? Why give the image significance? She circled the photo and wrote

luck of the Irish? next to it. Jacob was the common dominator of the group. He knew Ron through his work as a medical examiner. He had kept in touch with Parker, the childhood friend. He was Matt's best friend.

Birdie's eye traveled back to the top line. Matt committed suicide. Of that she was certain. "But," she said aloud, "he would know that self-death would void his life insurance policy. He wanted to leave me money. His death would have to look accidental so the benefits would pay out." She picked up a pencil and tapped the board with the eraser. "So, if you wanted to die successfully how do you do it? Hire Jack Kevorkian." She cackled at her own little joke then suddenly stopped. "Jacob is a doctor. He'd know how. He could help his best friend with a physician-assisted termination." *Holy shit.* She put her hands on her head and spun around in shock. "Jacob could've Kevorkianed Matt. And they'd arrange it on a day when a friendly detective would be working."

She talked as she walked to the kitchen to refresh her cold coffee. "Okay, let's say Jacob helped his best friend. So what? Kevorkian famously said, 'Dying is not a crime.' And even Ron remarked, 'Aren't cops allowed to die?' What does that have to do with Paige Street? Were the two events even related? Matt was organized. If he planned his death in a way that would provide me with monetary security, why not also give me the answer to my greatest desire? Paige Street. He must've known something. In his journal entry regarding our abruptly halted make-out session from eleven years ago he wrote about a choice I'd have to make. He worked side-by-side with Arthur. Did he discover that Arthur really was the second suspect? The one the cops think escaped through the park?"

She emptied the cold coffee into the sink and poured a steaming cup, took a refreshing sip before returning to the office. "So ... what choice? Everything circles back to Paige Street. Matt decided to end his life and arranged it. Organized it good. Since he was going to die anyway why not give me ... something ... what something? What's the key, Birdie? Think."

She moved a magnetic hook next to her work on the dry erase board and attached the DO NOT DUPLICATE key next to the Latin phrase he'd snuck into her pocket. "What do keys work? Duh. Locks. Okay, which lock? What location? Is it to a door or a padlock?"

Birdie sighed and sat at her desk to get a wider perspective of the giant board. She rested her head on her hand and mindlessly looked at the map book open on her desk. On the preceding pages he had written notes in the tiny margins. An address of a good restaurant in Los Feliz. The location of a favorite bookstore in West Hollywood. A cheap parking garage. Some notes were directly on the page. Always in pencil. As evidenced by smudges he had erased and remarked. She smiled. Such a low-tech way of keeping track. She had a GPS navigator in her car. Matt was old school.

Little circles and squares and stars surrounded oblique locations and intersections—some with address notations, some not. Man, how could he see what he had written? She ran a lighted magnifying glass over sections. Some pages had many marks and some were completely blank. Others were flagged, or a rare Post-it note would make an appearance. One street, Santa Monica

Blvd., had a lot of pencil marks. Made sense, it was a long street. She noted that it was historic Route 66. A fact she knew, but had forgotten. She flipped pages forward and back, slowly moving the lens over the entire street as it cut across the city. Then she came across an odd notation written in the margin on the ring side of the page. The gutter, if you will. It stuck out because he had not marked up the gutter of any other page. It read: **EZ-Stor/66#B19**.

EZ-Stor was a franchise of storage units. Birdie looked up at the key on the board. How are units secured? *With padlocks.* She rolled her chair to the shelf containing a collection of phone books. In this way, she was old school, too. She flopped the heavy tome on her desk and flipped to storage. The first listing was located on Santa Monica Boulevard. It was simple: the EZ-Stor on Route 66, unit B19.

Could it be that Matt had left her something hidden in a storage unit? Something to do with Paige Street? Only one way to find out.

Birdie drove carefully: she avoided drawing attention—excluding the massively stupid road trip in the rain last Saturday to get to Lake Henshaw—she drove the speed limit, properly maintained her car, made sure the lights and indicators were functioning, made sure her cell phone was off. She drove defensively with two hands on the steering wheel safely placed at nine and three.

Forget a fix-it ticket for driving without a license. She couldn't even afford to get pulled over. A standard check would reveal she had a suspended license for DUI. Further checking would show she was on probation: if caught driving she'd go straight to jail for one year. Not a harsh sentence considering that she tried to kill Denis. Still, she was thankful the negotiation point allowed her to skip a rehab facility, months of psychobabble, and a twelve-step program in exchange for at-home detox and no driving for two long years. So she took her chances and drove like a saint.

The EZ-Stor was surrounded by a cinder block wall topped with razor wire and a screened rolling gate with a keycard console. Access to the entrance was only available via a right turn. She made a U turn at the next traffic signal hoping to catch a vehicle at the gate.

A ratty blue sedan made the turn in her wake and sped around her when she slowed to check out the facility again. A glimpse between the gate and the wall revealed drive-up units. After a succession of U turns she abandoned hope of following a car in. She parallel parked on a side street right in front of the same ratty blue sedan. A man sitting in the driver's seat looked up as she parked, then returned his attention to a foldout map. As she turned the corner a black car drove through the gate. She jogged down the street and jumped in sideways just as the gate closed.

Large numbers were painted on the end units designating rows. The units were numbered like a residential street: 1, 3, 5 … 13, 15, 17 … by the time she came to number 19 she had stopped breathing. She leaned her forehead against the metal door and took deep, cleansing breaths.

The large convex traffic mirror at the end of the row reflected no approaching vehicles. She was completely alone on row B. The roll-up door had locking eyes at waist height that were secured with a square padlock. Brass. Much larger than the average gym-sized lock. She palmed it. Heavier, too. She slipped the DO NOT DUPLICATE key into the hole. It slid in easy. *Easy now*. She turned the key to the right and the link clicked open. She opened the door.

It was empty. Completely and utterly empty.

Not a trick of the light.

No trinket lay hidden in a dark corner.

No Latin words on the walls or ceiling or door.

She ran her hand across the steel walls. They were bare. The floor wasn't even dusty.

She hated Matt right then. Matt knew her to prefer logic over emotion, fact over supposition. It's what made her a driven journalist. He'd know that she would follow his clue A to Z. So why deliver a cipher that would end on this hollow errand? What would have happened if she didn't see the EZ-Stor reference in his map book? How long would she have looked for a lock that fit the key? She didn't know what protocols Matt left in place.

Birdie slammed the door shut. The metal siding shook and clanked and popped back open. She slammed it again. Then kicked it repeatedly and punched it a few times. Arthur was right. Hitting was an excellent stress releaser.

"I'm sorry," said a voice behind her. Familiar. Yet out of place here and now.

She chilled down to the bone with the all-knowing sensation that her life was about to make another permanent change—in a way she didn't see coming nor could have predicted. Still, she didn't flinch. Her skin didn't itch. Her hands didn't quiver. She didn't even need to contemplate this change of course or her calm reaction. Birdie simply got into the zone. Imagined press credentials around her neck. Put on her game face.

She turned around to face a man she knew, but didn't know well. Ralph Soto.

TWENTY-FOUR

INSTEAD OF TALKING AT the storage facility, Birdie and Ralph Soto arranged to meet at Kipling's Koffee Kasbah. Birdie entered the café. The warm aroma of ground coffee and just-baked spice cookies filled the entrance. She felt a glimmer of resilience, a can-do attitude she hadn't felt in over eight months. It manifested in her assured stride across the rugs covering the floor. She spied Soto at a tiny table in the far corner. He was speaking with a server and waved her over.

"Double espresso with ginger, and an order of cinnamon cookies," said Birdie.

"Whole or half order?" said the server.

"Whole." Breakfast and lunch.

Something in Soto's life had changed since Tuesday night. He wore the stress in the sag of his shoulders, the purple half moons under his eyes. Birdie wondered how she wore her own stress and if Soto could see it.

"Thank you for meeting with me," said Soto. "I know the timing's bad, but it's important we have a discussion."

Birdie moved the chair to the side so that her back wouldn't face the door. Soto smiled with amusement. "Gerard taught you well. I read that you'll be seeing Alejo tomorrow."

"He was happy to meet me on a Saturday. Fewer admin around."

"No doubt."

"Where do we begin?"

"With the acknowledgment that this conversation is off the record and confidential."

"Okay. I agree. How'd you know I'd be at the EZ-Stor?"

Soto's eyes scanned the ceiling. "This is difficult to say. Please, don't take this the wrong way." His mouth formed a tight smile of embarrassment. "I'm having you followed."

Birdie squinted her eyes in displeasure. "The guy in the blue sedan?"

"Affirmative."

"Why?"

"I'm looking for evidence connected to an old investigation that was in Matt's possession before he died. And I'm not the only one looking. Your safety is part of the surveillance."

Birdie hugged her messenger bag. Visualized the gun inside. "Paige Street?"

"No."

"What then?"

Soto sighed. "It's complicated."

"Alright, let's try another question. Why do you think I'd have the evidence?"

"You're Matt's beneficiary."

"How did you know?"

"He told me."

"Why didn't you simply ask me?"

"I didn't want to involve a civilian."

"So you sent O'Brien to my house to look for this so-called evidence?"

"God, no." Soto seemed genuinely put out by the suggestion. "He was sent by the people we're investigating."

"Who exactly?"

Soto held up a finger. The server came and placed their items on the table. Soto had ordered black tea. Birdie noted the deliberateness with which he poured hot water from the tiny teapot, scooped tea into the spoon, snapped it shut, placed it in his cup, and gently swirled it to brew.

Birdie took a burning sip of espresso. It was like swallowing a shot of whiskey. She involuntarily quivered at the strength.

Soto lowered his voice. "Since Matt trusted you with the key to the storage unit, he obviously trusted you with the contents."

Birdie looked at him wide-eyed. "The storage unit was empty."

"Matt's death was sudden … took me by surprise. So I emptied it."

Birdie leaned away from Soto and stuffed a cookie into her mouth.

Soto split the difference and leaned in. "After Paige Street Matt agreed to work undercover. We had strong convictions that the second suspect was Arthur so I put him and Matt together at Rampart. We hoped Arthur would eventually learn to trust Matt and reveal his role in the incident. But Matt discovered something bigger.

More sinister. More terrible than Paige Street. Bigger than the CRASH stuff."

CRASH was the acronym for Community Resources Against Street Hoodlums comprised of cops that worked out of Rampart. It was a member that accused some CRASH officers of misconduct that dominoed into the Rampart Scandal and forced the department to operate under a consent decree.

"Are you saying Arthur is involved?"

"I still think he was the second PS suspect. But this is something else entirely."

"Go on," she said.

"For many long and painful years Matt and I whittled away, chip by chip, from the inside. The investigation often crawled, stalled, and then picked up, and so on. It was torturous. We had the storage unit tricked out with fireproofing and a battery operated alarm. That's where we stored the evidence. Don't be offended, but I had a feeling you'd find it, and I didn't want a civilian contaminating our evidence and chain of custody."

Birdie's hibernating journalist ambition stuck its nose out of a hole and began to sniff a story. A big one.

"You followed proper police procedure without involving the department? There has to be some kind of official directive higher than you. Unless … the person with the oversight was involved … oh, no … bad cops."

"At the highest level. Secreted into administrative divisions. We didn't know all the players and couldn't take the chance of discovery. So I devised this plan."

"You're retired."

"The case isn't."

"Let me get this straight. Matt left me a key to a storage unit containing evidence of bad cop behavior, but you already took it. So what do you need me for?"

"On the Friday before he died, I got a call from Matt about a box he was going to put in the unit. He seemed hurried. Unfocused. He couldn't give me details except to say that it contained the key piece of evidence that would take our case to the next level."

"Indictments?"

Soto nodded. "He died before dropping off that last box."

"Someone thought the boxes I received from Martin Reidy were the actual evidence?"

Soto sipped his tea. "I believe so."

"Matt would never put my life in jeopardy by getting me involved with dirty deeds."

But Matt had done exactly that when he slipped a mysterious message into her back pocket. And why Birdie felt inclined to defend him after his betrayal was beyond logic. Except … a small part of her clung to the belief that Matt had a purpose she wasn't yet aware of.

"Please look at it from my perspective," whispered Soto harshly. "There's a box of evidence missing. I have no clue where it is." He looked at her with weepy eyes and held up a key. "It's the same as yours."

She held the key next to the one Matt sneaked into her back pocket. It was an exact duplicate. "So?"

"It's a demonstration that we were partners. Since you've been to the EZ-Stor," said Soto, "you know what the padlock looks like. Have you seen another?"

"No. Why?"

"Matt had two locks custom made. They're tamper resistant with an exploding dye that doesn't wash off if the lock is improperly opened. I don't know where the other one is."

"Two different locks keyed exactly the same?"

"Fewer keys to keep track of."

"That's logical. But why would Matt leave me a key with no instructions for its use?"

"I thought he must have. Something went amiss after he was shot last year." The words came out slow. Almost like an afterthought.

"It was a domestic," she offered. "You know how dangerous they are. Emotions all fired up. Altered states generating hatred and despair and absolute strength. And he was working alone that day." She felt the enormity of the words even before she spoke. "Arthur was out sick."

The shooting was still under investigation. No suspect has been named. Just like the Paige Street murder. And Arthur was involved by his noninvolvement. But Soto had already stated he wasn't involved in this new thing. The thing involving bad cops.

"The call for service was bogus," said Soto. "A chance to kill a cop. Any cop. But Matt felt differently. While he was still in the hospital he told me he felt it was an ambush. That's why he wrote his will. I beg you to help me as Matt's trusted friend. Matt may have died protecting that last box. We can't let his death be in vain."

"Are you suggesting his death was anything other than an accident?"

"All I know is that Matt was out of contact the week before he died."

That's right, thought Birdie. She ate a bite of her cookie and washed it down with espresso, deep in thought. She'd also tried to reach him that last week. He hadn't returned her calls and he'd missed appointments.

"He finally called me on Friday, but he died before giving me the last box."

"It might be at Henshaw House," Birdie said, all the while hating the thought of having to go back to the place Matt spent his last moments on earth.

"It wasn't in either residence. I've looked."

Birdie veiled her anger. "I'm Matt's heir. No one, not even his family, has the right to search his homes or his possessions. Was it breaking and entering or trespassing?"

Soto nodded his head in contrition. "No property was damaged. Nothing was taken."

"It won't happen again."

"Of course," he said. "I was desperate. I didn't want you or his family involved."

"But now you have no choice. You told me the box contained evidence that would break open the case. You've told me of the pains taken to conceal and secure the evidence. Yet you conducted an illegal search. If you'd found it, you wouldn't be able to use it."

Soto rubbed his face. "It had been such a long fight that I figured I'd discover a way around that fact. I'm truly sorry for invading his privacy. And yours."

"I'm not sure there's anything left to say. If I find the box I'll let you know." Birdie rose, but had one last thing to say before she departed. "Cease the surveillance."

Soto took out his phone. "Consider it done."

TWENTY-FIVE

BIRDIE STUCK HER NOSE in the lovely arrangement of pink sweet peas and inhaled the candy-like scent. She thanked the floral delivery guy and shut the door. She sat on the lower step and pulled out the card. *Thank you for everything. I'm ready when you are.* ♥ *Ron.* How did he know sweet peas were her favorite? And what did the heart mean? She carried the flowers upstairs and positioned them on the kitchen bar so she couldn't dwell on them or the man who sent them.

She sat back at her desk, twirled a pencil, and looked up at the white board. Priority one: zero in on how to approach Matt's quest—Paige Street for sure; the money an obvious indicator. Priority two: find out why he committed suicide. Three: determine if Soto and Matt's investigation was connected. Soto, the notorious hard-liner, was so hungry to get his hands on that last box of evidence that he actually broke the law.

"Why?" said Birdie aloud. "It contained the key piece of evidence." She flicked the pencil in the air like a baton. Caught it.

"The one that would break open the case." Twirled the pencil between her fingers. "The one that would bring indictments." She bounced the pencil on its eraser. "Indictments of what?" She broke the pencil in half.

Bad cops ... highest level ... secreted into administrative divisions.

Birdie continued the linear thinking in her head. So what if the conversation was off the record and confidential? If you need advice and have to break your word—on which you've built your reputation—who do you call? Simple. Deputy District Attorney Daniel Eubanks, a Major Crimes prosecutor.

Birdie initially met Daniel when she interviewed him for a feature story for the cop magazine *Blue Beat*. Then their paths often crossed in the hallways and elevators of the Criminal Courts Building. Even though he later came to know her intimately, he never stopped calling her by her professional name. For her part, she dropped all formality once they started having sex.

She and Danny had dated hard for six weeks. Spent all their non-work hours together. Screwed like crazy. Gerard didn't like that she dated a black man. Her father's disapproval was part of the appeal during her rule-breaking, alcoholic days. Danny's tough good looks didn't hurt either. He had a rugged, incorruptible, oh-so-sexy, don't-get-in-my-way look.

Birdie reached him on his cell.

"Elizabeth Keane," he said. "What a nice surprise."

"Hi, Danny. How are things up on the seventeenth floor?"

"The air is good. How are you?"

"The best I can be. You heard about Matt?"

"Couldn't avoid it. How are you and Jorge managing?"

"Come on Danny, you know he prefers George. Doesn't matter anyway. We broke up."

"And now? Another cop or would-be cop?"

Would-be cop directly referenced Denis. He was aware that Denis had once applied with the LAPD but failed the psychological and didn't get hired. Birdie detected a bit of jealousy in the slam because he never liked Denis.

"I'm not dating. You?"

"You know how it is. The job," said Danny.

"Same old excuse."

"I made time for you."

"And we had a lot of fun, but it was doomed from the beginning."

"Right. Prosecutors and journalists don't mingle well. Too much opportunity for conflict of interest. So, talk to me. Is this call personal or professional?"

After establishing that neither was dating she could play it personal, but Danny kept everything close to the chest. That trait made him a good poker player. And extremely trustworthy. But he wouldn't respond well if she jumped right in and asked him for advice about indictments of bad cops and Soto and Matt's long-time investigation.

"I'm not entirely sure," said Birdie, "Ever since Matt died a lot of weird stuff has been going on. Shit. Where do I begin? For starters, Matt made me his heir and my house was broken into and this guy, this thief, rummaged through his things and then shot himself. And then—"

"Hold on, Elizabeth. Not on the phone. Come to the office?"

"No way I'm driving into downtown on a Friday. Too much traffic."

Her doorbell buzzed. "Hold on, Danny, someone's at my door." She pressed the intercom button. "Yes?"

"Hi, Birdie," said a voice squeezed by electricity. "It's Emmett Whelan. Do you have a few minutes?"

"Sure, Emmett, I'm on the phone right now. I'll buzz you in. Help yourself to coffee in the kitchen." She pressed the electronic lock. Then back to Danny, "Sorry 'bout that."

"Did I hear correctly?" said Danny. "Emmett Whelan is there? At your house? Are you home alone?" Birdie detected a sliver of anxiety in his voice.

"Yeah."

Danny was silent for a few beats before saying, "What are you doing tomorrow?"

Just then Emmett walked past the opening to her office, drummed his fingers against the wall as he continued toward the kitchen.

"I've an appointment at the PAB to see Narciso Alejo."

"The Paige Street taskforce lead?"

"Yeah. That's part of why I'm calling. Seems Matt wanted me to get back into it."

Then Birdie remembered the sweet pea arrangement on the bar in her kitchen. Emmett couldn't avoid seeing them. Would he look at the card? Did she need to ask that question?

"Danny, I better go. I'll call back."

As she hung up the phone she thought she heard him say, "Tomorrow."

Birdie jogged toward the kitchen. As she rounded the corner she could smell the leftover booze mixed with stale cigar smoke emanating from Emmett's skin. It was a sickening combination that made her stomach churn. He waved the card.

"Heart Ron. What does that mean?"

She snapped the card from his hand. "I don't know, Emmett."

"Seems you're already over my brother." He said it with a slight slur. Still drunk.

"I loved Matt. I love him still. Nothing's changed. What brings you here, Emmett?"

"The offer of a cocktail would be hospitable."

"I'm an alcoholic. I don't have liquor in my house," she lied, opening the fridge. "I have bottled tea or Coke. Or coffee."

"I'll take the soda."

Birdie opened the top, surprised the leftover rum mixer still had fizz. She gathered some ice into a glass and poured it slowly, then motioned him to the living room.

Emmett sat up straight and purposefully proud, just like his father. Birdie sank into a chair, hugged her knees and wondered why he came. If she wanted to know what it was, she'd have to wait or bait and throw line.

She was impatient as usual.

"I assume you know Matt left you out of his will. What are your thoughts about that?"

Emmett shrugged his shoulders. "I'm not surprised. It's just that ... I'm in a financial bind and Matt agreed to loan me some money. He didn't get the chance before he died."

"Liar. Matt was a prolific writer and I have his journals. I've been spending a lot of time with them." Let him come to his own conclusion about what that meant.

"You know?" he said.

"I know his side of the story," she bluffed. "I'd like to hear yours."

He drained the Coke and poured more into the glass. He drained that one too and put the glass down. He leaned forward as if talking to a friend. It was an awkward contrivance.

"Linda and Eileen remained friends after the annulment," he said. "She's a regular at our house. One night years ago she had too much to drink and Eileen insisted I drive her home ... I didn't intend ... she started it." His lips split into a thin smile as though reliving the memory. "She's a beautiful woman ..."

This was about screwing Matt's ex-wife. Emmett's ex-crush.

"Matt found out?"

"Yeah," came out with burped Coke bubbles.

"Why would he care?"

"Seems they were testing reconciliation at that time. Linda was thrilled when she became pregnant. She always wanted Matt's baby and finally got her wish. Matt never wanted children. That was one of many problems in their marriage." He sneered at Birdie. "Had I known she was re-involved with my brother, I wouldn't have had sex with her."

Birdie held her hands so tight together she felt the blood pooling in her wrists.

Emmett continued. "Matt was convinced the baby wasn't his. He demanded a DNA test. After a long go around with the lawyers, he got his test. It proved he wasn't the father."

Birdie exhaled and let go of her hands, allowed the feeling to return to her fingertips.

"The test suggested a high probability that a male relative fathered the child. It didn't take him long to figure it out."

"Linda seduced you to get pregnant and pass the baby off as Matt's?"

He nodded. "I believed Linda when she said it wasn't mine. She convinced Matt that it was my idea to pass off the baby as his in order to get a settlement."

"Why? Linda is a trust fund baby."

"It wasn't really about money. It was about love and entrapment. She wanted Matt back and was convinced that his sense of obligation would bring them together. When that didn't work, she blamed me for forcing her into a lie. All I'm guilty of is an adulterous one-night-stand. As for the rest, it was all her."

Birdie wondered if Emmett could see the relief on her face. She reflected on April's green eyes. Looked into Emmett's. Both brothers inherited their mother's intense color. If April were Matt's child, he would have provided for her, regardless of his relationship with the mother. And neither April nor Linda were left a penny. Emmett returned Birdie's gaze with welling eyes.

"I saw Linda sitting nearby at the funeral Mass. How does that make you feel?"

"Afraid. Eileen doesn't know. When Linda is drunk her tongue gets loose. I feel a constant threat."

"Who does know?"

"Junior of course. Arthur."

"Arthur?"

"He was Matt's partner for all those years. Matt must've told him."

Birdie remembered the way Arthur squeezed Emmett's shoulder at the wake. "Is Arthur blackmailing you?"

"Of course not." He chewed on the words just long enough for Birdie to detect the lie. About Arthur or blackmail?

"How much money do you need?"

"One-and-a-half large."

"Geeze. Why so much?"

"Debts. I'll pay it back with interest."

"How do you suppose you'll be able to pay off a loan of this size, even if I give you a good interest rate? You'd be chasing your tail."

His face glistened with evaporating booze. "I'm stuck."

Birdie mulled the options and came to a quick conclusion. "I'll tell you what. I'll give you the money with conditions. Secrets continually weigh you down with fear. Confront the issue and it will no longer have any power over you. With Linda being a presence in Eileen's life she will find out one day. The truth should come from you, not Linda or a bl—" she almost said blackmailer, "—anybody else. Respect Eileen. Tell her and your money worries will go away. Guaranteed. You have one week to confess."

"You're kidding, right?" Emmett's scorn was evident.

"I'm serious. The money as a gift with strings attached, or nothing. You decide. Matt made no arrangement with you. I know this for a fact." Her eyes bored into his.

Emmett looked at her sideways, his eyes fixed at the periphery of her face.

"Do you accept my terms?"

Emmett sucked his upper lip. "I accept."

Later, she watched from the living room window as Emmett left with a check safely tucked into his pocket. As he turned to get into his car, she was struck by the look on his face—absolute hatred. Aimed at himself for having to let go of his pride and ask for a handout? Or directed at Birdie for reasons unknown? It was then she realized he hadn't even said thank you.

Birdie returned to her office and erased the April notation. What a relief.

The board changed with Soto's revelations. There was a second padlock that secured evidence of bad cop behavior. O'Brien was hired by bad cops. Two suicides: Matt's might have been assisted, O'Brien's was not. One murder: Reidy. Soto brought up murder in reference to Matt. Birdie discounted it then and now. She had insider knowledge. Still ... she dialed Ron's number.

"Hello, Birdie."

"I met with an associate of Matt's," she said. "He suggested murder."

Ron took a deep breath. "Right to business then? Elizabeth?"

"For now."

"Alright. I can't prove murder. There's no evidence. Hoy told me of your suicide theory at the cemetery. I can't prove that either."

"What about assisted termination? Jacob would know how to do it."

"I've confirmed his whereabouts Friday afternoon through eleven o'clock Sunday when he left his home in San Diego to drive to Lake Henshaw. He didn't have the opportunity."

"How did you know to do that?"

"Wow. You have no faith in my investigative skills. Remember what I said, I prove my conclusion and disprove all other explanations. Besides, I'm already getting to know how you think. How you process. You'd come at me with that new-and-improved theory sooner rather than later and you'd give me hell if I didn't check it out."

"I'm that transparent?"

"Either that or I'm extremely good."

Birdie heard his grin.

"So he did it on his own."

"I'm an hour away from filing my final report. It's going to state that Matthew Whelan died of an accidental overdose. The coroner will have the final say. As much as I like you I cannot change my conclusion based on your emotions."

"I guess there's nothing more to say then. So, what does the heart mean on the card?"

Ron raised the pitch of his voice to sound female. "Thanks, Ron, for the lovely sweet peas. They're gorgeous." He lowered his voice back to normal. "Insert adjective of choice here." He raised his voice again. "They're my favorite. How did you know?" He lowered. "Father Frank told me. I'm glad you like them."

By now, Birdie was laughing.

"Oh, good, we're back to Birdie now. I like her better."

"Really, Ron, thanks. They're awesome. How's that adjective? Now answer my question."

"The heart means affectionately."

"Why not just write the word?"

"Because the heart would compel you to call me."

She appreciated his cleverness.

TWENTY-SIX

Saturday, January 14

BIRDIE KINKED HER NECK to look up at Narciso Alejo: freaky tall, skinny, and preacher-like in all black attire with a buttoned jacket that ended at a mandarin collar under his goateed chin. His hair was a bit long and tucked fashionably behind his ears. He wore overpriced, hip designer eyeglass frames. There was nothing stylish about the permanent grim expression chiseled into his face. He cut an imposing figure.

Alejo's hand completely enveloped hers when they greeted and shook. "Do you remember when we first met?" he said.

"I do. My dad had picked me up from school and had business downtown before going home. I begged him to let me go inside with him instead of waiting in the car. I marched into your office and demanded you tell me everything to do with Paige Street."

"You were what? Seventeen?"

"Sixteen."

"I didn't take a girl in Catholic plaid and braids seriously."

"Everyone underestimated me."

"A cute girl that age should be hanging out at the mall with girlfriends and flirting with boys. How did you come by that drive so young?"

"I was a bad girl. Constantly on house arrest or restriction. Being an only child with no sibling diversions I had a lot of time to spend on the computer so I wrote."

"How'd you outgrow the bad girl behavior?"

"I didn't. I became an alcoholic."

"No shit? I just had my fourth birthday."

"Congratulations. I'm 246 days in."

"You in the program?"

"I'm on my own."

"Brave."

The compliment marked the end of further conversation and Alejo escorted her to a windowless meeting room in silence.

The Paige Street murder books had been brought over from cold case and were stacked up, awaiting her attention. Her inspection. She had begged and cajoled for years and years for this opportunity granted no one outside law enforcement. She gazed lovingly at the notebooks on the business-gray table.

Alejo gave her complete autonomy to look through the files with a few rules: no copies, no recordings, no notes, a short time limit, and a brief Q&A. All-in-all very generous. To make sure Birdie played by the rules he confiscated her electronics, the yellow pad, a pen, and broke the tips of her No. 2 pencils.

Birdie opened the first notebook. The separating dividers were no longer crisp and efficient. She could almost see the fingerprints that had worn the edges fuzzy, smelt the stress of frustration as investigators studied page after page after page, looking for an answer, convinced it lay hidden inside.

She started with the summaries.

Hugh Jackson had a college education and thought he was too cool for a black-and-white. He kept applying for advancement, but continually performed poorly on the tests. He broke rules, was overly boastful, and had a raunchy lack of respect for women and members of his own race. All of it earned him poor evals from his supervisors.

Matt was the opposite. After graduating from the academy, he hit the streets under the watchfulness of Commander Ralph Soto, who took a personal interest in yet another Whelan. During friendly competitions, Matt out-ran, out-shot, and out-tested nearly all his peers, earning him a reputation as an ass-kissing showoff.

Matt and Hugh rolled together for five years before their lives changed forever on a triple-digit, smoggy Tuesday when they responded to a hot shot.

The communication tape transcription:

OFFICER: *4Adam-19 clear from code 7.*

DISPATCH: Three shrill beeps, then: *all units, 211 in progress, RD 402, code 3, 8-9-3-zero Paige Street.*

OFFICER: *4Adam-19 in route, 8-9-3-zero Paige Street, ETA 5 minutes, going code 2.*

RTO: *Roger that.*

OFFICER: *4Adam-19, code 6 hot shot.*

OFFICER: *4Adam-19, two heavily armed masked men, requesting backup.*

RTO: *Backup on the way.*

Birdie grew up surrounded by cops and their stories. She immediately detected a wrong. Matt and Hugh rolled code 2, arriving in silence and taking the suspects by surprise. No cop passes an opportunity to roll code 3 with lights flashing and sirens blaring; especially to a hot shot. Had they rolled code 3 the suspects would have been alerted and the whole scenario could have ended differently. As it happened, it was over before backup arrived.

They observed the homeowner being severely beaten by two masked men—an exigent circumstance which demanded immediate action to prevent an irreversible act from happening. Matt and Jackson stormed the house. Jackson never had a chance to fire his weapon: he received a double-barrel shotgun blast to the chest. Matt took a grazing hit to the head, but was able to return fire and kill the man who shot Jackson.

One uniformed cop dead. One injured. One masked, off-duty cop dead. One masked man escaped. The homeowner died the following day from his injuries.

That's the story Matt told the FID (Force Investigation Division), PSB (Professional Standard Bureau), the Chief of Police, the psychologist from Behavioral Sciences, and Lt. Narciso Alejo, who headed the taskforce. It never wavered.

Alejo thought the officers should have retreated and reassessed. Waited for backup and Air Support Division. At the very least, one of them should have covered the back door. In the end, a suspect used it to elude capture and make off with over a million dollars cash.

Included in the case file was a recommendation by Alejo that Matt be declared unfit for duty. OSS rejected the request:... under the intense circumstances, any police officer could make the same mistake. Instead, Matt was awarded a Medal of Valor.

Imagine: a cop killed another cop and got a Medal of Valor. Yeah, the dead guy was off-duty out of Van Nuys. Yeah, he was performing armed robbery, but still, there had to be some pissed-off brothers. And she wondered if this was why the bad package rumors originated.

8930 Paige Street was a home owned by Martine and Monica Alvarado. Monica identified Officer Antonio Sanchez and Officer Arthur Keane as the cops who came to the home two days earlier looking for drugs. They didn't find drugs, but they discovered three-point-four million dollars in the house. Sanchez and Arthur couldn't seize the cash because it wasn't covered by the warrant's search parameters.

On the day of the robbery, two million in cash was checked into evidence from the Alvarado home, which left a deficit of one-point-four million. The day after Martine died of his injuries Monica held a news conference and accused the Los Angeles Police Department of murder and theft. She hired a lawyer and filed a wrongful death lawsuit. The press ate it up. And while Monica was talking to the press, so was the Chief of Police. He asked for the community's help in finding the second suspect and challenged the citizens of L.A. not to judge the whole police force because of the actions of one rogue cop. The FBI was invited to run a concurrent investigation. A reward was offered.

Arthur swore he wasn't with Sanchez that day. At the time of the home invasion, he was at the family's boutique doctor. Dr. Ryan supported Arthur's alibi, no physical evidence placed him at the scene, not even a drop of spittle or sweat. Still, Alejo wasn't discouraged by two circumstantial tidbits. One, Arthur was Sanchez's partner. Two, Monica identified him despite not being able to see his likeness through the long sleeves, gloves, and mask. She couldn't even properly identify his eye color. But she had been there at the start; a compelling fact that always seemed to slip behind the others. She had been beat up, too. She faked unconsciousness and while the two men assaulted her husband she snuck out and ran to a neighbor's house and called 9-1-1. Still, not a credible witness, and she prejudiced the process with a lawyer and a news conference just two days later.

The taskforce didn't hide the fact that Arthur was their number-one suspect. Yet Birdie was shocked that so many resources were spent investigating all the members of her family in law enforcement—including her mother, a non-sworn employee—as possible co-conspirators, along with Dr. Ryan. Their alibi sheets were thick with confirmations and triple checks. The Keane family presented a united front and made it clear that when you mess with one Keane, you mess with them all.

And the story got stranger. Nine weeks after the Paige Street murder, Matt resumed work and transferred to Rampart Division where Arthur had transferred in from Van Nuys. Their partnership was assigned. After all these years she finally knew why.

Birdie knew the story better than any reporter in the city. Still, she liked visuals. The murder books filled the requirement. She flipped through the photographs, autopsy photos, sketches, and floor plans. She speed-read as much as she could before her allotted time expired. Without the benefit of notes, Birdie had laid out the notebooks, pages carefully curled to secure her place so she wouldn't forget what she wanted to ask.

Alejo returned and sat at the far end of the table. She tried to ignore him as she furiously flipped for the same thing many investigators before her had sought: the identity of the second suspect. Without him, this case couldn't be closed. She found tidbits that would add flavor to the true crime novel in the works. She learned new investigative tactics, scanned the interagency memos full of law enforcement who-ha.

Birdie lingered over press clippings. At the top of one of hers someone had written "check this out" in red felt tip. It was a human interest story about Hugh Jackson's wife. On the morning her husband was shot to death she had taken a home pregnancy test and got a positive result. In one of Matt's many sworn statements he said that Jackson was upset by his impending fatherhood and that may have contributed to the recklessness of their actions—Matt never singularly blamed Jackson and he took his share of the blame for that awful day.

Birdie felt Alejo's leer. Seriousness personified. Heard him clasp and unclasp the watch on his wrist. His gum chewing equivalent? Or the not-so-subtle signal that her time was nearly up? She dared a peek in his direction through the hair that dangled over her face. He returned the gaze with a grin that said, *I see you*. At least Alejo was capable of smiling. And that he had big white teeth. Just like the wolf.

Alejo said, "Why Paige Street now?"

She flipped her hair back and secured it into a loose bun at the base of her neck with one of her stunted pencils.

"You know that crime solving moves slowly," she said. "In this business, the science and the courts have to catch up with the detection so I have several investigations going simultaneously and work on whichever one is currently hot."

"It's true what Soto said. You have something new. How can you be neutral with family involved?"

"I stick to the facts."

"We'll see, won't we?" said Alejo, crossing his arms. "I understand that Matt Whelan was a close friend of yours. He was too smart for patrol. By all accounts he should've been a detective, but he chose to stay on the streets. I distrust cops that prefer to stay on the street."

"You made that opinion quite clear in one of your many reports. But it's where he did the most good," she said. "He was fluent in Spanish, Korean, and Mandarin. He was a street cop, from a family of street cops. The hard work would be done before the detectives arrived on-scene. His work could make or break a case, and he was in the line of fire every day, where all the action was. The one, unwavering constant in his life was his love for the job. It was a calling, almost like a ministry. He loved the people. He never lost faith. So many street cops become jaded. Turn into hateful men. Or suited slags. Not Matt."

"That was almost the exact same way he put it. I believed his assertions until I found out he was undercover."

"Soto told me. Matt was teamed with Arthur so he could earn Arthur's trust and get a confession or something. I didn't know Matt was undercover until Soto told me. But I knew Matt well enough to say with the utmost confidence that it was secondary to his patrol job."

Alejo shrugged in dismissal then twirled his watch. "What blanks can I fill in?"

"Looking at the autopsy photos of Sanchez, I noticed a tattoo near his groin. A double B. Do you know what that signifies?"

"It represents membership in the Blue Bandits."

Birdie spat out an absurd laugh and her gum popped out of her mouth. She picked it up off the table, stuck it back in her mouth and wiped the spittle with the side of her hand. "Once upon a time, long ago when the department was corrupt, a small group of cops formed a secret society and called themselves the Blue Bandits. In the beginning, the Bandits acted like Robin Hood—they stole from bad guys and gave to good guys. Churches and men's shelters were the usual benefactors. As time went on, the society became a notorious gang that dealt in prostitution, kickbacks, extortion, and even murder for hire. Eventually, the members were flushed out, prosecuted, or fired. I've investigated the Bandits as far back as the 1920s. It was a small band of men. Old and nearly forgotten history. Rumor and exaggeration grew into urban legend."

Alejo scowled. Clearly not amused.

"Look," she said in her defense, "the story of the Blue Bandits is a fairytale told to criminals. The moral is 'don't mess with the LAPD. We've been there once. We can do it again.'"

Alejo didn't move. Give him a hood and a sickle and he'd be the reaper.

She erased an imaginary chalkboard. "Okay, Alejo, let's say the Blue Bandits have reemerged and Sanchez was a member.

And Arthur—because of his association with Sanchez—was suspected of Paige Street. Does it follow that he was a member of the BBs as well?"

"You tell me."

"Arthur is a MMA celebrity. He fights and trains. Quite the obsessive. He's not shy or modest. I've seen him naked. He shaves head to toe before a bout. He has no tats on his body. No Double B is hiding underneath the pubes because he shaves them too. His moniker is The Ghost. He's a fair-skinned white boy with no tats. He's pure like Casper."

"If you think Arthur is innocent and pure, then you're deluding yourself. He just hasn't been caught yet."

"Let's forget that for now. Soto told me he put Matt undercover with Arthur to get information about Paige Street. He said Matt found something bigger. Bad cops secreted into every administrative division. The Blue Bandits?"

Alejo nodded. "'Fraid so."

"Come on, Alejo. Don't screw with me. This is huge, if true. But look. Couldn't the Double B stand for something else? I mean, this Sanchez guy had a huge penis." She tapped her finger on the autopsy photo. "Maybe the BB stood for Black Beauty."

That almost brought a smile to Alejo's face. "Sanchez was Hispanic."

"Barrio Brother? Work with me, here."

"Work with me. This is my day off and I'm doing a courtesy. Don't debate me."

Birdie sighed. "Why Rampart?"

"The mastermind of the Bandits worked out of Rampart."

"Why not bust him?"

"There's a difference between knowing a thing and proving a thing. They're buried deep. Well organized. Disciplined. They're like evaporating vapors—impossible to catch. Much like that ghost of yours."

"Matt kills a member of the Blue Bandits whose boss worked Rampart, then transfers to the same division to do Soto's spy work? Did he know how much danger he was in? I mean, why not just paint a target on his forehead? Did Matt take the assignment willingly?"

Alejo looked at his watch. "He knew what he was getting into."

Birdie wasn't getting hard facts so her brain juggled the supposition. The Bandits must have discovered Matt's evidence gathering, but probably didn't know what he had or where he had it. When Reidy delivered Matt's boxes to Birdie, they dispatched O'Brien, not knowing that the evidence was already safe with Soto. Or maybe they knew Soto had the evidence stashed, but found out about the last box and wanted it as desperately as Soto did.

"Whelan and Keane were untouchable at Rampart," said Alejo. "They only worked days, no nights, no holidays after their first year together, they got a new car, always had the best rovers. The brotherhood didn't hassle the new guys. Someone high on the food chain had a hands-off policy for those two."

"That doesn't make any sense," she said. "The BBs knew Matt was Sanchez's shooter, and yet they had a hands-off so he could go about and collect evidence? He was a rat and rats get caught. Why are you telling me?"

"You asked. Soto asked. My bosses said okay. This is eyes only. You're being read in. You can't repeat or write anything." Alejo looked at his watch.

Then it became clear. The department took this opportunity to use Birdie. As an investigative journalist she could get away with stuff they couldn't. She would pursue it even if she couldn't write about it. She'd help them with their cause. That's why Soto had her followed. Showed up at the EZ-Stor. Her right hand began to shake. She sat on it. And though she was excited about getting information that the public and her journalist compeers didn't have access to, she still didn't have what she wanted.

"I looked at the ballistics summary," she said, getting back to the Paige Street murder books. "Jackson was hit with a single trigger, 10-gauge double-barrel shotgun loaded with double-ought shells, both barrels fired almost simultaneously. It takes a lot of skill to fire in quick succession like that. And it's an awful lot of firepower for a robbery. Double ought—nine pellets per shell, times two, is like eighteen bullets hitting Jackson at a range of fifteen feet. He didn't have a chance. But I'm confused. There seems to be a discrepancy about the other rounds. The report says that Matt's grazing hit to the skull was a 40-caliber round and that Jackson was also hit in the face with number 8 lead shot. Fired out of what and at what range? Sanchez had to have both hands on the shotgun. So there were three guns, but only two suspects?"

"The second suspect was a two-fisted shooter. According to Whelan's statement, he fired from the kitchen."

"Let me get this straight," she said, glancing down at the floor plan of the Alvarado home. "The second suspect had a handgun in one hand and some kind of gun that shot shells in the other.

He was thirty feet away, aiming at two different targets, six feet apart and hit both in the head? What kind of shell and casing?"

"None were recovered," said Alejo.

"The second guy shoots, collects his shell, collects his casing, and makes off with his gear and thirty-one pounds of cash—"

"Allegedly," interjected Alejo. "There was no proof that more than the two million was in the household. A portion could have been removed between the time Sanchez and Keane searched the home and the time Sanchez came back. The amount could never be verified."

"—and disappeared into thin air," she countered. "You're looking for Superman."

"That's why we haven't found him. He's still out there somewhere. But I promise you, I will close this case if it's the last thing I ever do."

"What was Matt's assessment about Arthur's involvement?"

"He never said for certain."

In a journal entry, Matt mentioned a choice Birdie would have to make. *My cousin or him?* Did he know and yet didn't dare write his knowledge?

"I know my cousin," she said. "He lives small."

"Maybe he used the alleged money to buy his alibi. If the second suspect were ever caught, he'd likely be charged with felony murder for the homeowner, felony murder for Jackson under aiding and abetting, felony murder for Sanchez under the provocative murder act, and felony robbery. There could also be attempted murder of a peace officer. Tack on all the special circumstances and special allegations, the suspect, if convicted, would likely get LWOP. The DA would have a great shot at the death penalty. Is freedom worth a mil?"

Life without the possibility of parole or death? Definitely worth a million dollars cash. And who better to hide it than a boutique doctor like Dr. Ryan? But there were no witnesses, no weapons, no evidence. Even the FBI never identified a suspect in the case. "Was the money checked into evidence stolen?" she said.

"No." He flipped another glance at his watch. "It was returned to Monica Alvarado."

She didn't misunderstand what Arthur said about Matt stealing evidence money. "Are you certain?"

Alejo smirked. *Oh, yeah.*

She felt pressure behind her eye. The start of a headache. Then a thought struck her. "Soto said that the domestic shooting that nearly killed Matt wasn't actually random. Is it possible that the shooter was the missing second suspect?"

Alejo shrugged. "Maybe it was our vanished superhero that sniped Whelan. In any case, we have no viable suspect. Time's up. That's all the consideration you get."

"Oh, come on. What a shitty way to end. Who benefits most from Matt's death?"

"From what I hear, you do."

Birdie's thoughts were troubled. Something hovered around her, nameless, formless, on the outskirts. She couldn't reach it. The radar pinged, but didn't zero in on a target.

The inspection of the Paige Street murder books was nearly anticlimactic. Yeah, the Blue Bandits element was new. Frightful even. But that didn't bother her. She wasn't even concerned about being used by Soto and Alejo. She foresaw the backend benefit. After all, she didn't sign a nondisclosure. Didn't even shake on it.

Her head hung downward, eyes watching the Wolverines scrunch her pale shadow on the sidewalk. Despite the steel toes these were her most comfortable boots. They were required equipment for a two-week stint where she lived on a deep-water oil platform while she researched a *Time* feature on offshore drilling. The posture was not only bad for the spine it meant she wasn't paying attention. She heard her father's admonishment in her ear, "Bird, walk with your head upright. Shoulders back. Be alert to your environment." At that moment an abrupt greeting shook her from her disconnectedness. "Yo, Tweety Bird."

Anyone who ever had the nerve to call Birdie "Tweety Bird" only said it once. But there was one person she allowed to get away with it. Pearl Eubanks. Adopted brother to DDA Daniel Eubanks. Private Investigator. Daniel's go-to man. Birdie's friend and unofficial sponsor. He spread his fingers in a subverted wave holding the line of forward momentum. "Keep walking," he said. "Don't look at me." They were nearly shoulder to shoulder when he said, "Danny sends his regards. Says your house might be hot. I'll come at midnight."

It took a few steps before the gravity of the message processed, yet she didn't look back even as her stride compulsively quickened. At least she felt grateful to be on 1st Street. If she'd been on the other side of the PAB, on 2nd Street, there'd be plenty of activity due to the loft dwellers that turned the PAB lawn into a dog park and where she'd feel exposed.

Pearl's message served one good purpose. It shed light on the *it* that bothered her.

Why would the department so diligently pursue a cop as the second suspect in Paige Street without the associative evidence to put him at the scene? And why would they spend precious resources investigating every member of his family?

Because they were fishing.

And maybe still fishing. Was that why Rankin was at her house after O'Brien broke in?

Birdie needed the 411 on Rankin.

And she knew whom to ask.

TWENTY-SEVEN

By the time Birdie passed Pearl and reached the safety of her car, she managed to transform three pieces of Doublemint into a grape-size piece of concrete. She got in, buckled up and immediately drove to the roof of a parking garage where she'd have a clear sight line of cars coming and going. She retrieved her travel gun from under the seat and placed it on the passenger seat. She sat upright behind the steering wheel. Windows up. Doors locked.

Her automatic response was culled from an organic desire for security. Danny wasn't a paranoid and wasn't prone to letting his imagination control his sixth sense. He would only be concerned if he had cause, which meant he knew something relevant based on two small bits that Birdie communicated: she is Matt's heir; someone broke into her house.

Meanwhile, with unknown listeners she didn't feel comfortable working at home, she'd work out of the Ford and conduct a bit of back checking. Housekeeping first. She removed a steno pad from the back pocket of the passenger seat and recorded in shorthand everything she could remember from the murder books. She'd learned the Gregg method from an old nun in seventh grade during a semester's worth of after-school detention. Few people used it anymore so there'd always been a level of security. Then she wrote her impressions. These would come in handy when the book reached the final stages of completion—should that day ever dawn.

She called her cousin, Thom, and invited him out for dinner. He insisted they meet at her house and, because she didn't cook, he'd bring Japanese. She couldn't shake him of his resolve to meet at the house and figured she might have to blow off the Rankin discussion and keep him sober enough to leave by midnight in time for Pearl's visit.

Her next call went to Monica Alvarado. They spoke often during the initial research stages of Birdie's investigation, during which Birdie disclosed that she was related to Arthur. Monica welcomed her anyway. She'd thought she could manipulate the teenage Birdie to provide her with familial confidences that would forward her lawsuit against the city. Years after the incident when reporters moved on to other business, she'd call Birdie to give her updates in hopes of getting coverage that would heat up the unsolved case. Eventually, they both moved on.

"Hello, Mrs. Alvarado, this is Elizabeth Keane. It's been a long time. I'm hoping you can answer a few questions regarding the Paige Street incident."

"Has there been an arrest?"

"Unfortunately no. I'm calling to ask about the cash checked into evidence. Did you ever get it back?"

"I had to sue. But I never got the rest that crooked cop took."

"It's never been established that another cop was present."

"The man walked like one. Talked like one. Hit like one."

"Who can argue with that logic? Mrs. Alvarado, please clarify. Did you receive the evidence money back?"

"I didn't have it long. The IRS robbed me of everything I had left. Said I wasn't paying taxes. Said I got that money dealing drugs. That's a lie. Me and Martine didn't do nothin' illegal. Then those government thieves took everything but my house. And now it's haunted by my beloved husband."

At least Birdie learned that Monica got the evidence money back, and she still lived in the Paige Street house. That was enough for now. "Thank you for your time, Mrs. Alvarado."

Her next call went to Arthur. She left a message on his cell. "I met with Narciso Alejo and spoke with the Alvarado widow. Both confirmed that the Paige Street evidence money wasn't stolen. It was returned. I expect you to counter any future bad package rumors with that double-checked fact. Matt's integrity on this issue has been restored."

Then she called Jacob Hoy to see how he was faring and drop a line into the water regarding assisted termination. After a bit of small talk Birdie finally got to the meat.

"Were you aware of strain between Matt and Emmett?"

"How could I not? They've been hot and cold since we were kids. There was an intense competitive streak between them that often got physical."

"Did any of their conflicts involve women?"

"Only Linda. Bad news from day one. Emmett and Linda had a past connection and he told Matt to lay off. Of course, that prompted Matt to pursue her harder. Hey, Hughes filed his report yesterday," he offered.

"Anything unexpected?"

"No. He did his job. Even investigated my whereabouts. Never thought I'd have to have an alibi. I know what he was looking for. He wondered if I helped Matt along."

"He said that?"

"Of course not. It's the next logical step up from your suicide theory and you should be ashamed for ever thinking it."

"I might have thought it, but I never mentioned it to Ron. He did that on his own."

"Just so we're clear, I didn't help Matt self-terminate. Okay, Birdie?"

"Alright. We're clear."

Birdie threw a tablecloth over the round table in the lanai and set out the everyday china. She put the sake she purchased on the way home on ice. She turned the gas warmers to low, lit candles, and flipped on the mini white lights circling the columns supporting the deck above. Of all the rooms in the house this would be the least likely to be hot. Birdie had just finished getting ready when Thom arrived. Right on time. He buzzed the door and she answered through the intercom, "The postern's unlocked. Come 'round back."

A few minutes later, Thom rounded the corner of the house.

"Look at this," said Thom placing the handled bag on the bar before kissing his cousin. "It's not often we're down here. It's a nice space. You really should use it more often. Too bad the death plot is in plain sight."

Birdie frowned at the sight of the yellow tape that marked off the location of O'Brien's final place on earth. Definitely a downside to the choice of the lanai for their mealtime discussion.

Birdie opened a Kirin for Thom while she transferred the food to covered serving dishes.

"What's the update?" she said.

"Wilshire checked a mile radius and found no abandoned cars."

"He had a wheelman."

"Not so fast. There's a Metro station nearby."

"Thom, the station is at Wilshire and Western. Trust me I've done the legwork. A guy from Belfast wouldn't know the short-cuts, which means a rough route of twenty-five blocks, depending on whether he took Wilshire or 3rd. Like I said before, he'd need a transport. Unless—"

What if he wasn't looking for something? What if he was adding something? Wire taps? What if the mess of Matt's things was merely a diversion? No. She quickly dismissed the theory. He had no possessions when he died. No ID, no keys, no paper, and no tools or equipment.

"Unless what?" said Thom.

"Nothing," said Birdie, shaking her head. "I was just running the Purple Line's timetable through my head. I have that sake you like. Let's eat."

After dinner Thom stretched out in a lounger with a cigarette and nursed another beer. Birdie curled up on the corner of the couch and sipped tea. Her phone rang repeatedly during their meal. Birdie screened and let them go to voicemail, but Thom had had enough when the phone rang again and she got up to check the caller's number.

"Damnit," he said, "does your phone ever stop ringing?"

"Not really, no." Since she was up she grabbed the photo of Rankin she'd downloaded from the department's website and tossed it in Thom's lap.

"So?"

"I remember him bringing you to the Manor after you'd been shot."

"And?"

"He tried to ask me questions the night O'Brien broke in. He wouldn't identify himself so I refused."

"And?"

"You tell me."

"You want to know what happened the night I got shot. Why is it relevant?"

"Matt died and cops are calling him a bad package, a Belfast jobber came to my house looking for something in Matt's things and then blew his brain to smithereens. Rankin showed up almost immediately afterward. Then you showed up. I was so happy to see you that I didn't have the wherewithal to ask how you knew what happened. Your past connection—"

"Okay, okay. But it stays there," he said, pointing at her head.

"Agreed."

"It was a night of no action," said Thom. "A bunch of us drove our radio cars to a hole where we went for naps or to shoot the shit. One guy picked up a couple of working girls. We drank and had a little adult fun. Next thing I know we're being approached

222

by a gang of Chicanos. Shots were fired and the group scattered. When it was over, the blue shoes were gone and I had one in the side. Mom used to be a surgical nurse, so I convinced Rankin to take me to the Manor. The rest you know."

"That's it?"

"That's it? Maybe I didn't stress that we were getting blown by street whores and fired our weapons at a group of guys that were probably just passing through."

"Who knows about it?" she said.

"Mom, Dad, and Rankin. You. And Madi of course."

"None of the other cops knew you were shot?"

"Think I'm crazy? When it comes to a conspiracy, the fewer people the better."

"How did you find out about O'Brien?"

"One of the patrol officers is a pal. He called."

"And Rankin?"

"I didn't know he was here prior to my arrival."

"I saw the two of you exchange eye contact."

"We have a mutual incident that could destroy our careers. Dad's, too."

"Why was he here?"

"You're related to one of his captains? I don't know."

"Have you had much contact with him since that night?"

"Naw. We took different career paths. Now he's more politician than cop."

"Okay, you're off the hook."

"Thank God," Thom said in mock relief. "Your dinner mission has been accomplished. I can go home now."

Thom had been gone a few minutes when the phone rang. It was Denis Cleary. The message of condolence he left after Matt's death was sweet. Their brief phone conversation had been civil. And now a third contact. Of all the calls this evening this one she'd answer.

"Do you still go to nine o'clock Mass?" he said.

"Yes."

"Would you meet me for breakfast afterward at our old place?"

Their old place was a quaint breakfast café off Sunset that started life as a kit home from Pacific Ready Cut. It rated high on atmosphere and privacy with its shroud of ivy and greenery.

Birdie had always desired to mend the fence with Denis. But forgiveness is given, not earned. The only way to receive it was to put herself in front of Denis and hope that his invitation was a step toward that goal. His voice was bright and friendly, so she agreed.

TWENTY-EIGHT

Sunday, January 15

MIDNIGHT. THE CLOCK START to a significant day.

Matt's birthday.

Like Birdie, he was born during the season of Epiphany. Catholics all over the world celebrated this as the time in history when the Magi bore gifts to the infant Jesus. She'd light candles today at the prie-dieu at the eastern corner of her living room. She'd celebrate this day as the day of his re-birth into heaven.

Birdie spied through the peephole and then opened the Judas hole just to be sure it was Pearl standing on her front porch holding a suitcase. She opened the door and he quickly entered.

"Girl," he whispered, "what mischief you into now? I can't believe some whack job broke into a crib in this 'hood. You attract all the crazies. I'm sayin' ya gotta fix that karma. Sober?"

"Hello to you, too."

"Sorry. Gotta find a sweet spot. Where's your bedroom?"

"Third floor. First door on the right."

"Stay here. I'll check that room first."

He loped up three stairs and disappeared up the turret. Birdie waited in the dark.

When Pearl was twelve his mother shot her abusing husband. With a father in the grave and a mother in prison he became homeless. He lived on the streets in South Florida where tall black boys stood out against the Cuban immigrants. With the help of a Catholic charity, he got adopted by the Eubanks family. Like a rescue dog, Pearl knew a good situation. He had a safe, loving home and new brothers with the same skin color.

A rare arthritis settled into his hips, crippling his high school basketball career and he became addicted to pain relievers. It took nine years, a few stayovers in county, and two titanium hips to get clean. And now he was a licensed investigator working for his brother.

Pearl tapped Birdie on the shoulder and gestured at her to come up. They entered her bedroom and he shut the door. "This room is cool. Stay in here until I finish the rest of the house and then we'll have a talk."

At 3 a.m. Pearl shook her awake. "We're clear. Let's go to your office and call Danny."

Birdie followed Pearl to her office. The always-open curtains across the French doors were closed. The suitcase was open and shoved against the wall. A red felt cloth was piled with plastic bits she wouldn't even pretend to identify. Her right hand twitched. She reached for an open pack of gum while Pearl punched a number into a smart phone and set it on the edge of the desk. The ringing phone echoed once before Danny answered.

"I'm here with Tweety," said Pearl. "We're clean."

"Elizabeth, let me be clear," said Danny. The words were serious, but the voice was lazy from recent slumber. "Though you may be participating in this conversation, it is between me and my brother and is strictly confidential. This is important and I need you to understand. I'm your friend but that takes second position to my job as a prosecutor and as such I can't put myself in a position as witness."

"Don't try to freak me out," said Birdie. "What the hell's going on?"

"Pearl?" said Danny.

"The car had a tracker. Same as law enforcement uses. Home and office phone lines were hot at the box. Here's where it gets crazy. The office had a pickup monitor. The kitchen and livin' room had two monitors each, the library one. The rest of the house was clear. The setup was designed for short-range monitorin' and there was a booster on the back wall of the house and another at the property line. Illegal as hell and old school. Like from the '60s or '70s old. And way too obvious. A savvy seventh grader could do better. And her computer and cell were clean. Doesn't make sense to me. It's like someone put it here to say, hey, we can get in."

"There are other ways to do that," said Danny.

"Sure," said Pearl. "Someone could open drawers, move stuff around. But Tweety is a techie girl and this would be guaranteed to get her attention. It's a one-man operation. My guess is the receiver is close. Either at the end of 2nd Street or at the Wilshire

Country Club. By now the monitor knows his operation is blown because of the massive equipment failure. He's already packed up."

"Unless he's dead," said Birdie. "The guy who broke in, O'Brien, could he have done it?"

"With the exception of a gun he had no possessions," interjected Danny.

"How do you know that?" said Birdie.

"I have sources. If he's the guy, you can bet he had help."

Birdie sat down on the couch in a daze. Now would be a good time for a drink. She looked up at the wall of numbers. She had made it through another day. She got back up and ripped off a page. 247. Today, Sunday, was the start of day 248. If she made it through she'd rip another page. The thought of starting over was dreadful so she quelled the I-wanna-drink sensation with a spit, a wrap, and a fresh piece.

"What was that?" said Danny.

"Tweety ripped a piece of paper off a big pad of numbers," said Pearl. "She's keeping track of sober days."

"Elizabeth? I didn't know you needed to be sober," said Danny.

"No one did."

"Pearl, did you know?"

"Afterward," said Pearl. "Goin' straight is a private journey for Tweety. She on the righteous path. Gotta say, though, the girl is skinny. She's got a white-girl ass now."

"I appreciate the levity at my expense," said Birdie. "But someone has to tell me what the hell is going on. Danny, you obviously knew something was amiss when I said my house was broken into. So give."

"I need more information. When did you last see Matt?"

"Friday, the sixth."

"Tell me everything that's happened since," said Danny. "Even if you think it's unrelated or minor. I need to know what you did and who you've seen and spoken with."

"Is this really necessary?"

"In more ways than you know."

"Send him the workup, too," said Pearl.

Before Birdie could stop him Pearl rolled up the shade exposing Birdie's contorted math formula and theories on the dry erase board.

"Hey! That's private."

"Girl, you gotta trust us. Danny might see somethin' important. So, bro, I'm going to send you a photo of Tweety's work board." He picked up the phone and snapped several shots.

Birdie felt a pulsing throb behind her left ear. No one gets to see her work. The madness behind the method. She plucked a bottle of Excedrin off the desk, shook one out, and swallowed it with day-old coffee.

"Got the photo," said Danny. There was a long pause. "What does the piece of paper say?"

"It was wrapped around that key you see next to it," said Birdie. "Matt snuck it into my pocket on the night of my bir—"

"Not the paper by the key. The other one."

"Oh, that. It's his last journal entry. Dated three weeks before he died. It reads: 'It's done. The project is complete and I am renewed. The agility and flexibility I once had is slowly returning.

Labor at Bird's house has helped my strength. Her gym is a work of art. The lumber for the gazebo is being delivered tomorrow and the blueprints are straightforward. I'll keep trying to convince her to build a pool.' You know what? The odd thing about this note is that he and I have never discussed building a pool."

"What does the rest mean?"

"Just what it says. He was feeling better. You know, physically. He finished building my gym and it's fantastic. The next project was a gazebo. The lumber was delivered. It's here under a tarp in my backyard."

"Could there be anything hidden in the lumber pile?"

"No. I supervised the delivery. I watched the workmen offload and stack the lumber. And because we—meaning Matt and I—didn't know exactly when we'd start the project, we covered it with a tarp."

"Alright. Now tell me everything since the sixth."

"Danny, give me some reassurance. Extremely personal stuff has happened since then. I trust you and I trust Pearl. But really, my antennae are up and vibrating."

"Elizabeth, I get it. We're two sets of fresh ears and eyes."

"If you screw me, I'll make sure you don't ever practice law again in the state of California. I will strip you of your livelihood."

"We have your back. Or perhaps I should say your flat white ass."

Pearl guffawed.

"Alright," said Birdie. "It started Friday night before midnight when Matt finally arrived at my birthday party…"

Birdie delivered a narrative version without personal commentary and she didn't leave anything out. Other than a few hard swallows of air Danny was silent. Several times Birdie had to ask if he were still listening. When she'd finished Pearl shook his head in wonderment and she could've sworn she heard Danny hiss an expletive.

"So?" said Birdie.

Danny was silent a few more beats before asking, "Pearl, is Elizabeth's home secure?"

"Not really. She needs to upgrade the security system. Put in some lighting. Cut back a few hedges. Key logs and surveillance would be good. The girl has an arsenal in the garage that won't do no good without easy access. At least the house ain't hot."

"Danny?" said Birdie. "Talk to me. Why were you concerned when Emmett came to the house?"

"Please understand the position I'm in. I'm standing on the line." He sighed deeply. "It's clear Emmett is being blackmailed about April. He came to my attention awhile back because he's on the hunt for money and now I know the reason. This is a bad place for a cop to be. It can make one desperate. Unpredictable. Who knows how far he'll go to keep that knowledge from his wife."

"What about the Blue Bandits? Do you think they've reorganized?"

"I can't speak to that. But I'll give you this warning. Don't let your guard down. If you pursue it, be prepared for any situation."

"Okay, I get it. It'll be dangerous. What about that last box of evidence? Any clue to its location?"

"You have everything you need."

"I don't see it."

"Because you're too close. Matt's death makes it personal to you."

"Help me see it."

"Alright. Tell me again all the parts regarding the boxes."

"Reidy delivered six boxes to me on Monday the ninth. They contained Matt's personal property. When I returned from the movies on Tuesday night I found O'Brien in my house. He had rummaged through them. I re-packed them on Wednesday the eleventh and hid them under the stairs. I lied to S&M when I said they were no longer in my possession. Then on Friday Soto surprised me at the storage unit where he and Matt had hid the evidence. He told me that he hoped I could lead him to the last box—"

"Do you hear yourself?" said Danny. "You told me the boxes Reidy delivered contained personal matter. Where's the rest?"

"Soto has them. He's looking for the last one."

"How many boxes does he have?"

"He wasn't specific."

Danny was silent once again. The silence was like a vacuum sucking the air out of the room. "Soto doesn't have the boxes."

"Then where are they? Why would Soto tell me he had them?"

"You know where they are."

"Danny! Quit messing with me. I don't."

"How do you know that it's the last box and not all of them?"

Birdie felt like she'd just been scolded. "Because Soto told me."

"Exactly. All he wanted was information. Now he knows you don't have the boxes. He also knows that you'll find them."

"He told me he has them," she repeated. "Soto's a legendary cop, well respected in the law enforcement community."

"Who are you trying to convince?"

Danny was leading Birdie to a conclusion. The rusty hinges were loosening.

"Are you telling me that Soto is dirty?" she said. "That he had my house wired in the hope I'd lead him to them?"

"Make your own conclusion. Tell me again. How many boxes did Reidy deliver?"

"Six."

"How many?"

"He delivered six."

"How many boxes?"

"Damnit, Danny! He delivered six boxes!"

"Don't you see the problem? The personal issue clouding your mind?"

"I didn't make it personal. Matt did."

"And you've invested in the emotion of the situation. Take a deep breath. Why did Reidy come to your house on Monday?"

"To go over Matt's estate." The door was finally opening.

"How many boxes did he bring?"

"Six ... No. Seven! He brought six boxes of personal stuff. The last box had all the legal documents and such."

"I swear, Elizabeth. You are a hard-headed woman. That seventh box is where you'll find your answer."

TWENTY-NINE

BIRDIE DUMPED THE BOX of Matt's legal documents onto the dining room table and made piles according to subject. Will and trust were pile one, financials two, deeds and ownership papers three. And so on. Considering the surreptitious nature of the evidence in Matt's care, what she sought was likely a small mention buried deep in a document. There were keys, too. None of them had designators and even Reidy hadn't been sure what they worked. She added the padlock key to the ring and placed them with her own to carry at all times.

She re-read and scanned documents. There was no mention of evidence boxes. Or a hiding place. Or bad cop behavior. Or Paige Street information. Just legal babble. She continually licked her index finger and flipped page after page. A sharp edge of paper sliced her finger. She cursed first and sucked second. The abrupt stop made her think. Danny was right. She had become too invested in the emotion of Matt's death. Dawn would break soon. She needed to decompress and reflect. A run would do the trick.

Birdie pressed the up arrow, increasing the speed of the tread-mill's belt rotation. She closed her eyes and eased into a rhythm. Matt encouraged her in all physical pursuits since becoming dry. If she were healthy, he reasoned, she'd be more likely to stay dry. She preferred the forward movement of running outdoors, but Matt didn't like her running on the streets. So he bought her a treadmill and set it up in the corner of the lanai facing the yard. Then one day, he said, hey, why not build a gym?

Birdie opened her eyes and admired his handiwork. It started life as a brick-lined carriage house that had been converted into an oversized two-car garage. Matt tore down the drywall, took down the old garage door and put in sliding French doors, re-placed broken bricks, restored deterioration caused by the pas-sage of time, put hardwood down, installed industrial lights in floorless bird cages. Mirrors were in wide gilded frames and se-cured to the walls. It was a work of art: a combination of Old World and modern. He was justifiably proud of the work he had done practically single-handed. The *coup de grâce* was a *Gray's Anatomy* poster of a skinless woman's body. He'd made a big deal about hanging it; he called it art.

Some art, she thought.

Yes. Art. A work of art. She stopped the treadmill and jumped off before the belt had ceased to turn. She unhooked the poster. Skinny nails held a piece of foamcore backing onto the frame. She carried it to the garage and used a pair of needle-nose pliers to remove the nails. On the inside of the foamcore Matt had writ-ten: *See Daniel Eubanks. No one else.*

Her heart leaped. Matt had been working in association with Danny. Of course, Danny couldn't tell her that. Or that he was aware of evidence in Matt's care. Birdie clasped her hands in thanks that she hadn't mislaid her trust in seeking Danny's input. Sure, he couldn't help her beyond pointing her in the right direction. Like he said, he couldn't be a witness. Birdie bit her lip in concentration; thought back to the conversation that took place a few hours ago and how Danny had glossed over the question regarding the Blue Bandits.

She thought about the last note. When she first read it she noticed its difference as compared to the journal writings. More like an instruction. Yet she didn't react to its simplicity. What else did he write? *The blueprints are straightforward enough.* Her eyes shot to the plans on top of the Sears workbench. She unrolled them. Tucked inside was another set that appeared to be an expansion of a house that included a pool. *A pool.*

The house didn't look familiar. There were several outbuildings laid out in a rambling pattern that reminded her of an industrial complex. Or maybe a farm. The existing home was compact and the add-on was expansive and aggressive. The pool piqued her interest. It'd be in the middle of the finished property. Henshaw House had a well. Water to fill a pool would be a problem, and maintenance would be difficult considering its remoteness. The Koreatown house had a lot large enough for a pool but the original house on the blueprint didn't match.

Was there another option? Maybe. Matt had property in Indio, a city in Riverside County, east of Los Angeles. There was no deed in the papers. She only knew it existed because the property was listed with other holdings and Reidy had given her a set of random keys. Birdie wasn't worried about missing paperwork. Matt would've paid taxes on the property. She'd find its location through the assessor's office.

Birdie paced in the garage. The quest gained momentum. She was keyed up in the same way when an investigation took a turn. Her brain fired on all cylinders. Yet she was very aware that the threat level had been increased. O'Brien's handlers were unknown. Soto's role and status unverified. She might have won this round with the destruction of the listening devices, but she felt confident that *they* would make a renewed effort to get at the hidden evidence.

Sunday morning breakfast at the garden café was as popular as ever and impacted the limited parking in the area. With a suspended license Birdie had to be extremely careful about how she drove and where she parked. She made several slow trips around the block until she was blessed with the luck of the Irish. A Hummer pulled away from the curb and left her plenty of room in which to parallel park. There were three parking signs, stacked vertically, on a nearby pole and it took a few minutes longer to verify the rules and determine she could park here. She had two hours.

Denis sat in the far corner at a round cocktail-sized table. He smiled and waved. He wasn't particularly handsome. Birdie considered his five-foot-eight height short for a man. He had a bouncy stride boastful in nature. His dark hair was thick and in frequent need of a haircut, and his bushy eyebrows had strays that stuck straight out. He had nice hands though—small, compact, strong. He was smart, enjoyed movies and music, he was Catholic—always a plus. She liked him immediately when they first met and they quickly became lovers. A major downside to the relationship—at two years, her longest—was that they constantly fought; usually over trivial matters like how much to tip a waitress or the best route to drive. The fighting was actually a power struggle. A sign they weren't compatible. So it was fitting that at the end they had the mother of all fights.

Despite Denis' welcoming smile Birdie felt awkward as she approached. Should she hug him, shake his hand, or kiss his cheek? Denis took the lead by patting her hips.

"You've lost a lot of weight," he said, pouring her a cup of coffee from the carafe.

"A side effect of sobriety."

"It looks good on you." He handed her the cup. "And your hair is wavy today. That means you didn't have time to straighten it. I like it in its natural state." He reached out and wrapped a finger around a soft wave. "It's beautiful."

Birdie almost recoiled. She tried to relax her mouth into a polite smile. "Thank you."

"Hungry?"

"Thom and I had a big dinner last night. Maybe fruit and toast."

"Why would you eat a big meal knowing we had a date for breakfast?" he said with a disapproving sniff.

Classic Denis. Passive aggressive. Straight out of the gate he set the temper of the morning. Birdie hoped she hadn't made a mistake in desiring his exoneration. The old Birdie would've told him to shove the attitude up his ass. The new-and-improved sober Birdie sighed with resignation. Forgiveness was worth an hour of her time considering the crime.

Birdie picked up a menu. "What looks good? Oh, homemade yogurt with fresh berries and granola. That's new since I've been here last." She snapped the menu shut.

Denis focused his attention on the menu before the fast-approaching server reached their table. Birdie placed her order. Denis settled on an egg-white omelet with asparagus.

"How's business?" Birdie said.

"Better than ever. I lost a contract, but picked up another one, a try-it. It went so well that we're renegotiating a fixed contract that promises to be much more lucrative. The future looks bright. And, oh, I paid off the third bird. No more debt."

"I bet that feels good."

"Not as good as you'd feel." He reached out and wrapped his hands around hers. "It's nice to see you."

"Denis—" She gently eased her hands away.

"What?"

"*Mica*?"

"We still work together, but, you know, things were pretty good with us."

"Until they weren't." Birdie worried her bottom lip. "You always considered me an emotional shrew."

"Yeah, but Matt was alive then."

She was repulsed. She should've known that he'd consider Matt's passing as the destruction of the Berlin Wall. Now there was nothing to prevent her from falling in love with him.

Birdie leaned forward and lowered her voice. "Denis, I tried to kill you because you cheated on me. And now you want to cheat on Mica? You're not a good boyfriend."

"I'll break up with her if you'll take me back."

His words chilled her. That's exactly what she'd done to George. With Matt's encouragement, she intended to break up with George to pursue a long-desired relationship. He just beat her to it.

"I'd be willing to break up with Mica if you loved me back—" Birdie shrank. That was almost exactly the way she'd said it to Matt. She felt guilty about George. Was Denis capable of any measure of guilt? "—even though you cheated first," he continued.

"Despite being a drunk, my memory is clear on the fact that I never, ever, slept with any other man while we were together."

"An emotional attachment is just as hurtful. You led me astray with great sex and the promise of marriage and family. The whole time you were in love with Matt and unavailable to me. When I finally saw it, I got involved with Mica."

"I never made you any promises."

"Your actions spoke louder than words."

Thus they settled into an old pattern. This discussion had no resolution and stirred up resentment and created heat where none was needed. When Birdie and Denis first started dating they had a stop-loss conversation. They agreed that their relationship would be an at-will arrangement. At any time one of them could simply say, "It's not working for me anymore." The six-word safety phrase would end the relationship with no-fault. Birdie mentally conjured up a revised version and was about to say, "I can't go back to something that ceased working for me," when the food arrived and interrupted the moment.

Breakfast seemed to last forever. Denis, perhaps sensing Birdie's reluctance to resume their relationship, continually reworked the angles to finesse his way under her skirt. Birdie managed to tiptoe through the minefield of innuendo by gently steering the conversation to neutral topics like the ongoing restoration of his Spanish colonial in Echo Park or his ferry business in the gulf. She politely shrugged off his assertions and couldn't wait to get the hell away and never take another of his calls. She was even willing to forgo her desire of forgiveness.

Birdie managed to catch the server's eye and motion for the check. When it arrived Birdie whipped out her wallet and offered to pay before looking at the total. Denis, always chivalrous, snatched it away and said, "Birdie, you know better." He set it on the table and then ignored it.

Birdie checked the time. She was okay with parking, but her grace was exhausted. She leaned over and thanked him for breakfast, making a show of gathering her purse, straightening her dress. She explained she had work to do.

He got the hint and pulled out his wallet. "I'll walk you to your car."

She begged him off. "Sit. Take your time. I'm not drinking anymore. I can walk a straight line. Even in high heels." She stuck out a long limb and rotated an ankle to show off the shoe.

"I always liked those legs," said Denis, flicking his tongue across his teeth.

Now you've done it. Birdie conjured another forced smile. "Thank you for the nice meal. I appreciate that you made the effort to reach out."

Denis stood. He counted out some cash and took her elbow. "Let's go," he said. As soon as they were outside he lit a cigarette. "One of these days, it will be illegal to smoke in our own homes."

"I'm this way," she said, pointing down the block. They walked the distance in silence. She leaned against the car, getting comfortable enough to make one last nudge. "So, Denis, since you obviously want to get back together I take it you don't hate me."

"My leg has healed. You made restitution. Paid my bills. I mean, come on, you were totally off-the-charts wasted. Shit happens."

"You forgive me?'

"Isn't that what you want?" His smile was part charm, part menace.

"Yes. But what's the price of forgiveness, Denis? You've made it clear that you want me again. Is that what I have to pay?"

"Would you?"

"Matt's death doesn't change how I feel. I also don't like going backward."

"So getting back together with me is beneath you?"

"That's not what I said. Nor is that what I meant."

"You know what your problem is? When you were an alcoholic it was all about you. Now that you're clean it's still all about you. You're selfish and smug."

Birdie felt strangely underwhelmed. Denis knew how to push her buttons, but unlike the past, she wasn't going to issue the usual retort. So she said: "You're right. It is all about me. When I was liquored up I worked hard, played hard, and paid an awful price for the unfathomable extremes of that life. I'm still paying a price. Since I've been sober I've not written a single word. I am the sole proprietor of my life. I am financially responsible. I'm it. There's no script and the closest thing I had to a backup was my best friend. And now he's dead. So, yeah, it's still all about me. Instead of being a lecherous shit, you might try a little compassion."

Birdie had a rich, raspy voice. There was a raw authenticity to it—like running on fumes. As she spoke, her voice pitched in a way that drew looks from passersby. Denis didn't like the exposure of standing on a busy sidewalk being bitched at. He glared, smoked, and pushed gray smoke from his nose. He looked like a miniature bull. Birdie realized that she sounded arrogant without meaning to do so. She was about to issue an apology when he unexpectedly shoved her against the car. He pushed his body onto hers and kissed her ferociously on the mouth.

"Consider that the big kiss off. Have a nice life." Then he briskly bounced away.

"Guess he's not gonna forgive after all," she said to herself. Thing is, she wasn't upset.

Then another inexplicable thing happened. She thought of Ron.

THIRTY

BIRDIE PRACTICED CONVERSATIONS ON the way home. "Hi, Ron, it's Birdie. I had breakfast with an ex-boyfriend. The one I tried to kill." No. Violence bad. She'd already mentioned something terrible happened with an ex, the details weren't necessary. "A funny thing happened today…" Without the context what's the real value of the story? "I was thinking about you this morning…" Totally not Birdie. "Remember what you said about skipping the audition and going straight to the play? We should audition. Get to know each other better." Yeah, that worked.

Once Birdie pulled onto her street she relaxed her driving paranoia and dialed Ron's number. She stuck the phone between her ear and shoulder. She got his voicemail as she turned onto her driveway. Emmett sat on her front porch. He stood and started walking toward her when she turned the engine off. She got the beep as she exited the car. "Hey, Ron, it's Birdie. Remember—"

Emmett shoved her. She fell to the ground and dropped the phone. It skidded across the brick of the front walkway. "To hell with you, bitch! It's been two days. You were gonna give me a week!"

"What the hell?" She scrambled to her feet.

He was drunker than before. "You couldn't just give me the money. You had to act high and mighty and put restrictions on it. Then you didn't give me the time you promised. You're a piece of work."

"I don't understand."

"You will pay for this." He spit into her face.

No one spat on Birdie Keane. No one called her a bitch. She wiped the mucus from her cheek and turned her back on him, headed for the front door. He grabbed her arm and pulled. She used the momentum of the swing and shifted her weight. Her right fist hooked him square on the chin. "AHHH." Blood sprayed from Emmett's mouth. She pushed him backward and he slumped into a heap on the grass.

Birdie shook so hard from the shock that it took several attempts to get the key properly fitted in the lock to open the door. She raced up the stairs into her office, grabbed the cordless and dialed Emmett's wife. She ran to the living room window to keep watch.

"Eileen, your husband attacked me. I hit him. He's passed out on my lawn."

"He can rot in the gutter."

"What happened?"

"I got a call. Linda's daughter is Emmett's child."

No wonder he was so pissed. "I'm so sorry, Eileen. It's the Goliath in his life."

"You knew?"

245

"I just found out." Birdie told her about Emmett's visit and the money she had given him to pay a blackmailer.

"I don't care. Linda is … was my friend. I'm April's Godmother. They betrayed me."

"He's torn up."

"Screw him," she sobbed. "He should have thought of me before he made love to another woman and fathered a kid."

"Eileen … he hasn't been a bad husband or a bad father. He gave in to temptation."

"That's not an excuse."

"I know this is hard," said Birdie. "Thing is, blackmailers never accept payment in full. They probably put the squeeze on him by telling you. If you let this destroy your marriage, they win. Please don't let that happen."

The only sound from the other end was Eileen's wails.

Birdie stared out the window at the man passed out on her lawn. "What do you want me to do with Emmett?"

Eileen sighed. "I'll come pick him up."

Birdie babysat Emmett from the safety of her home while she iced her knuckles. He hadn't moved and she began to worry. It seemed a long time to be passed out. About fifteen minutes later he began to stir. He managed to stand just as Eileen arrived. She threw water on his face. He gestured wildly and stumbled toward his car. Eileen tried to grab his keys and he fisted his hand as if to hit her. Eileen backed away and watched helplessly as he stumbled into his car and sped down the street.

Birdie ran outside and hugged Eileen. "I'm sorry for you both."

Eileen held onto Birdie and sobbed. When she had somewhat recovered she said, "I'll call his brothers. They have to get him off the street." She made call after call to her brothers-in-law in hopes one of them could manage to pull him over before he got into a career-damaging accident, or worse, killed someone.

Birdie's house phone was ringing when she finally made it back inside. It was just about to go to voicemail when she picked it up.

It was Jimmy, the bartender at the Westend.

"Still interested in stuff about Matt?"

"Absolutely. What do you have?"

"Photographs of his dead body."

"What the—? Where? When?"

"Here at the bar. Some dudes I don't recognize are smokin' him."

"Asses. Photos or downloads?"

"Definitely downloads, but the quality is good. No doubt on identity."

"Can you get your hands on them?"

"No problem."

"I'm on my way."

Birdie stood in the women's bathroom for what seemed liked hours, dumbstruck at the one image that Jimmy had managed to pilfer.

She already saw the remnants. Heard the gruesome details. But nothing prepared her for the visual she held in her hand. Matt died with open eyes. His lovely, shamrock green eyes were opaque. His dangling feet were swollen and reddish in color.

Stringy vomit covered his mouth and nose. A thermometer stuck out from his liver. His chest—scratched with red scars from the domestic—was bare. Urine and solid waste had oozed from his boxer briefs.

She couldn't believe she had been upset for not making it to Henshaw House in time to see this. Or that she was offended that Parker Sands hadn't let her see Matt at Holy Cross Mortuary. If a photo of it unleashed this kind of drink-craving horror, what would the Technicolor version have done? It was shockingly grotesque. She'd seen many offensive crime scene photos, seen more than her share of violent deaths at active scenes, but never had she seen the freshly dead body of a person she knew and loved. The eyes disturbed her the most. Vacant. Dead. She couldn't take her own off them.

After a long while she thrust the nasty image into her bag, walked back to the bar, slammed a ten on the oak, and said, "Black Bush, Jimmy."

"You outta your mind?"

"Give me a drink," she said between clenched teeth.

He shook his head. "I should've kept my mouth shut."

"Are you gonna pour?"

"Hell, no."

"Fine," she seethed. "I'll go somewhere else."

She stomped out of the bar and bumped right into her dad.

"Jimmy called. Come on. I'll take you home."

Birdie sat in the passenger seat of her own car while Gerard drove like a typical cop: quick accelerations, hard stops, fast and jerky weaving around traffic, running red lights, tailgating. Buildings and cars passed her periphery in a frenzied blur. The rhythmic boom-boom of rubber tires driving over street grooves became a calming lullaby that seemed special-ordered.

"How can cops celebrate the loss of a fellow officer?" she wondered. "I bet most of them were at his funeral—black bands around badges—and they probably went to the wake, too. Hypocrites. And I don't need to hear your sibling rivalry brotherhood bullshit."

"I don't think they were cops," offered Gerard.

She thrust three pieces of gum in her mouth. Spittle oozed from the corners of her lips as teeth worked through the tough sugar until it became soft. The action of chewing calmed her and the brief encounter with a scotch craving abruptly ended.

"I can't believe you asked Jimmy for a drink," said Gerard.

"It was stupid. I'm okay now."

"So fast?"

"The immediacy of the craving was delayed."

Gerard reached out and squeezed her hand.

The landscape became greener. The street smoother. And soon they were at Birdie's house. Gerard slowed and pulled the car into the driveway. His stealth car pulled in behind, driven by his devoted adjutant.

Ron paced the walkway, distraught expression on his face, phone pressed to his ear. Birdie's cell in his free hand.

"Hey," said Gerard. "That's the detective you were introducing at Matt's funeral."

Birdie jumped out of the car before Gerard had an opportunity to put it in park. Ron relaxed for a moment until he saw her aiming straight for him. She thrust her body toward his chest. He swiveled his torso, deflecting her.

"Whoa," he said.

"What is this?" She held up the photo of Matt's dead body and thrust it in his face. "How the hell did this get into cyberspace? Huh? It's your job to serve and protect. This kind of shit isn't supposed to happen."

Ron held up his hands. "Calm down. I had nothing to do with that photo. We'll figure it out."

"*We'll* figure it out? Who? You and me?"

"The sheriff's department."

"You played me. Took advantage of my grief. You had enough prior knowledge of my personality to know how to twist me. You're the type of guy I go for. You knew that. You romanced me. I'm ashamed to think how we tortured my sheets."

Birdie turned away from him.

Gerard and his adjutant watched with keen eyes.

Ron snatched the photo from her hand. "I'm sorry you had to see that." He rolled it up and slid it into the breast pocket of his suit jacket. "I'll find out who's responsible. And about the other stuff … don't think you're the only one vulnerable to hurt. Your problem is power."

Birdie sneered. "What?"

"You get into nowhere relationships with men you don't love. Date guys that swoon for you so you'd have the upper hand. But Matt was different. You two never took the final step of physical intimacy because then you'd be linked in an adult relationship. You can't handle that."

"How dare you make assumptions about Matt and I. You have no right."

"I may be overstepping, but it's the truth and you know it."

"You two got off topic," interjected Gerard.

"Stay out of this, Dad."

"Can't. It happened right in front of my eyes." Gerard extended his hand.

Ron shook it and said, "Nice to see you again, sir."

"Oh, *puh-leeze*," said Birdie, "Is this some hug party now?"

"My daughter is distraught." Gerard smacked Ron across the upper back. "But it's nice to meet a boyfriend of Bird's that's not a faggot. I like you."

"He's not my boyfriend," said Birdie. "Just someone I had sex with."

Gerard winked at Ron and said, "Stubbornness eats up her college-earned brain cells."

The sound of screeching tires distracted them all. A car hit the curb and bounced onto the lawn. Emmett got out, obviously not having been pulled over, and madder than ever. He pushed Gerard and charged Birdie. Ron stepped into his path. He was taller, heavier, and didn't yield when Emmett attempted to shove him away. "You'll pay for this," he screamed at Birdie.

"Hey," said Gerard, drawing his gun, "back off, Emmett."

If Emmett could slay a man with one look, Gerard would be dead.

Gerard and his adjutant moved closer, guns aimed. Ron put a protective arm around Birdie and pushed her out of the line of fire. Neither of them would actually shoot Emmett so long as he was within two feet of Birdie, but that didn't ease the tension of the situation.

"Calm down, everyone," said Birdie, jumping around Ron. "He doesn't have a weapon."

"What do you call the car?" said Ron.

"Look, Emmett, I get your anger, but I didn't tell Eileen anything. She told me."

"You told her about the money," he hissed.

"I helped because you asked, but I'm not going to take your abuse. Deal with the ramifications of your own actions."

Emmett's face contorted from hate to pain. "I really want to kill you right now." He said it low and deliberate as if on the verge of tears.

"You're drunk," said Gerard. "That's the only reason you're standing right now."

"Piss off, Gerard, you self-righteous bastard."

Gerard jiggled the gun. "Go for it. I'll put you out of your misery."

"So will I," added Gerard's adjutant.

"Alright. Alright," said Emmett, holding his hands in submission. "I'm going." He retreated. The car bounced backward into the street, leaving a big black scar on the curb and two swatches of muddy grooves on the grass. No one relaxed until he accelerated away.

Gerard ticked his head at the adjutant. "Have him picked up before he kills someone."

"That's it," declared Birdie. "I'm done. You guys can chase Emmett, have a nice little chat on my ruined lawn, get to know each other, psychoanalyze me all you want." She twirled her arms in a big circle. "I'm through with all of this."

"Wait," said Gerard. "What the hell was that about?"

"Leave me the hell alone."

"Birdie…" said Ron.

By then Birdie had already opened the door and crossed the threshold. She pushed it closed with a dull thud that echoed in the entryway.

Birdie was tired. *Tired.* A condition of extreme mental and spiritual distress. Hibernating was her preferred method of mental detox. She'd sleep. Lie in bed, look up at the stars on the ceiling and dream a new existence; a reality different from the one she was experiencing. Fantasy and reality intermingling to give birth to a new creation. Eight months ago, she would've been recreated by liquor. Nowadays, it was sleep. Sometimes she felt guilty for the self-indulgence, but not today. No, today she had earned it and had justification. She turned the phone ringer off, muted the door buzzer, pulled down the blackout shades, got undressed, placed the loaded Sig under her pillow, and covered herself with a soft cotton blanket. Her body jittered as it recovered from the adrenaline dump and want of a drink. No, she'd not go downstairs to get the bottle of B&B in the library. She threw the blanket off and got up to lock the bedroom door. Then she plopped back into bed and covered her head.

THIRTY-ONE

Monday, January 16

BIRDIE'S EYES POPPED OPEN midday. Her thoughts stretched out to Matt. What he must have endured with all those years of sneaking around and collecting evidence of a cop gang and then called out to a bogus domestic dispute and shot by an unknown assailant. Even near death Matt never let Birdie see the crisis of heart. And when he did call on her to finish, or find, something that was extremely important, she allowed her personal grief to impede her. She had let him down. Well, no more. With renewed vigor she got out of bed.

Some life experiences can be real shitty, hard to get through, but she had no legitimate reason to feel sorry for herself. Yeah, her heart yearned for Matt, missed him with every cell of her body, but she would not allow his task to go unfinished. She owed him that much. Yes, he had betrayed her, but it was for a reason. He had a plan. He always did. And the reason would likely be discovered when she found the evidence boxes.

See what a day in bed could do? Add perspective. Birdie had a rich life. A loving family. Trusty friends. A spiritual community. And she had herself. A woman who had the strength and will to push on.

After a hearty breakfast another page came off the wall. Day 248. Miracle.

Jacob had left a voicemail: "Now, Birdie, Ron Hughes told me about the photo. I can only think that someone hacked into the county's computer for some malicious purpose. Please don't think I or Hughes had anything to do with it. The data card from his camera went directly to an evidence envelope. The chain of custody was intact. I am extremely sorry you saw Matt that way. Please be assured that an investigation has already been launched." Well, that's one way to get ahead of the shit, thought Birdie.

After listening to all the messages, she was surprised that Ron had not called. So she called him.

"Did you drop everything to race here when you thought I was in trouble?"

"My weekend is Monday and Tuesday. I'd already considered breaking off early anyway. I'm glad you're okay."

"How long did you and Dad talk about me?"

"Talk? He interrogated me. He took me to the Westend where we met up with Thom and Arthur. They gang raped me. Right there in the bar. My ass is sore."

"Nice metaphor. My dad will do background."

"I've nothing to hide, but they pushed me hard anyway. Gerard wanted to know why I was at your house. Wanted to know all about Emmett. I couldn't offer anything more than what I heard on the message. Later they wanted to know my intentions."

"What did you say?"

"What could I say? You told your dad that we'd already had sex, and he told your cousins. So I said that we intended to get to know each other by dating."

"Humph. Now the whole family knows."

"Yeah, I got that dynamic."

"Why didn't you call after what happened with Emmett?"

"Gerard said not to. And Arthur said that when you got out of bed, you'd call."

"I hate being predictable. On a first-name basis with my dad?"

"And with Thom and Arthur. I think I'm in."

"You've schmoozed my family, but you have a long way to go with me."

"That's why I stayed in town. Can I come in?"

"Come over in two hours."

"Why not now?" he said, disappointed.

"I'm going on a run. It helps me think."

"I'll go with."

"I have only one treadmill."

"We can run outside. It's a beautiful day."

"Yeah, okay. That'd be nice, but I'll be ready in a few minutes and I really don't want to wait."

"No problem. I'm in your driveway."

Birdie opened the door. Ron shrugged. "I wanted to keep watch in case that asshole came back."

She looked at the duffle bag in his hand. "What kind of gear do you keep in your car?"

"Everything I need and then some."

Birdie watched Ron strap on a suspender rig made of neoprene. It crossed in an X over his back, down his chest and wrapped around his waist. All of it to conceal a tiny BUG at the small of his back. He jumped up and down to make sure it fit tight and didn't chafe. "What?" he said, "It's what the Secret Service uses."

"Yes," she countered, "but I'm not a jogging president and you aren't my protection detail." In the end, she couldn't convince him not to pack a gun. He explained that he felt naked without one. The Marines taught him to be prepared for any circumstance.

They walked briskly to 2nd Street, and then started a light jog. It was clear from minute one that Ron was the faster, stronger runner, but he humored her. The air was crisp and bit her cheeks, her nose began to drip. She ran her sleeve across her nose and concentrated on the soft squish of running shoes hitting the pavement, the ponytail slapping her back, the glint of the engraved ID tag attached to her shoe. It felt good to be outdoors for a change.

They turned eastward on 3rd Street, moving to the sidewalk and upping the pace. They ran in silence. Occasionally, Ron would sprint ahead and double back, laughing and smiling. He reminded Birdie of an overgrown puppy at play. Turning left on Rossmore Avenue, she thought about the joy he brought to her. How much his mannerisms reminded her of Matt.

She was now certain that Matt wanted her to find the evidence boxes. She also hoped they'd give up an answer to why he died. Despite Danny's assertions of danger, she felt that as long as she knew more than *they* did, she'd be okay. Knowledge gave her a safety net.

Ron fell in next to her. "May I make a suggestion? Relax your shoulders." That's it. "Now try to breathe through your belly, not your lungs. You're puffing too hard."

"I'm puffing because I'm not in good shape."

"You have a beautiful shape."

"You know what I mean."

"Oh, you mean cardiovascular shape?"

"Ha, ha."

"I'll teach you how to belly breathe when we're not running. It will be easier to explain when I can touch you."

"What a lame excuse."

They turned left on Beverly Boulevard.

Ron laughed. "What can I say in my defense?"

"*Nada*."

They eased into a comfortable rhythm. The only sound was Birdie's breathing. Ron was silent. He hadn't even broken a sweat.

Pass the Wilshire Country Club, then another left and they were back on her street. She kicked it.

"Ho, ho," said Ron. "It's like that."

Ron gave her a significant head start and then easily passed her, sprinting the distance to the house. She moved into the street, huffing and puffing, determined to give it her all. She didn't see the van. But she felt the front grill, the warmth of the engine. Her body bounced, limbs twisting in an unnatural way, skidding, somersaulting. A kaleidoscope of colors bloomed when Birdie hit the curb and her body abruptly stopped in the gutter. This was bad. She frantically gasped for air, felt like a thrashing fish on a dock. The silver van screeched to a stop. A white man jumped out from the side door to render first aid.

She heard Ron's voice, "BIRDIE … NO."

Birdie attempted to form the words that would express an apology for running in front of a moving vehicle. The man yanked her up by the ponytail. He put his hands under her arms and jerked her toward the open van door.

The driver yelled, "Hurry up." The van jerked forward.

"BIRDIE."

The man fell back into the van, dragging Birdie along. He wrapped a hand around her thigh and pulled her in. "Go. Go. Go."

"Who is that guy?" said the driver.

"Just go," said the white guy, slamming the door.

Through her fuzzy-head, Birdie realized these men weren't overzealous in their attempt to help. They hit her on purpose. Birdie was being kidnapped. She tried to scream, but still hadn't caught her breath.

She heard a POP as the back window exploded into a gazillion pieces of safety glass. The van rocked as it accelerated down the street. Two more POP-POPS as bullets hit the van.

"BIRDIE. NOOOOO."

"The jerk is chasing us," the driver screamed.

"Get the hell out of here."

Finally Birdie managed her own scream—the best she could muster.

The man and she got tossed sideways as the van took a fast turn.

The driver yelled, "Shut her up."

Birdie was still screaming when the gloved fist hit her face.

THIRTY-TWO

I AWOKE WITH A *primeval instinct to be absolutely still and assess the situation. Not an easy deal. Every nerve in my body screamed uncle. My right shoulder lay crumpled under my clavicle. Blood glued my cheek to the filthy concrete floor. Acidic goo coated my teeth. My eyes throbbed. And worse, my abdominal muscles were in a sustained state of contraction. My body was getting ready to vomit or shit. Retching or Expulsion? Guess it didn't matter. My detritus would blend with the stale piss, decomposing rodents, gastric chunks, and moldy fast food of my prison. I lay in odiferous hell and cursed my keen olfactory system. Even the clotted blood of my broken nose couldn't filter the odor of raw crude that fought for a presence among the miasma. How long had I been here? A day? Three? I had no sense of space or time.*

I wasn't alone in this nasty place. Two male voices: one harsh, one softer, engaged in argument. I couldn't make out the content, but they were clearly unhappy. Their voices were in front of me, so I dared to move my hands positioned behind my back. The fingers wiggled slowly. All ten intact. My wrists were handcuffed. That'd put a damper on any active plan of escape.

A sudden heat, like a fever, overwhelmed me. The peristaltic activity had reached its climax. An involuntary moan escaped through my clenched teeth just as my bowels emptied. The smell was quick to spread as excreta oozed underneath my running tights, warm and liquidly against my thighs. My thoughts reached deep inside my brain. As I drifted back into blessed unconsciousness I recalled the leftovers on Matt's death bed.

Sour water streamed onto my face, stinging. I lapped it up, desperate with an unquenchable thirst.

"Wake up," said a man.

When the water stopped I managed to open my one good eye. A dim light source barely illuminated white hands pulling up a pants zipper. The indignity of drinking piss didn't bother me. I had other pressing concerns. Like survival. I rolled over on my belly and tried to get up. The man pushed me down.

"I said wake up, not get up."

Then he stomped my kidneys. The pain was what I'd imagine a lightning strike to be like.

I had gone to hell. Not limbo. Not purgatory. Straight to hell.

A man drummed on my body. "That's it," he said. "Get the blood moving. Attagirl. Time to wake up for your company." He smacked the crook of my arm. Tap, tap, tap. A prick preceded a quickening of awareness. My heart beat faster. My brain fired up. What had he given me? I lolled my head side to side. Look around. Where am I? Feel the environment.

Someone kicked my face. No pain. Just a snap like a soda cracker. The darkness closed around me. A blackness hijacked my heart. All I saw were eyes. Matt's eyes. Dead eyes.

There was a long hallway. The door at the end was carved marble with a warm candlelit glow. That was the door to heaven. I, Birdie Elizabeth Keane, had an appointment with God. I wasn't afraid. I was at peace, ready to accept my fate. I stood in front of a tall pulpit. I felt the presence of a judge full of intense power and true, unconditional love. Deliverance from this earthly hell waited for me. I looked down on my body. Eyes open. Glassed over.

I'm coming, Matt. I'm coming.

THIRTY-THREE

St. Peter washed Birdie's feet with warm water. He poured rose-scented oil on her skin. The oil warmed as he gently massaged the vamp, toes, ankle, and calf. His hands were soft as they pressed into the flesh. He gently worked his way toward her knees. *Okay, he's getting frisky,* thought Birdie.

Then she heard Madi's voice. "Your skin is so dry. The hospital staff doesn't do anything to keep a girl looking good. Well, Dr. White is the exception. He's the plastic surgeon that fixed your face. Guess what? You got Botox in your cheek to keep the muscles relaxed while you heal. He said it will keep the scarring down. What about that? Get the shit beat out of you, get Botox."

Ron's rummy voice interjected, "Dr. Keyes said to keep it light and positive."

"Don't censor me, Muscle Man. I know my cousin. She'd want to know everything."

Birdie was stuck in the twilight between sedation and wakening. She heard their voices and the steady beeps and whirling of

264

hospital machinery, but couldn't respond. Not that it mattered. She wasn't in heaven after all.

Madi continued. "Just so you know you're in ICU at USC Medical Center. A patrol cop from Central found you naked and crumpled on the street in Little Tokyo. Three days ago. Remember the lawyer, Martin Reidy? Well, you were found in the exact same spot. So of course, the detectives are thinking that the bastards are connected. Anyway, the Central guy thought he saw a sign of life so he started compressions. He kept you going until the paramedics arrived, but you were given an overdose of drugs and you had what's called pull … ah … plum—"

"Pulmonary edema," said Ron.

"Yeah," said Madi. "What he said. Anyway, they kick started your heart. Gave you two injections of adrenaline, but you couldn't breath on your own because of fluid in your lungs, so you were put to sleep with a breathing machine, but you can breathe on your own now. As soon as you wake up Maggie and Gerard are moving you to Cedars-Sinai. I suppose you might remember that you were hit by a car, but you don't have any broken bones except the ones in your face. Mostly it's really bad bruises.

"You've had 24/7 security. A bunch of Hollywood uniforms are in a rotation. It was wild at first. Everyone was going crazy because you were missing for a week and Uncle Gerard and Ron and all the Keanes and half the Whelans were out looking for you. That pissed off some detectives named Morgan and Seymour. They're treating this like a homicide because your captors meant to murder you. Anyway, they want to talk to you because they figure you'll make a good witness."

Madi finished massaging Birdie's legs and started on her right arm. "You were so dehydrated when you came in that they had to put a catheter in your chest because there were no veins. And guess what? While you were captive, you lost a ton of weight. You look anorexic now. Did you know that a corpse loses five pounds a day? Well, you were mostly dead.

"I haven't told you the biggest scoop of all. Emmett is missing. Everyone thinks he's the one who took you because of the threats and all. Patrick is out of his mind. It's been hell. Our guys are supporting the Whelans even though some of us think its Emmett's doing. We've had lots of prayer circles. You know how I hate that shit. But what can I do? I have to support my boyfriend and his family, too. Family is the most important. We've all learned that lesson this past week. Did I tell you that Father Frank administered last rites? It was real sad."

Birdie was fully awake now. Madi was right, of course. She knew Birdie would be calmed by the clinical objectivity. It'd give her some small degree of control over her emotional status. Birdie'd want to know everything. Sooner rather than later. And not dipped in chocolate sauce. *What* happened to her wasn't the most pressing thought on her mind. Nor the *why*. Mostly, she had spiritual business with Father Frank.

She tried to open her eyes, but felt nothing more than a flutter. She quickly became frustrated due to an urgent desire to get up and take action. Her brain functioned, but her body wouldn't cooperate. She tried to speak, but felt nothing except tiny knives lining her throat. She wanted fresh, cool water. She wanted fat, ripe, juicy navel oranges. She felt Madi put warm socks on her feet. She heard Madi prattle on about having to work with her high profile actor client for the Golden Globes while Birdie was missing and how difficult that had been. She heard the apology behind the words. Birdie didn't care. Her circumstance had been a reprehensible reality. Every individual who cared for her should have the freedom—without judgment—to cope in any manner they saw fit.

When the first words came from Birdie's mouth it took the three of them by surprise. "Where's Matt?" she mumbled.

Madi jumped up. "Yes!" She opened the door and announced, "Birdie's awake."

Ron was instantly at her side, a pained expression on his face, the line between his brows a bit deeper. He placed a hand on her cheek and said, "Welcome back."

"Father Frank," said Birdie.

A nurse rushed into the room. "It's about time," she said. "You've been off sedation for twelve hours. Dr. Keyes will be thrilled you're alert. Let's sit you up some." She raised the head of the bed and adjusted the pillows. "Your husband hasn't left your side. He and your cousin can keep you company while we wait for the doctor."

"What husband?"

"Sore throat? That's from the breathing tube."

"Oranges?"

"Not yet, honey. I'll be right back with some ice chips."

Birdie looked at the bandages circling her bony wrists. She squinted at Ron, who leaned over her as if admiring some priceless porcelain doll.

"Ligature wounds," he said.

"Husband?" said Birdie.

"Gerard wanted another set of ears when he talked to the ER doc. Only family was allowed so he appointed me your husband. We've been married a month."

"What about Mom?"

"Maggie was too emotional."

"How do you feel?" said Madi.

"Twisted inside out."

"You look like it too, but it will get better. How about a warm blanket? They keep this room so goddamn cold that you're constantly shivering." She removed the top blanket and gave it to Ron. Then she removed a fresh one from a container that looked like an oversized chafing dish. She laid it over Birdie. "Feels good, huh? I'm going to make some calls and let the family know you're back with the living. Love you." She kissed Birdie gently on the forehead before departing.

Ron kissed her lightly on the lips. "I'm so sorry, Birdie."

"Why?"

"I couldn't stop them." A tear fell on her forehead. He turned his head away and wiped the back of his hand across his eyes, cleared his throat. "I got the plate. We tracked it to a young couple with twins. When we arrived at the house, the van seats and the baby restraints were sitting in the driveway. The couple didn't even know their vehicle had been stolen."

"Prints?"

Ron nodded. "Two sets not belonging to the family. One was a hit on AFIS: Carl Raica, DOB 5/16/82, five-eleven, 200, wanted in Louisiana for felony drugs. The other is unknown."

"Photo?"

Ron pulled it from his back pocket and held it up. She studied it. He was bald, dark skinned, round faced with a broad nose and widely spaced brown eyes. She shook her head. "I only saw a white guy. Van?"

"Abandoned near the tar pits."

"Seymour and Morgan?"

"Investigating your abduction. The cops posted outside your door have been instructed to call them as soon as you woke up. Gerard's in the lounge. Louis dragged your mom and Nora home."

"And you?"

"I refused to budge."

"What time is it?"

"0845. Saturday, January 28th."

Gerard entered the room. He had aged ten years. His mouth had jowls like parentheses. His eyes red with too much drink, too little sleep, and more than enough worry. And if possible, his hair seemed whiter. "Sweetheart." He collapsed into the bedside chair and leaned into his daughter. Kissed her forehead.

Birdie patted his arm. "I'm okay, Dad. Let's do this."

Gerard shot a look of confusion at Ron. Ron shrugged.

"I'll play witness," clarified Birdie. "But first I need that ice."

Ron nodded and left the room.

"Your poor mother has been an absolute wreck. Had to be practically sedated."

"Not unlike yourself? You look old, Dad. I'm sorry to put you all through this hell."

"The only people who will be sorry are the sonsofbitches who took you."

Ron returned and fed her a few pieces of ice from a plastic spoon. The ice slowly melted in her mouth like a magical elixir. Nothing had ever felt better. She took a shallow breath and slowly told them what she could. "Two men. One was white, but I didn't get a likeness. Neither man had an accent or speech pattern. I was held in a pump house. Smelled crude oil. Music played nearby all day and night.

"A third man came. They called him 'company.'" Her lip trembled. She touched the swelling, felt the stitches. "He…" She trembled. "I never saw … never heard his voice … just smelled him … cigarettes, rancid oil—almost feminine … I … I felt him …"

Ron's scowl turned murderous.

Gerard said, "Its okay, Bird, you're very brave."

"They kept me drugged." She rested a moment. "The company man wasn't Emmett."

Gerard once again looked at Ron for clarification.

"Did you hear everything Madi said?" said Ron.

Birdie nodded.

"How can you be so sure?" said Gerard.

"I just know."

A man and the nurse walked into the room. "At last you're awake. I'm Dr. Keyes and this is Rosanne. I'm going to ask your father and husband to leave so I can examine you."

"I love you, sweetheart," said Gerard.

Ron leaned over and whispered, "We'll be back later."

"Feeling pain?" said Dr. Keyes.

"Discomfort mostly. Give me the rundown. No candy coating."

"Yeah, your father said it'd be like this. He said, 'she'll wake up and start bossing everyone around.' Well, I'm glad you're here to do the bossing."

He talked as he poked, listened, and prodded. "You came into the trauma unit in critical condition. Hypothermic, dehydrated, with an excess of fluid in your lungs. Your respiration depressed and irregular. We kept you sedated and intubated. You also came in with many body contusions, which caused an abundance of bleeding. We've given you vitamin K. We also administered pressors to stabilize your blood pressure and you've been receiving fluid resuscitation."

"What happened to my face?"

"Your right zygomatic arch was fractured. You have a broken nose and some facial lacerations. Don't worry. Dr. White is the best plastic surgeon around."

"What about down there?"

"Deep abrasions to the vulva. Indicative of nonconsensual sex. A team did a complete exam and collected evidence for the police. Your family is going to transfer you to Cedars-Sinai. I've already made contact with a crime counselor to meet with you there."

"When will I be going?"

"It depends on how stable you are. Your blood pressure is still low. We'll take a chest x-ray to check on the fluid in your lungs."

"I feel something between my legs. Pressure."

"It's a catheter," said Rosanne.

"I'd like it removed," said Birdie.

"It needs to stay for now," said Dr. Keyes. "Your condition is still serious."

"Can you tell me what I was drugged with?"

"Preliminary tests indicate an opiate. We're waiting on the finals."

"Alcohol?"

"Negative."

"Who knows I was raped?"

"The detectives, your father, and your husband. There's no shame."

"I don't want the stigma or pity. What about pregnancy?"

Dr Keyes squeezed her hand. "We didn't take chances. We administered drugs to prevent pregnancy and treated for STDs. We'll monitor your blood for HIV and hepatitis."

"What else do I need to worry about?"

"There's still a chance of pneumonia. Your kidneys are bruised. Your body was traumatized. It needs lots of rest and recovery."

Rosanne said, "That's hard information to take all at once. We're here if you need anything. You're getting some pretty serious pain meds so you shouldn't feel any."

"I'm hungry. Thirsty. Can I eat?"

"Not yet," said Dr. Keyes. "Ice is okay. Maybe some bland food tomorrow. That will be up to your doctor at Cedars. Your physician, Dr. Ryan, is up to speed and will take over your care at Cedars. There are two detectives who've been anxious to talk to you."

"Might as well get it over with. When they come, send them in."

Dr. Keyes patted her arm. "You're doing great. Your father said you were stubborn. That, I think, is what saved your life. Keep up the good work."

"Wrong," she said. "I'm not stubborn. I'm around for an entirely different reason."

Dr. Keyes just smiled.

It didn't matter why Birdie survived. She was just another life saved.

Broken. But saved nonetheless.

THIRTY-FOUR

DETECTIVE MORGAN'S STRAIGHT LIPS expressed condolence. Pity. "Dr. Keyes said you granted permission to talk. Thanks for that."

"So you're going to be nice to me now?" said Birdie.

"We're nice all the time," added Detective Seymour, "but not everyone sees us as the good guys. What can you tell us?"

She prepared to tell them the same information she already gave Gerard and Ron when Seymour's cell interrupted the anticipation. He looked at the number, raised an eyebrow, and flipped it open. He listened intently for several minutes and said, "Thank you. We're on our way."

"You already talked to your father and Ron Hughes?" said Seymour, accusingly.

"Yes."

"Don't you just love those jurisdictional crossovers?" he said to Morgan.

"Who?" said Morgan.

"County," said Seymour

The two detectives huddled and had a whispered conversation.

"What's going on?" said Birdie.

"Your crime scene's been found," said Morgan. "With three DBs."

"I don't believe it," she said. "How can this be?"

"It does seem suspicious," said Seymour.

"Yes, it does," said Morgan. "Finding it first before anybody else? Someone knew where to look, huh? If we get the tiniest whiff that any Keane or that San Diego cop had anything to do with those three bodies, we won't cut them any slack—no matter the provocation."

They turned to leave. "Wait," she said. "How do you know it's my crime scene?"

"Running shoes with your ID tag were found," said Seymour.

"As was Emmett Whelan's dead body," said Morgan.

Nothing could cheer Birdie. Not the rose-colored walls in the spacious room at Cedars-Sinai. Not the flowers or cards or balloons. Not even the company of her mother, Aunt Nora, and Madi. The women were trying to help, but Birdie felt overloaded by their constant chatter of distraction while helplessly tethered to a hospital bed by tubes and a catheter. She wanted to get up and walk. She'd been bound in the pump house for a week. Couldn't anyone understand that she wanted freedom?

The men were out conducting cop business and her nerves were hyper-firing. She wanted news from the crime scene so badly that an electric-charged anxiety made her restless. Cranky.

Then there was the other stuff. Not the violence done upon her. Bodies are designed to heal and repair. Hers would be okay. No, the spiritual journey mattered most. The torment of arriving in heaven and then delivered back to earth, memories that tortured her—the profound revelation of a big lie and the deliverers of that lie, the raw betrayal and hurt embellished upon her by people who claimed to love her. It was too much to bear. She needed to speak with Father Frank. He alone would be able to guide her through this crisis.

Birdie woke in the middle of the night to find Ron slumped in the bedside chair, head on the edge of the bed, his hand placed over hers. Her fingers moved and he became instantly alert.

"Shouldn't you be home by now?" she said.

"I took vacation time." He raised his arms and stretched.

"Some vacation. Is it true about Emmett?"

"Yeah."

"And the other two?"

"The guy from Louisiana. The other is unknown."

"Do you have a photo?"

"I knew you'd ask." He picked up his camera off the tray table and clicked through the images stored in his camera. After finding the white guy, he held it up for her.

She shrugged. "I don't know. Does he have a name?"

"Not yet."

"How is it possible you found the exact pump house? I mean, there are so many in the Southland. Some are nothing more than cinderblock rooms while others are hidden inside clapboard bungalows."

"The music you heard was a clue. Gerard's adjutant was aware of a 24-hour music store that had speakers outside the store. He didn't know the name or location, only the reputation. Gerard made a few calls. We were directed to a place near Compton Airport. Once we found the music store, he drove a grid until we found a pump house. Neither of us wanted to touch it, so he called L.A. Sheriff."

"How long had they been dead?"

"Couple days."

"I don't understand," she said.

"The theory is that the two guys dumped your body in Little Tokyo and came back for either payment or maybe a debriefing when Emmett murdered them and then killed himself."

"That would mean Emmett was my rapist, and I can tell you absolutely that it wasn't him. He's not that kind of guy."

"You mean the kind who threatens to kill you in front of three cops?"

"It was pure evil and hatred. Methodical. Planned. Organized. Not heat of a moment. Emmett and I had our differences, but he wasn't capable of this."

"The evidence will tell us what happened. And there was a lot of it to be had." Ron squeezed his eyes shut. "It was damn awful to visualize you there. It was the most disgusting and filthy crime scene I've ever witnessed."

"All neatly contained inside a single location with four walls."

"Why are you being cynical?" he said. "You should be happy there's not going to be a trial, that you won't have to be a witness in open court, or that the bastards that did this got their due."

"Then what was Emmett's role in Reidy's murder?"

"It's too early to say. There may not be a connection. Perhaps the body dump location was picked to throw off suspicion."

"Is that the theory being knocked around?"

"I don't know," he said.

She shivered. "I think the company man is still out there."

Birdie became tired halfway down the hospital hallway. She white-knuckled the walker and turned around. The grip of the non-skid socks forced her to pick up her feet. No shuffling allowed. After several long minutes she turned into her room. Father Frank sat waiting in the chair by the window.

Frank had lost another earthly brother in the span of three weeks and the grief was clearly evident. Burdens were etched in the lines of his face. His shoulders fell forward. His Roman collar sat askew. His whole presence seemed shrunken and he clutched a wooden cross as though his life depended on it. Seeing his suffering, Birdie made an instant decision not to burden him with her crisis.

"Frank!" said Birdie, trying to keep it light.

He jumped up to help her into bed. She waved him away. "No, no, no. Let me do it myself."

"That's my Bird. How's my favorite parishioner?" he said with forced gaiety.

"I didn't know you were allowed to have favorites."

He winked and said, "Don't tell anybody."

She backed onto the mattress and grimaced in pain.

"Shall I call the nurse?"

"I'm determined not to use the pain meds. They're weaning me off."

"For God's sake, why?"

"I'm afraid of becoming an addict."

"Oh, Bird," he said sadly.

Once Birdie managed to get her legs up on the bed she fought the pillows into position and then struggled with the blanket. Finally she allowed a sigh of tiredness and settled back.

"What a process," said Frank, sitting in the chair closer to the bed.

"It sucks."

They eased into a quiet equilibrium as they so often did. Requiring each other's company, but not needing to speak. Frank held her hand. After a long while of reflective silence Birdie said, "I went to heaven."

"Oh?" Frank's attention piqued. "Any revelations?"

"Yes. God doesn't provide virgins for Islamic radicals."

Frank's instant laugh lightened his dark mood momentarily. Then, too soon, it morphed into a sob. He covered his face with his hands. Birdie let him have his cry without shushing or offering words. Here sat a simple man. He did God's work and was enlightened in ways Birdie'd never understand, but a man nonetheless. Birdie felt blessed that Frank trusted her enough to let her experience his grief instead of holding it deep inside and whispering in the darkness of his small room at the rectory.

After he recovered and blew his nose Birdie took his hand and kissed it. "I'm so sorry, Frank."

Frank acknowledged her with a smile and pressed the cross he'd been clutching into her palm. It was carved from a single piece of wood that had crescent-shaped tool marks rubbed smooth by constant fingering.

"You touch this a lot," said Birdie.

"Yes. Emmett gave this to me when I took my vows. He made it himself from olive wood. I keep it on the bedside table next to my books. It represents pure faith. The kind that doesn't need gold inlay or gems or silver or brass. Made and presented with love."

"It's beautiful in its simplicity." Birdie handed it back.

Frank held up his hand. "I'd like you to have it."

"No, Frank. I can't accept something that means so much to you."

Frank shook his head refusing her refusal.

"Alright. Thank you, Frank."

She'd take his generous gift and in return she'd give him what he'd given her in big heaps over the years—comfort, peace of mind, and an ear to listen.

THIRTY-FIVE

Saturday, February 4

RON GREETED FATHER FRANK with a firm handshake and closed Birdie's front door. A panting black pug bounded down the last few stairs of the turret and skidded across the entry floor, nails scratching the wood for purchase. When she recovered she performed an excited doggie dance around Frank.

"Why, hello Louise," said Frank, rubbing the dog's neck. "When did you arrive?"

"She's been staying with my neighbor. I asked him to bring her up along with some clothes."

"How did Bird react?"

"She tolerates her exuberance." Ron picked up Louise who squirmed in his arms. He kissed her nose, patted her flank. "You missed your daddy. Didn't you, baby?"

Frank chortled. "Where is Bird now?"

"Napping," said Ron, tucking Louise under his arm.

"Good. I'm sure she needs it."

"She knows."

"She knows what?"

"She *knows*."

Frank took a step back. "How is this possible?"

"I don't know. The first words out of her mouth when she woke up from sedation were, 'Where's Matt?' I ignored it, but it hovers between us. She knows that I know that she knows."

"Does she know you called me here to mediate?"

"No."

"Oh, my," sighed Frank. "This is going to be fun. You best open a bottle of wine."

Birdie sat on the couch, bundled in a thick robe, and still she shivered. Ron held his arms tight across his chest and paced the living room.

"He's constantly shoving food at me," said Birdie.

"It's basic math," said Ron in his defense. "Frank, when she arrived at the trauma unit she weighed 96 pounds. Her body is burning up calories as it heals. The rehabilitation exercises burn calories. She doesn't cook. She forgets to eat. So, yeah, I serve her a proper diet of complex carbs and proteins and good fats. And she gets food often."

"Is this really about food?" said Frank. He uncrossed his legs and reached for the wine glass only to discover it was empty. Ron refilled it.

"No, it's not just about food," said Birdie. "He's micromanaging my life. He answers the phone, takes messages, gives my parents daily updates. I move slowly, but I'm not an invalid. Ron hovers over me like some fragile piece of china with a fracture that will break at any moment. And the lights. He's constantly turning them off."

"You complain about your electric bill, yet you burn kilowatts as if they're free."

"I can't be in the dark," whispered Birdie. "Not anymore."

"Hell, Birdie," said Ron. "Why not say so? That I get."

"What does the counselor have to say about that?" said Frank.

"Birdie fired her," said Ron.

"A certificate from a tech school doesn't mean she understands what I've been through."

"As a man of war I understand. You can talk to me." Ron sat next to her on the couch, picked up her hand and kissed the bandaged wrist. "I've been around that shit all my adult life. It leaves a mark." He gently pressed his palm against her damaged cheek. "And not just physical wounds. The Corps calls it stress inoculation. Troops are put through training and classes to teach them how to be survivors in combat scenarios. I've seen the aftereffects of simulations on the psyches of the toughest bastards. But you Birdie? You've been immunized in a real-life situation. I'm more than impressed by your strength of will. I can help."

"I'll drive you crazy," said Birdie.

"I can handle crazy. It's the anger that's hard. I bring a blanket and you yell at me for coddling. I hear you weeping. I see the pain. When I offer the meds you scream at me."

"I don't want to become addicted," said Birdie. "I've told you that."

"He understands your point of view," added Frank. "You need to see his. Addiction grows from abuse. Not occasional use. But what's going on here isn't about taking a pain pill or blankets or food or lights or therapies. It's about your feeling of helplessness. You think Ron belittles you. He wants to mollify your burdens. Tell her why, Ron."

Ron got up shaking his head. Resumed pacing.

"Tell me what?" said Birdie, flicking her eyes between the two men.

"Why does he make sacrifices in his life to help you with yours?" said Frank.

Ron looked at Birdie with wistful eyes.

"He couldn't have stopped my abduction," said Birdie. "He has nothing to feel guilty about."

Ron turned away to hide his disappointment. "It doesn't matter, Frank."

"Yes, it does," added Frank. "What can crush a man of war?"

"Enough," said Ron. "Let's move to the topic that's the real source of her anger. "Her—" he winked his fingers, "—spiritual conflict. That's why you're needed here."

"What would an agnostic know about that?" challenged Birdie.

"Because he's observant," added Frank. "And you should have more faith in—"

"Faith?" Birdie seethed. "You question my faith?" Birdie reached out to push herself up. Ron instinctively held out an arm of support, then recoiled to allow her to get up on her own.

"I was going to say you should have more faith in Ron. But since I've hit a nerve, keep going. What do you want to say, Bird?"

Birdie shuffled toward the window, aware of Frank and Ron's concerned eyes on her. She looked down at the lawn; the grooves from Emmett's car tires were barely visible. The incident seemed ages ago. A lifetime had passed since then. Truly. Her life had been stolen and by some miracle regifted. Only, she came out the other side with an adamant and profound knowledge that upset her more than the violence. The distance of days from this one to that one added doubt, and now she was uncertain. She threw a quick glance over her shoulder. Ron knelt next to Frank. They whispered conspiringly, comfortable with each other's company. Like old friends. Louise rested her head on Frank's thigh. He absentmindedly rubbed her ears.

Birdie turned away. Her eye caught the sunlight on the glass in such a way that her warped reflection bounced back at her. She had tasked Ron with covering all the mirrors with newspaper so she wouldn't have to see the horror, but now her freakishness was validated like the quick click of a camera shutter. She moved her head side to side, but the image vanished in the time lapse along with the light. Like unremembered memories, it might come back when you least expect it. Just like the one of Rankin and Thom and the kitchen surgery. She thought of Thom now as he told her the true story of that night. He had said something curious, "When it comes to conspiracy, the fewer people the better."

It finally became clear. The thing that niggled her brain, the thing she couldn't realize or reach. Until now. Her world wobbled. She leaned into the window to keep balanced. She wanted to throw up. To laugh. Cry. Scream with joy. A confusing mix of emotions left her breathless and curious and relieved and happy and … devastated.

Birdie hobbled back to the couch. She'd need to sit. Frank and Ron were trying hard not to look anxious. Ron took to pacing again. Frank flicked his finger through a bowl of nuts looking for a cashew. Louise wagged her tail.

"I'd been bothered by a photo Matt had tacked up in the shed. Four guys in the snow," she said. "When I pressed Ron, he explained that the photo was taken on a ski trip to Mammoth. Matt, Ron, Jacob, and this guy named Parker Sands were standing side by side like old friends." She gazed up at Ron. "Please get the photo for Frank. You know where it is."

Of course he did. The photo was on the dry erase board next to her notes that were read by him and Gerard and Patrick when they searched the house looking for a clue to why she was abducted.

"Why Matt would purposefully display an unimportant photo next to ones picturing milestones confused me," said Birdie.

Ron returned with the photo and handed it to Frank. His eyes dilated with recognition.

"Matt knew I'd go to Henshaw House after his passing," she continued. "He knew the exact location in which to hide a photograph in plain sight. Sometimes obvious isn't always so. He said that to me a long time ago and I've utilized that obviousness in my work. I wondered … why this photo? I stared at it for long stretches of time looking for some revelation. All three men pictured happened to deal with his body. Patrick called it luck of the Irish. But we all know that Matt made his own luck. Now I know that the revelation is behind the scene. Unseen. The picture taker. You, Frank. You accompanied Matt on that trip. I had forgotten because it was inconsequential. After all, you and Matt took many trips together. But see, Matt not only wanted me to find the photo. He wanted me to know the truth. Many truths in fact. And I will continue to seek them out until I'm satisfied that I've learned everything.

"So here you are. Two of the four conspirators." Birdie waved her finger at Frank and Ron in warning, met their gaze evenly. "You two want me to talk about my spiritual conflict? I know Matt's still alive, but I don't know why. But you do. Be thorough in your confessions."

THIRTY-SIX

"Why do you think Matt's still alive?" said Frank.

"He wasn't in heaven," said Birdie.

"Maybe he's in hell," offered Ron.

"Nice try," she said. "Frank can accept the purity of that truth."

"Unfortunately, yes," said Frank. Then to Ron, "Birdie questions everything. Even divine inspiration. She needs proof."

"That's not true," said Birdie. "I feel the truth of my experience in every cell of my body. But there's more here. I thought Matt tasked me with one mission: to finish a job he started years ago. But he also wanted me to question why he gave up his life. He laid enough bread crumbs. It started with his late visit to my birthday party. Do you remember, Frank? I called you the next morning."

"I recall being at a loss for words," said Frank.

"Because you knew what was about to happen. And you wondered why he'd make a promise he had no intention of keeping. On my birthday nonetheless. That was the first clue to task number two. The gibberish on the office wall is my effort at cobbling together the puzzle."

"I hear wishful thinking," said Ron. "I saw nothing in that so-called gibberish to explain why Matt would still be alive."

"Perhaps I'm not properly articulating the reasons why I know what I know. So let's say Frank is right and that I need proof. I mean, he knows me better than any human on this earth. Trust me, Ron; I can prove my theory very easily. All it will take is enough fuss, to the right authority, to cause enough doubt, to get an exhumation. Done deal."

"A hollow threat," said Ron.

"No, it's not," said Frank. "When Bird puts her mind to something she'll move a mountain to get what she wants. An exhumation won't be necessary. We'll tell you everything."

"NO," said Ron.

"I know you're afraid, my friend," said Frank in the most soothing way possible, "but she has to know to protect all of us."

"What do you mean, 'protect all of us'?" said Birdie.

"We broke the law. Jacob, Parker, Ron, Matt, and myself. The empty casket of a popular police officer would reach the public domain the way a spark turns into a wildfire by a fierce Santa Ana. Our lives would be ruined. We'd go to prison. And Matt's life would be in more danger than ever. Only you can save us, and in the process save yourself.

"Ron, you promised," continued Frank. "You said that if Birdie were found alive that you'd come clean. Isn't that why you called me over?"

"I can't," said Ron. The words came out in an anxiety-laden whisper.

"What are you afraid of?" said Birdie.

"He's afraid of losing you," said Frank. "Don't you see that he's in love with you?"

Birdie knew. She'd known almost from the start. Did she love him in return? She didn't want to, she fought the emotion, pushed it back.

"I was heartbroken when you were snatched," said Ron. Pain broke in his voice. "I felt as if a giant hand squeezed my insides. Frank is right. I made that promise because if we are to have a chance at a life together then it'd have to be clean. No secrets to destroy it later."

Just like Emmett's, thought Birdie. "You best talk to me then," she said.

"It was Matt's idea," said Ron, pacing again. "Conceived and organized by him, carried out by the rest of us. Except Deputy Santos. He wasn't in on it. His role was to authenticate Jacob's findings. The guy had his fingers on Matt's jugular and was so freaked out that he couldn't feel his sedated pulse."

"From the beginning?" said Birdie.

"It's true that Matt and I met for the first time in Mammoth. But I lied about knowing him. We became buds. Spent time together. Fished in Cabo, drank in Tijuana. One weekend he came to my house. Totally wasted. Depressed. That weekend, I met you. Matt showed me photographs. Lots of photographs. I must have lingered over them too long because he said, 'You can fall in love with her just like that,' and he snapped his fingers. Then he said, 'I'm going to make provisions for her and I want you in her life.' When I pressed him for details, he said he was going away. He was going to turn in some evidence on a long investigation and enter the witness protection program. He made me swear that whatever happened, I would look after you. He even offered to pay me."

"You took money?" said Birdie.

"I'm not a mercenary. I didn't take his money."

"The man I loved for fifteen years is alive," Birdie spat. "How can I put that aside?"

"You can't," said Frank. "But your heart is big enough to love two men."

"Frank, why are you pushing this agenda?" said Birdie.

"I love my brother. I love you. I loved the idea of the two of you together in marital bliss, but Matt never took that step and one is left to ponder why."

"He didn't love me enough."

"Not true. He loved you more than life itself. But his journey wasn't going to lead him to a proper relationship with you or anyone. His is to take a different pathway that he has yet to discover. When he does, his life's purpose will be fulfilled. The point is he made this sacrifice so you'd have the freedom to find love. Live love."

"Yes," said Birdie sadly, "but the bottom line is that he left on purpose." She sighed heavily. "Please tell me the specifics."

Ron sat next to Frank. "Matt had already begun preparations, but the so-called domestic shooting accelerated his plans. His life was in extreme danger. He believed that he couldn't live without constantly looking over his shoulder. If he were dead, he wouldn't have to. But he didn't like the government's requirement of turning over the evidence before getting his new identity. That's why he planned his own death. He and Jacob worked out the scenario."

"What was your responsibility in this mad scheme?" said Birdie.

"To do my job. Jacob and Matt did the makeup, set the scene. Jacob called the Sheriff. The rest you know. I did keep something out of the official report. You already know I found vials of methadone in the bathroom. Methadone usage is regulated by the federal government. Each vial is microprinted with a tracking number. So I did what I'd do in any investigation. I tracked the numbers. His doctor on record is the same as yours, Dr. Ryan, which is peculiar on its own. I learned that Ryan is the private physician of the entire Keane and Whelan families. He has no other patients."

"I could've told you that," said Frank. "Dr. Ryan and I are the keepers."

"In my world that looks suspicious, like the families have something to hide."

"He's a boutique doctor," added Birdie.

"Well the numbers weren't a match to Ryan as dispenser. Their origin is still unknown."

"Those methadone vials are another clue Matt left behind," said Birdie. "I bet you money that when my tox report comes back it will show methadone was used to murder me." She shook her head. It was a lot of information to process. "What about the photo I saw? There's a thermometer sticking from Matt's liver."

"Jacob released it as proof of death for those with unfriendly intentions. He didn't expect that you'd see a copy and he feels really bad."

"An optical illusion. What about the vomit and waste?"

"Oh, that was real. You don't want to know the process."

"The blood for the coroner?"

"Jacob drew a pint of blood, mixed it with a drug concoction and pre-loaded a heart syringe. Jacob used sleight-of-hand and I did a clever job of videoing what looks like an actual recovery of blood from the heart."

"This is so crazy. Who knows he's alive?"

"Just us."

"He used close friends he trusted."

"Matt didn't want to involve Parker," said Frank, "but we needed his services."

"He filed the burial certificate with the state," said Ron. "Neither Jacob nor I could falsify that document. Matt also didn't want to involve his brother, but a priest coming to retrieve his dead brother's body wouldn't seem suspicious."

"I'll be damned," said Birdie. "Matt thought of everything. Is there a money trail?"

"No," said Ron. "Nor a paper trail."

"Where is he?"

"We don't know," said Frank. "He made those arrangements himself. He has a new name, a passport, social security number, an entirely new identity. He didn't tell any of us. Safer that way."

"I can't believe its true," said Birdie. "Matt and I have a second chance. All I have to do is find him."

"You don't get it, do you?" said Ron, tension oozing from his pores. "Matt left you behind so that *you* and *I* could have a chance together." He pointed at her to drive the point home. "He. Left. You. Behind."

"Have you heard nothing we've said?" said Frank. "Don't you think he worked this through? He knew the consequences. He didn't walk away from you lightly. Do you think he wanted you to live an underground life? Away from friends, family, work? Never write another article or book? He loved you too much to put you there. Give him the benefit of doubt and know he made the right decision."

The words spoken so plainly stabbed her heart. She coughed out a cry.

Ron wrapped his arms around her. "He can never come back."

Her body shook and shuddered. The girl in her cried because Matt left her. The investigative reporter in her wanted to find him. And the woman in her was crushed because he didn't love her enough.

"When you were at Henshaw House and clutched that picture to your chest I witnessed the love you have for Matt. I've seen it in him. I've never experienced a love that deep. I wanted what Matt had. It was the *possibility* of you that was the motivator for agreeing to Matt's insane plan. Love is here. Wrapped around you." He whispered in her ear, "Let go. Feel it."

Birdie did feel the warmth of Ron's love. But would it ever be enough?

Birdie locked the bedroom door. She needed to escape, shut down. The whole of the world's experiences since January 6 crushed her. She couldn't process. She fell into the bathroom and locked that door, too. In a violent, wracking grief her body shuddered with spasms like dry heaves. She wept with incoherent rage. How could Matt do this? Whatever the boxes contained surely couldn't be bad enough to betray the woman you love and leave a life behind.

Birdie wasn't nearly ready to own the atrocities of her confinement, but she'd take a peek. She ripped the newsprint off the bathroom mirror, shrugged off the robe, stepped out of the flannel pajamas, and stared at her naked image. Madi was right; a textbook anorexic stared back, bug-eyed and shrunken with skin of kaleidoscope colors in huge overlapping patches. The image struck hard. Forget the drug overdose. She had taken such a horrific beating that she'd nearly bled to death from the inside.

She examined her once pretty face. She gently pressed the red cut across her cheek, felt the hard stitches underneath the red line. Even in its current state of medicinal immobilization and swelling she could foresee what the end result would be. A thin scar would bisect the right side of her face.

Birdie wondered where she'd find the courage to continue what she knew she had to do. Her own words to Eileen replayed in her head, "If you let it destroy your marriage, they win." *If I let them destroy my spirit they win. I will not end up a worthless piece of collateral.*

THIRTY-SEVEN

Sunday, February 5

BIRDIE SHUFFLED DOWN THE hall toward the service stairs. Yesterday after she locked herself away she ignored Ron and Frank's through-the-door pleas to come out and talk—or at least eat. Eventually they left her alone to process in her own way. Even now she felt their nervous strain hanging over the house.

Birdie had thought long and hard. She decided not to punish Ron or Frank or Jacob or Parker for a decision that rested squarely with Matt. When she rounded the corner and entered the kitchen she saw Ron shouldering the worry and guilt. He thought he'd lost her a second time—it was in his posture, etched into his face. But when he saw her concern for him in her expression, his smile was quick and it warmed her marrow. She went straight to him and hugged him, pressing her head against his chest; listening to the lullaby of his heartbeat. Ron held her and sighed with relief. She reached up and gently kissed him on the lips. She felt the press on the stitches, but there was no pain, just a slight tugging sensation.

"Thank you," he said, "I figured I'd be lucky to get a cold shoulder today."

"You're not responsible for Matt's choices. I don't like it, but I understand that you guys wanted to help. Besides, Matt could be very persuasive."

Birdie's stomach growled and Ron was quick to respond, having already put together the makings of skillet eggs. As he went about preparing breakfast, Birdie poured herself a cup of coffee and huffed and groaned her way onto a bar stool. Ron was already dressed in a pair of tan slacks and shiny black pullover. A tan and black checked jacket hung on the back of a chair.

"You look nice," she said. "What's up?"

"Nora called to make sure we'd be at the Manor after Mass."

Birdie had lost track of days and didn't realize it was Sunday. "I'm not ready for a public debut."

"Oh. Okay."

"I hear disappointment."

"I'm back on the job Tuesday and have stuff to get caught up. Louise and I bounce at dawn. I wanted to see your family before I left."

The blood drained from Birdie's face. Yes, Ron drove her crazy with his intense nursing and attention, but she'd begun to feel a rhythm when he was around—like a new dance beat she hadn't heard before. Just as well, she told herself. She had to put this business of Matt's behind her and finish the mission, but as long as Ron was around he'd make sure that she was distracted from the task. With him out of the way she'd be free of his over-protective-ness. No, she determined, his departure was a good thing. But she couldn't be over-enthusiastic or he'd get suspicious.

"Patrick's going to be there, too," continued Ron.

"I heard that you two got close while I was missing. Madi said that Dad partnered you two and assigned a city grid."

Ron busied his hands with toast. "I don't want to talk about that. But, yeah, we get along great. And with the Emmett situation he needs all the support he can get."

"How about after breakfast you help me with my exercises. By then Mass will be over and you could still go to the Manor. I'll be fine for a few hours. I've been thinking about trying to shower anyway and this'd be a perfect opportunity."

"I don't think I should let you shower for the first time without help."

"Come on, Ron. Have you learned nothing? Please stop treating me like an invalid."

Ron turned off the gas and scooped the eggs, peppers, and potatoes on top of the toast. He purposely dropped a bit on the floor and Louise scarfed it up immediately. "Okay," he finally said, "Only if you promise to use the grab bar."

Later that day Ron and Birdie sat in the library. She sat on the couch, rubbing Louise's ears as the dog snuggled against her thigh. Ron sat in the opposite chair going over the schedule. "The refrigerator's full with pre-made meals. Re-heating instructions are on the lids." He handed her a paper. "Here's the exercises you're to do and when to do them. Dr. Ryan wants you to drink two eight-ounce glasses of cranberry juice per day. It will help with kidney function."

As he went on and on Birdie wished she could tell him that she loved him back. Give him something to take away in payment for all he'd done for her and her family.

She just couldn't do it.

THIRTY-EIGHT

Monday, February 6

BIRDIE AWOKE WITH THE violent shiver of a nightmare. She rolled over and caught the time: 6:30 a.m. She picked up the phone and dialed Pearl's number, asked him if he could come back today to search her house again. He said he'd be by later. She pulled the covers tighter around her body and had just fallen back asleep when at straight-up seven the phone rang. She'd had the ringer off. Ron must've turned it back on before departing. He had recorded a message: *Good Morning, Birdie. Don't be mad at me for not waking you. You were resting peacefully for a change. But it's time to get up and eat. Today's breakfast selection is whole wheat pancakes, maple syrup, egg white scramble, turkey sausage, and an apple muffin. You may also have coffee or tea. Don't forget your exercises. Have a good day.*

Ron's cleverness made Birdie smile. Then the loneliness immediately set in. No cute dog padding down the hallway. No former

Marine to encourage her to stretch farther, lift a heavier weight. No one to force her to drink the prescribed cranberry juice. She already missed him.

She sat up on the edge of the bed and circled her ankles, slowly turned her head and stretched her neck side-to-side, rolled her shoulders. Mornings were the worse. Her muscles were stiff, circulation sluggish. At this time of day she felt like a ninety-year-old. She stretched her hands over her head and grimaced from the discomfort of the stretch against the ribs. Then she got up and gently swung them forward and back. Then she shuffled into the bathroom for her morning rust-colored pee.

By the time she ate breakfast and did the required amount of treadmill walking and the resistance and weight training, it was nearly ten before she entered her office. Pearl had already arrived and was diligently checking the house.

Birdie hadn't been keeping track of her sober days so she had to count them out on the calendar and rip off the pages until 269 appeared. She sat at her desk and bounced into the chair; her bony butt acutely feeling the mashed, practically nil padding from long hours of butt time. She powered up her computer and launched a de-bug program that detected any hidden and/or encrypted files that keylogged.

Her cell rang. *Time for a snack*, said the recorded message. *Greek yogurt. A pre-mixed topping of almonds, dried cranberries, and granola is in a baggie in the bread box. Don't forget your first serving of cranberry juice.* Now that her body was loose with the exercise she could walk to the kitchen almost normally. She downed the juice like medicine and ate the yogurt.

Back in the office she raised the screen covering the dry erase board. While her computer did its work, she reviewed the notes on the board. The convoluted math formula was no longer relevant. She knew what happened to Matt. The key worked a padlock at an undisclosed location she guessed to be at his property in Indio. The hidden evidence probably contained information on Paige Street as well as the Blue Bandits. She had yet to find out who had bugged her house. And the big question of the day... who was the ringleader of the kidnap crew and why did they take her? Because unless they questioned her while she was drugged and unaware they hadn't spoken to her. They sexually abused her and beat her, but why? Just for jollies? The third man, the company man, had a purpose. But what?

"My computer's clean," said Birdie to Pearl when he re-entered the office. "This anti-spy program you installed is really cool."

"Glad to hear it. Your house and car are squeaky," he said.

"I'm sorry to drag you out here for nothing."

"Tweety, don't worry none. Let me call Danny now and get you set up. Are you sure you want a web call? He's gonna be upset by the way you look."

"That's the point. My appearance will make an impact on his emotions."

"For the record, I'm against this manipulation of yours."

"Yeah, well if I hadn't been murdered this little manipulation wouldn't be necessary. Danny knows more then he's telling me and he must cough it up."

"You're playing hardball."

"Something he does every day."

"He has legal constraints."

"I have safety issues. Besides, I'm not here," said Birdie. "He's having a conversation with his brother who happens to be a trusted investigator on his payroll."

"I'm gonna catch hell for this."

Birdie could see the framed quote that hung behind Danny's head. It read: *I don't play politics with the truth*. He took a healthy swig from a bottle of Wild Turkey: 101 proof with a flavor of tobacco and molasses—Rotgut strong. Birdie had had her fair share of swills in that office. As if to honor that past, Danny nodded as he put the bottle back in his desk.

They'd been hooked up for nearly a minute and still he said nothing. He looked over her face as if reading a seismograph.

"You know," he finally said, "you really know how to pull the heart strings, showing yourself all beat-up and bruised and swollen just to get something out of me."

"You need to know about my abduction."

"I already knew. I didn't need to see your face."

"How could you have known?"

"Very little happens in this city without my knowledge. Just because your family can conceal details from the media doesn't mean it escapes my attention. The Irish Mob and one San Diego detective were tearing this city apart looking for something precious."

"Oh-oh," said Birdie, "I detect a preachy tone in your voice. The media is usually respectful to crime victims, especially when the victim is a member of a cop family."

"True. But they also love the gritty details when said family member breaks the law. As I recall, you've been on the other side many times and were still spared the watchful eye."

"Is Matt's unfinished business related to my abduction?" she said.

"That's tricky. Instinct says yes. On the other hand it's extremely personal. Your abductor wanted to control you. He needed you broken, passive. It's someone you know."

Danny was right. The third man never spoke. In case she survived? "Leave it to you to scare the crap out of me just when I'm resolved to finish this shit. They make Emmett Whelan for it. Any thoughts?"

"Emmett's not that stupid. Here's something that'll fry your brain. Why go to the trouble to set him up?"

"Jesus, Danny! Why indeed? He was being blackmailed. Maybe that's a message to all the other schmucks being blackmailed. Pay up or we'll tell your loved ones the truth and make you pay big time. So, Soto's dirty business is extortion then?"

Danny winced. "We're back to him are we?"

"Why the hell not? Matt and you were working together. It's been confirmed by a hidden message from Matt since we last talked. Soto was Matt's mentor. It's a classic tale of the pupil turning on the master. Come on, Danny. Do you want the stuff Matt hid or not? Please don't let what happened to me mean nothing. By God, there's got to be some good that comes from it." Birdie's eyes pooled with pain and grief.

Danny let out a quiet, tortured sigh. Then his eyes grew hard. "There are many reasons why this investigation was buried so far underground. I couldn't even get sealed warrants because of the threat of leaks. My job is to take the best case to my boss. One that is winnable. Let me stress that we'll only have one shot. If Matt's evidence is compromised in any way, it's over. We won't get another chance."

"I understand," said Birdie.

"Where's Pearl?"

"Here, bro," said Pearl, leaping up from the couch.

"I can't do this," said Danny, "but I certainly can't control what my brother might say. Elizabeth, I leave you with this warning, don't trust anybody." Then he turned off the webcam.

"Danny always makes me the heavy," said Pearl, slapping his head. "I hate this shit! Okay, buckle up, Tweety Bird. I'm gonna rock your world. Matt discovered that Soto is dirty. His partner is Deputy Chief Theodore Rankin and a third man of unknown identity."

Birdie took a deep, painful breath of excitement. "That explains Rankin's appearance at my house the night O'Brien showed up. Why don't you know the name of the third partner?"

"Matt never told Danny and he never directly referenced him. He even refused to give an explanation."

"I think I know. It's a family member. Matt didn't want to force me to divide my loyalties. But if Matt knew Soto was dirty, then why did he continue to work with him?"

"Soto let loose his prodigy early in the Paige Street investigation. He wanted to see how aggressive Matt would be and if he would manufacture evidence against Arthur."

"To protect the true Paige Street suspect?" said Birdie.

"Most likely. During his unofficial investigations Matt discovered Soto's true nature, but played along as long as he could. It wasn't until Matt moved the evidence that Soto knew Matt knew. Shortly after, Matt was ambushed on a domestic call. Danny doesn't think Soto was the triggerman, but he ordered the hit for sure. So, you see, Tweety Bird, Danny is just as anxious as you are."

This seems right, thought Birdie. Matt directed Reidy to deliver the personal boxes so that she'd be curious and find the letter with the clues. The grand goodbye and the delivery were designed to pique her inquisitiveness sooner rather than later. Anyone looking at the transaction from the outside would see a lawyer delivering personal effects. Except that's not how it happened. Because the whereabouts of the evidence boxes were unknown, Matt's personal boxes became the subject of speculation and inadvertently acted as decoys to flush out interested parties.

Birdie was spent with worry. Matt had left her with a devastating authority: the power to destroy her family, the power to further break down a police department, the power to destroy evidence.

She had the power.

How she'd wield that power had yet to be determined.

THIRTY-NINE

Tuesday, February 7

DAY 270. BIRDIE AND Detectives Seymour and Morgan huddled in the living room.

"You look much better," said Seymour. "How are you feeling?"

"Every day is better than the last," said Birdie.

"Glad to hear it. We'd like to clear old business before continuing. We've positively determined that the fugitive John O'Brien killed Martin Reidy."

"*Fugitive* O'Brien? Not unexpected, but I thought you had determined a connection with Reidy on January eleventh."

"You have a good memory," said Seymour. "The use of the same weapon didn't necessarily prove who pulled the trigger. We had a ballistics match; nothing more at that time."

"Do you have a motive?"

"Not at this time. Also, FID concluded that O'Brien shot himself."

"As expected."

Morgan pulled a document from his jacket. "We have a warrant for those boxes that belonged to Matt Whelan."

She didn't bother looking at the paper. "I already told you that the boxes are no longer in my possession. A warrant can't make them materialize, but you are more than welcome to search my home."

"Where are they?" said Seymour.

"Father Frank Whelan has them," she said. *Forgive me, Frank.* "Father Frank is ... was Matt's confessor as well as brother. He has the protection of privilege. I don't think any court could compel the release of personal property from a priest. Besides," she added, "I'm not sure what he did with them."

S&M communicated with nonverbal signals in a manner all partners share. She detected they weren't surprised. "We'll come back to that issue later," said Seymour. "During our investigation into your abduction, we found a room rented by Emmett Whelan at the Cecil."

The Cecil was a rundown, extended-stay hotel full of junkies, prostitutes, transients, and poor families. Its new owners refurbished the lobby and raised the rents in hopes of moving out the lowlifes and attracting tourists to downtown.

"The desk clerk positively identified Emmett from a six-pack as the man who rented a room. Inside were items relevant to the murders."

"Such as?"

Seymour looked at Morgan, who shook his head.

"Everybody's dead," she said, directing her comment to Morgan. "What harm can come of it? Are you going to put dead men on trial?"

"Okay," said Seymour. Morgan gave him a *why do I bother* stare. "Names, home addresses, work addresses, vehicle plate numbers and descriptions, photos of all the parties involved. O'Brien's fake passport, a boarding pass, clothing, maps of the city, cash."

"How much cash?" she said.

"A hundred K," said Seymour. "Money for a quick hit?"

"But not enough to kill yourself. Can't take it with, ya know?" Birdie didn't hide the sarcasm. "I gave Emmett a check for a hundred and fifty thousand dollars on the thirteenth. That was after Reidy's murder. My take is that he was being blackmailed. According to my bank statement, he cashed it the same day."

"Three days prior to your abduction," interjected Morgan.

"So what? It's all nice and tidy, isn't it? At the pump house, you happen to find three dead guys. At the Cecil, you find after-the-fact evidence pointing to Emmett. He was a cop, forcryingoutloud. Do you think he'd be dumb enough to house O'Brien? I bet you don't even have a credit card or cash receipt."

Birdie continued with a bit of flourish, "My guess is that Emmett used the money to pay off the blackmailer. That person planted a hundred as proof of Emmett hiring O'Brien and the other fifty was used to pay off the desk clerk. Oh, and let's not forget the probable anonymous tip leading you to the Cecil in the first place. In one swoop you have the perpetrator for Reidy's murder; O'Brien's death—because Emmett must be blamed for abducting me—one identified, the other not—and Emmett. It makes a complete circle. Emmett did it all!"

By the time Birdie finished, S&M stared at her as if she were a crazy woman.

"That was a grand demonstration, Miss Keane," said Seymour. "But we have other evidence. The gun recovered at the pump house was Emmett's service weapon. He was the only one that tested positive for GSR."

"Emmett was set up."

"Okay, here's a tidbit for you," said Seymour. "How can a person force a cop to shoot two men and then himself without a struggle? Emmett was ambidextrous. He shot left-handed, wrote right-handed. That's not common knowledge."

"I disagree. He wore his gun on the left side. That's a simple observation. But there's one piece of irrefutable evidence yet to be revealed. When the rape kit is processed, and the DNA doesn't match, how will you explain your hurry to convict a dead man for a crime he didn't commit? Murder is messy. Rape is messy. And yet, you show up at my door with a tidy package. It's much too convenient. What is the broader issue here? It's *why*. Why would Emmett hire a guy to break into my home and look through boxes that he likely could've gotten from his own brother?"

"Actually," said Seymour, "they were in the possession of Martin Reidy prior to Matt Whelan's death."

"So? It still doesn't answer the question."

"We go where the evidence leads," said Morgan.

"I know," she said. "But don't you think that two smart RHD detectives are being hand-fed a case? But like you said, you go where the evidence leads."

Morgan looked like he wanted to tell her off. Instead, he turned away.

Seymour said, "We're doing a courtesy by being here to give you an update."

She threw her hands up. "I appreciate that. It's just a little frustrating. How would Emmett know a jobber from Ireland? How would he know the guy from Louisiana? What is the connection? It's like a completed test with an A, but no one has bothered to check the answers."

Morgan snorted and shook his head.

"We know about the minor child," said Seymour. "Emmett was angry with you for telling his wife. He wanted revenge. He wanted you to suffer. During your captivity he became despondent and finished it off."

"There's a major flaw in your why. I didn't tell his wife."

"She's the one who told us you did."

"*What?*" said Birdie, dumbstruck. "Why would Eileen lie?" Was she so angry at Emmett for what he had done, or was she mad at Birdie because she knew about April before Eileen did? "Okay," said Birdie, "you're going to believe whatever you want. Just do me a favor. Get a subpoena for the local call log of my house from the phone company. You'll see that I never called her. And the closing date for my cell phone is the fifth, which means I'll have my bill in a few days. You'll see."

"We already have the records," said Seymour. He flipped through his portfolio of notes. "We have a call originating from your home phone to the Whelan household on Sunday, January fifteenth."

"Wait ... I called Eileen because Emmett was passed out on my lawn."

"And why was that? He was upset with you for telling his wife and he got drunk and confronted you. You had opportunities to call her previous to the lawn incident. You had been out that morning."

"Are you kidding me? I didn't tell her. Why would she say something that wasn't true?"

"Why does anyone lie?" said Morgan.

"We also have Deputy Hughes' statement," said Seymour. "He witnessed Emmett threaten your life later that same day. 'I really want to kill you right now.' Isn't that correct? And there were other witnesses: your father, Captain Keane, and his sergeant."

Birdie nodded in defeat. They wouldn't believe her, no matter how much she protested. Their minds were set. "You better leave now."

Seymour said, "We'll be in touch."

Morgan softened and gave her another of his pitiful smiles.

"Seymour," she said as she escorted them down the turret toward the front door, "tell me one thing, did you get an anonymous tip about the room at The Cecil?"

He turned and said, "Yeah. We did."

Birdie hobbled up the stairs to catch the ringing phone. She caught it before it went to voicemail.

She huffed out a breathless hello.

"What's wrong?" said Ron.

"Whoa. Hold on." Birdie wheezed until her breath grew shallow. "Sorry. I hurried to get the phone."

"Why were you hurrying?"

"I escorted S&M out. They just left."

"What did they have to report?"

"Evidence of Emmett's malfeasance."

"Credible?"

"After-the-fact from an anonymous tipster."

"Hum. The worst kind. How can you be so certain it wasn't Emmett?"

"Because the man was a smoker. Emmett's not. And there was a particular smell about the man that's … I don't know … familiar … but not. It's hard to say. I spoke with my ADA friend yesterday. He doesn't think it was Emmett either, but he says it's somebody I know."

"You already knew that … because of the personal nature."

"In my heart."

"What else is going on? Are you eating? Exercising?"

"Such a nag. By the way, the recordings were endearing the first day, but now they're intrusive and irritating and beginning to piss me off. Being helpful is okay, but I'm getting control vibes and that is the fastest way to chase me off. I don't live my life with a set of rules and a fixed schedule. I'll eat and exercise when it fits into my ev—" She almost said "evidence recovery plan," but she didn't want Ron to know that she'd hatched a plan. He was now in the men's gossip circle and she didn't want any babysitters.

"Yes?" said Ron. "When exercise fits into my what?"

"My everyday life."

"Which is, at least for now, rest, therapy, and recovery, so what are you up to?"

"Nothing strenuous. Matt's estate paperwork mostly. You know, paying bills, making arrangements for the sale of the Koreatown house." Birdie spent the next few minutes trying to convince him. By the time they disconnected she wasn't sure he believed her cover story.

FORTY

THE MOMENT BIRDIE PLACED the phone back in the cradle, it rang again. "What'd you forget?"

"*Gracias a Dios que he podido comunicarme contigo,*" said the frantic voice on the line. It was Denis' girlfriend, Mica. Birdie didn't have the energy.

"Mica—" Birdie protested.

In Mica's panic she reverted to her native Spanish; her cool and seductive voice hidden in angst. "*Es urgente. Necesito verte ahora mismo. Encuéntrame en Casa Cleary.*"

Not wanting a repeat of her breakfast with Denis, Birdie asked with trepidation, "*¿Estará Denis allí?*"

Mica started to cry. "*Ven ahora mismo. Necesito tu ayuda. Trajiste la llave.*" The line dropped dead.

"Why me?" said Birdie aloud. "Why now?"

Birdie's harsh treatment of Mica after the sex episode hadn't fazed her. So, her current distress had to be seriously big to rattle her. Maybe if Birdie comforted Mica, Denis would return the favor and consider forgiveness without conditions.

Good karma trumped Birdie's trepidation.

As Birdie backed out of the drive, a Crown Vic pulled in and blocked her departure. Thom jumped out from the passenger side.

She threw the Taurus into park and opened the door. "What's going on?"

George stepped out of the car, trying hard not to stare at Birdie's damaged body.

"What?" insisted Birdie.

Thom and George had a silent discussion. Finally, George said, "Denis is missing."

"That's why Mica's frantic. She just called me."

"Mica filed an MP. He's MIA for almost two weeks," said George.

"She's his handler, manages his life. Since when does she not know where he is? Better yet, why does she think he's missing?"

"She had him scheduled for a hitch," said George. "When Denis didn't return and wouldn't answer his cell she contacted the customer. Apparently, he never showed for the assignment. She called the airport and was told that his helicopters were grounded. And he's missed an important meeting."

"Oh-kay," said Birdie. "Why are you here?"

"You two were close at one time," said Thom. "We thought you'd like to know."

"Fine," she said. "You drive. Mica wants me to meet her at Casa Cleary."

From the cramped back seat, she said, "There's an entire division for missing persons. Why are you two involved?"

"My sister, Gloria, works in that division," said George. "She came across the name and thought it sounded familiar."

"Why would she know the name?" said Birdie.

"I may have mentioned the name in reference to you," said George.

"And George thought you'd like to know," added Thom. "He tried to call, but the line was busy and you never pick up call waiting. He thought about coming over, but didn't want to come alone in case the new boyfriend was still here."

"You lie," said George.

She had to smile. Cops were the biggest gossips *and* the biggest babies.

"It's likely Mica didn't know you've been indisposed of late so I wonder why she didn't try and reach you prior to now," said Thom.

"Notifying the ex-girlfriend was probably a last resort," said Birdie. "Denis cheated on me with her."

"He cheated on you?" said George, surprised.

"It didn't help that she tried to kill him," said Thom.

"That was after, and besides, the details of the incident are unclear," said Birdie.

"Right," said Thom.

"George, wait till you see Mica," said Birdie. "She's beautiful and even-tempered. Not at all like me."

"She can't be as beautiful as you," said George.

"Give it up, Georgie boy, Bird's out of your reach now," said Thom.

317

George shot Thom a dirty look, then looked in the rearview mirror to catch Birdie's reaction. She smiled. George smiled back.

"Tell me about Casa Cleary," said George.

"It's on a hill in Echo Park. Not far from Arthur's place. At street level there's a short driveway and a two-car garage, then up forty-two stairs to the house."

"Forty-two?" said Thom.

"Hey, I've been up and down them enough times to know how many stairs. Anyway, it's an authentic Spanish colonial with a gorgeous view."

By the time they arrived, they knew as much about Denis' house as Birdie did. George parked the CV against the curb. Thom opened the back door and helped Birdie out. Thom and George walked up the stairs as Birdie slowly hobbled behind. Mica sat on a step crying. She looked up at Birdie, seemingly incognizant of her damaged appearance. "Thank God you're here. *¿Trajiste la llave?*"

"What key?" she said.

"The key to house. Denis said you never return."

"*¡Cómo que no!*" protested Birdie. "Ages ago. Besides, you never said anything about a key." Or did she? *Llave*. Key. She had lost it during the translation. Didn't matter anyway, she didn't have it.

"*Señorita,*" said George, "*¿Es usted la que hizo el reporte de la persona desaparecida?*"

"Speak English," said Thom.

"Yes," said Mica. "I file report. My boyfriend, Denis, live here. I thought ex-girlfriend would have key to *casa*. I can't get in to check for him."

Thom and George exchanged looks. George nodded and headed back to the car and retrieved an apparatus designed to pop locks. Thom frowned as he followed George toward the house.

Mica took Birdie into an unexpected hug. "Thank you for coming. I'm so worried."

Birdie immediately felt suffocated. Mica held her too tight. Then she realized that she wasn't holding her hard at all.

It was her smell that bothered Birdie. Hemp oil. In her hair and on her skin.

Birdie pushed her off and Mica landed on her ass. She screamed. Birdie hyperventilated.

Thom and George rushed back down the stairs.

Birdie's body convulsed. She leaned over the edge of the stairs and vomited onto a blue agave. Thom rushed to her side and held her hair while she heaved.

"Bird," he said, his voice far away—in a cave.

"The smell," Birdie managed to wheeze. "That smell. It was on the man … the company man." She upchucked again. "Ohmygod … Denis. It was Denis."

Thom grabbed her around the shoulders and pulled her down the stairs. She stumbled. "Thom," she pleaded, wiping vomit from her mouth, "you're hurting me."

"Shut up," he said, dragging her farther down the stairs.

"Thom, please listen. It was Denis. Not Emmett. Stop."

"No," he scolded. "You stop." He grabbed her shoulders and squeezed. "Listen to me. Emmett was the third guy. End of story."

"No, Thom," she wailed. "It was Denis. I remember now. The man … the scent on his skin, hemp oil, it was transfer. Mica."

Thom slapped Birdie hard across the left cheek.

"OW," Birdie yelped. "Why—"

"Shut up."

George closed in. Thom pulled her body up and held it tight. He hissed in her ear, "Don't say a word. Hear me?"

"Birdie? Thom?" said George.

"She's sick George. That's all. Right, Bird?"

Thom held her hard by the shoulders. She felt her heart beating in her neck. She looked up at George, pleading silently for help. All she could manage was a nod.

George wasn't sure. "Birdie?"

Thom shushed in her ear.

"George … I'm okay."

"Good girl," Thom whispered.

George slowly nodded. "Okay then. Are we going to check the house?"

Thom said, "I'll take care of Bird. You check."

George turned and walked back up the stairs.

Thom led her down the last of the stairs and pinned her against the garage. He leaned his body against hers. It hurt, but she couldn't catch enough breath to tell him so. His face was flushed. "It's for your own damn good that you not repeat to anyone what you just said. Have I made myself clear?"

She nodded.

"Good." Thom kissed her cheek and released his grip.

Birdie crumpled.

Thom pulled her up. With the other hand he punched a number into his cell phone. "Hey," he barked, "You know where Denis Cleary lives? Get your ass here pronto. We have a problem."

She was tempted to scream out, but she'd never seen Thom this angry before and didn't know why her assertion set him off.

Mica tentatively made her way down the stairs, her eyes full of concern. "Birdie?"

Thom released Birdie's arm and gave her a knife stare. "English only."

"I'm sorry for pushing you, Mica. The sickness came on fast and I didn't want to vomit on you. I'm sorry about the mess."

"No worry," Mica said, then to Thom, "I stay with her if you want to help other policeman."

"No. Wait for Detective Silva on the lawn."

Mica huffed, turned and went back up. Birdie's legs gave way again. This time Thom helped her to the lower step. Feeling that she could pass out, Birdie leaned against the rail for support. Thom paced anxiously.

Birdie shut down. Nothing was as before. Thom's body turned into a shadowy vapor and there was a buzzing in the air like a beehive. The trees, the bushes, all the living things suddenly seemed evil. Life had turned against her. Her hands vibrated with a mesmerizing rhythm.

She couldn't fathom the amount of hate required for Denis to abduct, abuse, and rape her. And if that weren't bad enough, he murdered her and dumped her naked body on a city street.

The wicked world spun faster as if to throw Birdie off.

"Well?" said Thom, his voice bringing her back to reality.

George arrived with Mica in tow. "Denis isn't in the house or on the grounds. No sign of a struggle. His girlfriend has the remote code for the garage."

"She has the code to the garage, but not a key to his house?" said Thom.

George looked at Mica.

"Sometimes I drive car here when he goes away for long time." She punched the code on the keypad. The wood door slowly rolled upward. Denis' Saab was parked inside. George motioned Mica to stand near Birdie. He entered the garage, checked the car and trunk. Sans Denis.

Arthur screeched to a halt in his F-250, exactly like Matt's except for the color. He was pissed about being ordered around by his brother. Thom took Birdie's arm and urgently walked her to the idling truck, opened the door and pushed her in the front seat. Arthur wore workout clothes, no shoes, and he was covered in sweat. He hated when his workouts were interrupted.

Thom belted Birdie into the seat and leaned toward Arthur. "Your cousin here swears she remembers that it was Denis who was the third man. Not Emmett. Says she remembers a smell. Denis is missing."

Arthur nodded in confirmation and accelerated. Birdie attempted to look back at George, but Arthur scolded, "Keep your eyes forward."

"Did you and Thom set up Emmett?"

"Don't be stupid," Arthur said. "We didn't set him up."

"You were blackmailing him about April."

"Not true."

"But you knew about her."

"So."

"Thom's reaction to my declaration is indicative of the truth. He slapped me and pinched me and threatened me."

"Bird, I'm sorry for Thom's inappropriate behavior." Arthur was uncharacteristically cool. "Emmett was his friend—have some compassion for the way he must feel."

"That doesn't make any sense! And don't talk to me about compassion. The Whelans are our friends. Our second family. We owe it to them to support Emmett. I don't understand why no one besides the victim is speaking out against the injustice."

Arthur glared.

"If you found out that Thom was involved in something illegal, would you tell?"

"No," he said.

"You think I should do the same?"

"Thom hasn't done anything illegal, but let's say he did. Then, yes, I think you should keep your mouth shut."

"Is that what you and he are asking me to do in regards to Denis?"

"Yes. But for a different reason. We're concerned about your safety. If you were to start mouthing off about Denis—"

"If Emmett's guilty, then why would it matter what I say? Why do you and Thom care so much?"

"It's clean. Who knows what else Emmett was involved with. Or with whom. You're safer to say nothing."

"You're full of shit. The bottom line is that Denis was the third man, the company man, the ringleader, and he's unaccounted for."

FORTY-ONE

BIRDIE YEARNED TO KICK Denis in the nuts with her steel-toed Wolverines and ask him how he liked drinking cranberry juice and pissing blood. Then she wanted to shoot him in the balls and watch him bleed to death. But too soon the bravado vanished. Alone and uneasy in her big house Birdie jumped at the slightest sound. She checked every window, door, and slider at least three times and carried the loaded Sig in the pocket of her robe. She put off the inevitable as long as she could, but she finally caved and called Ron, hoping his rum-infused voice would put her at ease.

He answered in an abrupt whisper. "I'm in the middle of something," he said, "I'll call you back."

"I know who the company man was."

"Hold on." After a minute of muffled conversation, he came back. "Who?"

"Denis Cleary."

"The boyfriend before George?"

"Yes, and he's missing and his girlfriend called me and I went to his house with Thom and George and her scent triggered the memory of his smell and I had a violent reaction—"

"Slow down, babe. Take a breath."

"Thom and Arthur want me to hush it up. Today's confrontation confirms that one or both of them are a part of this."

"Maybe it was another man with the same smell."

"It was him. No doubt."

"I'm sorry doesn't cover what you must be feeling."

"When Denis shows up, we'll get a blood sample and check it against what was collected. That will prove me right."

"What if he used a condom?"

"I don't think he did. Besides, in a rape exam they comb for foreign hairs and stuff." She stifled a cry and tried to push the thought away.

"Being right doesn't help if he's unaccounted for," he growled. "He or his cronies already murdered you once. I'm coming up."

"NO." The word surprised her. She'd been frightened since Arthur brought her home, and yet, as soon as an offer of assistance presented, she no longer wanted it. "And don't call my dad and have him send a cop over for protection. I need to get through this on my own."

"I'm not comfortable with you being alone and him on the loose."

"I'm locked in. I'm okay, I promise."

When she hung up the phone, she burst into tears. What a liar.

Late that evening Birdie lay in bed clutching the Sig to her chest. She looked up at the glow-in-the-dark stars and prayed for the courage to get through the night. When the doorbell buzzed, she sat straight up and wide-eyed. Ron must've come to town after all. She wrapped a throw around her shoulders and tiptoed down the two flights. She spied out the peephole. George stood on the stoop, flooded in light from the motion detector. She opened the Judas hole.

"What are you doing here?" she whispered.

"I wanted to know that you're okay."

"Are you with Thom?"

"I'm solo."

She opened the door. At the second floor landing, he rubbed the head of St. Joseph, as he always did.

She curled on the sofa, keeping the robe pocket open and thus the gun handy. George sat in a chair, resting his arms on his thighs. He should say something. She should say something. But they sat there and said nothing. She wished that Ron hadn't taken Louise home with him. The diversion of a cute dog would cut the awkward silence. As it was, the only sound in the room was the quiet ticking of the mantle clock.

"What do you want to know?" she finally said.

"Nothing you don't want to tell."

"You make Emmett for it?"

"It doesn't matter what I think."

"What about Denis? What's up with that?"

"He's an LAPD contractor far enough up the food chain to be a priority. He'll be found."

"Dead or alive?" she said.

"I don't think any of us will ever see Denis again."

"Good riddance."

"Is that how you feel about me now that you've got Ron?"

"I'm fond of you, and I was happy while we were dating. The thing is … I don't know."

George looked at her incredulously. "Tell me what happened between you and Thom."

"I was sick. I guess the Denis thing upset me more than it should."

"You're a liar. I saw Thom's handprint on your face."

"I've said all I'm going to say."

"Is there something I can do?"

"Actually, yes. Will you sleep on the other side of my bed?"

"You never let me in your bed and now that we're not together I get to stay?"

"You're right, it's a crazy request. I can't explain it." Sure she could. She didn't want to be alone.

George took her hand and led her upstairs. He tucked her into bed, flipped off the hall light and slowly moved to the other side of the bed. He sat on the edge for a long time. Some time during the night he eventually lay down.

FORTY-TWO

Wednesday, February 8

DAY 271. THE DAY Birdie had planned to launch her evidence recovery plan.

At six a.m. Birdie awoke alone. George left a note next to the clock. *Call me if you need anything. Love, George.* His absence was a good thing. One, she had a schedule to keep and didn't want to kick him out after he'd graciously agreed to stay. Two, she'd have plenty of time for breakfast and the required exercise before departing.

Birdie couldn't believe her stupidity. She'd been so overwhelmed with the Denis thing that when Arthur delivered her home she scurried inside and locked herself in. She never moved her car off the driveway to the security of the garage. It sat on the driveway all night. *They* could've had complete access and privacy in which to place another tracker. A massive wall covered with ivy separated her property from the neighbor's on the right side. Waist-high hedges on the other side of the drive separated it from the lawn. The landscaping provided cover for someone with unfriendly intentions. She didn't want to impose on Pearl for a third time.

Time for plan B.

She needed new wheels for the cargo that others were willing to kill for. She couldn't trust her cousins. She could rent. But rental companies had trackers on their vehicles to keep tabs of their property. No, she wouldn't take chances. She'd err on the side of paranoia. What to do? She had emergency cash. And she knew where to spend it.

She drove to parking lot C—long-term parking—at LAX and left her Taurus. She caught the airport shuttle and disembarked at the always-busy Tom Bradley International Terminal. She walked inside, mingled with the crowd, then casually strolled to the curb and took a place in the taxi queue.

Business at Mario's Car Sales was brisk today. Mario and his family were parishioners at St. Joseph. Birdie had known the family for years.

She waved at Mario as he concluded a sale with a young couple. She cruised the lot to determine vehicle choices and found an older model Chevy van with an airbrushed desert scene painted on the side. Perfect. When Mario finished, he greeted her like an old friend.

"My favorite reporter," he said, squeezing her arms. He studied her damaged face and frowned. "*¿Cómo estás? ¿Te pasa algo?*"

"*Peilgro,*" she said. "I'd like that Chevy van. I can pay cash. *Sin trámites. Sin preguntas. No estuve aquí. Si no lo puedes arreglar, lo entiendo.*"

Mario agreed immediately to her proposal of cash. No papers. No questions.

Birdie made him promise not to mention that she'd been there. In the worst-case scenario he'd have her cash and could file an insurance claim for theft if she didn't return. She stepped up into her new wheels and started the engine. The Chevy rumbled to life. She eased the van out onto the street and headed for the freeway.

Less than two hours, three freeways, and one highway later, she checked into a Polynesian-styled hotel on East Palm Canyon Drive in Palm Springs.

Birdie knew what to expect in regard to Matt's property. She had used one of her many database subscriptions to access the Riverside County Assessor's office to locate the address of the property Matthew Whelan paid the taxes for. Then, with a few keystrokes, an overhead satellite image of the property could be found. And a street view, too. With time and anonymity on her side she decided to check it out personally.

Indio was located in the southern desert of California with the distinction of being the first city in the Coachella Valley. The old slowly succumbed to the new as a cheap housing market for retirees and weekenders spread from hip Palm Springs to the golf course-heavy communities of Palm Desert and Rancho Mirage.

The property wasn't a house. It was a big chunk of agricultural property at the edge of the city. Date palm stumps in neat rows were all that was left on the eastern half. On the western half, cultivated rows contained giant green tumbleweeds. The abandoned farm was surrounded by houses on two sides. A major thoroughfare lay on the third side. More houses and a date packing plant with a tourist store were on the fourth.

Located inside the compound, directly across the street from the packing plant, were a series of wood-slatted buildings; the blue paint faded from the desert heat and sun. Near the single-story buildings were hundreds of wood crates stacked in columns. Large crates. Four stacked together were taller than the hurricane fence, topped with razor wire, which enclosed the entire plot. Four large barrels of liquid were at the far end of the closest building. Birdie drove slowly around the perimeter of the property and stopped to take pictures from the window. There was one entrance. A gate held together with a heavy chain and a large lock. She saw no vehicles or signs of life. There was one large wire to the property. Probably electricity.

After another pass, she drove to the date farm and tourist center and headed into the store.

There were lots of cars in the front parking lot, but not many people inside. A plethora of date food products, nuts, dried fruits, culinary crap, and tourist souvenirs packed the store. She walked over to a deli counter and asked an old man, "Where are all the people? The lot is packed."

"On a tour of the packing plant. Busy this time of year, ya know. National Date Festival and all." He pointed to a poster that advertised the ten-day event. Right next to it was a poster for the upcoming Coachella Music Festival. "It's a big deal around here," the man continued. "Brings in two hundred thousand visitors during the whole festival. The music brings in even more." He scratched his chin.

"Do you know anything about the property next door? I'm in the market."

"It used to be a date farm. The owner died and the place was bought and sold a few times. It's closed now. Some developer is trying to buy it. Build more houses, ya know."

She had to credit Matt. The man could sniff a good business opportunity. He bought a huge chunk of land, sat on it, waited for it to appreciate.

"Have you ever met the owner?"

"Nope. Get my information second-hand. The owner should sell though. It's worth millions."

"Do you know the developer?"

"Naw. But it's probably the same company that built the houses on the other side."

"Anyone work there?"

"Not that I've seen."

"How long have you worked here?"

"Four years."

"In four years, you've never seen anybody over there?"

"Doesn't mean no one ever does. I just don't see it, that's all."

Birdie bought a bottle of water and thanked the man for his time.

She leaned against the outside wall. Studied the property. A dark shape ducked behind a stack of crates. She watched a big black dog emerge from the other side. The man may not have seen anybody in four years, but someone must feed the guard dog.

Birdie drove back toward the center of town and dropped into a drug store. She used the self-help digital processing machine to develop the pictures. Then she went to a grocery store and bought a hunk of meat for the dog.

Back in her hotel room she compared the photos and the printed satellite images to the blueprints. She pieced together the layout. It fit quite nicely. The stacked fruit crates were outlined on the blueprint as new construction. The existing buildings matched. But there was one crucial feature missing. A pool. None was visible from overhead or from the street. She hoped all the computer research and surreptitious activity led her to the right place. All she could do at this point was pray that she hadn't got it wrong.

At ten p.m. Birdie was wide awake, lying on a too-soft bed with a too-fat pillow. She couldn't get comfortable. Intrusive thoughts of her captivity and Denis' role kept creeping into her brain. The minutes ticking past on the clock just made her more agitated. So she made a call.

"Silva," answered George.

"Did I wake you?"

"No, I just got home. Been working all day. What are you doing?"

"Calling to say thank you for staying with me last night."

"You're welcome. Where are you? Your cousins are looking for you."

"I know. They've been leaving messages on my cell."

"Thom wants me to call if I hear from you."

"I don't want to be found."

"Going to tell me where you are?"

"No."

"Hold on. Someone's at my door." George put the phone down and Birdie didn't hear anything for a moment. Then she heard shuffling. George cussing in Spanish. A Caucasian voice cussing in English. The conflict moved closer to the phone. It sounded like a fight. She heard a crash like a fallen lamp, a body slammed against furniture, cluttered noise, objects being broken. Then she heard a sound she knew too well. A gunshot.

She covered her mouth and suppressed a cry. Then the call dropped.

She screamed into the fat pillow.

Her cell rang.

"OHMYGOD. What the hell happened?"

"Birdie?" said Ron. "Why aren't you at home? What's wrong?"

She screamed at him. Told him something about being on the phone, a home invasion, fighting, a gunshot. Get help for George!

"Give me his address. I'll take care of it," he said in a calm voice.

She rattled off the address.

"I'll call you back. Don't answer for anybody but me. No matter what." He rang off.

How far was this going to go? Did someone else have to die?

FORTY-THREE

Thursday, February 9

DAY 272. AT 4 a.m. the vibrating cell phone shook Birdie from slumber. She couldn't believe she'd actually fallen asleep. It was Ron.

"George is going to be okay."

"What happened?"

"Two guys came to his door looking for your whereabouts. He was caught by surprise. Mostly his pride is hurt. He took one in the abdomen with his own damn gun in his own damn house. It was a clean exit."

"This is my fault," said Birdie, holding the phone away from her mouth to swallow the guilt that lodged in her throat. "He came by to check on me after I got sick at Denis' house. I asked him to stay. I never thought that it would put him in danger."

"Yeah, he told me you'd feel responsible."

"You spoke with him?"

"I've seen him. I'm here in L.A."

"Why would they go after George? What does he have to do with this?"

"Nothing. I suspect your house is being watched. They saw him arrive late, leave early, and go straight to work. The first opportunity to catch him alone was when he went home."

"What about Arthur?"

"No one knows where he is. George told me that Denis is missing. I didn't tell him I already knew."

As Birdie gathered gear together and stuffed it into her backpack, she confessed to Ron all the details about her evidence recovery plan.

"I knew you were lying! I never should've left you alone!"

"Calm down. I'd figure out a way to get this done anyway."

"You're in no shape to take this on alone. I'll meet you."

"No. I need you to stay. Keep my cousins diverted. I don't know for certain that the evidence boxes are here. I know you're worried. But please, please, I need your support right now, not your condescension."

"Look, Birdie, I'm impressed by your abilities as a journalist to dig deep at stories and uncover the truth. To keep you safe is asking you to deny who you are and what you're compelled to do. But this is dangerous. Don't you see?"

"You must respect my independence. I have to do this. Sooner rather than later. I won't be able to heal until this is behind me."

"Do you honestly think your life will magically return to normal if you do?"

"Tell me, Ron, what's normal?"

There was a long silence before Ron finally said, "Assure me again you didn't tell anyone about Matt's property."

"No one."

"Let's hope the damn boxes are there. Do you want me to call your ADA friend?"

"No. He has to stay completely clean."

"Keep a low profile. Don't answer your cell unless it's me."

"Understood." She double-checked the backpack contents, scooped up the recon photos, opened the mini fridge and grabbed the meat. Her senses worked at a heightened level. She felt the adrenaline pump through her veins, firing nerves, making her feel like she could fly. At that moment she could conquer anything.

"Go now while it's still dark," said Ron. "Kill the headlights before you get to the property. Park the van out of sight. Get in, get the boxes, get out."

"I know what to do."

"Do you have your Sig?"

"Loaded and ready to go."

"Do you have a flashlight?"

"Stop it. I have a flashlight."

"Be smart. Be safe. Don't do anything stupid."

As Birdie hung up the phone, she was glad she hadn't mentioned the guard dog. He'd really go off on that tidbit.

FORTY-FOUR

BIRDIE CAUGHT ALL GREENS and pushed the van to nearly eighty mph on Highway 111. She parked on the street near the farm. It was dark, but there weren't any darker shadows lurking. She got out of the van and pulled on the padlocked chain securing the gate. Reluctantly, she turned on the flashlight and held it between her throat and chin and flipped through Matt's keys until she found one that looked right. Not the right one. She tried another. And another. One more. This time, the padlock popped open with a slight tug. As quietly as she could, she unwound the heavy chain and pushed open the gate. She drove the van through and wrapped the unlocked chain back around the fence.

She visualized the layout from the photos she'd studied. Straight ahead was a stack of fruit crates four high. Behind them were two more. On the right, crates were stacked eight high. She gently steered the van to hide it behind the taller stack. She backed it between two stacks. She slung the backpack over a shoulder, checked the gun under her left arm, grabbed the Maglite, rested the meat on top of the pack.

Okay doggie. I'm ready for you.

She stood still, listening, and allowed her eyes to adjust to the darkness. Dawn would break soon. Taking a deep breath, she crept from crate stack to crate stack until she was closer to the farm's buildings. According to the blueprint there was a pool. That's where she wanted to start. It was the Big Kahuna clue. Was there one here? With her back to the nearest building she moved farther away from the street.

On the left was an unmistakable light shining from underneath a door. She squatted to look under, but couldn't get the angle. She knelt down on her knees, lowered her torso forward against the ground and pressed her damaged cheek into the dirt.

She peered under the door but didn't see anything except bright artificial light. Then she heard it. The sound of a dog sniffing. A big black nose explored the bottom of the door. It started to growl. A man's groggy voice said, "What do you smell boy? Got yourself a rat?" The dog started barking.

The light was extinguished.

The man on the other side of the door probably knew the layout of these buildings better than she. Birdie got objective with her situation. What were the options? One: she could wait for the man to come out. Two: there could be another door and the man would come in behind her. Three: he was waiting for her to enter. Four: he could have taken off, leaving the dog. Five: she could turn and run like hell.

She went with five.

Birdie dumped the meat out of its plastic bag and ran. She wasn't even to the first crate stack when the door creaked open and the dog ran after her, ignoring the select piece of meat. She decided to run toward the van. Thirty yards at most. It never occurred to her to turn and shoot the dog following her. She ran around a crate stack and another until the back bumper came into view. Just when she thought she'd make the van, the dog clamped his mouth on the heel of her steel-toed Wolverine boot. He brought her down. She rolled over to reach for the gun tucked into the holster under her left arm. Just as she got her hand on the grip, the dog jumped up on her chest. She was certain the dog was going to tear her face apart. She screamed bloody murder.

Then she heard the pumping of a shotgun and the words "Don't move."

A dark figure stood behind the gun.

It's not like she had anyplace to go. A big-ass dog was on her chest, his teeth inches away from her face.

She challenged the man. "What the hell are you doing?" she demanded.

He chuckled. "What the hell are *you* doing? Can't you read?"

"Read what?"

"The signs on the fence. They say private property, no trespassing."

Of course. "That's right," she said with as much authority as she could muster. "I own this property. You're the trespasser."

The man commanded the dog to retreat. It took a position three feet away and bared its teeth in a perverted dog grin. "Git up," the man said. "Toss the pack. Put your hands on your head." She did as told. He took her gun and pack, then motioned with the shotgun and marched her back. "Open the door and slowly step into the room," he said. "Turn on the light."

"What about the dog?"

"Don't worry 'bout the dog."

She felt the wall for the switch. She squinted into the light and turned to face him, slowly backing farther into the room, hands still up. The man was maybe twenty-five, shaved head, dragon tattoo on his neck, no facial hair. Probably had a mug shot.

"What's your name?" he said, gun still pointed at her chest.

"None of your damn business."

"Lady, let's git on with this. What's your name?"

What did she have to lose? "Birdie Keane," she said.

"ID?"

She ticked her head toward the backpack hanging off his arm. "In there. Front pocket."

He put both guns on a table and held up his hand in warning. He pulled out a passport and compared the image with the one standing before him. "I'm Warren. I've been expecting you for weeks. What took so long?"

"I don't know you," she said, relaxing a bit. "What are you talking about?"

"I'm the caretaker. Was told that a woman named Birdie would be coming to git something." He tossed the backpack to her and she hooked it over her shoulder.

She looked around the small square room. It contained the basics: a cot, table, two chairs, a mini fridge, microwave, a plastic water jug on the edge of the table. The dog sat at attention, eyes glued on her. He had picked up the meat and it sat nearby; ready to be eaten when given permission.

"Who's your employer?" she said.

"Don't know. I git a check from a lawyer in Beverly Hills. Look lady, just git what you need. I wanna go home."

"Show me where."

Warren shrugged his shoulders. "I don't know what you want. Or where it is."

She anxiously studied Warren. He looked untrustworthy, yet she needed to believe that Matt had arranged for him to protect the property until she arrived.

"Okay," she said, "Is there a swimming pool on the property?"

"An empty one. I'll show you."

The pool was covered with a massive desert camo tarpaulin rendering it invisible to the satellite. With Warren's help they rolled it up.

"Start packing," said Birdie.

Warren gave a nod and turned toward the building. Before her was a classic kidney-shaped swimming pool with about a foot of muck at the bottom. Now what? She leaned on her knees and sat back on the heels of her trusty boots. She spread the blueprints on the dirt and flipped the pages. She didn't understand. The buildings, pool, and crate stacks were on the blueprints, but where was the evidence? She looked around in all directions. Crates. More crates. She didn't bother inspecting them; Matt would've protected the evidence from the elements.

She studied a decrepit tractor: an old John Deere row-crop that had once been bright green. She climbed up in the seat and pressed the start button. Nothing. Not like she could start it anyway. She didn't have the key. Or did she? She pulled out Matt's key ring and looked for an uncommon one. There was an extra long one with a rubber cap. She removed it from the ring and poked it into the ignition and turned the key to the right. She pressed the start button again and the tractor thundered to life.

Warren came out to watch, shotgun over his elbow, broke open in safe position. He stood next to the tractor and yelled, "I figured this thing didn't work."

"Just because something is old and rundown doesn't mean anything. Where's the dog?"

"Eatin' his treat. Do you know how to drive it?" he said.

"It has a clutch and gears. How hard can it be?" She gripped the gearshift and ground it to what she believed was first. The tractor argued and spat out black smoke, but it slowly jerked forward.

Warren turned his interest behind the tractor. Buried under the ground, a heavy chain attached to the back of the tractor snapped out of the dirt as the vehicle moved. It was attached to a large metal plate that slid forward to reveal an opening in the ground.

Warren ran toward the plate and disappeared. He popped back up and came out shouting. "It looks like a bomb shelter."

"What's down there?" Birdie said anxiously.

"A door with a lock."

The second padlock.

She turned the tractor engine off and was about to get down when Warren snapped the barrel of the shotgun in place. Damn. Her gun was on the table. "I'll take it from here. I know you have the key. Gently now. Toss it down."

"You're double crossing the man who's been paying you?"

"Stupid shit, I was told to take whatever it is you find."

Soto. He knew she had the key. How did Soto know about the Indio property? Did Matt tell him? Maybe when they were still friends? No. If that were so, Matt would've hid the boxes elsewhere.

"I changed my mind," said Warren, his eyes growing squinty. "Git down nice and slow."

How did Soto know about the property? She'd seen him twice recently. At the EZ-Stor and later at Kipling's. Prior, at the Westend on the night of her dinner date with her dad.

"Git your ass down here," hissed Warren. "I'm not gonna ask again."

Something snapped inside Birdie. She had had enough. Like a sudden injection of a warrior gene she felt the rage pump through veins, servicing every nerve, muscle, tendon. She channeled all the hate and sized the distance. Warren was close. But not close enough. She held the steering wheel with her left hand for support and reach. "Okay," she said. "I'm coming." She pretended to slip sideways. Warren jumped forward in a reflexive move to save her from falling. Those few extra inches were all she needed. She swung her right leg with super strength rage. The toe of her boot caught him on the chin with such force that she heard his jaw crack. His head spun and his body slowly slumped. She didn't give him a chance to recover. She jumped off the tractor and with both feet, smacked him square on the chest.

Birdie scrambled for the shotgun and rolled over and over until she was far from him. She jumped up and pointed the gun at his head. He didn't move. She kicked him in the side. Blood and dirt covered his face.

She didn't take any chances. Retrieving a roll of duct tape from her backpack she wrapped it around his left hand several times then twisted the roll again and again until she had fashioned duct tape handcuffs. She repeated the process with his feet. Only when she was certain he couldn't move did she check his pulse. Alive, but unconscious.

She didn't know how much time she had. While she'd farted around with the blueprints, he could've called Soto from a cell phone. The threat of someone arriving thrust her into overdrive.

FORTY-FIVE

Birdie flipped on the Maglite and inspected the opening. Steep concrete steps led to a small ante chamber. A thin layer of dirt covered the concrete walls. A metal door with a thick iron bolt across the front was secured with the EZ-Stor padlock mate. The key that she'd been carrying around was finally going to unlock a secret.

Her hands shook with stress. When she managed to slip the key into the lock it snapped open and she pushed the door open. A loosely woven camouflage net covered eight coolers of various colors and sizes. Each wrapped with evidence tape and signed by Matt. Additionally, each cooler was bound with one or more metal straps like the Postal Service use to seal mailbags. Each strap had a dated seal. Birdie could only speculate as to the exact contents of the boxes. What she did know was that someone was willing to kill for the contents and Matt gave up his life to protect them.

Ringing in her ears signaled that her brain had caught up with the agony she just put her emasculated body through. She wondered how she'd get the coolers up the steep steps. Just then, the cell phone in her back pocket vibrated. She went up the steps to answer.

It was Ron. Urgency in his voice. "Denis is dead."

Birdie felt off balance. She'd been taught to forgive-and-forget and to forgive those who trespassed against her. But now, she could not grasp these righteous attributes. Not only could she not forgive Denis—there was a part of her that was happy.

"I have something to say," continued Ron. "It'll be difficult to hear. While you were missing, I witnessed your dad reload shotgun shells in his garage. He had four of them. They were pink with yellow stripes. Unique. Gerard told me they were for the sonsofbitches who took his daughter. One was found concealed in the brush near Denis' body."

Gerard taking revenge against the man responsible wasn't hard to hear. What father wouldn't do the same for his daughter? "Are you telling me that my dad murdered Denis?"

"You'll have to come to your own conclusion."

"Tell me everything."

"The body was recovered less than a hundred yards from Denis' house by a neighbor's dog. It was hidden in some brush. He's been dead awhile. The police are canvassing. Denis was shot more than once. So far the only evidence recovered at the scene was the one shell."

"Dead awhile?" she said, confused. "I only discovered myself that Denis was the company man the day before yesterday. The only way my dad would know is if Thom or Arthur told him. And that's not likely because they wanted it quiet. I don't care what you saw, or what he said while I was missing, Dad didn't do it. He couldn't have known it was Denis."

"I hope you're right," said Ron.

"Have you seen my dad since you've been in town?"

"No. Remember when I said no one knew where Arthur was? Well, he called Thom to check in and said he was out looking for Gerard."

"Have you told anybody about the shell?"

"No."

"Good. Keep it to yourself. I have work to do. I found the boxes and I have a prisoner that might wake up any moment."

"Prisoner? What the hell?"

"Gotta go." She punched off before Ron could get in another word.

Pure instinct and presence of mind took over her emotions and actions. She had something to fix. She called her parents' house.

Maggie answered. "Gerard?"

"No, Mom, it's me. Where's Dad?"

"I don't know. Where are you?"

"I'm busy. I need you to do something important for me."

Maggie hesitated. "Okay."

"I'll walk you through it step-by-step. First thing I need you to do is go into the garage, pick up the extension and put it on speaker."

"Bird, what's going on?"

"Mom, time is vital. Please just do as I say."

"Okay. I'm in the garage. Picking up the extension and turning on speakerphone. Hanging up cordless. What next?"

"Put on a pair of latex gloves. Dad has a box on top of the filing cabinet. On the workbench is a gray plastic box with tiny clear drawers. Inside the lower left one is a key. Make a note how it's placed in the drawer and make sure you replace it exactly as you found it."

"Okay. Found the key."

"Unlock the padlock on the cabinet to the left of the workbench. Notice how it's hanging. Dad knows when someone has been snooping in his stuff."

"It's unlocked. Now what?"

"On the bottom shelf, on the far right is a brown coffee can. Open it up and tell me what you find."

"I remember these. You collected them on one of our deer hunting trips in Utah. You said they were pretty."

"Pink shells with two yellow stripes?"

"Yes."

"Count them. How many?"

"There are twelve."

Twelve. Birdie collected sixteen. Four were missing.

"Mom, you need to wipe down each shell with an oil rag. There's a clean stack to your right. Wipe the can, inside and out and don't forget the lid. Lock the cabinet and replace the key. You need to dump the can. Do you still get trash pick up on Thursday?"

"Oh! I haven't put the cans out yet."

"Good. Shake out the shells into a bag of garbage. Put the can in the recycle bin. Do it now, Mom, before the garbage truck comes. When you're done, take the gloves and put them in the cross shredder Dad has in the office. Collect the pieces and flush them down the toilet."

"Am I destroying evidence?"

"I don't know. Do it just in case." Birdie hung up.

Warren mumbled. He was coming to. She grabbed the tape rope around Warren's ankles and dragged him farther behind the crates. Her whole body screamed in pain. She had to drag, rest, take a breath, drag, rest, take a breath.

She squatted next to Warren's blood-encrusted face. "Who do you work for?"

He tried to say something.

"I suppose it's hard to talk with a broken jaw? See that van over there?" She took his face in her hands and turned his head toward the direction of the van. "I'm going to move it. If you squirm from this spot, I'll run over your head. Do you understand?"

Anger seeped from his eyes.

"Whatever you feel, times it by a hundred, and maybe you'll come close to what I've been going through."

FORTY-SIX

BIRDIE'S SUPERHUMAN STRENGTH WAS replaced by excruciating pain. Her weak body wasn't functioning. Nervous energy was the only sensation left. The immediate danger to her person had passed and without benefit of the adrenal hormone, she wondered how she'd muster the muscle stamina to get the coolers up the steep flight of stairs and into the back of the van. She rooted through the pack and found the in-case-of-emergency pain pills. She popped two and washed them down with the leftover water from the tourist center.

Time was no longer on her side. She didn't know if Warren had notified Soto, but she had to operate under the assumption he had. It was urgent Birdie find enough vigor to move the evidence. More importantly, she had to drum up the courage. Once they were loaded, she'd be on the freeway driving the van to the Criminal Courts Building to deliver them to Deputy District Attorney Daniel Eubanks. Soto and Rankin would likely go down for something yet to be revealed, perhaps Thom and Arthur, too. Her role? The destroyer of a cop dynasty. Or, she could cut the seals, contaminating the evidence, and become a tainted journalist.

Birdie wished there were a way to assign a value to love. How was she to balance her love for Matt with the love for her family? Were her feelings for Matt strong and deep enough to make her cousins suffer by finishing his work? Even the innocent of her family would be affected by the consequences. And the Whelans? The pain of losing Matt, and now Emmett—a son who was by all accounts a good cop, a husband, and father to four—would not be less.

She had a task to complete and if she took much longer to decide, the decision would be taken from her. And this, after all, was the gift and the power Matt left her. If she continued to stall, then surely Soto would show. And then what? Would he kill her and destroy the evidence?

Destroy the evidence. What did that mean exactly? Whose sins besides Soto and Rankin's would be buried? What would the final outcome be if she turned it in? Could she live with the thought that she helped further destroy the trust the citizens of Los Angeles placed in the LAPD—a department that has provided livelihood for her entire family? A department that had a history of corruption that no one would let it forget? Wasn't it time to move forward and forgive and forget? A motto to live by.

She had no idea how it was going to end, but there was one certainty: She had to be prepared to make a final decision and she couldn't do that until she took the first step.

The bright light of the Maglite illuminated the coolers. She tugged at the camouflage netting. What looked loosely woven and lightweight was actually stiff and heavy. It was a net of colored wires. Now she was in a bigger pickle. How would she remove the heavy net? She came across a round disc about the size of a hockey puck that had five thick wires coming from it. These led to another round disc and more wires. They stretched on and on around the entire bundle of clustered coolers like a giant Tinker Toy blanket.

Birdie fell back against the wall when she realized she was looking at a bomb. The coolers were rigged to explode. But why? Wasn't it her choice? How could she make a decision now? Surely, Matt would've left more instructions. She frantically waved the light around the room. On one wall he had written in black marker the same Latin words on the note that enclosed the padlock key: *Judex ergo cum sedebit, quidquid latet apparebit, nil inultum remanebit.* The Latin contained the answer. *Matt wants me to make every secret known.* Then why rig it to explode? There had to be another explanation.

Birdie searched farther into the room. On the far side of the bundle was a pair of wire cutters with a tag that read: cut blue wire to deactivate. Next to it was a covered box. She opened it to reveal a red button. Inside the cover of the lid was written: press to activate. Close door. 90 seconds to boom.

Birdie needed to think. She ran up the steps for fresh air. Warren was still in his spot, but she could see he had been working at his bonds. Didn't matter. He was secure. Birdie collapsed in the dirt. She lay there on her back, immobilized by fatigue and pain pills. She gazed at the brightening sky and wished she were safe in her bed looking up at glow-in-the-dark stars. She wanted to blink herself to a different time and place.

Time moved so swiftly it seemed not to pass at all and she was no closer to an answer to the question: What now? How long had she lain in the desert-baked soil? An hour? White clouds slowly collided. Two? The sun shone brightly and the dirt warmed under her body. Three?

Warren's screams woke her from the drowsy trance.

"What the—?"

The gate chain rattled. She jumped up.

"You little shit," she hissed, picking up the shotgun. "Who'd you call?"

He cackled.

She jammed her boot between his shoulder blades and pointed the gun at his head. "Give me a reason."

She could only hope that whoever was at the gate couldn't see the van. She dropped to the ground and slithered to the end of the row to see which direction the intruder was moving. A car slowly pulled forward in her direction and stopped. She jumped up, aimed the shotgun at the driver.

A man got out and waved.

FORTY-SEVEN

"Bird," said Gerard, "I've been worried. You went missing again. What are you thinking to be out here by yourself?"

Birdie gazed into her dad's vibrant clear blue eyes—strong eyes full of thought, concern, and love for his daughter. He took the shotgun from her hands and pulled her into a hug and gently rocked her. "Oh, this feels nice. I'm so glad I'm able to do it before the end."

It took a few seconds for Birdie to comprehend what he said. "What do you mean?"

Warren's screaming caught Gerard's attention.

"Did you do this?" he said.

"Yes, sir."

"Gerard … cut me loose," grumbled Warren.

Gerard? He knows my dad? He could talk the whole time?

Gerard stepped on Warren's neck. "Boy, you have a big mouth." He pulled a small caliber pistol from his jacket, and before Birdie's brain caught up with the visual, he fired one shot into Warren's head. The sound echoed in the stacked crates. Bright red blood slowly oozed from his skull. Warren's body froze in death.

The landscape morphed into the melting colors of a watercolor and slowly bled out of focus. Birdie's legs gave way.

Gerard toppled a crate stack and placed one upside down. He helped her to sit. He sat on another, across from her, lit a cigarette and dragged deep. He didn't speak as she tried to understand the events of the last five weeks. He allowed the reporter in her to put the facts in place and compartmentalize the brain files.

Pearl told her that there was an unnamed third partner in the Soto and Rankin triangle. He said Danny didn't know the person's identity. Matt never told him. Whether that was true or not didn't matter now because Birdie knew who the third leg was.

Gerard led her down a path by responding to her thoughts and theories the way any father would. He misled her by telling her untruths with a twinkle in his eye, as if he were speaking gospel. Why wouldn't she accept anything out of his mouth as anything but the truth? He was the teacher, the disciplinarian, the role model, the one she looked up to. They had an unbreakable love that could never be doubted. Even now, she didn't love him less. Gerard Keane's heart may be cold enough for murder yet it was warm enough for love.

It was there all along.

She just didn't see it.

Matt wanted to save Birdie from having to choose between her father and himself. How terrible it must have been for him when he found out who Gerard really was. How long did Matt know? When she thought about Matt's notations in his personal journals, the hints of her having to make a choice between him and family were there. It went all the way back to their sexually charged tussle in his new house. She was nineteen and Matt took himself out of her emotional life so she wouldn't have to make a choice. He made that one for her.

Matt encouraged her to date and took his sex elsewhere. But he couldn't fully let go. He was always in her life. They still did the things couples do—saw movies, ate at restaurants, went dancing, traveled together, shopped, they spent *time* together. They were a couple by all accounts; except they didn't speak about their emotional attachment nor did they have sex. Every one of their acquaintances knew about their love. And no one understood why they didn't take that last step to make it official. Except Matt. And Gerard. He knew why Matt kept his distance.

"You're the bad package," whispered Birdie.

Gerard simply nodded.

"How did this happen?"

Gerard looked up at the bright sky and wiped his brow. Looked over at Warren's lifeless body and frowned. "It's a long story, sweetheart."

"We've got plenty of time."

"Unfortunately for me, we don't." He pointed at the van. "You'll find out soon enough. I'm just here to say goodbye to my girl. I'm going to be dead soon." He took a shallow puff off the cigarette and snorted smoke out his nose.

"I don't understand."

"Keep going, Bird, riddle it out. Ask the small questions, because I don't have time for the big ones."

She wanted to know about the Blue Bandits. She wanted to know what would rock the LAPD. She wanted to know how many other men her dad murdered without flinching, and with no apparent moral dilemma. But she knew the coolers would contain those answers.

The coolers. Now she knew why they were rigged to blow.

The storm clouds of concealment parted and the sun shone on the answers. It was her dad, not Arthur, who was the at-large Paige Street suspect.

And it was she who filled in the blanks for her father when they met for dinner at the Westend. On the night that O'Brien rummaged through the boxes at her house, Gerard made sure she was out long enough for a search. They were supposed to meet for dinner. Not dinner and a movie. But during the conversation, he learned about the boxes and the property and persuaded her to stay out longer so that he or his partners could arrange for O'Brien to search the house. This meant he knew about Matt's evidence boxes beforehand. Just as Soto did.

"You were in with Antonio Sanchez to rob the Alvarado's on Paige Street?" she said.

"Yes."

"What happened to the money?"

"It's best you not know."

"Dad—"

He waved his hand in dismissal. "Keep going."

"S&M said O'Brien killed Reidy. True?"

Gerard nodded.

"But why? He didn't know what was in the boxes."

"We couldn't take that chance."

"Why didn't you just kill Matt?"

"You loved him. He loved you. You two were good for each other. Had circumstances been different, I really would've liked him as a son-in-law."

"Did you kill Denis?"

"Oh, boy. If you know about Denis then I have less time than I thought. I made a promise that I was going to get the bastard responsible. I screwed up. I used those pretty shells you collected in Utah. Figured it'd be divine justice. Recovered three out of four. Ron saw me reload those shells. I shouldn't have allowed that. In my grief, I got sloppy. You should've seen the look on Denis' face when he saw me staring at him through the sight. I never liked him anyway."

"How did you know it was Denis?"

"Denis was an employee we recruited after you and he broke up."

The new contract.

"We utilized his flight services. He was well paid, but he was overly greedy and cocky. He wanted more. We refused. He threatened." Gerard flicked an ash and took another drag.

"So he sent you a message by abducting me. That was why the kidnappers didn't want anything from me. Denis used me to send an 'up yours' and took his revenge in the process."

Gerard grimaced. "Since the day I met Maggie and fell in love, I wanted to do right by her. For years we tried to have a baby. Your mom had four stillbirths before you came along. You were our miracle. The only child we'd ever have. I wanted to take care of my girls. In all the years I've been doing bad business, no one has ever threatened my family. It's just not done. Until that sonofabitch Denis with the bushy eyebrows had no sense to play by the rules. Even bad guys have rules, Bird. He crossed the line and he had to pay. The fact you lived was another miracle."

It was too much to bear. The woman in her was overwhelmed; the reporter in her wanted more.

"And Emmett?" she said.

"Soto did that one. Emmett was a patsy. Rankin was blackmailing him about April. When you were first snatched, I thought it might have been Emmett because he threatened you. Come to find out he had nothing to do with your abduction, but we couldn't let him go. Soto did a brilliant job in whacking Denis' two goons and pinning the whole thing on Emmett. Very impressive work. Soto got a tremendous amount of pleasure in framing Matt's brother. Retribution, man."

"But the timing—"

"It's like this … Denis threatened me, so I had a tracking device put on his car. I tracked all his movements. After questioning Emmett, Denis became suspect *numero uno*. But he was a greasy sucker and found the tracker, thus removing him from my reach. He had his goons drop you at the same spot where O'Brien killed the lawyer." Gerard waved a finger. "Now that was a clever diversion. But one of Soto's men waited and the stupid bastard led Soto straight to the pump house, but Denis saw his tail before going in. Didn't matter. Soto used the opportunity to set up Emmett. And then we waited for Denis to go home."

"There's forensic and DNA evidence to put Denis in the pump house. Then the truth about Emmett will surface and it'll be all over."

"You're right. There's a shit-load of evidence in that awful place. The lab is great, state-of-the-art, but it's also understaffed.

By the time it's analyzed, categorized, studied, compared, and such, us three top cats will be long gone. Rankin took his own life last night. I took Soto's. I've dispatched a letter of confession and named all the others involved. There were eight of us."

"Were Arthur and Thom involved, too?"

"No. But they knew. They've been silent for the family's sake. I wanted to come clean after Paige Street. I just didn't have the balls and Arthur took it for me. I'm ashamed."

"Why, Dad? Why get involved with bad business? Tell me."

Gerard hung his head. "I'm sorry, sweetheart; I have to die with that answer. I'll be judged as a man should be. I'm prepared to pay in full." He dropped his cigarette butt and lit another.

"Then why are you here?"

"To say goodbye to my girl."

Birdie told Gerard about how she had Maggie destroy the leftover shells. And the next words that came out of her mouth surprised her. "Don't do it, Daddy."

Gerard's cigarette dropped from his mouth. He looked at her with sad blue eyes.

"Don't you see?" she said. "That's why Matt gave me the key with the clues. He could have sent it to Danny with instructions. But Matt gave me the power to decide all our fates. It's my decision! The evidence is rigged to blow. No one will ever know." She popped up off the crate. "All you have to do is deny everything. Soto and Rankin are gone. There will be no proof. Say that Soto wrote the letter and it's a pack of lies."

Gerard hung his head. "I'm disappointed in you, Bird." He looked up at her, eyes weepy. "That's not the way I raised you. You have a solid moral spine. You may flirt with rebellion, but you always do the right thing and I know you'd be doing it for me, but that's not right and you know it. You'll live to regret the decision and you'll come to hate yourself. Besides, there's plenty of proof to be found. Even without Matt's stockpile."

He picked up his cigarette from the ground and puffed. A familiar sound shattered the desert sky. Gerard searched the shiny blue sky for the approaching helicopter.

"Well, Bird, that'll be the cavalry. I'm sorry I didn't have more time." He pulled her into a last hug. She whiffed his woodsy aftershave, the one he'd been wearing her entire life. "You're my girl forever. No matter how weak I was as a man, as a cop, I'm your father and I love you more than words can say." He held her tight. "You girls are going to have to take care of each other from now on. I'm so sorry that you and your mother will have to live with my rotten legacy."

The large LAPD helicopter made a wide circle above them. A silver and black bird, it banked and circled again.

Gerard leaned over Warren and mumbled a Latin prayer for the departed. He got into the car. Birdie ran to the driver's side door and leaned in the open window.

"Please don't leave, Daddy," she pleaded.

The helicopter descended into the date palm stumps. Dry, biting dust swirled in the rotor wash.

"You haven't called me Daddy since you were ten." He patted her arm. "Bird, you have to make sure the boxes get to Daniel Eubanks. Promise me. I'm going to make sure it ends for good. Make me that promise." He gave her the blue-fire look of seriousness.

She nodded.

"Good girl. I'm proud of you and everything you've created. You're a strong woman."

Three men jumped out of the police helicopter, heads bent, and ran toward them. Gerard put the car in drive, made a three point turn, and began to accelerate.

Birdie ran alongside the car. "Dad, you aren't going to leave me." He didn't slow or look her way, but she saw the tears streaming down his profile. She ran faster. "Don't leave like Matt did. Stop. Please!"

He sped off.

"DAAADDY!"

A man caught her arm. She spun around and saw two men lunge back in the cabin of the helicopter. The third held her in place.

It was Ron. "Birdie—"

"Let me go." She hit Ron in the face with her elbow.

Ron's face distorted with the blow. But he didn't attempt to stop her. Then she threw a punch into his chest. Then hit him again, and again, as if hitting would focus her rage. He absorbed the blows with grimaces and grunts, but he took them nonetheless and continued to do so until she was completely broken and had nothing else to give.

FORTY-EIGHT

BIRDIE LAY ON HER side on top of a crate. The helicopter returned to make a landing and the whirling pulled her away from unconsciousness. The rotor blades swirled the dust like a devil wind. A figure stood near the entrance to the shelter, held something to his head—a phone?—then threw it. He moved like a mirage through the dirty haze. The wavering figure drew closer. Ron. He knelt before her and brushed the hair from her face.

"You're one filthy girl," he said. He helped her to sit and handed her a bottle of water.

"Did I faint?"

"Exhaustion. Drink."

Birdie held the plastic bottle to her mouth and swallowed. The water cleansed the dust from her throat. The earth rumbled. The crates shuddered. The ground bounced with the earth's vibration.

Earthquake, thought Birdie.

A plume of white dust billowed from the bomb shelter.

She shot up. "The evidence!"

The white dust became black smoke. The ground shook violently with another eruption. She stumbled. Ron pushed her to the ground and shielded her body with his. A series of thunderous explosions filled the air. The black smoke choked the air. A crate stack toppled. Ron grabbed her shirt and pulled her up. They ran away from the smoke and were met by Thom and another man with the insignia of the Indio P.D. on his sleeve.

"What the hell?" said Thom.

"Evidence," screamed Birdie. "It was rigged to explode. It's gone."

The Indio P.D. conducted dead body business. The California Highway Patrol and the LAPD chased Gerard. Thom videotaped the crime scene and the remnants of the bomb shelter.

"So this is it," said Birdie. "How am I supposed to live with the loss?"

"Enlightenment will come later," said Ron. "You're strong and stubborn and brave and one day you'll be able to draw on that strength and see yourself through this darkness."

"That from an agnostic," she said. "All this time I thought it was Arthur or Thom. I never would've imagined that it was Dad. Did you know?"

"Sort of. I wasn't completely honest … the methadone vials? They led to a drug treatment facility named Janko Medical Center. Patrick and I surveilled it when you were missing. I saw two men go in with a small package and come out empty handed.

One of them was Gerard's adjutant, and the other ended up on the security detail at your hospital room."

"That's not enough proof of Dad's guilt."

"Not by itself. Add inductive and deductive reasoning. Knowing how criminals behave. Twenty years of experience. I used it all to come to a conclusion."

"But there were inconsistencies with Arthur's and Thom's behavior. Thom hit me."

"We need to discern what is life and what is criminal. I know you'd rather believe one of them dirty before you could believe the same of your father. They've been trying to keep it from the family."

That's why Arthur mislead her with his bad package comment?

"They told you?"

"Not exactly. I cornered Thom in a moment of weakness and he told me about what happened at Denis' and what he and Arthur did to you. If you look at it rationally then you'd see they were shielding you from the truth about your father and to protect you from Soto and Rankin. After George was shot and I came up to L.A. it all came together. Your cousins were tired. They were burning both ends. Arthur doesn't have a social life. Thom and his wife have serious marital issues. Those two were trying to keep the family in the dark. But events escalated and some terrible things happened. It promised to get worse unless it was stopped for good."

Thom approached, cell to his ear. Birdie saw the pain on his face. "At least it happened before the news helicopters arrived," he said.

"What happened?" said Ron.

"Just what you'd expect," said Thom. "Suicide by cop. When the pursuit ended he blasted his way out of the car. The CHP had no choice. Leave it to Uncle Gerard to save himself from Death Row."

Birdie's lips trembled. "He ended his life on his own terms. Controlled the manner of his death. To spare us a trial. He may have been a bad package, but he was a damn good dad."

FORTY-NINE

Friday, February 17

ABSOLVE, DOMINE, ANIMAS OMNIUM *fidelium defunctorum ab omni vinculo delictorum. Et gratia tua illis succurrente mereantur evadere judicium ultionis et lucis æternæ beautitudine perfrui.* Release the souls of all the faithful departed from every bond of sin, O Lord. Enable them by the help of your grace to escape the avenging judgment that they may enjoy the happiness of eternal light.

The crowd at Gerard Keane's funeral was small. There were no police escorts, helicopters, black-banded police shields, uniformed cops, nor adoring and thankful public, just the Keanes, Whelans, and a smattering of friends. Though the Keanes and Whelans had cause to war, there was no moral high-ground on which to plant a flag. The Irish Mob was down three men. They'd suffer and heal as a unit; still unified by shared religion, heritage, and occupation. It bound them together and gave them strength.

Birdie and Maggie would never forget their rock. They'd go to Mass, say their prayers, and light candles in his memory. No matter what would be revealed about his illegal activities in the days to come, his memory as a father and husband would never diminish.

FIFTY

Ron prepared dinner in Birdie's kitchen. Louise paced the floor in hope of a fallen scrap. Birdie sat in the library, mesmerized by the city lights, lost in a meditative nothingness.

Frank entered the room swirling the contents of a wine glass and took residence in his favorite chair. Birdie inhaled the essence. "Black plum and licorice. Flavors usually associated with scotch."

"Your nose is like a bloodhound's," said Frank. "You must do something productive with that ability. Perhaps the perfume business? As an aside to writing true crime?"

An appropriate analogy, thought Birdie. She'd been thinking about tracking lately. There were too many unanswered whys and only one person to provide the answers. The one who collected the evidence. But she'd have to find him first.

"Madi's branching into clothing design," said Birdie. "If she goes into fragrance, I'll be her nose."

"She'd be happy to have you." Frank took an appreciative sip of wine and set the glass on the side table. He removed his sweater and gently tossed it to the couch. "Thank you for the invitation. It's not often I have the privilege of dining with my favorite parishioner."

"That's because she doesn't cook."

Frank sighed contentedly. "Isn't it amazing how love and grace transforms us simple humans? We suffer. We grieve. Then one day we self-actualize."

"Wow, Frank. That's random."

Frank smiled mischievously. "This scene . . . a man in the kitchen cooking, a dog wandering around . . . it's domestic. He'd be happy for you. He wants you to love this man and make a life."

Birdie's radar pinged with Frank's use of the present tense.

"Why is it he always *wanted* for me, yet couldn't *provide*?" Birdie waved her hand in dismissal. "Doesn't matter anyway. I've acknowledged my feelings to Ron."

Frank's eyes glowed. "This pleases me."

"But you know, Ron has secrets. He blew up the evidence."

"All men of a certain age and occupation have something to conceal. As for the other, it was redundant at the end."

Birdie froze with a sudden realization. How could Ron know of the evidence's redundancy? She thought back to that day in Indio, to the mirage-like image of Ron throwing something into the shelter moments before it blew. She thought it had been a phone. She went further back and remembered a two a.m. call.

Birdie knelt in front of Frank and looked up into his eyes "You've talked to him," she said. "Ron's talked to him, too."

"Bird," said Frank sternly, "be careful."

She grasped his hands. "Do you know where he is?"

"No."

"Does Ron?"

"I doubt it."

Birdie let go. "For a divine man you don't know much do you?"

Frank smoothed a wave from her face and gently traced the scar on her cheek. "I'm sorry, my child."

Birdie pushed up and sat back on the couch, crossing her arms in a sulk. Her priest, her friend, her moral barometer could not offer the solution. She understood the burden of truth. How hard it is to know everything. All the secrets. Bound by covenants.

Ron called out from the kitchen, "Dinner in five."

"That's my cue to wash up," said Frank, picking up his wine glass. "See you in a few."

Birdie sat for a moment more, then cracked her neck and stood up. She grabbed Frank's sweater and draped it over her arm. On the couch lay a cell phone that must've slid out of the pocket. When did Frank begin carrying a cell phone? She picked it up off the couch and noticed it was cheaply made. Like a burner. Yes, thought Birdie. Just like that. She greedily clutched it to her belly and looked over her shoulder. She checked the phone log. There had only been one call—incoming from a blocked number. She felt a rush of excitement. There was no way to track the number, but she might be able to track the phone. Find out where it was purchased. She quickly punched her own cell number. When it began to vibrate on the desk, she answered it and quickly disconnected the call. Now she had a record. Then she erased the outgoing call on Frank's phone. She had just finished putting the phone into the sweater pocket when Frank returned. She placed the sweater over his shoulders.

"Thank you," he said. "Shall we eat? I'm so looking forward to Ron's meal. He's such an excellent cook. You are one lucky woman."

As Frank escorted Birdie to the dining table, her heart beat with a silent hopefulness. She knew one thing for certain. There was no way to disappear in a technological world. There are traces. Electronic fingerprints. She'd begin tomorrow. Because sorry simply wasn't good enough.

THE END

ACKNOWLEDGMENTS

Failure is private. Success is not. My team is right here. Thank you all for your support, guidance, and expertise.

LAPD: Robert Bub, Dominic Licavoli (Ret.), Peter MacDonald, Victor Marin, Larry Nolan (deceased), Steve Rose (Ret.), and Scott Smith. Latin: Ilona Thompson (too bad most of it got cut). Legal: Ron Bowers. Medical: Rebekah Halpern PA-C, Dr. Eva Heuser, and Dr. Greg Thomas. Spanish: Robbin Ward. USMC: Richard Barry (Ret.). I am solely responsible for stretching or altering the facts in service of the story.

To my drinking group with the writing problem: Linda Cessna, Anna Kennedy, Kurt Kitasaki, Doug Lyle, Rob Northrop, and Theresa Schwegel. I am grateful for you all even when you ripped apart my favorite passages.

Editor Kristen Weber forced me to break down the process, rethink, and dispose of waste. Lessons I'll never forget. I am indebted to my literary agent, Kimberley Cameron, who loved the novel and became its advocate. Thanks to Terri Bischoff at Midnight Ink for signing an emerging novelist. Thank you also to the helpful staff at Llewellyn.

Sue Ann Jaffarian's no-nonsense advice and counsel gave me hope during times of despair—of which there was plenty. The wisdom imparted by Melissa Orcutt gave me the courage (and permission) to pursue my dream and passion. Without her, I would not have taken the opportunity to recreate my life.

My parents, Pat and Margie, were forced to listen to a daily regalement of my nightly dreams. They encouraged me to turn that creative recall into stories. My son, David, is always quick with a hug to condole or celebrate. David hugs are a good thing. My daughter, Brenna, is my first reader and editor; her pencil is sharp and she wields it deftly. My husband, Scott Bozanic, always has my back with unconditional love and support. It hasn't been easy, but he never lost faith.

And to my future self: You're a lot better than you're allowing yourself to be.

ABOUT THE AUTHOR

Terri Nolan lives in her native Southern California. She earned a B.A. in Radio/Television from the University of Texas at Arlington. She is a freelance crime reporter, and her short fiction has appeared in the anthology *Murder in La La Land*. Visit her at www.terrinolan.com.